He was standing close enough to Pegeen that ~~she~~ the heat from his body, but she wouldn't move away. She kept her hands on the balustrade, her chin turned up so that she could look into his frank, laughing eyes.

"I beg your pardon, Lord Edward," she said. "But speak for yourself. I may not be a saint, but at least I'm not a lecherous spendthrift."

"And at least I," Edward said, suddenly uncrossing his arms and laying one hand on the balustrade on either side of Pegeen's waist, effectively trapping her within his broad, muscular arms, "am not a penny-pinching hypocrite."

"And what is that supposed to mean?" Pegeen thrust out her chin indignantly, her emerald eyes blazing. She tried to ignore the fact that his face loomed just inches above hers, and that one of his knees had insinuated its way between her thighs, despite the sturdy wires of her crinoline.

"I think you know very well what I mean," Edward said, with another one of his devilish smiles. "For all your miss-ish protestations, you want me, Pegeen, every bit as much as I want you."

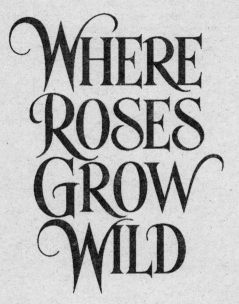

WHERE ROSES GROW WILD

PATRICIA CABOT

St. Martin's Paperbacks

WHERE ROSES GROW WILD

Copyright © 1998 by Patricia Cabot.

ISBN: 0-312-96489-7

Printed in the United States of America

St. Martin's Paperbacks edition / March 1998

St. Martin's Paperbacks are published by St. Martin's Press, 175 Fifth Avenue, New York, NY 10010.

10 9 8 7 6 5 4 3 2 1

for Benjamin

Chapter One

England, 1860

Lord Edward Rawlings, second and only surviving son of the late duke of Rawlings, was unhappy.

It wasn't just that Yorkshire wasn't the most pleasant place to spend the winter, though there were entire weeks when it seemed as if the sun never shone. It wasn't just that Lady Arabella Ashbury, whose husband owned the estate neighboring Rawlings Manor, was currently too self-absorbed to turn her prodigious attentions to him.

No, Edward was unhappy for reasons he couldn't have put into words had he wanted to, and he didn't want to, because the only person at hand was the viscountess of Ashbury. While the viscountess was well-known throughout England for many of her fine attributes, including her fair coloring and slim, elegant ankles, a sympathetic ear was not one of them.

"I'll have Mrs. Praehurst order enough foie gras for fifty people," Lady Ashbury said, scratching away at the list of assorted last minute items she wanted Edward to bring to the attention of his housekeeper before their friends from London arrived in Yorkshire for a weekend hunt. "I've found that in the country, not everyone cares for foie gras. The Herbert girls wouldn't know a foie gras from a hole in the ground."

Edward, stretched out on a chaise longue in front of the fire in the Gold Drawing Room, let out a yawn. He tried not to, but it escaped, just the same. Fortunately, Lady Ashbury, not used to men yawning in her presence, wasn't paying attention.

"I don't see why you have to invite the Herbert girls at all," Lady Ashbury went on. Her tone wasn't petulant, but it wasn't playful either. "Their father may be your estate agent, but I can't say that I feel he's done you any good, Edward."

Edward leaned forward on the chaise longue to pour himself another snifter of brandy from the decanter he'd placed within arm's reach on the side table. He was quite drunk already, and intended to get even drunker before the afternoon slipped into evening. One of the viscountess of Ashbury's finest attributes was that this sort of behavior did not bother her. Or at least if it did, she never mentioned it.

"After all, Edward," Lady Ashbury continued, "if it weren't for Sir Arthur Herbert's so-called tireless efforts on the behalf of the Rawlings estate, you'd be duke now, and not that brat of your brother's."

Edward leaned back, sipped his brandy, and stared heavenward. The Gold Drawing Room's ceiling was painted a muted yellow to match the heavy velvet drapery over the windows. He cleared his throat noisily and said in his deepest voice, the one that frightened the Rawlings Manor stable boys, "Everyone seems to forget that John's son is the legal heir to the title and to the estate."

Lady Ashbury affected not to notice his warning tone. "But no one even knew the whereabouts of the boy until Sir Arthur started his vile nosing about—"

"At my request, remember, Arabella?"

"Oh, Edward, don't patronize me." Lady Ashbury threw down her pen and rose from the ivory-topped secretary, the skirt of her pale blue satin gown rustling noisily. She strode towards the chaise longue, her pale skin and white-blonde ringlets making quite a pretty picture against the tawny drapery in the background. That, of course, was the reason why the viscountess always demanded that they be seated there, rather than in the more comfortable, but less complexion-flattering, Blue Morning Room.

Arabella declared, "It would have been the easiest thing in the world for you to simply tell the duke that John's son was dead too, like his mother and father, and then assume the title yourself."

Edward raised a mocking eyebrow in her direction. "The easiest thing in the world, Arabella? To lie to my father on his deathbed? He spent the past ten years cursing John for marrying a Scottish vicar's daughter, wouldn't allow their orphaned brat to be brought to Rawlings even though he was, in fact, the proper heir to the title. And then, when the duke relented at the eleventh hour . . . Faith, Arabella! It would have been damned dishonorable of me not to at least *attempt* to grant the old man's dying wish."

"Oh, hang honor," Lady Ashbury exclaimed. "You've never even met the boy!"

"No," Edward agreed. He'd finished his fourth brandy and poured himself a fifth. "But I will when Herbert returns with him tomorrow." Smiling to himself, Edward mused, "What you can't seem to get through that lovely head of yours, Arabella, is that I don't *want* to be a duke. Unlike yourself, and, I'm certain, your mamma, who made it her life's ambition to snag you a husband with a title, I would be perfectly content to be merely a mister."

Lady Ashbury let out an exasperated snort. "And how, pray, could you afford the kind of horseflesh you keep in your stables on the salary of a mere mister, Lord Edward? Or the house on Park Lane in London? Not to mention this drafty monstrosity you call a manor. The only mister I know who can afford all that you have is Mr. Alistair Cartwright, and as you well know, his wealth is every bit as inherited as yours. No, Edward, you are a duke's son, and, accordingly, you have the tastes of a duke's son. Your only misfortune was that you were not born before your miserable brother John.''

Edward glanced over at her, one eyebrow raised sardonically. ''Damn, Arabella. Do you honestly think I'd enjoy being duke? Brooding over estate business all day long? Forever being hounded after by men like Herbert, who'd want to take up all my time with account-keeping? Having to muck about with the tenant farmers, seeing that their roofs are freshly thatched each year, their children educated, their wives happy?'' He heaved his wide shoulders in a shudder of distaste. ''That kind of life made an old man out of my father, killed him before his time. I won't allow it to happen to me. Let my dear departed brother's brat have the damned title. Herbert will see that Rawlings doesn't burn to the ground in the meantime, and, in ten years, when the boy's left Oxford, he can return here and assume his rightful place in the hallowed halls.''

''And what do you intend to do with yourself, Edward?'' Arabella inquired, her asperity ill-disguised. ''You can only hunt from November to March, and London's beastly in the summer. What you need, my darling, is an occupation.''

''What do you think I am, an American?'' Edward laughed, not very nicely, and drained his glass. ''I adore it when you condescend to advise me, Arabella. It always puts me in mind of the difference in our ages. Tell me, does it bother your husband that you're always sprinting off across the moors to visit a man half his age and a decade younger than yourself?''

''Must you drink so much?'' snapped the viscountess of Ashbury, and Edward, with a resigned sigh, mentally subtracted one of her attributes. "It's quite revolting to see someone so comparatively young getting so bloated and paunchy."

Edward looked past his white, expertly tied cravat at his powerfully built chest and lean, waistcoated torso. "Paunchy?" he echoed in disbelief. "Where?"

"You've got bags under your eyes." Arabella stepped forward and snatched the brandy snifter from his hand. "And it's plain to see that you're starting to get jowls, just like your father."

Edward cursed and leapt up from the couch, the brandy making him a little unsteady on his feet. Standing several inches over six feet tall, Edward was always an imposing figure, but in the Gold Drawing Room of Rawlings Manor, he seemed doubly so. His large frame dwarfed the delicate gilt and green velvet furniture, and his feet, in well-shined black riding boots, trod heavily upon the carefully combed Persian carpets.

Striding to a beveled mirror that hung on one wall, Edward examined his reflection for paunchiness.

"Faith, Arabella," he said, looking from his own reflection to that of the viscountess. "I don't know what you're talking about. What jowls?"

He was certain that it wasn't vanity that kept him from seeing any signs of dissipation. Surely if they were there he'd notice. Edward wasn't that interested in how he looked, though he knew from having been told by so many women that the way he looked was pleasing. Of course, he was quite conscious that despite the fine cut of his clothing, he looked out of place in any drawing room, gold or not. He had the dark, saturnine complexion of a pirate or brigand, and longish jet-black hair that had a tendency to curl raffishly against his coat collar. In sharp contrast to the Lady Ashbury, who was as fair as a lamb, only Edward's eyes were light-colored, a grey that seemed to echo the mists that were forever pouring off the moor on the edge of which Rawlings Manor was situated.

"I didn't exactly mean that you had jowls now," the viscountess of Ashbury said, suddenly quite busy with something over at the ivory-topped desk. "What I meant was, if you're not careful—"

"That's not what you said."

Edward wasn't sure what dismayed him more; the fact that she'd startled him into rising from the couch or the fact that now that he was up, he might as well as go upstairs. He could be unhappy more easily in the comfort of his library, or even the billiard room, where he could smoke and drink at his leisure without any harping females to warn him about paunches.

But before he had a chance to formulate an excuse that would mollify the easily offendable viscountess, with whom he'd already shared a few pleasant hours of titillation in a third-floor guest room earlier in the day, Evers stepped into the room and cleared his throat noisily.

"Sir Arthur Herbert to see you, my lord." The butler, who had served Edward's father for fifty years and would undoubtedly serve the new duke of Rawlings for another twenty, did not raise an eyebrow at his employer's obvious intoxication so early in the afternoon.

"Herbert?" Edward echoed, in disbelief. "What's he doing back so soon? I wasn't expecting him 'til tomorrow at the earliest. Is the brat—er, His Grace, the duke, with Sir Arthur, Evers?"

Evers' gaze never left a spot somewhere above the green marble mantel. "Sir Arthur is alone, my lord, and, I might add, in a state of considerable agitation."

"Damn!" Edward reached up to rub his chin, which, even though it was only just past midday, was already rough with dark stubble. If Herbert was alone, it could only mean that the report they'd had from Aberdeen had been a false one, like all the others. And Herbert had sworn the source was reliable! Now Edward was going to have to expend more effort—and money—in the search for the heir to the Rawlings dukedom. How was it that a ten-year-old boy could virtually disappear off the face of the earth?

"Damn," Edward said irritably. "Show him in then, Evers. Show him in."

The viscountess heaved an exaggerated sigh the minute the butler was out of earshot.

"Oh, Edward, really. Must you entertain that loathsome man in here? Couldn't you have had him wait for you in your library? It's not as if I particularly enjoy listening to you two drivel on about that wretched child—"

"Yes, wretched!" Sir Arthur, portly and gregarious as ever, hurried into the room, hardly waiting until Evers had fully opened the doors before bustling past the butler and his stiffly raised eyebrows. "Oh, a most wretched child indeed, Lady Ashbury! Truer words were never spoken!"

Sir Arthur was so distraught that he had not even allowed the footman to remove his cloak and hat, and now snow spilled from the middle-aged man's sloping shoulders. Evers hovered close by, his face a pained mask as wet spots grew on the carpet beneath the solicitor's galoshes.

"Good God, man," Edward blurted, startled by his estate agent's unkempt appearance. "Have you just come from Scotland, sir, or from hell?"

"The latter, my lord, the latter, I assure you."

Before Evers could stop him, Sir Arthur sank into the very green velvet chaise longue that Edward had only just abandoned. Snow fell to the deep cushions and began to melt immediately in the warmth cast by the generous fire. "Never, in all these months of searching for your father's heir, have I encountered anything quite so disagreeable, Lord Edward."

The viscountess, having watched the proceedings with faintly curled lips and delicately arched brows, glanced at the butler. "Evers, I believe Sir Arthur is in need of a brandy."

"No, no," Sir Arthur cried, holding up a fat hand. "No, thank you, my lady. I never touch spirits before noon. Lady Herbert would not approve, not at all."

"But, Sir Arthur," Arabella's smile was decidedly mocking, "it's past one, after all."

"Ah. In that case—" But Evers was already at the solicitor's elbow with a full snifter. "Oh, thank you, Evers, my good man. Ah, quite hits the spot, that . . . And there's no reason Virginia need ever know, now is there?"

Edward, who almost always felt like smashing something breakable whenever he was in the presence of his late father's most trusted advisor, asked through gritted teeth, "Am I to take it from your complete lack of composure that we have been duped yet again?"

Sir Arthur looked up from his brandy, his plump, bland face almost comically surprised. "What? Duped? Oh, no, my lord. Not at all. No, this is the lad. Oh, yes, we've got the right lad at last." He heaved a shuddering sigh that was as dramatic as it was noisy. "More's the pity."

As Sir Arthur reached out a trembling hand to pour himself another brandy from the decanter on the gilt end table, both Evers and Edward stepped forward to stop him, the butler out of an outraged sense of duty, Edward out of sheer frustration. Edward wasn't so drunk that he couldn't outmaneuver a fifty-year-old father of five and a seventy-year-old butler. Falling to one knee alongside the couch, his fingers closed around the neck of the brandy decanter. He was so tall that only kneeling could he look the seated Sir Arthur in the eye, and he did so now, unaware that his own grey eyes were glittering dangerously with suppressed anger.

"What . . ." Edward said, enunciating carefully, "happened . . . in . . . Scotland?"

Sir Arthur stopped looking mournfully down into the

bottom of his snifter, his gaze arrested by Edward's menacing glare. "Well, I, er," stammered the solicitor. "Well, you see, my lord, it's him. The duke, my lord. Young Jeremy of Rawlings—"

"You found him?" Edward's relief was palpable. "Thank God." But his relief soon turned to impatience. "But if you found him, why in the hell didn't you bring him back with you to Rawlings?"

"Wouldn't come," Sir Arthur shrugged simply.

Edward wasn't certain that he'd heard the solicitor correctly. "I'm sorry, Sir Arthur. Could you repeat that?"

"He wouldn't come," Sir Arthur said again. "Was quite adamant about it too, my lord. Wouldn't budge from the spot without—"

"Wouldn't come?" Edward bellowed. He sprang to his feet, his fingers balled into fists at his sides. He noticed that Arabella was staring at him with some alarm, but he couldn't control his sudden compulsion to pace the room like a caged animal.

"Wouldn't come? The boy was told he is the heir to a fortune, the owner of an estate that is the jewel of Yorkshire, that he is, in fact, a duke, and he *wouldn't come*?

"Is the child an *idiot*?" Edward roared, startling Evers, who'd been endeavoring to clear away the now empty brandy decanter. It would have been just like John to produce an idiot heir, Edward thought furiously to himself.

"Oh, no, my lord," Sir Arthur winced. "Quite the contrary. Healthy as a pony, ten years old, full of the devil. Hammered the back of my head with an egg the moment I descended from my carriage."

Edward fought for patience. "Then why wouldn't he come with you?"

"Well, it wasn't so much the boy, my lord, as his aunt."

"Aunt?" Arabella looked up from a close examination of her cuticles. "The boy has an aunt?"

"Yes, my lady. He's an orphan, don't you know, what with Lord John's untimely demise ten years ago. I believe his mother, Lord John's unfortunate wife, passed on shortly after that. The duke has been raised by his mother's sister and his maternal grandfather, who also passed away about a year ago now, I think. Dreadful thing, I understand. Dropped dead in the pulpit. A vicar, you know."

Edward was beginning to feel as if he was the only person in the room, with the possible exception of Evers, who still had some grasp on reality. "What about this aunt?" he demanded, attempting to steer the conversation back to the point at hand. "The aunt won't let the boy come?"

"Not precisely, my lord. The boy won't come without his aunt. Quite devoted to her he is. Really quite touching, in this day and age, to see a boy so close to his—"

"Hell and damnation, Herbert," Edward thundered. "Why didn't you tell the bloody aunt that she could come along with the boy?"

Sir Arthur looked startled. "I did, my lord. Indeed, I did. I extended an invitation to her to come and live at Rawlings Manor for as long as she liked. For the rest of her life, if she cared to." The solicitor broke off and suddenly began removing his outer wraps. "Is it warm in here, Mr. Evers? I think that fire is too high."

"Well?" Edward had quit pacing and now stood leaning an elbow against the mantel. He did not find the fire too hot at all. "Well, what did the blasted woman say to that?"

"Oh, she quite resolutely refused my invitation, my lord. Wouldn't even hear of it. And of course, the boy wouldn't stir without her." Herbert shrugged. "And so here I am."

"Refused your invitation?" Edward really did feel like thrusting his fist through something. Evers had just that moment set up a firescreen between Herbert and the hearth, so he took out his wrath on that, smashing the delicate, hand-painted screen to the floor with a powerful blow.

Arabella let out a little startled shriek and Herbert looked stunned. Only Evers calmly retrieved the screen, righted it, and cast his employer a disapproving glance.

"Is the *aunt* an idiot?" Edward demanded.

"Oh, no, my lord, quite the contrary." Sir Arthur had begun to sweat profusely, either from the heat of the fire or from nervousness at Edward's behavior. Perhaps he thought one of those great fists would be hurtling in his direction next. In any case he elaborated quickly, his broad face shiny with perspiration, "No, my lord, not an idiot. A Liberal."

If the portly solicitor had spat upon the parquet, Edward could not have been more astonished. "A *what*?" he breathed.

"A Liberal."

Sir Arthur smiled thankfully at Evers, who had stepped forward to remove his cloak and hat from the wet bundle in which the estate agent had piled them on the chaise longue. "Quite the anti-royalist, my lord. Won't have a thing to do with the titled gentry. Says they're responsible for the lack of reform that would aid the common man. Says it's the Conservatives who are keeping the masses in abject poverty, so that one percent of the population can enjoy ninety-nine percent of the wealth. Says landowners like yourself are nothing but ne'er-do-wells without a thought in their heads save hunting and whore-mongering—" Breaking off in embarrassment, Sir Arthur glanced at the viscountess. "Begging your pardon, Lady Ashbury."

Arabella raised a single eyebrow and said nothing.

Edward listened to the solicitor in a state of disbelief. This couldn't be happening. It simply couldn't be happening. The heir to the duke of Rawlings had been found but the boy wouldn't come because his lunatic aunt was a *Liberal*? How was this possible?

"I don't understand," Edward said, fighting for calm. He was afraid of losing his temper again. There was nothing left for him to smash but Sir Arthur's fat, smiling face, and since he really did like the old windbag, Edward didn't want to hurt him. Much. "You say this woman turned down an invitation to live in one of the greatest houses in England because of her *political sentiments*?"

"Quite so, quite so," Sir Arthur chuckled. "And of course, the boy wouldn't come without her."

"And this . . ." Edward swallowed hard. "This woman. Hadn't she a husband who could be appealed to rationally?"

"Oh, no, my lord. Miss MacDougal is unmarried."

"Miss MacDougal?"

"Yes, my lord. Pegeen MacDougal. Has lived in a cottage near the vicarage since her father died—she and the boy. I believe they are sustained by a small allowance left by her mother. God knows the vicar left them nothing—"

"A spinster," Edward hissed through clenched teeth. "Thwarted by a spinster aunt with Liberal leanings. Hell and damnation, man!" Edward was ready to tear his own hair out, but instead he bellowed at his estate agent loudly enough to startle even the unruffable Evers.

"You couldn't convince a maiden aunt surviving on a pittance that the best thing for her beloved nephew was to let him come live in splendor in a Yorkshire manor house?" Edward demanded incredulously. "Are you daft, man? What could have been simpler? Do you know *nothing* of women? Couldn't you bribe her? Charm her? Win her over with flattery? Is there nothing in this world that the bloody woman wants that we could provide her with in exchange for the boy?"

Sir Arthur had leaned back as far as the chaise longue would allow, but still he couldn't escape the menacing glare that burned through him hotter than any fire. Inserting a

plump finger beneath his cravat, he pulled on it ineffectu-
ally, gulping.

"But my lord, I told you! She wouldn't have anything
to do with me! Turned me out of the house, she did. Even
threw a pot at me!" Sir Arthur was almost whimpering.
"And the boy, my lord! Not a proper boy at all, but a
hellion. Slipped a horrible weasel in my pocket and put a
burr beneath the harness of one of the carriage horses. I
thought I'd never get back to Lady Herbert in one piece!"

Abruptly, Edward turned away from the solicitor, his
broad shoulders slumping. Well, it was quite obvious what
needed to be done now. His mistake had been to send an
agent to perform a task that could have been done more
properly by him. Hadn't his father always said that it was
invariably simpler to do a chore oneself than to explain to
a hireling how it ought to be done properly? This was a
classic example. What did Sir Arthur know about women,
for all his five daughters? He had courted and wed the first
woman who'd have him, and while Virginia Herbert was a
fine creature, she certainly hadn't posed anything like a
challenge to the bumbling knight.

No, there was only one thing for it. Edward himself
would have to make the trip to Aberdeen and fetch the boy,
as well as the blasted aunt.

A Liberal! God spare him from overeducated women!
What had that vicar been thinking, letting his daughter read
the newspaper? She shouldn't even know the difference
between Liberals and Conservatives. It wasn't any wonder
the woman was a spinster, and she was doomed to remain
so, if what she'd spouted off to Herbert was any example
of her conversational technique.

Evers, in the doorway, cleared his throat. "Excuse me,
my lord, but will that be all?"

Edward, who'd been standing before the fire with his
hands clasped behind his back, turned suddenly.

"No, that will not be all, Evers. Inform my valet that

we shall be leaving for Scotland posthaste. I shall need enough shirts packed for a stay of no less than three days. Have Roberts bring around the brougham. I shall depart as soon as I am packed.''

Over by the secretary Arabella laid down her pen. ''Edward, are you mad? You cannot be thinking of going to see that dreadful woman yourself.''

''I most certainly intend to,'' Edward declared. ''Why? Do you think I lack the necessary powers of persuasion? Is a Liberal Scottish spinster beyond my capabilities?''

Lady Ashbury laughed. Her laughter, Edward had once noted, was a cold, tinkling sound, like a dinner bell without resonance and rather demanding. ''Oh, no, my lord. We all know how persuasive you can be, when you set your mind to it.'' Her glance flicked over him, and Edward did not fail to notice the appreciative widening of those fine eyes when they settled on the subtle swell at the front of his breeches. ''But you must be desperate, darling, if you'd go all the way to Scotland in weather like this. Whatever is the rush? We know where the beastly boy is and he's obviously not going anywhere.''

''I want this thing settled,'' Edward said quietly, turning back to the fire. ''My father's been dead nearly a year and Rawlings has languished without a duke all that time. That's quite long enough, I think.''

Arabella laughed again. ''Oh, la, since when do you care about Rawlings? Really, Sir Arthur, you're a bad influence on him. Next thing you know, he'll be wanting to tour the sheep meadows!''

Sir Arthur looked aghast at Edward's proposed trip to Scotland. ''I beg you, my lord, let it alone! Give it some time. Perhaps in a month or two, when they've had a chance to get used to the idea, they'll come around. You know, Miss MacDougal was most firmly convinced of your father's total indifference to the boy, and she was shocked to discover that the duke had not cut him from the will—''

"I do not have the patience to wait a month, Sir Arthur," Edward replied. "I shall leave today, and I wager I'll have the two of them—the boy and the maiden aunt—safely ensconced here at Rawlings within a fortnight."

"If you plan on doing any wagering, you'd best wake your old schoolmate Mr. Cartwright," Arabella remarked dryly. "He's sleeping off last night's billiard game in the library. Will you be taking him with you, Edward? You know how much he'd enjoy engaging wits with a Scottish spinster."

Edward growled, "I'll not be needing Alistair's dubious services this trip. You can keep him here, Arabella, to entertain you while I'm gone. See that he doesn't break anything too valuable, and that if he does, he replaces it."

"My lord, I really must beg that you reconsider." So flustered was he by his employer's plans, Sir Arthur actually heaved himself up from the chaise longue and went to stand beside Edward. "I fear that you do not ken how volatile this woman's temper is. She quite resolutely despises all gentry and adamantly refuses—"

Edward laughed and laid a heavy hand upon the knight's shoulder. "Herbert, old man, let me tell you something about women. They're all the same." The glance that he flicked at the viscountess was mocking. "They all want something. What we've got to discover is what this Miss MacDougal wants, and give it to her in exchange for her nephew. It's quite simple, really."

Sir Arthur did not look satisfied. "The problem, my lord, is that I believe what Miss MacDougal wants is—"

"Well, Herbert?"

"Your head, Lord Edward. On a stick."

Chapter Two

Pegeen cradled the newborn babe in her arms, bouncing it slightly and cooing to it as it wailed.

"There, there," she said, her breath fogging up immediately in the frigid air. "It's all right. I know it isn't nearly so pleasant out here as it was in there, but you're going to have to get used to it, you know."

On the bed, which really wasn't much more than a pile of sodden rags and straw, the mother of the newborn looked up with a weak smile. " 'E looks all right, does 'e, Miss MacDougal? All 'is fingers and toes?"

"Ten and ten," Pegeen replied with far more cheer than she felt. "What are you going to call him, Mrs. MacFearley?"

"Oh, Lord, I dinna know."

"Run out of names, 'ave you?" Mrs. Pierce, the midwife, turned from the sorry excuse for a fire she and Pegeen had been trying to build up for the past hour without much success. Without coal, fueled only by a few damp pieces of peat, such fires did not provide much heat, but the MacFearleys were luckier than some of their neighbors, whose lean-to shacks didn't even contain chimneys. "I canna say as 'ow I'm surprised. What is 'e, yer sixteenth?''

Mrs. MacFearley nodded proudly. ''Eighth son, if you dinna count the three what came out dead.'' Thoughts of her stillborn babies momentarily clouding the woman's exhausted face, she murmured, ''Would it be wrong, d'ye think, Miss MacDougal, to name 'im same as one o' the dead ones? I like the name James awful much, but the last one, what died, was called James. . . .''

Pegeen looked down at the wailing, red-fisted bundle in her arms and quite suddenly couldn't bear it a minute longer. It seemed as if the smoke-blackened walls of the single-room shack were pressing in upon her, and the smell, which was usually an unpleasant mixture of cabbage and human excrement, was now ten times worse, what with the stench of afterbirth.

Pegeen felt her breakfast of porridge rising in her throat, and with a small moan, she thrust the baby into the hastily held-out arms of the midwife and rushed outside into the yard.

Stumbling blindly through the snow, Pegeen made it to the slop pile before vomiting. When she was finished, she clung to the wash pole, laying her cheek against the cold, rough wood and closing her eyes against the brilliant winter sun. It didn't smell much better outside the lean-to, but at least she was away from that wan face and the rail-thin body wasted from producing child after child.

The door to the shack opened behind her and Mrs. Pierce came out holding a bucket that's contents steamed in the cold. Pegeen hastily reached into her reticule for her handkerchief, wiping her mouth with it and a little bit of clean snow she scooped up from the ground.

Mrs. Pierce approached Pegeen and the slop pile muttering to herself. When she was close enough to see the mess the young woman had made in the snow, she clacked her tongue disapprovingly.

''I dinna know why you insist on comin' wi' me every

time,'' the midwife declared, ''when all it does is sicken you.''

Abruptly, Mrs. Pierce turned over the bucket, emptying its contents over the vomit. Pegeen, recognizing the familiar odor of afterbirth, felt her stomach turn once more, and she quickly grasped the wash pole, clinging to it as if doing so could ward off her nausea. She pressed her handkerchief to her lips.

''Oh, Mrs. Pierce,'' Pegeen sighed miserably. ''It's so dreadful. How can you stand it? That woman is going to kill herself having a baby every year. Someone has got to speak to the men in this village. Can't you do it?''

''T'ain't my place to do so and you know it, Miss MacDougal,'' Mrs. Pierce declared reprovingly. '' 'Tis the vicar's duty. And if you think our new vicar's going to dirty 'is 'ands with the likes of Myra MacFearley, you're as daft as your da was.''

Rather than take offense at Mrs. Pierce's reference to her father's eccentricity, Pegeen merely sighed, tucking her handkerchief back into her bag. ''I suppose you're right. It just seems so unfair. Sixteen children, in as many years, and a third of them stillborn. And Mrs. MacFearley's only thirty, Mrs. Pierce! That woman in there is only ten years older than myself, and looks—''

''As old as me?'' Mrs. Pierce winked, her broad face beaming. ''Not a day over fifty?''

''You know what I mean.'' Pegeen looked glumly down at the tops of her boots, the hem of her brown wool dress damp from the snow. ''Perhaps if *I* spoke to Mr. Richlands,'' she suggested, not very hopefully.

''*You*?'' The midwife threw back her head and laughed. The rich sound was oddly muted in the crowded, dirty yard. ''*You* speak to the vicar about the village prostitute? Oh, that's rich, Miss MacDougal, that is!''

Pegeen frowned. ''Why is it so strange? After all, we're both adults. It's Mr. Richlands duty to speak to his brethren of such things. Lord knows, my father tried.''

"Mr. Richlands'd go green in the face and lose his own breakfast, were you bring up any such thing.'' Mrs. Pierce shook her head. "No, my love. T'ain't right for a young unmarried woman to speak to a single man—even a vicar—about such things. Especially a woman like yourself.''

"What do you mean, a woman like myself?'' Pegeen demanded, instantly taking offense.

"Dinna look so stricken,'' Mrs. Pierce laughed. "I mean a woman what looks like you do. Why, you're fairer than any of them actresses what's in the papers. Beautiful woman like yourself tries to speak to a man like the vicar about things most married ladies dinna mention in front of their own 'usbands . . . Well, it just ain't seemly, Miss MacDougal, even for you. I know your da wouldna like it, despite them fancy books 'e always made you read. . . .''

Feeling a little better, Pegeen released the wash pole and shook her head gloomily. "I don't know what you're talking about, Mrs. Pierce. I'd best be getting back now. Jeremy will be home for dinner soon and I haven't set a thing on the fire. Please tell Mrs. MacFearley that I'll be back tonight with some broth and bread for her and the children.''

"That I'll do, love.'' Mrs. Pierce winked again, patting Pegeen on the shoulder. "That I'll do.''

It wasn't a long walk from the end of the village where the poorer families lived to the vicarage if one took the shortcut through the cemetery, which Pegeen, not being at all superstitious, did, walking briskly to keep her mind off the extreme cold. In her haste to get to the MacFearleys' cottage before the birth, Pegeen had forgotten her bonnet and now she had only her loose, dark brown hair to warm her ears. Keeping her arms tucked within her threadbare pelisse, Pegeen listened to her feet crunching on the snow. She idly read the epitaphs she knew practically by heart,

which was what came of having lived in a village her entire
life.

Here lies Enid, read one that had always unsettled Pegeen. *My Wife, My Love, My Life.* What would it be like,
Pegeen often wondered, to care about someone like that?
She couldn't imagine caring about any man that much. She
loved Jeremy, that was true, and was quite certain that if
asked she would give her life for his. But care for a man—
someone outside her own family—so deeply that she'd
consider him her life? How frightening to love someone so
fiercely! She felt quite sorry for Enid's poor husband,
who'd been so bereft at the loss of his wife. How much
more sensible it would have been for him to have maybe
loved her a little less.

"Miss MacDougal!"

Pegeen froze, mid-stride. Oh, no. It couldn't be.

"Miss MacDougal!"

But it was. She saw him pop out from behind a particularly large tombstone, brushing snow from his knees.
What had he been doing back there? Had he seen her pass
by the vicarage earlier and now awaited her return? Odious
man. She thought about hurrying forward, pretending she
hadn't seen him, but he was upon her at once, and she had
to force a smile.

"Good morning, Miss MacDougal!"

Mr. Richlands swept off his tall hat and bowed with
comical zeal, although Pegeen did her best not to laugh at
him. He was, after all, her father's replacement, and the
spiritual leader of the community. It wasn't Mr. Richlands'
fault that he sometimes reminded Pegeen of a marionette,
with his gawky frame and ungraceful movements.

"How well you look on this cold winter's morn," the
vicar gushed, his breath coming out of his mouth in great
white puffs.

Pegeen kept the false smile pasted upon her face.
"Good morning, Mr. Richlands. I wish I had time to visit,

but I must get back to the cottage to prepare Jeremy's dinner.''

"Then you must allow me to escort you," the vicar declared, holding out his arm for Pegeen to grasp. "The way is slippery, and I would not have you fall and perhaps turn an ankle."

Pegeen wasn't altogether sure she appreciated the vicar making reference to her ankles. He was a tall young man—Pegeen stood only as high as his shoulder—and, though clumsy, well formed, with blue eyes and russet hair. But unlike every other unmarried woman in the village, Pegeen wasn't attracted to him, and couldn't ken what all the fuss over him was about.

Seeing that she could not possibly refuse to accept his arm without appearing rude, Pegeen slipped her gloved hand into the crook of the vicar's elbow and allowed him to escort her through the cemetery. As they walked, Mr. Richlands spoke at length about the changes he'd made in the house Pegeen had grown up in, the house that, after her father's death, had been turned over to the new vicar. Though she was quite content with her own small cottage on the far reaches of the church's property, Pegeen could not help feeling proprietary towards the vicarage, and it angered her to hear that Mr. Richlands had repapered the walls in the sitting room. Foolish man. Didn't he know the chimney smoked and would only soil the paper within the year?

Mr. Richlands' inanities lasted almost to the cemetery gate. Pegeen, who had been debating the matter to herself for several yards, suddenly blurted, "Mr. Richlands, I have just been at the MacFearleys', down in the village, attending the birth of Myra MacFearley's sixteenth child—"

Before she could finish, she felt Mr. Richlands stiffen and pull away from her in astonishment.

"What?" he cried, looking quite dismayed. "Are you

joking, Miss MacDougal? Though I must say, if you are, it is in poor taste.''

Pegeen stared up at him, frowning. ''No, it isn't a joke, Mr. Richlands. I have been talking it over with Mrs. Pierce, the midwife, and we feel that it is your duty as vicar to speak with the men of Applesby. They have got to stay away from Mrs. MacFearley for at least a year. Otherwise, at this rate, she'll never regain her strength. And we've got to supplement her lost income as best we can from the collection plate.''

''Miss MacDougal!'' Mr. Richlands' pale face had gone a shade paler and was now very nearly the same color of the snow all around them. Pegeen realized with a sinking heart that Mrs. Pierce had been right. She'd shocked the vicar and now she was going to have to bear the brunt of it.

''I am astonished, truly astonished to hear that you, a young, unmarried woman, attended a birth! I have never heard of such a thing! And the birth of a bastard child of the village slut! What could the midwife be thinking, allowing you to do such a thing? I have a mind to speak with that woman. Such a thing is so disgraceful that I—well, I hardly know what to think!''

The memory of Myra MacFearley's wan face was still fresh in Pegeen's mind, as was the noxious smell of afterbirth. She stamped an impatient foot, angry that the vicar should obsess over the propriety of her attending a birth when there were so many more serious issues with which he ought to be dealing.

''Oh, come, Mr. Richlands. Young and unmarried I may be, but I am not a child, nor am I ignorant. I know how babies are made and I know how to deliver them, and I'm asking you, as vicar of the parish, to help Mrs. MacFearley—''

''I will do no such thing,'' Mr. Richlands exclaimed. ''I would not lower myself to come to the aid of a woman

so licentious that she cannot keep her legs shut long enough
to recover from childbirth.''

''But it is your duty to do so! My father—''

''Your father! Your father! Have you any idea, Miss
MacDougal, how tired I am of hearing about your father?
Your father was hardly the enlightened thinker you seem
to believe. If he was so forward-minded, why did he leave
you and your nephew alone in the end with only the charity
of the church—*my* charity—keeping you from the workhouse?''

Pegeen blinked up at him, her eyes suddenly filled
with tears that she angrily dashed away. ''If that is the way
you feel, Mr. Richlands,'' she said, in a tight little voice
she hardly recognized as her own, ''then I bid good day to
you.''

Turning on her heel, Pegeen began to stalk stiffly
away. Of all the nerve! Kept from the workhouse by *his*
charity! Tired of hearing about her father, was he? Well,
he wouldn't have to hear another word about him, not another word. Pegeen would never speak to the obnoxious
man again. See if she would!

The vicar called her name, the agitation in his voice
extreme. He stumbled after Pegeen, and when she didn't
stop, suddenly laid both his gloved hands upon her shoulders, spinning her around to face him. Pegeen was surprised
by this gesture. The vicar had almost assiduously avoided
touching her, even at the evening balls they'd sometimes
attended at the homes of well-meaning neighbors who
wanted nothing more than for the late vicar's attractive
daughter and the good-looking new vicar to come to an
understanding.

''Miss MacDougal,'' Mr. Richlands panted, his fingers
cutting through the material of her pelisse. ''I apologize for
offending you, but please hear me out. For a long time I
have felt that your father, good man though he was, was

far too liberal in his dealings with the parish, and particularly in his upbringing of you—''

When Pegeen drew breath to hotly deny this, the vicar hastily continued, ''What may be unsuitable for a young girl to know, however, is ultimately essential knowledge in the wife of a vicar, so I am willing to overlook this lapse in taste that you've exhibited—''

Pegeen stared up at him, her lips falling open. ''Mr. Richlands,'' she managed to gasp. ''Are you . . . ?''

''Yes, I am. I don't suppose it comes as much of a surprise to you, Miss MacDougal, that for some time now, I have come to admire you as more than just a friend. I hope that you will do me the honor of becoming my wife.''

Pegeen was so taken aback that she almost burst out laughing, but she managed to control herself in the nick of time. Good Lord, she'd just been proposed to for the very first time in her life and her first reaction had been to laugh! How unseemly.

Mr. Richlands face was deadly serious, more concerned, she thought, about the topic she'd introduced earlier than in whether or not she'd accept him. And of course that was something she had absolutely no intention of doing.

Reaching up to pry his fingers from her shoulders, Pegeen said, ''Mr. Richlands, you are mistaken if you think I ever suspected the true nature of your feelings for me. I'm sorry if I misled you into believing that my own were anything more than feelings of friendship. But as they are only that, I'm afraid I cannot accept your generous proposal. Now, please release me.''

When he still resolutely refused to release her, she began to wriggle in his grasp. ''Did you hear me, Mr. Richlands?''

''Call me Jonathan,'' the vicar said, leaning down to kiss her. ''Pegeen.''

Pegeen was so surprised when his mouth closed over hers that for a moment, she froze, conscious of the hot dryness of his lips and the sudden, startling introduction of his tongue as it attempted to dart past her firmly closed lips. Her next reaction was not nearly so passive. Drawing back a foot, she launched the sharp toe of her boot at the vicar's shin.

He released her with a yelp, and Pegeen, lifting her skirts, took off like a colt, tearing down the cemetery lane as fast as her slender legs could carry her. Though she heard him call out her name, Pegeen kept running, slipping on the icy surface of the snow. She dared not slow down for fear he'd catch up with her and apologize, an act which, even after having lost her breakfast earlier that morning, she wasn't certain she'd be able to stomach.

She kept running, the cold wind cutting through her open pelisse and causing her eyes to tear. She nearly collided with Mrs. MacTurley, the baker's wife, on the village lane but only shouted, "Sorry!" over her shoulder. She didn't care if the entire village got an eyeful of her ankles and calves. She was intent on escaping. She ran past the vicarage, through her garden gate, and she would have made it to her front door had she not been stopped there by a large, dark impediment. She hurled herself against the obstacle full force and it let out a surprised, "*Oof*," as she careened into it.

Stunned, Pegeen would have fallen from the force of the impact, but strong hands reached out to steady her, and the same deep voice which had uttered the, "Oof," chuckled, saying, "Ho, there, sweetheart. And where do you think you're going, so hell-bent for leather?"

Panting to catch her breath, Pegeen pushed some of her dark, windblown hair from her eyes and looked up. . . .

Into the most astonishing face she had ever seen.

Clear grey eyes laughed down at her, crinkled within folds of lightly tanned skin that instantly reminded Pegeen of summer days, of purple heather blowing in the soft evening breeze. In sharp contrast to the light-colored eyes was

the jet black hair curled about a chiseled face distinctly
saturnine with its heavy dark brow and sensuous lips.

Staring breathlessly up at this Vulcan-like apparition,
Pegeen thought that the man was like a pirate out of one
of the books Jeremy was forever clamoring for her to read
to him. She found herself intensely conscious of the strong
arms that held her upright, of the broad, black-cloaked
shoulders that were so wide they blotted out the view of
anything around them, of the masculine odor that seemed
to emanate from the confines of his waistcoat, of leather
and tobacco and, faintly, horse.

Pegeen was suddenly aware that the grey-eyed gaze
had dipped boldly down to where her pelisse had parted to
reveal her narrow waist and trim bosom, which was still
rising and falling heavily as she tried to catch her breath.
With a quick shake of her head, she came to her senses.
What was she doing allowing a complete stranger to hold
her like this when she had only just kicked the vicar for
attempting to do so? With a gasp Pegeen made a sudden
motion to be free, and the chuckling stranger set her at
liberty at once.

"Is there a fire somewhere, sweetheart?" the man inquired, with a quirk of one of those dark eyebrows. "Or
are you being pursued by some lovelorn shop clerk?"

Pegeen stared up at him, still too breathless to speak.
She knew that her cheeks had turned a deep crimson and
she was thankful that, what with the cold, he couldn't possibly think she was blushing, though, of course, she was.
He was the handsomest man she had ever seen. How could
she help but blush?

"What's the matter, child? Cat got your tongue?"

He grinned down at her, and the sight of those rakishly
curled lips caused her heart to turn over in her chest.

"I've been standing here some time, trying to rouse
your mistress," he went on. "If she isn't at home, could
you at least let me step inside to warm myself while I wait?

I believe I've caught a chill standing here, banging on the door so long—''

Pegeen heard someone call from the lane. Standing on tiptoe, she peered over the dark-haired gentleman's arm and saw Mr. Richlands limping towards them, waving his hat in one hand.

''Oh, no!'' she groaned.

Her visitor glanced casually over his shoulder and said in his rumbling voice, ''That man seems to want you.''

''I know,'' Pegeen moaned. ''That's the problem.''

She threw herself against the door, which she never locked, and stumbled across the threshold. Hurrying into the parlor she worked the togs that fastened her pelisse with one hand and threw aside her reticule with the other.

''Stuff and bother,'' Pegeen muttered, hardly noticing that the broad-shouldered stranger had followed her inside and now stood peering out a window at Mr. Richlands, who'd paused at the garden gate, suddenly seeming to realize his presence was not wanted. ''And Jeremy will be home any minute!''

''Is that man bothering you, love?'' asked the dark-haired gentleman. ''Because if he is, I'll gladly get rid of him for you.''

''Oh,'' Pegeen moaned, laying her pelisse over the back of the settle and then putting a hand to her forehead as if to ward off a headache. ''You can't get rid of him. Believe me, I've tried.''

The tall man looked out the window once more. ''I haven't fought anyone since college—leastwise, with fists— but he doesn't look like much. He might have youth on me but that's all. How do you think he'd fare with pistols at dawn?''

Pegeen looked at him and laughed, a bright, bubbling sound that seemed to spill out of her. She had no idea where it came from. ''You can't be serious! He's Mr. Richlands, the vicar.''

"Serious as death. I wouldn't care if he was the Archbishop of Canterbury. I'd be happy to kill him for you. Just say the word."

She saw the grey-eyed gaze flick quickly about the cheerful if sparsely furnished room, only to settle on her. Pegeen was suddenly conscious of her slightly damp brown wool dress with the snow-stained hem and tight-fitting waist.

"On second thought," the stranger said, reconsidering, "rather than killing him, which might offend someone and bring a whole mess of people about, why don't I just frighten him away, and then you and I can light a fire and sit in here and get to know each other better. At least until your mistress returns, that is."

"My mistress?" Pegeen echoed. "Whatever are you talking about?"

At that moment, the door flew open and the vicar limped into the room. Throwing back his shoulders, Mr. Richlands said with wounded dignity, "Pardon me for intruding, but I believe I owe you an apology, Miss Mac-Dougal."

"*Miss MacDougal?*" the stranger repeated, glancing sharply at Pegeen.

Before she could reply, Mr. Richlands continued. "It is, I believe, customary for young women to turn down a gentleman's first proposal, and so I shall not take your rejection too much to heart. I will ask again though, never fear, and again and again, until you do me the honor of becoming my wife."

Now Pegeen was clearly blushing. She had never been so mortified in her life. How could the vicar carry on so in the presence of a total stranger?

"I assure you, Mr. Richlands," Pegeen began hotly, "that no matter how many times you ask, my answer will always be the same. Do you think that I am some foolish young girl who trifles with men's affections as if they were trophies? If so, you think wrongly." With an imperious finger, Pegeen pointed towards the door. "Now I would thank you to leave this house."

Mr. Richlands started to do so but stopped suddenly and stared at the tall stranger.

"And might I ask what brings this gentleman to your cottage?" The vicar's voice was querulous with emotion. "It is unseemly of you, sir, to call alone upon a young, unchaperoned woman such as Miss MacDougal."

The grey-eyed man looked excessively startled, and it was only then that Pegeen herself began to wonder what he wanted. No one ever came to call upon her and Jeremy, except for a few of the parish women who joined Pegeen in her charity work. Who could this handsome stranger be? In her consternation over Mr. Richlands' proposal, it had never occurred to Pegeen to wonder.

The gentleman was clearly at a loss for words. "There seems to be some sort of mistake," he said at length.

"Mistake?" Pegeen stared at him. He was well groomed, caped in the finest cloak she'd ever seen, and his high boots fairly glowed, they'd been polished to such a sheen. His cravat was snowy white and expertly tied. All in all, he was an extraordinarily attractive man, but suddenly Pegeen began to see that there was something a little familiar about him as well. Something about those grey eyes. . . .

"I'm looking for a Miss MacDougal," he said uncertainly. "But the Miss MacDougal I seek is the aunt of one Jeremy Rawlings—"

Pegeen felt a sudden weight in the middle of her chest. "Yes, that's me," she sighed and her shoulders slumped tiredly. "What's Jeremy done now? Whatever it is, I swear we'll make it up to you. Was anyone hurt, sir? I can't tell you how sorry I am—"

"Uh, no, you misunderstand me." The stranger looked her straight in the eye, his discomfort readily apparent. He said, "I believe, madam, that I am your brother-in-law, Edward Rawlings."

Chapter Three

For a moment Edward thought the girl was going to faint.

All the bright color left her cheeks, rendering her as pale as a marble sculpture, and she seemed to sway a little on her feet. Moving hastily to her side, ready to catch her in his open arms if she fell, Edward cursed to himself, wishing he had killed Herbert when he'd had the chance. Of all the idiocy, to let him think the boy's aunt was a dried up old spinster when in reality she was the choicest piece of womanhood Edward had seen in, well, a good long time.

And he'd thought her nothing more than a fetching parlor maid when she'd come careening into his midsection like a cannonball! With her trim little figure and ivory complexion, she was certainly prettier than the parlor maids his friends kept in their London townhouses. Prettier, but no older. He ought to have known the moment she'd opened her mouth that she was no common housemaid, lacking as she did a traditional Scottish accent. Her English was as refined as any schoolgirl's. Damn that Herbert! And when she'd lifted that tussled mane of dark hair and he'd gotten a look at those emerald green eyes, well, he'd thanked his lucky stars she was only a servant or he'd have been in serious danger.

But she wasn't a servant. She was his sister-in-law.

And that information was apparently causing her to faint.

She didn't, however. Instead of slumping to the floor, or even into Edward's waiting arms, the girl fell back onto the settle, burying her face in her hands with a moan.

"Oh, no," Pegeen cried, in the throaty voice that Edward had found quite charming—until he'd found out who she was. "Somebody wake me. This day is turning out to be a nightmare."

Trying to disguise how deeply offended he was at being referred to as a nightmare—and wondering why it should bother him so much—Edward gazed down at her.

"I beg your pardon, madam, but . . . shall I ring for your maid?"

"Maid!" cried the vicar contemptuously. "She hasn't any maid. Just a charwoman who comes in once a week to help with the heavy work, and then only because I pay for it, out of my own pocket!"

Edward looked down at the bent head, trying to catch a glimpse of the face hidden beneath that curtain of red-brown hair. "No maid? You mean she and the boy live here—all alone?"

"Quite alone," Richlands replied with the relish of a born tattletale. "Not even a woman to look in on them at night. But she wouldn't have anyone, even though I offered the services of my dear widowed aunt, Mrs. Peabody. Miss MacDougal said there wasn't room and she wouldn't be bossed about. But then Miss MacDougal has always been highly unconventional, sir, most unsuitably so. It's disgraceful, I've said, from the very beginning. A young unmarried woman, living alone. Why, there's no telling what ideas the men in the village might get up to—"

"No," Edward said, shooting the red-haired youth a baleful glance. "There's no telling, is there? Why, they might even force themselves upon her, demanding that she marry them because they've paid for a charwoman to come in once a week." He had the satisfaction of seeing the young braggart flush angrily. Turning his attention back to Pegeen, Edward inquired, gently, "Is there anything I can get for you, Miss MacDougal? Smelling salts, perhaps?"

"Smelling salts?" Pegeen lifted her head, a chestnut-colored lock of hair falling over one eye. She fixed him with a disbelieving stare. "Smelling salts? You must be joking. A shot of whiskey would be more the thing, don't you think?"

Taken aback by her temerity, Edward raised his eyebrows. "Whiskey?" And then, when he saw by her expression that she wasn't teasing, he asked gamely, "Where do you keep it?"

"Miss MacDougal," exclaimed Richlands, in the same timorous voice that had earlier set Edward's teeth on edge. "I beg you to reconsider. Spirits are never the answer—"

"Oh, get away from me, the both of you."

Rising, the girl stalked disgustedly out of the room, her boot heels clacking loudly on the wood floorboards.

Edward stood staring at the vicar, feeling murderous. It was evident that he couldn't have come to call on Miss MacDougal at a more inopportune time. Perhaps if he came some other morning, when unwanted suitors weren't proclaiming their love for her, the girl might be more receptive to him. Certainly, before she'd known who he was, she'd been easy with him—friendly, one might almost have said. He flattered himself that he'd seen admiration in her glance and why not? He was clearly a magnificent specimen of a man. Or at least better than this self-righteous vicar.

But Edward certainly wasn't going to leave until the

other man left, and the besotted fool didn't look at all ready to depart.

Richlands fixed Edward with a challenging stare and said, "I don't know who you think you are, but you should know right now that I intend to marry Miss MacDougal, and if you have any, shall we say, less honorable designs upon her, then I suggest that you leave."

"I told you who I am, you bleating coxcomb," growled Edward, and he had the pleasure of seeing the smaller man pale at the threatening note in his deep voice. "I'm her brother-in-law, and my only intention is to get my nephew away from here and install him as the seventeenth Duke of Rawlings."

The vicar cleared his throat. "If that is your intention, sir, then you are going to be disappointed. Miss MacDougal would never allow anyone to take Master Jeremy from her. She loves him as if he were her own son. I, of course, would be willing to raise him like my own, providing she agrees to send him away to school."

"How noble of you," sneered Edward, "to put her wishes ahead of your own. What are you to her?"

The youth—for so Edward thought him, though the man was probably close enough to his own age—looked taken aback. "What am I to Miss MacDougal? Why, whatever can you mean?"

"You said you pay for her charwoman." Edward had a distinctly unpleasant taste in his mouth. "Is she your mistress?"

"Sir!" Richlands turned red as a pomegranate. "How dare you? My suit for Miss MacDougal's hand is completely honorable. If it weren't for the church's generosity—*my* church, sir—she and that blasted boy would be in a workhouse now, instead of living in this relative luxury—"

Edward glanced around the room, which, though attractively arranged, was quite cold and reeked of genteel poverty. "You call this luxury?" he smirked. "Why, I've been in tombs warmer than this. Don't you supply her with enough coal to heat this bloody hovel?''

''Sir!'' The thin-lipped vicar looked about to suffer an apoplexy. ''I might ask you, who claims to be her brother-in-law, why you haven't seen fit to supply Miss MacDougal with a single ha' penny in support of her nephew! Had I any idea her relations were so well-off, I most definitely would have appealed to Miss MacDougal to write to you of her poverty!''

Sickened by both Richlands' insinuating tone of voice and the fact that he had him to thank, apparently, for the keep of his nephew all this time, Edward reached into his waistcoat and drew out his purse. ''How much?'' he demanded tersely.

''I beg your pardon, sir?''

''How much, total, has the church spent on Miss MacDougal and her nephew since the death of her father?''

The vicar looked nonplussed. ''I could not begin to calculate. You cannot put a price, sir, on Christian charity.''

''Tell me how much, damn you, or I'll wring that pious neck of yours.''

The youth stamped an irritated foot. ''Seventeen pounds, eight pence, sir.''

Edward counted out the money and stepped forward. Seizing Richlands by his coat collar with one hand, he dropped the coins into the vicar's pocket with the other.

''Now,'' Edward snarled, thinking that he really was enjoying himself far too much. ''If you're not out of this house by the time I count to ten, I'll drag you outside and thrash you within an inch of your snivelling life. Do I make myself clear?''

Richlands gasped. ''Do you, sir, know to whom you are speaking? I am the Honorable Jonathan Richlands, vicar to the village of Applesby, and I take deep offense at your—''

''One,'' growled Edward.

"—vile threats—"

"Two."

Richlands began to look worried. "I would not be a gentleman if I left a man like you alone with Miss MacDougal."

"Three. You aren't a gentleman, Richlands. If you were, you would not be attempting to blackmail an innocent girl."

"Blackmail? What are you saying, sir?"

"You tell her she owes you for your charity and then you propose. I call that blackmail." Lifting a quizzical brow, Edward demanded, "And what do you mean, a man like me?"

"Well, you're obviously a member of the aristocracy. I've heard what men like you do to pretty, defenseless girls like Pegeen. You think that just because you've got a title and some land that gives you the right to gallop about the countryside, debauching every woman you meet. Well, you won't have Pegeen. I'll . . . I'll fight you for her, I will! I did some boxing in seminary school. I was really quite good at it."

"Four." Edward had to admire the man for trying. "You're a Liberal, too, then, are you?"

"Absolutely. I'll always stand and fight for the good of the common man. Especially against lecherous woman-izers like yourself."

"Ten," Edward said, because he wanted to wipe the floor with the ignorant sod's face. Unfortunately, Richlands didn't possess the strength of his convictions, for he turned pale as a rabbit and ran out the door, shouting for help.

Edward followed him as far as the garden gate, but it was clear young Mr. Richlands had no intention of allowing himself to be caught. Sliding awkwardly on the icy lane, the vicar hightailed it to the safety of his own parlor. Shrugging philosophically, Edward went back inside the house.

A casual examination of the sitting room's furnishings

as he sought his reluctant hostess proved his supposition that Miss MacDougal, though proud, was living only just above the brink of poverty. However much her parents had left her—and Edward could not imagine it to be more than forty pounds a year—she was clearly not independent. The cottage itself was owned by the church and had undoubtedly been offered to her at a reduced rent because her father had died so suddenly, leaving her nowhere to go. While the furnishings were well kept and of good quality, they were old, probably handed down from some long-dead parishioner. Close scrutiny of the girl's pelisse revealed it to have seen at least a dozen winters, indubitably at the hands of a former owner. Even the newspapers, which Edward found tucked neatly away beside the settle, were twice creased, revealing proof of previous scanning at the hands of another.

　　After his inspection, Edward felt even more keenly the extraordinariness of the girl's flat rejection of both Herbert's offer and the vicar's proposal. While Edward himself could not picture a less worthy husband than the self-righteous Mr. Richlands, Pegeen MacDougal hadn't much to offer in the way of a dowry besides her pretty face and enticing figure. And she came saddled with a nephew. There probably weren't many men in Applesby who'd be willing to take on a penniless bride, however pretty, as well as a ten-year-old boy. Mr. Richlands might well have been her last hope. But she had rejected him as flatly as she had rejected Herbert. What ailed the girl? Edward had never met Katherine, his brother's wife, but he could only assume that lunacy ran in the blood of the MacDougal clan.

　　He found her in the kitchen, heating a pot of something that smelled delicious and making a great deal of noise slamming cutlery down onto a table pointedly set for two. She'd pulled her hair back and tied a shapeless apron around her reed-slim waist, but there wasn't anything she could do to make herself less attractive, if that's what she'd been attempting.

Scowling at him, Pegeen said, "I distinctly remember telling you to leave."

"Where did you learn your manners?" Edward inquired, leaning casually against the door frame. "A member of the family comes all the way from Yorkshire for a visit and you don't even offer him a cup of tea? Tisk, tisk."

"You're not a member of my family," she declared. She took a loaf of brown bread from a drawer and began to hack at it with a very large knife. "I've never seen you before in my life. How do I know you're even who you say you are? For all I know, you could be some stranger who wandered in off the street and wants to take Jeremy away to force him into child labor in London."

"Did you look out the window?" Edward walked over to her. She stood at a cutting board that was placed directly in front of a window. Through the fingers of frost that covered the glass panes, his carriage could be seen plainly.

"That's a brougham with the Rawlings crest on the door," Edward said, and because she still had her back stiffly to him, he leaned both of his large hands against the cutting board on either side of her narrow waist, trapping her within the confines of his arms.

"The footmen hanging onto that brougham are dressed in Rawlings livery, green and gold," he continued amiably, conscious that he was standing closely enough to her that his breath stirred the fine tendrils of hair at the nape of her neck. "And those horses—all bays, all perfectly matched. You couldn't find finer horses than that in all of Scotland, and I don't mean that disparagingly. Do those look to you like the horses of someone who would employ child laborers?"

She turned her head to look up at him, and he saw that her expressive green eyes were surrounded by dark lashes that had an insouciant curl to them. She smelled quite nice, of soap and something else. Violets, maybe. The column of her neck was so slender that he felt he could have circled her throat with a single hand. How would she react, he wondered, if he pressed his lips upon the whiteness of her neck, just below one delicately curving earlobe?

Pegeen found herself curiously affected by her brother-in-law's close proximity. She could feel the heat from his body at her back, and a glance at the hands on either side of her revealed fingers brown and strong from riding and hunting but uncallused, she thought wryly, by any sort of *real* labor. A sudden and unbidden vision of those hands on her body sent a rush of hot color into her face. Good God, what was she thinking? She had met the man hardly an hour ago and already she was fantasizing about . . .

Her fingers tightened on the knife handle. Damn him. So *that* was his game!

Since Edward had refrained from acting on his impulse to kiss Pegeen, he was more than a little surprised when she suddenly brought the knife down very hard not an inch from his right index finger. Barking a sharp interjection, he yanked the cleaver from her hand and spun her around by the shoulders to face him.

"You little hussy," he cried, glaring down at her furiously. "You could have cut my finger off!"

"Is it your intention, Lord Edward," Pegeen demanded with measured calm, "to seduce me right here in my very own kitchen? Because if it is, let me warn you right now that I have a great many more knives just like this one and I'm not the least bit afraid to use them."

When Edward only gaped down at her, the girl smiled a smile without any humor in it.

"Let me see if I can guess how it went." The bright green eyes were shrewd upon him. "Poor, hapless Sir Arthur returned to Rawlings Manor bemoaning the fact that the little duke's cruel aunt wouldn't allow him to be returned to the family seat. You berated poor, hapless Sir Arthur. 'What?' I imagine you said. 'You let a simple woman order you about? We'll see about that.' Accordingly, you arrived here in Applesby expecting to find a haggish termagant against whom you were prepared to pit your tremendous intellect and even more tremendous purse. What you found, however, was me, and you were forced to change tactics. From manipulation to seduction, am I correct?''

Edward was so angry he could only sputter. What sort of vicar's daughter was this, who drank whiskey and threatened him with a cleaver? Edward didn't have any idea how he was supposed to react to her shenanigans. He didn't know any young girls with the exception of Herbert's five daughters, and all of them seemed to go out of their way to avoid him whenever possible. He had a sneaking suspicion that they did so because Lady Herbert had warned them about his reputation as an unregenerate rake. Certainly, no well-meaning grand dames of society ever steered their virgin daughters in his direction. And had they done so, Edward couldn't imagine any of those whey-faced misses blithely brandishing bread knives.

But this green-eyed vixen had done so as casually as if it were a habit acquired in childhood. Hell and damnation!

''I was *not* trying to seduce you,'' Edward lied, his voice so low it sounded like a growl.

''Weren't you? I thought that's what I heard Mr. Richlands accusing you of trying to do directly before you chased him out of the house.''

Edward glared at her in annoyance. Vexing wench! And was she fey that she so perfectly captured the gist of his conversation with Herbert? That's all he needed, a witch for a sister-in-law. What had John been thinking, marrying into this ridiculously eccentric family? Granted, if Katherine had been anywhere near as pretty as her sister, he could understand the attraction. Nevertheless, it was no small wonder the duke had stricken John's name from the will.

Pegeen abruptly turned her back upon him again and continued hacking away at the brown loaf in front of her. "Let's not play games, shall we, Lord Edward? I know why you're here—"

"Do you?" Edward could not stifle a smile at her officiousness.

"I'm not a fool." She put away the knife. Folding her arms across her chest, she turned to face him again. "What I don't understand is why."

"Why?" The smile quickly turned to a frown. "What do you mean, why?"

"Surely it would have been a simple thing to assume the title yourself. Why did you go to all this trouble to find Jeremy? I'm quite certain if you had said the boy couldn't be found and was presumed dead, everyone would have believed you. No one would have questioned your right to the title. So why?"

"Why?" Edward shook his head irritably. "Everyone keeps asking me that. No one seems to understand that I cannot honorably assume a title that rightfully belongs to another!"

Pegeen's slender eyebrows rose. "Honor? That's a surprising virtue to find in a member of your class. I thought honor, like chivalry, died with the knights of the Round Table."

"You take a very dim view of my *class*, as you call it," Edward observed. "Might I ask what any of us ever did to you to warrant such censure?"

"Nothing. That's the problem. You have all the wealth and power and yet you do nothing for the thousands of people like me who haven't anything."

Edward straightened. "Now, see here—"

"Don't deny it. I don't see you sitting in the House of Lords striving for reform. I don't see you working for

the good of the common man. I'll wager the only reason
you wanted Jeremy found was so that you could continue
leading your hedonistic lifestyle uninterrupted by vexing
estate business.''

Edward was so taken aback that he could only sputter.
Never in his life had he been spoken to in such a manner,
not by a woman, and certainly not by one ten years younger
than him and so far beneath his social standing. Never mind
that what she'd said had a grain of truth to it. He was deeply
offended by her reference to his supposed hedonism.

''Very well, then, Miss MacDougal,'' he said stiffly,
folding his own arms in an unconscious imitation of her
stance. ''You said you don't want to play games. I think
it's time we discussed your future, don't you?''

Pegeen looked at him as if he were demented. ''I beg
your pardon?''

''Your future. Yours and Jeremy's. You've thought
about what's going to happen when your mother's money
runs out, haven't you?''

The dark, slender eyebrows descended in a rush.
''What do you know about my mother's money?'' she demanded.

''I know there isn't much of it and it isn't going to
last forever. Let's be frank, Miss MacDougal.'' He looked
her up and down with deliberate rudeness. ''You've already
shown me that you're good at that.''

He never would have thought it possible but suddenly
she was blushing. Hot color flooded those silken cheeks,
and she dropped her gaze down at his boot tops. ''Well
put,'' she acknowledged, without a smile.

He was delighted to discover that he had *some* power
over her at least. ''All right then. You've already turned
down both my agent's offer and at least one marriage proposal. Just what *are* your plans for the future? Do you intend to live upon the charity of the church forever?''

"Certainly not," she sniffed. "This is a temporary situation."

"Temporary? Then you are expecting other, more profitable marriage proposals?"

She stuck out her pointed chin. "Certainly not," she said again. "I shall never marry."

"Ah." He reached up to rub his jaw, studying her. "Because you hate men?"

"I do not hate men," she declared. "Only *some* men. But that is not why I shall never marry. I shall never marry because the laws governing this island upon which we live make married women nothing but subservient chattel to their husbands. Married women cannot own property, cannot divorce, even in the case of husbands who abuse or abandon them, and custody of any children of such a union is given to the husband, however big a bounder or cad he might be . . ."

"I see." Edward could not help grinning. "In your eyes, marriage is a very grim prospect indeed."

"Not just my eyes, Lord Edward. The eyes of many women here in England, as well as abroad. Why, anyone who has read Mary Wollstonecraft's *A Vindication of the Rights of Woman* can tell you—"

"That's all very well and good, Miss MacDougal," Edward cut her off. The last thing he wanted to hear was a lecture on the rights of woman. As far as he was concerned, the women in his life were perfectly content, and when they weren't, he bought them jewelry or a townhouse and that shut them up. "But I believe we were discussing Jeremy, not your views on the institution of marriage. Have you considered what, precisely, you're going to do about him once your mother's money and the church's charity runs out?"

Pegeen hesitated. Clearly she had not.

"The fact is, Miss MacDougal, while you are free to

go about decrying the injustice of mankind, there is Jeremy to keep in mind.''

Pegeen looked angry. ''I have always kept Jeremy in mind, Lord Edward! Unlike *some* people—''

''Jeremy is the heir to a very great fortune,'' Edward interrupted. ''There is nothing you can do about that, Miss MacDougal, whatever your political leanings. He must and will assume his responsibilities as the seventeenth duke of Rawlings.''

''Is that so?''

He should have seen it coming. He ought to have known that she would not stand meekly by while he lectured to her. But he missed the warning signs as he strutted about the kitchen, casually spinning a chair around and rudely straddling it without asking her permission or offering her the chair first.

''That,'' he said, enjoying himself immensely, ''is so, Miss MacDougal.''

''Tell me this, then, *Lord* Edward.'' She said the word 'lord' scathingly. The arms that had been folded across her chest now dropped and her hands went to her hips. ''If Jerry is the duke of Rawlings, where has this great fortune been up until now? I haven't seen a farthing of support from the magnificent house of Rawlings. My father and I raised Jeremy from an infant and this past year I've done it alone as well as I could. But you have the nerve to sit there and accuse me of not thinking of him!''

Edward began to realize that perhaps he had spoken rashly. ''Miss MacDougal, I didn't mean to imply that you weren't—''

''How do you explain your neglect of the past ten years?'' she demanded. ''You're his uncle, every bit as much as I'm his aunt. And yet where have *you* been?''

Edward twisted a little in his seat, a bit uncomfortable. He was a large man, and the chair was designed for a much smaller person. ''You know perfectly well—''

"I know perfectly well that when it's convenient for you Jerry is the duke of Rawlings. When it's convenient for *Jerry*, however, we don't hear a peep out of you."

"That isn't it and you know it," Edward said quickly. "My father wrote Jeremy's parents out of his will. When he heard they had died, he was, I'm sorry to say, glad of it. It wasn't until the old man was dying himself that he relented and agreed to acknowledge Jeremy as his rightful heir—"

"And because of your father's bitter disappointment that your brother married a Scottish vicar's daughter and not some society lady from London, Jeremy's had to sleep with me every night since my father's death, because we can't afford enough coal for two fireplaces." She spoke in a hard voice. "He's had to wear clothes handed down from other children because I hadn't enough money to buy him his own boots or trousers—"

Edward started to rise from the chair. "Miss Mac-Dougal—"

"He's had to have porridge for breakfast every day for a year, because I can't afford more than two eggs a week, and we eat those for supper what with meat being so dear—" Her voice cracked, and Edward was amazed to see that tears threatened to spill out of those jewel-like eyes. "And he's had to suffer the pity of odious people like Mr. Richlands! And you have the unmitigated cheek to think that after enduring what he has, he should sink down onto his knees and thank you for handing him a duchy? That after what your family put him through, put his parents through, that he should be *grateful* to you? You spoke of honor a little while ago. Do you think that Jeremy hasn't any? He does, my lord, and I assure you, it has been most sorely compromised these past few months. There aren't enough duchies in the world to make up for that!"

To Edward's astonishment, the girl turned from him

with a sob. "Oh!" she cried. "And you wonder why I support the Liberals?"

Edward was completely at a loss. It had never occurred to him that she might resent his family for their treatment of her sister and nephew, though, of course, he should have known. How else could she feel but resentful? The Rawlings family had brought the MacDougal clan nothing but trouble.

"Miss MacDougal, I can't tell you how sorry—"

Pegeen had turned her back on him, however, and was standing with shaking shoulders, at the cutting board. She could not believe she was crying in front of him, but for the life of her, she could not stop. The very last thing she'd wanted to do in front of this arrogant, cruelly handsome man was show any sort of weakness, but here she was, sobbing half-hysterically, as if all the grief that had been pent up within her for over a year was finally spilling out. She was mumbling through her tears and disjointed phrases came floating towards him. "—despicable old man . . . children to suffer for their parents' mistakes . . . expect us to just pick up and go with you like nothing has happened—"

Edward shoved away his chair and climbed to his feet. "Miss MacDougal, please believe me, I had no idea. We didn't even know where Jeremy was until just last month, and we certainly didn't know that all this time he was being raised single-handedly by a maiden aunt. . . ."

This only seemed to make the slender shoulders shake even harder. Edward had no more experience dealing with young girls' tears than he'd had with their impertinence, but he found that overall he distinctly preferred impertinence. Pegeen's sobs were heart-wrenching. Each one seemed to pluck at a separate chord within his gut.

"Please, Miss MacDougal! You must believe me. I'd give anything, anything I own to undo the hardships you've been forced to endure. . . ."

Not knowing what else to do, Edward approached her with the intention of soothing her some way or another, possibly by promising to buy her a bracelet. That had always worked whenever one of his mistresses burst into tears. He certainly had no other thought in his mind save placating her. Anything else would have been quite untoward.

But when he placed a hand on either of her slim shoulders and turned her towards him, looking down into her pretty, tear-stained face, something extremely odd happened.

Edward, who'd been with literally hundreds of women in his lifetime, and who'd always had perfect mastery over his own baser instincts, was struck by a sudden impulse to lay a kiss upon those moistly parted, beckoningly red lips. Never mind that kissing one's sister-in-law was singularly ill-advised under any circumstances, and under the present ones, absolutely disastrous. Never mind that he was a decade her senior and had probably already compromised her reputation by being unchaperoned in the same house with her. Never mind that she was alone in the world and that only a cad would take advantage of a woman in her current economical let alone emotional state. He felt an urge to kiss her that was stronger than any compulsion he had ever known, and without thinking further, he obeyed it.

Chapter Four

The second Edward's lips met hers, Pegeen stiffened with surprise. Her eyelids, which had been lowered, flew wide open. His fingers tightened on her shoulders as if he expected her to pull away, and though when similarly accosted but an hour before by Mr. Richlands, flight had been her immediate reaction, this time escape was the last thing on Pegeen's mind. Edward's mouth on hers was manipulative, making her feel things she'd never experienced before. Instinctively, her arms crept up to circle his neck. A heartbeat later, she felt his hands leave her shoulders, his fingers slipping beneath the heavy fall of her braid to cradle her head. When Edward's tongue met hers, the explosion of sensations within her nearly knocked her off her feet. A rush of warmth coursed between her thighs, and her nipples went taut in the lace cups of her camisole. Pegeen made a soft noise, not of protest but of pleasure.

Edward had expected a reaction from the outspoken girl, but not the kind he received. A slap, at the very least, and words of embittered reproach. Instead, he found himself holding a woman so soft and yielding that he felt he could have lifted her to the cutting board and had her, then and there, as many times as he pleased and never heard a negative word from her. How could he have known in the short time they'd been acquainted that beneath Pegeen MacDougal's prudish facade was a sensuality so strong that even now her eyes were half-lidded with desire, her lips raw from his savaging of them? He hadn't the slightest idea how he'd sensed it. He only knew that he wanted this woman more than he could ever remember wanting anyone. His erratically pounding heart was proof of that, if not the front of his breeches, which strained from the pressure of a rock-hard erection. . . .

There was no telling what might have happened next had not the back door to the kitchen suddenly been flung open, letting in an icy blast of wind. Before Edward had a chance to react, he found himself accosted by a four foot tall bundle of woolen mittens and scarves that seemed to have been blown indoors by the force of the wind.

"What are you doing to Pegeen?" a childish voice demanded from within the confines of a brightly colored muffler.

Pegeen sprang away from Edward as if he'd singed her. Her cheeks scarlet with embarrassment, she put both hands to her hair, straightening the mess Edward's fingers had made of her braid.

"Jerry, you're late," she said in an unsteady voice, stepping quickly forward to close the door behind the boy. "And where are your manners? That's not how we greet visitors."

Edward, completely unmanned by the interruption, had to turn away to hide his obvious state of arousal. He was panting as if he'd just run a race. More than anything, he longed to throw the duke of Rawlings back out into the snow so he could continue ravishing the boy's aunt.

"Did you wipe your feet, young man?" Pegeen demanded with a calmness Edward envied.

Steadfastly ignoring his aunt, Jeremy Rawlings glared

up at Edward, his grey eyes the only recognizably human trait visible through all the garments he wore.

"What were you doing to Pegeen?" the boy wanted to know.

"Now, Jeremy," Pegeen was saying, as she went to work unraveling the scarves. "That's no way to speak to your uncle Edward."

"My uncle *what*?" the boy echoed rudely.

"Your uncle Edward."

The girl whipped a wool cap from the duke's head, revealing a head of hair as dark and as curly as Edward's own. The child's face was rosy-cheeked and slightly freckled, not unlike his aunt's. The set of the mouth, Edward saw, was familiar as well.

"This is your uncle Edward. He was just, uh . . ."

"Kissing your aunt hello," Edward supplied helpfully. He still didn't dare turn towards them. "Haven't seen her in quite awhile."

Jeremy Rawlings was evidently not a dim child by any stretch of the imagination. He glared at Pegeen's blushing cheeks and said staunchly, "That didn't look to me like a kiss hello. It looked to me like the kind of kiss Mrs. MacFearley gives to men who'll pay her a penny—"

Pegeen interrupted hastily. "Take off your boots and sit down. Your dinner will get cold."

Studying the boy, Edward ran a hand through his hair and let out a ragged sigh. "I'll be sworn," he said under his breath. "If I didn't know better, I'd think I was back in the nursery being tormented again by my older brother John. That's his mouth, all right. I've never seen anything so cruel."

Pegeen overheard him and frowned. "Not Jeremy," she said. "Mischievous, maybe, but not cruel."

Jeremy fixed his uncle with a steely-eyed glare. "Is that your carriage outside?" he demanded, his cherubic face in stark contrast to the sneering suspicion in his voice.

Edward raised his dark eyebrows. "It is. Do you like it?"

"Better than Sir Arthur's," Jeremy muttered darkly. "I never saw a man with a redder face than his. Like a cherry. I thought he might spontaneously combust."

In response to Edward's quizzically raised eyebrows, Pegeen said by way of explanation, "Mr. Dickens' *Bleak House*. We've been reading it out loud in the evening. Several of the characters spontaneously combust. Jeremy, sit down and stop telling tales. And if you know what's good for you, you'll take off those boots or you'll be scrubbing the floor again come Saturday."

Edward hadn't the slightest idea what Pegeen was talking about. He knew only that she was looking more appealing than ever with her pink cheeks and mussed hair. The brown wool dress she wore was perhaps a size too small and fit her snugly, the bodice clearly revealing the hardened peaks of her breasts. Edward wished he'd fondled those breasts while he'd had the chance.

"Well, my lord, am I to take it that you're staying to dinner?" Pegeen inquired.

Startled, Edward looked down and saw that the table was only set for two. Whatever it was his nephew was devouring in large gulps smelled divine. Thinking guiltily of his footmen shivering outside, Edward said, "Well, I—"

"There isn't enough for all of you," Pegeen said, matter-of-factly. "You ought to send them down to the village pub. They've a very good ploughman's lunch there. In fact, you might want to join them."

"Witch," Edward accused her.

She smiled beguilingly. "Hardly. If I were, I'd make you disappear."

By the time Edward returned from dispatching his drivers and footmen to the pub, a third place had been set at the table and a pot of ale stood near his steaming bowl of stew. This small expense surprised and touched him.

Pegeen MacDougal hadn't much, but what she had she was willing to share. The woman was a confusing bundle of contradictions, and Edward found himself more and more drawn to her.

That fact, coupled with the discovery that her stew was delicious, led Edward to believe he was in very great danger indeed. He had already been fool enough to kiss her. He would not allow himself to be stupid enough to fall in love with her. Better to have her on the defensive, spouting her Liberal politics, than sitting across from him, daintily sipping beer and looking like an angel.

So he cleared his throat and said without preamble, "So, Jeremy. Would you like a carriage of your own like the one outside?"

Jeremy laid down his spoon, his grey eyes wide. "*Would* I?" he cried. "Why, I'd ride straight over to Brandon McHugh's and spit in his eye—"

"You'll do no such thing," Pegeen said, lowering her glass with a bang. "Lord Edward, I'd thank you not to put ideas into the boy's head."

"But Jeremy's the duke of Rawlings," Edward shrugged with mock innocence. "If he wants to purchase a carriage like mine and ride over to Brandon McHugh's and spit in his eye, that is His Grace's prerogative."

Pegeen's green eyes fairly crackled with fire. "Lord Edward—"

"A duke's got to have his own horse," Edward continued, as if he hadn't heard her. "So of course you and I will have to take a trip to London to secure a fine one, Jeremy."

"A horse?" For the first time since his arrival, Jeremy looked at his uncle with actual respect. "A horse of my own? A real horse? Not a bloody pony?"

"Jeremy," his aunt said calmly. "Don't say bloody."

"A real horse," Edward said quickly. "A hunter, sixteen hands high for you, and a . . . a dappled grey mare for Miss MacDougal.''

''Unlike a certain ten-year-old boy, Lord Edward, Miss MacDougal cannot be bought off by horseflesh,'' Pegeen said with a slightly bitter smile. Still, it was a smile, and Edward pressed his advantage.

''And not only that, Jerry. You'll have your own bedroom, as well as a schoolroom with the best tutors money can buy and a nursery full of toys.''

His cherubic face turned up towards his uncle's, Jeremy said, ''I never had any toys before. Grandfather said they were for babies.''

''Well, toys you shall have, Your Grace,'' Edward declared. He leaned down and lifted the boy up, setting him down on his lap. To his surprise, Jeremy didn't protest. ''The only problem, Jerry, is that your aunt Pegeen doesn't want you to go with me.''

Pegeen shot him a look that might have frozen volcanic lava. ''That is hardly the *only* problem, Lord Edward,'' she said.

''Isn't there anything,'' Edward wondered, ''that I could give your aunt that would make her want to come with us back to Rawlings?''

Jeremy regarded Pegeen from across the tabletop. ''I don't know,'' the boy said uncertainly. ''She looks angry. What'd you do to her, anyway?''

''How about a new gown?'' Edward ventured, ignoring the boy's query. ''Wouldn't you like to see your aunt Pegeen in a new gown, Jerry? A gown by Mr. Worth? Wouldn't she look like an angel?''

The boy nodded hesitantly, clearly not knowing what Edward was talking about, then wiggled to get more comfortable. ''I always think Pegeen looks like an angel, no matter what she's got on.''

''That is undoubtedly true. Oh, my, your aunt will have all the new gowns she likes, and the Rawlings jewels, as well. And her own maids, and—'' He tried desperately to think of something that might appeal to the wench. Unlike his mistresses, she looked completely unimpressed by the mention of Worth gowns and jewelry. Then he remembered the newspapers. ''And an entire library at her disposal, one of the finest in the country, and her very own newspapers, not previously read by anyone . . .''

That seemed to get her attention. She stared at him even more coldly.

''Oh,'' Jeremy said. ''Pegeen likes newspapers. And books, too. Did you hear what my uncle said, Pegeen? You're to have books and newspapers, as many as you like.''

''I heard him,'' Pegeen said tonelessly.

Edward hurried to add, ''And she'll have an allowance she can dispose of however she likes of no less than a thousand a year, and—''

''And a real horse?'' Jeremy asked again. ''Of my very own?''

''Yes. And a conservatory in which roses grow all year round, even in winter.''

Pegeen bit her lower lip, then released it from her small, even teeth, leaving it lush and red as blood. ''Now you're simply being ridiculous. Whoever heard of roses all year round in Yorkshire of all places?''

Edward tried not to stare at her mouth, which was bow-shaped and eminently kissable. He wondered if the vicar had kissed her and felt an overwhelming regret that he hadn't thrashed the man.

''We have them,'' he said, and had to clear his throat. ''At Rawlings Manor. I am not lying to you. Come with me and see for yourself. As part of the bargain, I'll gladly continue to chase away all of your unwanted suitors, free of charge.''

With a quickly suppressed smile, Pegeen said, ''Jerry, hop down from there. You have to get back to school.''

Jeremy didn't budge. "Can't we go with him, Pegeen? I want to see the roses that grow all year round, even in winter."

"Your uncle and I will discuss it," she said. "But I have to say, I don't think so."

Jeremy groaned with disappointment. "Why ever not?" he whined.

"Because it isn't that easy, Jeremy." Pegeen rose from the table and began clearing the dishes away, careful not to let Lord Edward get a glimpse of the tears that had gathered once more beneath her eyelids. "People . . . people can't just come swooping down with offers of hunters and year-round roses and expect us to forgive and forget." Pumping cold water onto the plates, Pegeen grumbled at the frost-tinged window, "I won't be bought, you know. Not for a pile of newspapers."

Setting Jeremy aside, Edward rose. Though he didn't know where they came from, a torrent of words left his lips rapidly and with much emotion.

"Miss MacDougal, please forgive me," he said to the girl's narrow back. "I know there is no possible way I can ever repay you for what you must have suffered raising Jeremy on your own this past year, but you must believe me when I say that had I known, I would not have allowed it. And I'm asking you—no, I'm begging you—to let me try to make it up to you by taking you both back to Rawlings Manor with me, where I swear to you there's enough coal for a fire in every room and Jeremy can have as many eggs for breakfast as he likes."

While this ineloquent though heartfelt speech seemed to have no effect on Miss MacDougal, who continued rinsing the dinner dishes, it seemed to please Jeremy very much.

"Eggs for breakfast every morning?" The boy went to his aunt's side and pulled on her skirt. "Did you hear that, Peggy? Eggs every single morning!"

Edward, seeing that he'd scored an unexpected advantage, hastened to remain on the offensive. "And meat at suppertime every night."

"Oh, can't we go with him, Peggy?" the boy pleaded. "Can't we go?"

"Maybe," Pegeen said. She wiped her hands on a dish towel and then, taking off her apron and hanging it on a peg by the pantry door, she said, "But right now you have to go back to school."

Jeremy looked up at Edward, his small face transformed by a smile of delight. "When Pegeen says maybe, she always means yes," he whispered. After imparting that useful piece of information, he went to put his boots back on.

It wasn't until Jeremy had safely passed through the garden gate that his aunt turned around and slapped Edward so hard across the face that he saw stars.

"That's for the kiss," Pegeen said tersely. Then, as if nothing had happened, she went calmly to the sideboard and withdrew a bottle of whiskey and two glasses.

Edward was still reeling from the blow, which had been a surprisingly hard one for so slight a wench. He hadn't been slapped by a woman since—well, he couldn't remember when—and the sensation had been distinctly unpleasant. Reaching up to rub his jaw, he eyed Pegeen as she poured out two generous dollops of whiskey, then slid one of the glasses towards him.

"Here," she said, sitting down in the chair directly across the table from him. "You look as if you need this as much as I do." And with a practiced flick of the wrist, the contents of her glass disappeared down her throat.

"Oh." Pegeen was coughing a second later. "I needed that."

Edward, still completely nonplussed by the slap, didn't trust himself to reply. What could the girl have been thinking? Hadn't she enjoyed the embrace every bit as much as he had? He couldn't have mistaken the lust in her eyes, or the desire on those sweet lips, or the way her body had swayed against his so readily. Was the girl mad? Or merely denying what she knew, in fact, to be true?

Lifting the whiskey glass to his lips, he drank, then proceeded to choke as if his gullet was on fire.

"What *is* this stuff?" he rasped, when he could bring himself to speak between coughs.

Pegeen looked down into her own empty glass, her eyebrows raised innocently. "Just some of the local peat whiskey, distilled right here in Applesby. What's the matter? Is it a bit strong for you, then?"

"Strong?" Edward's eyes had teared over. "It's like drinking vitriol . . ."

"Ah, well. Perhaps it's an acquired taste. I've been drinking it all my life." As if to illustrate this, Pegeen poured herself another glass. "It's mother's milk to me. Another?"

Edward, still hacking, shook his head. "You keep away from me," he warned, wagging a finger at her. "Since meeting you, I've been verbally assaulted by a man of the cloth, nearly had a finger cut off, my face slapped, and my vitals burned. I don't know if I can take much more."

She smiled at him pertly. "If you had listened to Sir Arthur and stayed away like I told him, you'd be enjoying a nice smoke and a brandy before a roaring fire, your head resting in your mistress' lap."

Edward glared at her. "And what do you know about mistresses?" he demanded with more suspicion than was perhaps necessary.

The pert smile turned wry. "Oh, why nothing, of course. What could a mere vicar's daughter like myself possibly know about the worldly ways of a gentleman like yourself?"

Edward glared at her, remembering the kiss they'd

shared. While he was quite certain it wasn't something she did on a regular basis, he was equally sure that she knew a good deal about kissing, though for the life of him, he couldn't figure out how. "I'll wager from that statement that you know a lot more than you're letting on. How old are you, anyway?"

She arched a single delicate eyebrow. "What impertinence. Why on earth should I tell you how old I am?"

Edward shrugged. "I'm family."

"Jeremy's, not mine," she pointed out. "Unlike my sister Katherine, I would never have married a member of the aristocracy, not for all the tea in China."

"I thought you were never marrying anyone at all. Remember?" He grinned. "I didn't think that sentiment only excluded men like myself."

"Oh, it doesn't. Though I do think men like you are among the most despicable of your sex."

He caught her studying his reaction like a schoolboy studies a spider whose leg he's just torn off, and though he knew he shouldn't, he asked, "Oh? And how is that, pray tell?"

"It's men like you who are holding back vital reforms that will help thousands of suffering women and children all over this country," she replied chipperly enough. "Perhaps even all over the world, since everyone looks to England as a bastion of morality."

Edward very nearly burst out laughing. "What in God's name are you talking about?"

"Don't you know?" Pegeen rolled her eyes at his ignorance. "I'm talking about young girls who are sent to London to learn trades and end up walking the streets because they've been raped or seduced by their employers—"

"*What*?" Edward cried incredulously.

"—and are considered soiled goods by their families and have nowhere to turn but prostitution," Pegeen continued as if he hadn't interrupted. Leaning her elbows on the table, she went on. "I'm talking about women who endure having baby after baby, year after year, because they are so uneducated they don't know how to prevent pregnancy, all because men don't think educating their daughters is a worthwhile investment . . ."

"Good God," Edward breathed, feeling himself turning red in the face. "What in the name of heaven was your father thinking, letting you read newspapers? That's like handing a box of chocolates to a dyspeptic!"

"I beg your pardon," Pegeen sniffed, leaning back in her chair. "I am telling the truth. I can't help it if you've been so busy hunting poor innocent foxes that you can't see what's happening right in front of you."

"You, my dear girl, have lived alone too long. When I get you to Rawlings—"

She glared at him with such venom that he broke off. "You'll what? Starve me intellectually, the way women have been repressed throughout the ages?"

"Take you over my knee and give you the thrashing you so soundly deserve. What could you possibly know about prostitutes, or about preventing pregnancy, for that matter? You can't be a year out of the schoolroom yourself."

"I happen," she declared, wide-eyed with effrontery, "to be twenty years old next month!"

Edward started to chuckle, sinking back into his chair. The girl eyed him wrathfully.

"What, pray, is so funny?" she demanded.

"You. I got you tell me your age after all, didn't I?" He slapped his knee with delight, as happy as if he'd just beat Alistair Cartwright at a game of billiards.

She continued to glare at him but then, after a philosophical shrug, turned her attention back to the whiskey.

Edward, though he knew he shouldn't, stared at her wonderingly. With her wide green eyes and pointed face framed by soft tendrils of dark hair, she looked innocent as a schoolgirl, all ivory-skinned and pink-cheeked. But when his gaze dipped lower, to the capricious set of that rosebud mouth, he knew the innocence was only a ruse designed to distract him from the fact that behind the angelic face lurked a woman with as rapacious appetite for sex as any he'd ever encountered. And she had a waspish personality to go along with it. God help him, what was he going to do with her?

And why was it that, irritating though she was, he still wanted to kiss that impudent mouth? Impossible creatures, these young girls. He infinitely preferred older women, and married older women above all others.

"If we're going to be living with one another under one roof," he began, "can't we at least be friends?"

Pegeen rose and crossed to the sink to rinse out the whiskey glasses. The glance she shot back at him was suspicious. "Living with one another? Whatever are you talking about?"

"You said you and Jeremy would agree to come back to Rawlings with me."

"I said no such thing!"

He knew he was frowning, the thunderous frown that had once sent one of the elder Herbert girls into an attack of hysterics, but he couldn't help it. "You said 'maybe'—"

"That I did. Since when does maybe mean yes?"

"Miss MacDougal." Edward was at a loss for words. All this time, he'd thought he'd won the war, but he hadn't so much as begun the battle. He wanted very much to thrust his fist through something but unfortunately, the vicar wasn't in sight. "I've apologized to you for my father's neglect. I've paid back every penny that damnable vicar says he lent you. I've done everything within my power to show you that I truly mean it when I say that there is nothing, nothing in this world, that I will deny you should you agree to come to Rawlings with Jeremy. What else is there

that I can do to convince you that I am sincere in my desire
to do right by you and our nephew?''

Her back to him, she said in a soft voice, speaking
more to the window than to him, ''Nothing. I believe you.
I know that you mean to do the right thing. Only—''

''Only what?''

''Only . . . How much do you know, Lord Edward,
about my family?'' When she turned towards him, her
green eyes looked unnaturally large. ''What do you know
about my sister?''

''Nothing,'' Edward shrugged. ''Except that if she was
anything like you, it's no wonder my brother died an early
death.''

Pegeen, not surprisingly, did not smile at his joke.
''Nothing? Nothing at all? You never met her?''

''You know I didn't. My brother met your sister here
in Applesby whilst enjoying a weekend hunt. They rather
ill-advisedly and certainly hurriedly eloped, and when my
father refused to acknowledge their marriage, they left for
the Continent, from which neither of them returned alive.
What are you getting at, Miss MacDougal?''

She didn't reply, at least not right away. Instead, she
looked down at her hands. Edward followed her gaze,
thinking about how those hands had fisted in his hair. He
wondered what it would be like to have them, small and
cool, working the buttons of his breeches . . .

''We'll go with you,'' she said suddenly, in so low a
voice that Edward wasn't certain he'd heard her correctly.

He looked up sharply. ''I beg your pardon?''

''We'll go with you,'' Pegeen said again, more loudly
this time.

''Miss MacDougal!''

''On several conditions.''

Edward frowned. ''Miss MacDougal . . .''

''I'm to have the final say in all matters concerning
Jeremy. I'll not have him cosseted and showered with gifts

by people who wish to win his patronage. He's to be raised as normally as possible—''

"That simply won't do, Miss MacDougal," Edward scoffed. "Jeremy is the duke of Rawlings. What, you want him to attend the village school with the ordinary brats?''

"Jeremy *is* an ordinary brat, Lord Edward. Or he was until today. I'd like him to remain so for as long as possible. And of course if I'm to go with him, I'll need something to do.''

"I beg your pardon?''

"I must have something with which to occupy my time, Lord Edward. Unlike you, I am not used to a life of leisure. Perhaps I could see to your household affairs.''

"I have a housekeeper," Edward grumbled.

"Then perhaps I could manage your accounts. I used to keep track of the church's financial records for my father. I've got a head for figures.''

"That doesn't surprise me," Edward remarked dryly. "However, Sir Arthur manages my accounts for me.''

"Well, Lord Edward." Her exasperation was apparent in her frown. "There must be *something* I could do at Rawlings Manor.''

Edward stared at her. He could think of any number of functions at which she'd perform phenomenally. None of them, however, was appropriate for an unmarried young lady, or at least an unmarried young lady who'd swallowed the whole of Mary Wollstonecraft's *A Vindication of the Rights of Woman*. So he said noncommittally, "We'll find something for you to do, never fear. Now, what else?''

She bit her lower lip. "Well, I suppose if I'm to be the aunt of a duke, I'll need . . . I'll probably need to look presentable. I mean, I have only this dress and one other, for church . . .''

Edward followed her gaze, noting as he did so that her cheeks had gone scarlet. He didn't know what it was that was bothering her. The gown was plain, true, but it fit her in a most delectable manner. He was acquainted with few women who wouldn't have happily killed to have looked so good in so drab a dress.

But he nodded seriously and said, ''Yes. A new wardrobe will, of course, be part of the bargain.''

Looking visibly relieved, Pegeen exhaled, then hesitated once more.

''I'll . . . I'll need to borrow some money.'' She lowered her gaze, and he saw her cheeks flame once more. ''To help a local family.''

Now really. This was going too far.

''Why doesn't that damned vicar of yours help them?'' Edward demanded irritably. ''That's his job, isn't it?''

''He won't do it.'' With a sigh, the girl looked up at him, her cheeks redder than he'd ever seen them, redder even than after they'd kissed. ''Mrs. MacFearley is the local prostitute, and I attended the birth of her sixteenth child this morning—''

''You *what*?'' If she had said she'd attended the birth of Christ, he could not have been more surprised.

Pegeen coughed uncomfortably. ''Well. There was no one else, you see, and . . . well, if I could give her just a little money, she'd be able rest awhile, regain her strength, before going back to work . . .''

Edward quirked up an eyebrow. ''That will be a novelty,'' he remarked. ''A man of my class paying a lady of the night *not* to sleep with anybody.'' When he noticed that the girl wasn't smiling at his sarcasm, he sighed and reached into his waistcoat pocket. ''How much?''

She was biting that succulent lower lip again. ''Would . . . would five pounds be too much? I swear I'll pay you back. I'm good for thirty a year . . .''

''Hmmm.'' He scanned the coin in his purse. ''Let's make it an even twenty, shall we? Who knows, perhaps she'll use it as a lure to catch herself a husband. I think Mr. Richlands is available now, isn't he?''

He was surprised at the amount of happiness his casual gesture aroused. Pegeen clapped her hands, all the embarrassment gone, and even twirled about the kitchen. ''Twenty pounds? Do you mean it? Will you really? Oh, thank you, Lord Edward, thank you!''

Before he knew what she was about, she had spun towards him, flung both arms about his neck, and leaned down to press that cherry-red mouth against the very cheek she'd slapped but half an hour before.

Edward started at the gentle pressure of her pert bosom against his shoulders. Before he could stop himself, he'd turned his face so that instead of his cheek, her lips met his, his arm snaking around her trim waist and pulling her onto his lap.

He felt her stiffen at once . . . but her mouth was sweet against his, so sweet that he couldn't let go of her, not just yet. He had wondered if she'd meant that slap and now he had his answer. She'd slapped him because that was what a well-bred vicar's daughter did when a strange man made advances. But in her heart, she'd welcomed those advances. And that was why now she seemed to melt against him, her eyes closed, her heart thumping wildly beneath her breast . . .

It wasn't until he raised a hand to cup one of those exquisite breasts through the wool of her tight bodice that she sprang back, leaping off his lap like a startled cat.

''Lord Edward!'' she cried, her pupils so dilated that her eyes looked black, not green.

Edward, still tasting the sweetness of her, reached out, wanting to draw her back, her warmth, her softness, her eager desire to learn. But she backed away from him until her spine came in contact with the sink basin on the far side of the room.

''Lord Edward,'' she said again, almost incoherently. ''Not again. I *told* you!''

He looked at her, thinking she was the most engaging creature he'd come in contact with in a very, very long time, and suddenly realized that if he didn't play his cards right, he'd lose her. She wasn't a married woman who knew her way around the bedroom. She was a virgin, though a highly sensual one, and she looked more shocked at her own reaction to his advances than at the fact that he'd made them.

"Miss MacDougal," he said, not recognizing his own voice, it was so rough. He cleared his throat and tried again.

"Miss MacDougal. I can't apologize enough. I don't know what came over me. You must believe me, it will never happen again." Even as he said it, he was staring at her bosom, at the fascinating way her nipples, like hard pebbles in the cups of her corset, were distending through the wool of her dress. "After all," he said with a grin, "You're my sister-in-law."

He ought to have been expecting it this time, but it still came as a shock, the sudden blow to his cheek. She hit him even harder than before, seeming to take out all her sexual frustration on his jaw. Damn, but she had a strong right cross!

"There's to be none of that at Rawlings," Pegeen declared angrily. Her green eyes were fairly flashing fire. "Do you hear me? You so much as lift an eyebrow at me, and Jeremy and I are coming straight back!"

"Absolutely," Edward said, ruefully rubbing his jaw. "You're quite right."

Without another word, she turned tail and stalked haughtily from the room, her backside swaying in a fetching manner that Edward was certain was unconscious.

"And it was *sixteen* pounds, eight pence, you milksop," she said over her shoulder.

Remembering the coins he'd shoved into Richlands' pocket, Edward began to chuckle, shaking his head. The damned vicar had overcharged him a pound.

Chapter Five

The bitter north wind flattened Pegeen's full skirt against the crinoline she wore beneath it, biting through the folds of her new beaver fur pelisse and causing tears to sting her eyes. She moved the handkerchief she'd been pressing to the cut just above her hairline and dabbed at her eyes with a clean corner of the monogrammed linen, hoping Jeremy wouldn't notice and think that she was crying. But too late she realized he'd been watching her, his bright eyes wide in his red-cheeked face.

"Hullo!" he cried, having to shout to be heard above the wind. "Now look what you've done, you louts! You've gone and made my Pegeen cry!"

The three men who were working desperately to lift the brougham from the ditch it had tipped into looked up from their labors, their ragged breath coming in great puffs of white from their mouths. In their green and white Rawlings livery, they were probably far colder than she was, but their exertions had brought a shine to their foreheads and the footman's hair was sticking to his neck.

Pegeen wished, as she'd been wishing for the past half an hour ever since the carriage slid off the road—if one could call this sorry excuse of an ice-covered dirt track that led to Rawlings Manor a road—that she and Jerry had never left Applesby. At this time of day back home they'd be curled up by the fire enjoying their afternoon tea, not shivering out on a moor so barren and cold even the highway robbers were staying away.

Next to her, Sir Arthur Herbert shifted uneasily in the snow and touched her arm with unctuous solicitousness.

"Miss MacDougal, I cannot apologize enough for this unfortunate accident." Sir Arthur had been apologizing nonstop ever since the carriage tipped over. Pegeen had hoped that the cold would still his tongue. Unfortunately, Jerry's indignant assertion that Pegeen was crying had reawakened all of the estate executor's concern. "Are you certain that you don't wish to sit down? Are you cold? Mayn't I loan you my cape?"

"Certainly not," Pegeen declared more stoutly than she felt. She did not point out to him that had she wanted to sit, there was no place to do so, since the brougham was half-in, half-out of a ditch and there wasn't a structure anywhere in sight. "I'm perfectly fine, Sir Arthur. Jeremy is mistaken. I am not crying."

Turning her head so that Sir Arthur could not see her face behind the wide brim of her new fur-lined bonnet, Pegeen shot Jerry her most disapproving look, her slender eyebrows slanted downwards over her straight nose. As soon as they got to Rawlings, she was going to have to find a private moment to have a little word with him. Ever since he'd learned he was the new duke of Rawlings, Jeremy had been nearly impossible to live with.

The new duke of Rawlings took one look at his aunt's face and shrieked, "It's bleeding again! Peggy, your head's bleeding!"

Stuff and bother. Pegeen pressed Lord Edward's handkerchief to the cut she'd received when the brougham tipped over. She wasn't in much pain and didn't see what all the fuss was about since it was a little cut hidden by her hair. But it had been bleeding rather profusely, enough to make Sir Arthur go rather white and Lord Edward insist on setting off on foot for help.

"That's better," Jeremy said, grinning impishly up at her, happier than she'd seen him since their long journey south had begun. Even their week-long stay in London hadn't been as exciting to Jeremy as this carriage accident. Jeremy's eyes sparkled as he related once again how Lord Edward had saved Pegeen from being crushed to death by Sir Arthur's girth when the carriage slid from the road.

"As soon as he felt it tipping," Jeremy gushed, reaching up to tug the sleeve of Pegeen's dark green traveling dress, "Uncle Edward pulled you on top of him, didn't he, Pegeen? I reckon he saved your life. I reckon Sir Arthur would have flattened you like a grape if he'd fallen on you."

"That's enough, Jerry," Pegeen said mildly. "I'm quite aware of the fact that Lord Edward saved my life. I thanked him once already."

Sir Arthur Herbert cleared his throat. He'd been listening to the young duke's comments on his weight with growing embarrassment and he seemed to have reached breaking point. "I say, Your Grace, why don't you run up to the top of that rise there and see if your uncle is returning yet with a rescue party?"

Jeremy needed no more encouragement to expend some of his seemingly limitless energy. He took off towards the snow-covered crest like a stone from a slingshot, and Pegeen used the opportunity to wipe her eyes again. The wind had picked up, hurling snow and small ice particles at them, and her cheeks and nose felt frozen. During the accident, most of Pegeen's long hair had slipped out of the net in which she kept it coiled, and her fingers were too numb with cold to tuck the unruly tendrils back into place. Now the curls were keeping her ears from becoming frostbitten. She stamped her feet, feeling her toes growing numb inside her kid leather boots. There was no place on this godforsaken moor, she realized, for them to take shelter from the wind. They may have survived the carriage accident only to freeze to death just a few miles from their destination.

"My dear Miss MacDougal," Sir Arthur admonished her. "You're fairly blue with cold. Please do allow me to loan you my cape. I'd be perfectly content with the lap blanket from the brougham. . . ."

"Don't be ridiculous, Sir Arthur," Pegeen replied through chattering teeth. "I am perfectly well. I don't know how many times I'm going to have to say it before someone believes me." The throbbing pain in her head belied her statement, but there was no reason to give Sir Arthur something new to lament. Pegeen bit her lower lip and bore the pain silently, glad to have the excuse of the wind for her watering eyes.

"I think we've nearly got it, sir," called one of the drivers, and Pegeen looked up hopefully. The footman had hold of the lead horses and was yelling encouragingly at the beautifully matched team, while the two drivers, down in the ditch, pushed the heavy black brass-trimmed vehicle with all their might. Pegeen thought that a man of Sir Arthur's size might have been a great deal of help down there at the pushing end of things, but the solicitor seemed to feel he was of more use comforting her. Even now, he was patting her shoulder and muttering, "There now, you see! They've almost got it. They're good boys, they are. Lord Edward only hires the best, you know . . ."

But it was going to take more than three of Lord Edward Rawlings' best to right his carriage. The fractious horses could not find their footing on the icy road, and just as the front wheels of the coach met the road, the lead pair stumbled, sending the whole vehicle crashing back into the ditch. Horrified that the drivers would be crushed, Pegeen screamed a warning and both men dove out of the way in the nick of time.

"Oh!" Pegeen cried. Now she really was beginning to feel like weeping. "Oh, this is terrible. Those poor men! And the poor horses! How long will it take, Sir Arthur, for Lord Edward and that other footman to walk to Rawlings Manor? I know it's barely tea time, but it's already growing dark . . ."

"Have faith, Miss MacDougal." Sir Arthur looked about as crestfallen as she felt. He too would most probably rather be lounging beside a blazing fire taking tea. "Have faith. Lord Edward Rawlings will not let us down."

Faith in Lord Edward Rawlings was something Pegeen completely lacked. Although in the fortnight that had passed since she'd first met him that horrid day back in Applesby he had refrained from making any more unwanted advances, she still wasn't at all certain she trusted him.

True, he had proved himself the perfect gentleman during their stay in his beautiful London townhouse. He had sent for Sir Arthur and his wife to act as chaperons, and although Pegeen didn't particularly care for Sir Arthur, she found that she quite liked his wife. Lady Herbert was everything her husband was not—attractive, good-humored, and sensible. Having five daughters herself, she took the seemingly endless stream of dressmaker's appointments that resulted from Lord Edward's promise of a new wardrobe in stride and remained far more cheerful than Pegeen after a half dozen visits to the milliner. Between fittings, Lady Herbert escorted Pegeen about London. She did not at all protest to a tour of the House of Commons, though Parliament was not yet in session, and she slipped in and out of museums as enthusiastically as if she'd never seen them before.

Lord Edward saw that the young duke was also well-entertained with riding lessons in Regent's Park, frequent trips to the zoo, and a shopping spree that resulted in a number of purchases that infuriated Pegeen, who disapproved of a boy Jeremy's age owning his own rifle, let alone his own sixteen-hand hunter.

But it was difficult to remain angry with a man who insisted upon escorting them all to expensive dinners every night in restaurants Pegeen had only read about, never dreaming she'd actually dine in them. And when, after each succulent meal of lobster and champagne and meringues, he invariably produced tickets to box seats at the opera and theater, how could she go on resenting him? The fact that shortly after dinner every night Lord Edward disappeared was hardly any of her business. As Lady Herbert pointed out with a shrug, Edward Rawlings was a man of the world, and it was a bit tiresome for such a man to spend all of his evenings with an old married couple—and, Pegeen added to herself, Lady Herbert being far too well-bred to say so, a prudish vicar's daughter.

Pegeen always felt particularly prudish each morning, when Lord Edward joined them again at the breakfast table. Though he was as fastidiously dressed as ever, there were unmistakable circles under his eyes, and sometimes she was quite certain she caught a whiff of last evening's whiskey on his breath. In short, she believed Lord Edward to be engaging in the sort of practices one would expect of a man of his age and class, and she wondered exactly how much he spent on the gaming tables each night and precisely how many mistresses he supported.

Still, despite her conviction that Lord Edward was becoming quite dissipated from a life of hedonism, Pegeen was unfailingly polite to him. She did not want Jeremy to sense her antipathy towards the man. It was important to her that her nephew, who had never really had a father figure in his life with the exception of his grandfather, look up to his uncle, and he would not do that if he knew how much Pegeen disapproved of the man. So, for the first time in her life, Pegeen kept her opinions to herself. Every time she saw Lord Edward drooping over his morning coffee, she bit her tongue to refrain from teasing him about his excesses.

But even Pegeen had to admit herself impressed by the manly display of courage Lord Edward exhibited during the carriage accident. The moment the brougham had begun to tip, he'd thrown his arms protectively about her and flung her out of the way of Sir Arthur's tumbling body. Unfortunately, he hadn't been able to protect her from ramming her head quite hard against the brougham's interior oil lamp. But Lord Edward's solicitous treatment of her, gently lifting her from the brougham and pressing his own handkerchief to a wound she could not see (and did not believe was as bad as everyone was making it out to be), his insistence upon making the walk to Rawlings Manor himself to get help, all had improved her opinion of him a hundredfold. She hadn't even the heart to complain of the cold, she'd been so touched by his concern.

But now he had been gone for some time. Pegeen was chilled to the bone, and headachy besides. How far from here was Rawlings? And how long would it take for another carriage to be dispatched to fetch them?

Pegeen thought about Sir Arthur's sweet-tempered wife, Lady Herbert, and the couple's five daughters, and how warm and happy she'd been staying the night before with them at their ramshackle country estate a dozen miles away from Rawlings. If only they'd known about this terrible winter storm before they'd started out for the manor house this afternoon. If only they'd left a little bit earlier, they'd have missed the worst of it. If only . . . if only her toes weren't so blasted cold!

"I say, hullo, there!" Sir Arthur raised an arm and signaled to someone—not in the direction that Jeremy had gone, but in the opposite direction from which their carriage had come. "Hullo!"

Pegeen turned her head, squinting into the wind, and saw a lone horse and rider approaching at no mean pace. In such weather, on such ice, it was pure foolishness to drive an animal so hard. She thought with a sudden faintness of heart that only a man who was escaping from someone—or something—would ride at such a speed, and that perhaps Sir Arthur was flagging down a highwayman. Swallowing hard, Pegeen stepped a little behind the barrel-bellied knight and found his body quite effective in shielding hers from the bitter wind.

"Ho, there!" Sir Arthur called. "Can you help us, sir?"

The horse and rider emerged from the swirling veils of snow and ice, and Pegeen found herself blinking up at an enormous, red-eyed stallion, steam rising from his black nostrils. The stallion's rider was no less intimidating. Cloaked all in black, the broad-shouldered, steely-eyed man grinned down at her, and with a start of recognition, Pegeen realized it was none other than Lord Edward. He handled the massive beast he rode with graceful strength, whistling between his white, even teeth as the horse stamped his heavy hooves in the deep snow.

"Lord Edward!" Sir Arthur cried in delighted tones. He reached up to sweep off his hat and laid a hand on the stallion's bridle. This was a mistake. The horse angrily tossed his ink-black head, flecking Sir Arthur's cape with foam and bits of slush.

"Oh, excuse me," Sir Arthur said, ostensibly to the horse, an act which caused Pegeen to hide a smile in the fur trim of her pelisse. "But from where do you come, Lord Edward? I saw you and young Bob set off in quite the opposite direction—"

"I know it." Leather creaking, Lord Edward swung from the saddle, landing heavily in the snow beside Sir Arthur. Sir Arthur, Pegeen had thought from the moment she'd met him, was an abnormally large man, but Lord

Edward stood a head taller, towering over Pegeen by almost a foot. In his riding boots and breeches, it was plain to see that Edward Rawlings was lean in all the places Arthur Herbert was fat, but he still managed to intimidate by his sheer size.

"The wind off the moor is not to be trifled with," Lord Edward tersely informed them. "There's no way a man on foot could survive it. So we made a detour and stopped at Ashbury House. I borrowed a horse and came as fast as I could. The carriage is going to take some time to get here. The roads are dead treacherous."

"Oh dear," Sir Arthur cried, dismayed. "How unfortunate. Miss MacDougal's head is still bleeding, my lord, and I'm afraid she is in a great deal of pain."

"Still bleeding?" Edward echoed, even as Pegeen's cry of denial was snatched from her throat and lost to the wind. His eyes, grey as the overcast sky above, raked her accusingly. "Lift that handkerchief," he ordered her. "Let me see."

"It's nothing," Pegeen insisted. "It's only Jeremy. He's overprotective of me." She was quite embarrassed at the fuss everyone was making over what was surely a tiny cut.

She was also more than a little conscious of the intensity of Lord Edward's gaze. Why was he always looking at her like that? He must know she could never be more to him than a sister-in-law . . . a particularly prim sister-in-law, at that. Stuff and bother! The man was a menace. The last thing she wanted was him cupping her face and peering at her at close range. His touch unnerved her, and his stare—well, he had better give over staring at her like that or she'd have a sharp lesson to teach him.

But he wouldn't let her alone until she let him look at her forehead and so with ill grace she took the wadded handkerchief from her head and tilted her face towards him, keeping her gaze carefully averted from his. He took hold of her chin between black-gloved fingers, and peered closely at her, his dark eyebrows furrowed. She would have survived the ordeal well enough if he hadn't felt it necessary to probe her hairline with yet another clean handkerchief, this one Sir Arthur's.

Pegeen's cry of pain was inadvertent. She bit her lower lip but could not keep tears from spilling at the tenderness of her wound. Her vision suddenly swam and her balance momentarily left her. Lord Edward instantly released her chin, and despite Pegeen's inarticulate protest, wrapped an iron-hard arm around her narrow waist as she swayed, dizzy from she knew not which—the wound on her head or his close proximity.

Sir Arthur immediately began to berate her for not telling him she didn't feel well, and she could only blink apologetically at him, not trusting her voice to speak. She leaned against Lord Edward, grateful as much for the warmth of his body as for his support. He'd wrapped his heavy black cloak around them both, and inside its confines Pegeen began to be able to feel her fingers and nose again.

It wasn't until the dizziness began to dissipate that she became aware of the hardness of the muscles beneath the wool upon which her cheek rested. Suddenly self-conscious, Pegeen slipped her hands from her muff and placed them against Edward's broad, inflexible chest. She was so small, and her strength so ineffectual, that he paid no attention to her urgent push.

"She must be very ill indeed," Sir Arthur kept saying, "but she never said a word, poor little soul."

"Stuff and bother," Pegeen managed to scoff, though her breath was still short and her heart was hammering against her corset stays. "It's nothing but a little bump—"

"Pegeen!" Jeremy's bellow was enough to wake the dead, and dazed as she felt, Pegeen lifted her head to see him barreling down the snowy hillside, his small face red with anger and his breath coming out as fast as steam from a locomotive.

"What do you think you're doing with my Pegeen?" Jeremy demanded. "You unhand her at once!" Long considered the scourge of Aberdeen, Jeremy Rawlings had been involved in more scrapes and fights than Pegeen could remember, many of them on her account. It had been her hope that bringing him to his ancestral home would help to civilize him. . . .

But it looked as if in his uncle Edward, Jeremy might have met his match.

"Silence, you impertinent pup," Edward growled. "or I'll take you over my knee."

"You can't do that," Jeremy declared. "I'm the duke!"

"Oh, Jerry," groaned Pegeen. The last thing she wanted was to be released from Edward's warm embrace to face that bitter wind once again, but it really wasn't the least bit circumspect to rest so intimately in his arms. Nor was it necessary, at this point. The pain in her head had returned to a dull but bearable throb, and she no longer felt the least dizzy.

But when she looked up, her lips parted to ask that Edward release her, she found that he wasn't paying the least bit of attention to her. For all the conflicting emotions his close presence wrought within her breast, it seemed he wasn't affected at all by her proximity. He was staring fixedly at the sky, his expression inscrutable.

"The snow is coming down harder," he observed. "I think it might be best if I take Miss MacDougal to Rawlings now. She ought not to wait for the carriage."

Pegeen glanced apprehensively at the black stallion, steam coming in great white puffs from his nostrils. "Really, my lord, I'm quite all right. I can wait for the carriage. And you needn't hold onto me as if I might blow away."

"You are not all right, and you will do as I say."

Edward's piercing gaze seemed to bore through her, and Pegeen looked away, another blush tingeing her fair cheeks. She'd never known a man, aside from the occasional anonymous admirer on the street back in Applesby, to stare at her so unabashedly. She must look a sight indeed, she thought worriedly, for him to stare like that.

As if sensing her discomfort, Edward withdrew his arm from around her waist but undid his cloak and placed it over Pegeen's narrow shoulders despite her protests. The heavy garment was so large that nearly a foot of material dragged on the snow. Free from that overly familiar embrace, Pegeen swayed a little in the wind, feeling as if all the places Edward had touched her had been branded. Her cheeks burned and she kept her eyes lowered to avoid meeting anyone's gaze.

Jeremy, however, knew her too well to be fooled by her attempt at normalcy. "You *are* ill," he declared, coming to her side. "Why didn't you say anything before?"

"Well, what good would it have done?" She reached out and adjusted his cap, tugging it down more firmly over his ears. "It wouldn't bring us help any faster."

Jeremy squirmed. "Quit fussing me. You're the one who needs fussing over." Puffing out his chest, he turned and addressed Lord Edward. "I think you had better take her, Uncle. She isn't as strong as she looks."

Pegeen nearly burst out laughing at that, but the laughter quickly died when she looked up and saw Sir Edward striding towards her, his expression one of grim determination.

"You're coming with me," he said flatly.

Pegeen instinctively stepped back, her gaze flying to the stallion. "Oh, no," she said, brandishing her muff as if it were a weapon. "That's quite all right. I'll stay here with Sir Arthur. Take Jeremy. He would probably love to ride on . . . on . . . that thing."

But her protests could not have fallen on less sympathetic ears. Even as she backed away, Edward's fingers closed over her wrist and suddenly she was gathered into his arms. As if she were no heavier than a child herself, Edward lifted her onto his saddle, his handspan so large that his gloved fingers nearly met around her tightly corseted waist. Pegeen could not restrain a gasp as she realized what a long way it was to the ground from atop the enormous horse's back.

"Are you all right?" Edward asked curiously, studying her face.

Pegeen swallowed hard and nodded, disguising her terror with an outward display of nonchalance, calmly arranging her skirts across the animal's neck. Inwardly, however, she was praying fervently that she wouldn't do anything stupid, like faint or fall off.

Edward swung himself up onto the saddle behind her, taking the heavy cloak from her shoulders and wrapping it about them both. His arm went brazenly around her waist again, but this time Pegeen was grateful for his support. This way, if she did faint, he'd catch her before she hit the hard ground so many feet below.

"Herbert," Lord Edward said, gathering up the stallion's reins. "You'll wait here with His Grace for the chaise. It shouldn't be too much longer."

"Oh," cried Sir Arthur. "Excellent, my lord. And perhaps on our way, we can stop at the home of the surgeon and bring him with us to the manor to see to Miss MacDougal's injury."

Cradled between Edward's strong, lean thighs, Pegeen sat as still as she could, her cheeks burning. Through her skirt and crinoline she could feel the bold outline of his manhood against her buttocks, the hardness of his chest against the curve of her back. She had thought his embrace intimate before, but that had been nothing compared to the familiarity with which they now leaned against one another. Pegeen tried to control the hammering of her heart, knowing full well that as a man of the world, this was probably all very routine to him. Oh, la, just a tear across the moor. What could be more dull?

"Good-bye, then," Edward called to Sir Arthur and Jeremy, reining in the snorting steed. "Until we meet at Rawlings."

And then they were off with such a burst of speed that Pegeen was once again left gasping. Withdrawing her hands from her muff, she wrapped terrified fingers round the arm with which Lord Edward held her, and he responded by tightening his hold on her waist with a chuckle.

"Not much of a horsewoman, are you?" he asked.

Pegeen bit back a sarcastic reply. It didn't seem wise to antagonize the only thing that was keeping her from certain death beneath those enormous hooves.

They thundered across the uneven plains of the moor, snow whipping against them and frigid air wreaking havoc with Pegeen's hair despite the wide brim of her new bonnet. Her eyes were streaming from the cold and she could barely see. She lowered her head against Lord Edward's chest and began to pray. Foremost amongst her prayers was the hope that she not fall off Lord Edward's horse. She had a secondary desire to see Lord Edward die of a particularly nasty disease, but that, she grudgingly admitted, could wait until she was safely at Rawlings Manor.

When the snorting black stallion had settled into a smooth canter, Pegeen felt Edward's grasp around her waist loosen a fraction of an inch. He asked into the fur trim of her bonnet, "You are well? This isn't too much for you?"

"Oh, yes," Pegeen said through gritted teeth. "I'm quite well, thank you."

"You aren't a very convincing liar, are you?" Edward chuckled.

"I'm a vicar's daughter," Pegeen replied tartly. "I'm not supposed to be good at lying. Jeremy, on the other hand, lies admirably."

"That particular trait must come from his father's side of the family," Edward said with a grin.

Pegeen shook her head. Her teeth were chattering, but she hoped Lord Edward would assume it was from the cold not her fear of his horse. "Oh, I wouldn't be so certain. Kathy's always had a talent for fabrication."

"No, Jeremy is his father's son, all right. The spitting image of John at that age." Lord Edward's voice sounded wry. "Your father must have suffered an apoplexy when your sister and my brother eloped. Do you remember it?"

"Of course I remember it," Pegeen said. She gulped, not at the memory, but at a large gully Lord Edward's horse leapt nimbly across. When she felt herself able to speak again, she said, "I was Jeremy's age at the time. Children do have the ability to form memories at ten years old, you know."

If Lord Edward heard the tremble in her voice, he ignored it. "What was she like, your sister Katherine? Not like you, obviously, if she was a skillful liar."

Pegeen shifted against him uncomfortably. She still could see nothing ahead of them but a shifting sea of white with grey sky heavy overhead. "Like me? No, nothing like me."

"Nothing like you? That's hard to believe. Surely Katherine was beautiful, like you."

Pegeen, had she been able to, would have craned her neck to get a look at his face then, since she could not tell by his tone whether or not he was teasing her. But the minute she tried to do so, she was struck full in the face by a curtain of snow. She ducked her head against Edward's chest. Damn him anyway. Why was he trying to flirt with her *now*, when her defenses were down? He'd had a week in London to try to woo her and instead he'd all but ignored her. Obnoxious creatures, men.

"Katherine's lovely," Pegeen admitted after a pause. While holding a conversation in this weather on the back of a horse was difficult, Pegeen had to admit that it was taking her mind off both the cold and her fear of falling. She added hesitantly, "But a beautiful face does not necessarily connote a beautiful soul."

Edward laughed. "Spoken like a true vicar's daughter. You disapproved of Katherine, did you? She and John, from what I understand, were not exactly retiring in their pursuits . . ."

"They most certainly were not." Pegeen snorted. "It was just one party after another for them. Never mind that it was their dissolute lifestyle that eventually destroyed them, leaving their innocent baby an orphan—"

"Whom you then took it upon yourself to raise." Edward was looking down at her now, his expression sardonic. "Small wonder you're a Liberal. You must have pretty low opinion of the gentry if my brother's all you've ever seen of it. John was not exactly responsible, fiscally or in any other manner."

"And who of your class is?" Pegeen demanded. "I can't think of one member of the House of Lords who is more concerned for the good of the common man than for the good of his own pocket."

"I do not relish arguing politics with a green-eyed vicar's daughter in the middle of a blizzard," Edward said and now there was definite amusement in his voice. "But in defense of my people, had you or your father ever once thought to contact my family, we would have seen to it that monies were supplied to you for Jeremy's welfare."

"Oh!" Pegeen interrupted, all her fear of being dropped forgotten. "You expected us to come crawling from Applesby, looking for scraps from your table, when everyone in your family made it so very clear when John and Katherine were married that none of you wanted anything to do with us? Why, without knowing the least little thing about us, you all hated us from the very beginning!"

"Easy, now," Edward chuckled, for all the world as

if he were soothing a nervous mare. "You throw all of us Rawlings in together like we're some great stew or something. I am not responsible for my father's actions, however much I might have protested against them." At Pegeen's pointedly disbelieving sniff, he insisted, "I speak the God's honest truth, Miss MacDougal. I was away at Oxford when John and your sister eloped."

"Oh, really? And he told you nothing of his plans?"

"He and I were never close. We had our differences—"

Edward broke off in surprise when Pegeen snorted rudely. She couldn't help it, though her father certainly wouldn't have approved. "What an understatement!"

"Am I so different from John?" Edward sounded dubious. She wondered what he meant by it. Didn't he know that his brother John had been an ill-tempered, foul-mouthed drunkard? Why, Pegeen would never understand what Katherine had seen in him with the exception of his handsome face . . . and seemingly bottomless purse, of course.

"You know you're nothing alike," Pegeen said, unwilling to coddle his ego by elaborating. She was certain that Lord Edward Rawlings had plenty of lady friends to coddle his ego—and other things as well. She was not going to succumb so easily to his charms. She stopped speaking, however, when she glimpsed something through the swirling snow. She stiffened unconsciously in Edward's grasp. He glanced down at her inquiringly and noticed the direction of her gaze.

"Ah," Lord Edward said with a laugh that held no warmth in it whatsoever. "Here we are, then. The incomparable Rawlings Manor."

Through the slanting curtain of snow, Pegeen saw that where the moor came to a straggling end, a line of ancient oak trees, leafless now, formed an allée up a gently sloping hill, on top of which rested the structure Lord Edward called Rawlings Manor. Three-storied, with numerous outbuildings making up the stables, carriage house, and tenant farmers' homes, the manor graced the surrounding landscape like a swan gliding on a silver lake. From the south-facing upper windows, Pegeen was sure that on a clear day one could see down the hillside to the local village, over which Rawlings Manor and its inhabitants presided.

"It's beautiful," Pegeen breathed, hardly realizing that she'd spoken out loud. She had never seen anything like it, and wondered whether things would have turned out differently for Katherine if John had ever brought her to his ancestral home.

"You think so?" Edward sounded amused. "I've always considered it rather a monstrosity. Rather unfortunately situated. The winds from the moor permeate its very walls in the winter. We've a devil of a time heating it. But my great-great-great-grandfather Rawlings hadn't the sense God gave a starling, and he *would* have a house that looked out over a moor."

Pegeen barely heard him. It just didn't seem possible that just a few weeks ago, she and Jeremy had been using up the last of their coal from the coal shed, wondering how they'd ever come across money to buy more. Now, with a suddenness that was making Pegeen's head spin, they would never have to worry about coal—or money—again. To go from genteel starvation to this, all in a fortnight. . . . It seemed like a chapter out of one of Jeremy's fairy story books.

Behind her, she felt Edward kick his horse into a gallop that sent snow and bits of gravel from the drive path flying. They careened between the line of oaks that led towards the mist-shrouded house, the lights from the manor's many windows making cheerful yellow patterns on the unbroken snow and the wide stone steps that led to the heavy double portals. Those doors began to swing open even before Edward had pulled his mount to a stop, revealing more brilliant yellow light and two men in powdered wigs and green and white livery who skittered down the snowy steps and ran towards them.

It took the strength of both men, plus all of Edward's equestrian skills, to steer the wildly excited horse towards the stone steps so that they could dismount. Apparently, Edward's horse was not as anxious to get out of the inclement weather as its riders.

"Oh, Lord Edward," cried a woman's voice. Pegeen could see a plump silhouette between the twin doors to the house. "I'm so glad to see you home safe, my lord. Such a dreadful accident, and such frightful weather! What a mercy you were able to find a horse. Tell me, how fares the young master and his aunt?"

"You can ascertain that for yourself, Mrs. Praehurst," Edward said, removing his heavy cloak from his broad shoulders and draping it entirely around Pegeen. "I come bearing one of the victims from the great Post Road brougham disaster."

With a gasp, the woman moved out onto the stone steps, and Pegeen could see that she was heavyset and middle-aged. Judging by the circle of keys she wore on a chain bob at her waist, the woman was obviously the manor's housekeeper.

The wind and snow tugged at the lace cap she wore over her greying hair, but Mrs. Praehurst hardly seemed to notice. She turned and cried into the house, "Mr. Evers! Rosie, go and fetch Mr. Evers. Tell him Lord Edward is home, and that he's got—" She paused, squinting through her gold-rimmed spectacles at Pegeen. "And who would that young lady be, my lord? Surely not little Maggie Herbert, not on a night like this!"

"Surely not," Edward said, with another one of his humorless laughs. He dismounted with what Pegeen was learning was characteristic agility and turned towards her, his arms outstretched, a mischievous glint in his clear, light eyes. Pegeen bit her lower lip, her gaze dipping apprehensively towards the ground.

"Come now," he said, his gloved hands prying hers from his horse's mane. "I shan't drop you, if that's what you're thinking."

That was so close to what Pegeen was thinking that she blushed, embarrassed. Fortunately, in the pool of light spilling from Rawlings' front doors, anyone seeing her red cheeks would mistake the color for windburn. Carefully, Pegeen placed her arms around Edward's neck, squeezed her eyes tightly shut, and slid into his warm embrace as if it were the most natural place in the world for her to be.

But instead of handing her down from his horse's back, Edward scooped her up as easily as if she were a child and turned to carry her up the stone steps and into the house.

"For heaven's sake," Pegeen protested, her eyes flying open wide. "I'm not an invalid! I can walk, you know."

"It's slippery here," was Edward's succinct reply, though he didn't seem to be having any trouble at all finding his footing. "And wet."

"I'm wet through," Pegeen informed him. "I haven't a dry stitch on. I don't know what difference—"

"Has anyone ever told you," Edward wanted to know as he climbed the steps to the manor house, "that you talk entirely too much?"

Before Pegeen could come up with an appropriately stinging retort, Edward was calling to his housekeeper. "Mrs. Praehurst! May I present His Grace's aunt, Miss Pegeen MacDougal?"

Mrs. Praehurst, when Edward brought Pegeen close enough to get a good look at her, was all astonishment behind her spectacles, but her good breeding forbade her from showing it overly much.

"Oh, my," the housekeeper said, bobbing a curtsy.

"Oh, dear. Miss MacDougal. . . . Do forgive me. Only in the light . . . and you look so young . . . I do hope. . . ." The housekeeper tried a different track. "You aren't too badly injured?"

"I'm quite well, thank you," Pegeen said politely, as Edward whisked her past the startled housekeeper. It was exceedingly hard to sound dignified while being carted bodily around like a sack of wheat. "It's terribly nice to meet—"

"Evers!" Edward's bellow made her wince. When she opened her eyes again, she saw that they had entered the Great Hall, a room so large, with ceilings so high, that the only structure Pegeen had ever been in that was of comparable size was her father's church.

Brilliantly lit by several chandeliers suspended from the rafters, the room was exactly what Pegeen had always thought a great hall would be . . . a vast, ostentatious space that served no conceivable purpose. It was furnished with a few sets of tapestry-backed chairs and there were several tolerably well-done still lifes on the walls, along with some ancient carpets on the stone floor. A set of double staircases curved around a wide door to the dining room and led up to an open gallery that lined three walls of the hall on the second floor. In all, it was an enormous space, and the annual cost of heating it would probably have fed an entire family in Applesby for a lifetime.

But Pegeen barely had a chance to take all of this in before Lord Edward's bellow caused her to wince once more.

"Evers!"

This time Edward was answered by a calm, somewhat elderly man who came shuffling into the hall from a side door. "My lord?" He looked neither surprised that his master was carrying a young woman nor particularly interested.

"Evers," Edward said. "There you are. Did Robert—"

"Young Robert did indeed arrive a few short moments

ago. I have brandy being warmed this instant. This, I presume, is the duke's aunt?'' Without pausing for an answer, Evers addressed Pegeen as if he were speaking to a queen, bowing at the waist. "Miss MacDougal, I am honored."

"I've had the Rose Room made up for the young lady," Mrs. Praehurst said, bustling past them, her keys clinking musically. She'd closed the front doors and had instructed a maid to mop up the melting snow that had blown inside. "There's a nice fire, and we'll heat up a bath at once. You'll both be wantin' toddies after bein' in that bitter cold. Rosie, run and tell Cook that the master—I mean, Lord Edward—is home and will be wanting something warm to drink—"

"Brandy's all I want," Edward said. He strode swiftly towards the double staircases at the end of the Great Hall. "Sir Arthur Herbert will be bringing the surgeon with him. Send Mr. Parks directly to Miss MacDougal's room as soon as he arrives."

Someone hooted from the gallery that overlooked the Great Hall and Pegeen looked up. A handsomely dressed man of about Edward's age, thirty or so, leaned over the balustrade, a glass of amber liquid in his hand.

"Heigh-ho, Edward," he cried good-naturedly. "Wherever did you run off to? Arabella told me to expect you a sennight ago." The fair-haired gentleman took a sip of his drink, then peered down at them. "I say, who's that you've got there? Is that Maggie Herbert? What the devil's that child been up to now?"

Edward shifted Pegeen in his arms, and she instinctively tightened her grip on his neck, thinking he was going to drop her. She then realized with a blush that he was simply wrapping his long cloak more firmly about her, since the trailing hem was in danger of tripping him. He looked down at her, a teasing smile on his uncomfortably sensual lips. Pegeen looked quickly away, trying to avoid his gaze. Unfortunately, in her current position the only way she could escape it was to fall several feet to the flagstone floor.

To hide her embarrassment, she inquired, "Who is that man, the one doing all that shouting?"

"That," Edward said, with a quick glance upwards, "is Mr. Alistair Cartwright, whom I met when I was sent away to school as a boy and have yet to shake off. He doesn't have a manor house of his own, so he makes free use of mine."

"And who might Arabella be?" Pegeen asked tartly. "Your mistress?"

The smile turned into a disapproving frown. "How," he asked drily, "could such a sweet face harbor such a prickly tongue?"

"I'm a Liberal, remember?" Pegeen replied. "My prickly tongue is my only defense, as I have no income or property to speak of."

Edward only frowned more sternly in way of reply. Oblivious to their conversation, Mrs. Praehurst bustled past them, lifting her skirt to hurry up one of the curving staircases.

"I'll just go on ahead, my lord, and turn down Miss MacDougal's bed. . . ."

"Miss MacDougal?" The fair-haired man Edward called Alistair Cartwright nearly dropped his drink over the side of the balustrade but with deft fumbling, he caught the glass before it fell crashing to the flagstones below. By the time Edward had followed Mrs. Praehurst up the stairs to the open gallery, his friend had pulled himself together enough to meet them with an easy smile along with ill-disguised curiosity.

"Hullo, there," he said, hurrying alongside Edward, his bright-eyed gaze fixed on Pegeen. "Allow me to introduce myself, since my impossibly rude host won't do it for me. The name's Cartwright. Alistair Cartwright."

Edward's stride quickened as he followed Mrs. Praehurst's rustling skirt along the open gallery. Pegeen found herself straining her neck to see Alistair around Edward's broad shoulder. "How do you do, Mr. Cartwright?" she asked politely. Alistair Cartwright wasn't as tall as his host, nor as powerfully built, and he was fair where Lord Edward was dark, but he was good-looking, and very dashingly dressed. Pegeen had never seen so many frills in a cravat.

"Well, I was only doing tolerably well, Miss Mac-Dougal, until you arrived." Alistair Cartwright trotted alongside them as they turned down a carpeted hallway as if he were a well-coifed lap dog. "Deadly dull it's been these past few weeks since Edward's been away. But I must say, your uncommon beauty quite lights up this dreary old—"

"Cartwright," Edward growled. She felt the disapproving rumble in his chest. "Don't."

"Oh, have mercy, Rawlings." Alistair skidded to a halt when Mrs. Praehurst stopped and fumbled with her keys in front of an ornately carved door at the end of the dimly lit hallway. "Miss MacDougal and I were just getting acquainted!"

"I said don't," Edward snapped. Pegeen glanced sharply up at the chiseled profile above her and saw that the square jaw was set. A dangerous light glinted in his eyes. "You forget that I dislike having to repeat myself."

Alistair looked completely unruffled by his friend's rebuke. He leaned against the elegant wainscoting and sighed. "I suppose this means farewell for now, Miss MacDougal."

"Off with you, Cartwright." Edward gave the door Mrs. Praehurst unlocked a kick, sending the portal crashing open. Pegeen glanced at the housekeeper to see what she made of this barbaric behavior, but Mrs. Praehurst only looked heavenward, in a manner not unlike Pegeen herself when Jeremy behaved foolishly.

The Rose Room, into which Pegeen found herself carried, had been aptly named. Sumptuously furnished in subtle tones of pink and mauve, the walls papered with a print of white primroses, the room fairly glowed with femininity. But although a bright fire crackled on the hearth and fresh flowers had been placed in a bowl by the large canopied bed, Pegeen had a feeling the room hadn't been occupied in some time. She guessed that the last occupant had been the Duchess of Rawlings, Lord Edward's mother, who had died nearly twenty years earlier.

If her guess was correct, Mrs. Praehurst certainly didn't let on as she bustled across the room, pulling back the heavy down-filled comforter to reveal a set of spotless white linen sheets. "There you are, Miss MacDougal," she fussed, fluffing up white pillows that had quite obviously been fluffed a few hours before. "I hope the room suits your tastes."

"It's lovely," Pegeen cooed, meaning it. She had never seen a prettier room. And the addition of the flowers touched her. She had no idea how anyone could come across full-blown roses in November and supposed they were some of Rawlings Manor's famous year-round blooms. Perhaps Lord Edward hadn't been lying, after all.

Edward didn't pause on the threshold but boldly crossed the thickly piled rug to the bed, where he lowered her with almost exaggerated gentleness. Pegeen would have laughed at his caution, comparing herself to a fragile piece of china, but as he drew his arms from around her, her bonnet slid off, revealing the gash in her hairline and making Mrs. Praehurst gasp.

"Oh!" cried the housekeeper. "What a nasty looking cut! The poor lamb. Why, she's gone white as the sheets below'er, I'll be sworn!"

"Where's Evers with that brandy?" Edward's voice was filled with annoyance. He must, Pegeen supposed, be a very exacting employer. She felt a little sorry for Mrs. Praehurst. "Cartwright, don't just stand there gaping. Get me some spirits, man. Can't you see the girl's fainting?''

Pegeen, whose eyelids had started to feel a bit heavy, lifted them with an effort. She wasn't fainting. Why, she'd never fainted before in her life. She was a hearty Scottish vicar's daughter, not a dainty society miss. Still, she had to admit she was feeling sleepy. Perhaps if she just closed her eyes for a minute or so....

''Here we are, my lord,'' called the singsong voice of the butler. Pegeen heard the clink of crystal glasses and the sound of a stopper being pulled from a decanter. ''Cook has sent up some toddies as well.''

''Blast the toddies,'' Edward swore. ''Just pour out some brandy. The girl's lost consciousness.''

Just to be contrary, Pegeen opened her eyes. She found herself looking up into Mrs. Praehurst's kind, concerned face as the housekeeper bent over her, peeling off her gloves, loosening the fasten to her pelisse, and untying the bow that had held her bonnet under her chin.

''There now, my dear,'' Mrs. Praehurst said, gently slipping the bonnet out from beneath Pegeen's head. With a cool, competent hand, the housekeeper brushed back some of Pegeen's tangled hair from her face. ''Oh, my. That cut does look deep. I do hope that—''

''Mrs. Praehurst, if you *please*.'' Edward edged past Mrs. Praehurst's generous backside, a snifter of the same amber liquid his friend had been drinking in his hand. Pegeen saw that his handsome features had tightened, but she supposed it was with annoyance at his servants and not concern for herself. After all, he'd only known her a scant fortnight, hardly enough time to develop any feeling for her other than, say, lust, which she knew quite well that a man like Lord Edward Rawlings felt for just about every passing housemaid.

''Drink,'' Edward commanded, not a trace of sympathy in his deep voice. He held a bell-shaped glass beneath her nose, and the fumes from the alcohol within it caused

Pegeen's eyes to water. She shook her head mutely. She wasn't touching a drop of that foul-smelling liquid.

"Haven't you any whiskey?" she managed to inquire weakly, noticing Mrs. Praehurst's startled glance and not understanding it.

"Drink it," Edward said again, and something in his tone of voice reminded Pegeen that he didn't like to have to repeat himself. She shot him an irritated glance, and, as ungraciously as she could, took the glass from him, closing her eyes as she took a sip of the fiery liquid. Her reaction was instinctive and immediate: She clasped the glass in both hands and swallowed the whole of its contents in a single, greedy gulp.

When the last drop of amber liquid was gone, Edward took the glass away and stared down at her as she passed a trembling hand across her smarting eyes. As if from nowhere, a clean handkerchief appeared in his hand, and he passed it to her, all the annoyance gone from his grey eyes.

"Better?" he asked, as Pegeen sniffled.

She nodded. The delicious brandy was warming her entire body, even down to her frozen toes, and the pain in her head didn't seem to matter so much. Why, brandy was better than whiskey!

"Good," Edward said, as he passed the snifter back to Evers, who handed him a second glass, this one containing significantly more liquor. Edward stared down at the glass, then glanced back at Evers. After wagging a long index finger at the elderly butler, Edward downed the entire contents of the glass in a swift gulp.

Mrs. Praehurst cast Edward a disapproving look over the rims of her spectacles, then, with the familiarity of a servant of long standing, shooed him out of her way as she bent back over Pegeen and began to undo one of the many rows of jet buttons on the front of her travelling dress.

"Now, Miss MacDougal," the housekeeper began, "I hope you won't mind the presumption, but Lady Herbert and I thought you'd be wanting a lady's maid, so I've engaged young Lucy Alcott from the Ladies Seminary. I know the fashion these days is for French maids, but we hadn't much notice, you know, and besides, Mr. Evers doesn't take kindly to the French. I didn't think you'd mind . . ."

As Mrs. Praehurst prattled, Pegeen saw Edward lower his brandy snifter and lift a quizzical eyebrow. Following the direction of his gaze, Pegeen realized that he was staring at the curves of her breasts, plainly visible through the thin muslin of her blouse. Her cheeks crimson, Pegeen glared at him until he felt her eyes on him, and he lifted his gaze to meet hers. He immediately blushed, an action which both surprised and confused Pegeen. If he was such a man of the world, why the embarrassment?

Her own embarrassment coupled with the alcohol she'd consumed had brought a good deal of color back into her face, and two bright spots of pink appeared on each of her high cheekbones. In a deceptively sweet voice, she inquired, "I don't believe the services of Lord Edward are needed any longer, are they, Mrs. Praehurst?"

Mrs. Praehurst looked up from the cuff she was unbuttoning, and her gaze swung accusingly towards the men hovering in the doorway. "Certainly not!" she declared.

Dropping Pegeen's hand, the housekeeper stalked towards her master and his butler. Neither man required further prompting. With respectful bows, Edward's face still red and expressionless, they retreated back into the hallway, where Alistair Cartwright greeted them with a cheerful, "Heigh-ho, there!"

Mrs. Praehurst shut the door firmly behind them and returned to Pegeen's side, shaking her head. "You'll have to forgive them, Miss MacDougal," she said, in her nononsense but kind manner. "There hasn't been a lady in residence in Rawlings for—oh, since the duchess passed years and years ago." So Pegeen had guessed rightly. She was staying in the duchess' old room, its first occupant since Edward's mother had died.

"Of course, Lord Edward's friends from London come to stay frequently, but what I mean to say is, we haven't had a lady in permanent residence in quite some time."

Pegeen asked curiously, "Does Lord Edward entertain large parties often?"

"Oh, when he isn't in London, it seems as if all of London is here." Mrs. Praehurst spoke of her employer with undisguised pride. "Of course, Lord Edward keeps an excellent table, and he's quite generous with his hunters. You know, Lord Edward's stable is one of the most respected in the equestrian world. Even the Prince of Wales—"

A low rap sounded on the door, and Mrs. Praehurst hurried to answer it. It was Lucy Alcott, the lady's maid the housekeeper had hired for Pegeen. A pretty, wide-eyed redhead, the girl smiled nervously at Pegeen and was immediately banished by Mrs. Praehurst into the adjoining bathing chamber to await the arrival of the housemaids who were transporting the hot water for Pegeen's bath.

The interruption had apparently sidetracked Mrs. Praehurst, because she forgot all about the Prince of Wales and began discussing, rather anxiously, Pegeen thought, a large party of Lord Edward's London friends who were to arrive next week for a ball and hunt. This party, Mrs. Praehurst took care to explain, had been planned weeks and weeks ago, and Lord Edward had seen no reason to cancel it upon learning from Sir Arthur the whereabouts of the Rawlings heir.

"For," the housekeeper said with evident embarrassment, "there was reason to believe at the time, Miss MacDougal, that you were not, uh, as young as you have turned out to be, and Lord Edward had thought you, er, would not mind. . . ."

Pegeen couldn't help smiling. What Lord Edward had

obviously thought was that, as a dried up old spinster, she'd have leapt at the chance to dine with gentry. "I see," she said. "And is the fact that I'm only just out of the school-room, as Lord Edward so tactfully put it, and have never had a season in London, going to put a damper on the festivities?"

"Certainly not," Mrs. Praehurst said, a little too heart-ily. "Why, there will be any number of ladies as young as yourself visiting. Sir Arthur's elder daughters, for example. You've met them already, I suppose?" At Pegeen's nod, Mrs. Praehurst continued, an unmistakable glitter of pride in her crinkly grey eyes. "They're fine girls. Lord Edward only invites the finest families in England to stay, you know. The earl of Derby and his family, the marquis and marchioness of Lynne and their children, the baronet Sir Thomas Caine, the dowager lady Seldon, and, of course, the viscountess of Ashbury. . . ." Mrs. Praehurst broke off with a good-natured laugh. "But then, I forget myself! None of those names can mean anything to you, my dear. You must stop me if I go on too much. I am an old woman and have a tendency to gossip!"

Pegeen smiled weakly. She was certain that if Mrs. Praehurst had any idea her proud recitation of the hunt's guest list was causing Pegeen dismay rather than pleasure, the housekeeper would have changed the subject. The pros-pect of having to rub shoulders with a dozen titled guests for the weekend caused Pegeen's heart to sink. What in heaven's name was she going to talk about with the dow-ager lady Seldon or the marchioness of Lynne? The sorry conditions of London poorhouses? The need for child labor reform? For of course she'd be included in all the activities from evening whist to riding with the hounds. Oh, bother!

There was nothing else for it. She was going to have to speak to Lord Edward. She couldn't possibly be expected to spend her days in idle chitchat with dowagers and their empty-headed daughters. She knew nothing of London society, and so would not have been able to join in with their gossip, even had she approved of such a pastime. She had no talent for needlework or music, hated hunting, and despised gambling with a passion. Heavens, what was she to do with herself? Perhaps she could contact the local vicarage and offer her services. She infinitely preferred tending to the sick than kowtowing to the rich.

The housemaids bearing steaming water for Pegeen's bath arrived, and Mrs. Praehurst led them into the bathing chamber, giving Pegeen a respite from the housekeeper's well-meaning chatter. Another rap was heard on the door and this time Mrs. Praehurst admitted a portly older man she introduced to Pegeen as Mr. Parks, the village surgeon. Mr. Parks brought with him a black bag, a cheerful demeanor, and the unmistakable odor of brandy—Evers had probably got hold of him on his way to Pegeen's room. Pegeen wasn't as much interested in his medical opinions of her injury than in the information he could bring her about Jeremy. Was he at Rawlings? Was he all right? When could she see him?

Mr. Parks answered affirmatively to the first two questions, and shook a finger at her for the third. "Not until I've discovered what ails you, little missy," he admonished, and when Mrs. Praehurst coughed, he corrected himself. "I mean, Miss MacDougal."

With Lucy's help, Mrs. Praehurst was able to comb enough of Pegeen's hair away from her wound for the surgeon to thoroughly inspect it, and it wasn't until Pegeen saw the maid's reaction to the sight that she felt the injury might be more severe than she'd thought. Poor Lucy gasped and stared, one hand flying to her mouth as the other hastily made the sign of the cross. Mr. Parks, however, showed no surprise, only a medical interest in Pegeen's injury. He rotated her head with gentle fingers, pressed on various spots on her skull, asking if they hurt, then asked if she'd experienced nausea or dizziness since the accident. At Pegeen's affirmative answer, the surgeon nodded, and set about cleansing the wound.

Mr. Parks was worried, he informed Mrs. Praehurst, about concussion, though the dizziness Pegeen experienced might simply have been due to the shock of the accident and the jolt of her subsequent trip to the manor house. Ignoring Pegeen, the surgeon went on to explain that his patient was to be wakened every two hours, and that if she seemed groggy or disoriented, he was to be sent for immediately. Tomorrow, Mr. Parks said, laudanum might be administered if there was any pain, and he went on to list things Pegeen was not to attempt to do for a week, such as horseback ride or attempt fine needlework. This last warning delighted Pegeen, who now had a perfect excuse not to join Lord Edward's hunting party.

Mr. Parks left after having given Mrs. Praehurst careful instructions involving Pegeen's laudanum. No sooner had Lucy opened the bedroom door to see the surgeon out than a four foot tall, dark-haired streak whizzed by them both, making a beeline for the canopy bed. "Pegeen!" Jeremy cried, diving onto the soft coverlets and jarring Pegeen enough to cause her to cry out. "Hullo! Did he bleed you?"

Recovering herself, Pegeen eyed Jeremy critically. His cheeks were very red, his eyes bright, but it appeared his heightened coloring was from excitement rather than illness. She reached out instinctively to sweep some of his dark hair from his sweaty little brow. In the doorway, Mr. Parks cried, not without some amusement, "Young man! What did Sir Arthur and I discuss with you in the carriage?"

Jeremy ignored the surgeon. "Did he bleed you, Pegeen?" he wanted to know.

"Certainly not," Pegeen said. "What do you mean, running about like a little ruffian? You can't go jumping on the furniture, you know. We aren't back in the rectory—"

Mr. Parks strode past a confused Mrs. Praehurst and

seized Jeremy by his shirt collar. "Young man," he said with mock severeness, "your uncle Edward told you that you were to leave your aunt be. She's had a terrible knock to the head, and she isn't feeling well—"

"I know it," Jeremy said, his voice sounding strangled because Mr. Parks was hoisting him off the bed by his collar. "If it wasn't for Uncle Edward, she'd be dead, you know. Sir Arthur would've squashed her flat. Pegeen, did you see that banister on those stairs on the Great Hall? Do you suppose Uncle Edward'd get angry if I slid down that banister just once?" As Mr. Parks steered him from the room, Jeremy craned his neck to look up at the surgeon. "See here," he said. "You unhand me at once. I'm the duke, you know."

Mr. Parks laughed as if Jeremy had told him a funny joke. "Say good night to your aunt, Your Grace," he said.

Jeremy cast Pegeen one last glance before he was hauled out of the room. "Don't worry, Pegeen," he assured her. "I'll get up to see you after supper!"

"Dinner," the surgeon corrected him. "And no, you won't."

Lucy closed the door swiftly after them and leaned against it, looking startled. Across the room, Mrs. Praehurst's eyes were very large behind her spectacles but she said only, "Well. His Grace seems a spirited young man."

Pegeen was too tired to argue. Jeremy's spirited, it's true, she wanted to say, but aren't all ten-year-old boys? What had they expected? A miniature Lord Edward? Ha!

Chapter Six

dward flung his cloak down on one of the overstuffed leather chairs in his library and asked Sir Arthur, "What happened to Katherine Rawlings?"

Sir Arthur choked on his brandy. Edward felt a twinge of sympathy for his solicitor. The poor man had just been through a carriage accident and had stood for two hours in a blizzard with an incorrigible young boy. All he wanted to do was enjoy a drink by the fireside and here was his employer, barking questions at him. Still, it had to be asked.

"What do you mean, Edward?" Alistair, deep in the confines of a neighboring leather chair, was cradling his own snifter. "She's dead, isn't she? She died after your brother John was killed in that duel."

"Yes, but how? From what?"

"My lord," gasped Sir Arthur, recovering himself. His large, beefy face had gone red as the velvet portieres at the window casements. "Your poor, departed brother's wife died of consumption in Venice, shortly following Lord John's death."

"Can you prove that?" Edward flung himself on a low hunter green couch, but he didn't stretch out upon it. He

sat leaning forward with his elbows on his knees, waiting
for his solicitor's response.

"I never saw the death certificate, no," Sir Arthur
said. "But Miss MacDougal assures me that her nephew
was left in her care some nine and a half years back, when
her sister returned briefly to England after Lord John's
death, and shortly before her own. . . ."

"That much is probably true," Edward snorted. "Miss
MacDougal seems to have good deal more maternal instinct
than her sister ever did. Leaving her son with his aunt was
probably the only sensible thing John's wife ever did in her
short life."

Alistair looked wistful. "And what luck for the boy,
too, eh? Wish *I'd* been raised by an aunt who looked like
that. Those eyes! And that tiny waist!"

Edward glared at his perpetual houseguest. This was
worse than he'd feared. "You keep your eyes off her waist.
That girl is here under my protection, and I can't afford to
lose her. She's all that separates me and the dreaded title.
Don't you dare offend her, Cartwright."

"Does she offend easily, then?" Alistair inquired with
a wicked smile.

Edward stroked his jaw, remembering the blows the
girl had planted there. "Easily enough," he said. "You've
got to remember, Alistair, Miss MacDougal's not one of
us. She . . ."

He paused, uncertain how to proceed. The gist of it
was, he didn't have the slightest idea how Miss Pegeen
MacDougal was to be handled. He had all the experience
in the world with women—the married kind, that is. He
didn't have a clue how one was to behave around proper
young misses, and though he strongly suspected that the
strong-willed Miss MacDougal did not fall into that category, he could think of no other in which to place her.

Still, he intended to treat her like the vicar's daughter
she was, and he'd expect Alistair to do the same.

"She's very young," he finished, feeling the inadequacy of the statement. "And inexperienced. So stay away from her."

Alistair quirked up a golden eyebrow. "Is that what you did in London, then? Stayed away from her?"

"As best I could," Edward replied with a grimace.

He had not particularly enjoyed the week he'd spent in London with his nephew and Miss MacDougal. For one thing, the season hadn't yet started, and almost all of Edward's friends were still in the country. He had already seen all of the shows and Arabella wasn't about, so he'd had no choice but to spend his nights at his club on Pall Mall, gaming with the few men still in town and occasionally hiring a hansom and slumming it in the Vauxhall Gardens until the wee hours for want of anything better to do.

The point, Edward had felt, had been to spend as little time as possible in the presence of Pegeen MacDougal. It had not mattered much to him what he did or where he went, so long as it took him away from her and her infernal green eyes.

He had at first tried to dismiss the kisses they'd shared in her kitchen, but the more he thought about it, the more he realized that Pegeen MacDougal was a very dangerous young woman indeed. Not because she kissed the way she did, though Pegeen MacDougal kissed the way none of Edward's mistresses had ever kissed him, like she meant it. No, Pegeen MacDougal was dangerous because she kissed like that and she wasn't anybody's wife or mistress.

Which meant that she was excessively free to fall in love. . . . Worse, she was free to fall in love *with*.

And one thing Edward had no intention of doing at this stage in his life was fall in love with a green-eyed vicar's daughter who called herself a Liberal and delivered prostitutes' babies. It simply wasn't going to happen. Because in the end, he'd have to marry her in order to have her, and marriage complicated things. Wasn't Arabella living testimonial to that?

And so, to avoid falling in love with her, Edward had been spending as little time as possible in the presence of the little chit. And it appeared to be working. In fact, he congratulated himself that he was now almost completely out of danger.

Almost.

"Just stay away from her," Edward growled at his guest. "Think of her as one of Herbert's daughters."

Alistair glanced at the portly solicitor. "You can't be serious."

Sir Arthur looked profoundly perplexed. He was gazing into his brandy as if it might produce the answers he sought. "My lord," he began slowly. "I'm afraid my slow brain cannot quite absorb the gist of this conversation. Has something that Miss MacDougal said given you reason to believe Lady Katherine is still alive?"

Edward hesitated. "No. Except I find it odd that she speaks of her sister in the present tense. 'My sister is lovely' she said. Not 'was.' 'Is.'"

Sir Arthur roused himself into something like indignation. He sat up in his deep chair and coughed loudly. "Lord Edward, I must take exception to these implications. I thoroughly investigated this family. Pegeen MacDougal is the second daughter of Gavin MacDougal, the late rector of the parish of Applesby near Aberdeen. Her elder sister Katherine left His Grace in the care of her father and sister when the boy was but an infant, shortly after Lord John's untimely death, and then returned to the Continent to die penniless in Italy."

Edward folded his arms and leaned back against the hunter green upholstery. "That I don't believe," he declared. "John must have had over twenty thousand pounds to his name when he died. How could she have died without a penny?"

"Pardon me, sir, but it appears that your brother spent his last days drinking and betting on horses without a thought to his family. Lord John, you'll recall, was tragically murdered with his affairs in scandalous disorder. What little money he left to Lady Katherine that didn't go to settle his gambling debts was used to pay off accounts at multiple clubs. The rest of it went to his tailor. I'm sorry if what I'm saying shocks you, my lord, but it's the truth. Your brother never adequately provided for his wife and child, and the poor woman died because of it."

Edward shook his head. It wasn't that he didn't believe Sir Arthur. John had always been a self-centered, womanizing drunkard, but Edward had never thought he'd so reprobate as to leave his family unprovided for. However, Edward wasn't at all surprised to learn that John had done exactly that. Twenty thousand dollars in gambling debts! No wonder someone had finally seen fit to shoot the man.

Unbidden, an image of Pegeen MacDougal as he'd last seen her sprang into Edward's head: a fragile, diminutive figure in his mother's massive four-poster bed, emerald eyes enormous in a pale face surrounded by an aurora of soft, dark hair. And the collar of her dress opened just enough so that he had glimpsed a soft, round breast, veiled in lace. . . . Edward unfolded his arms and leaned forward again, clearing his throat loudly.

"Katherine was very young when my brother married her, was she not? That's why they had to marry in Scotland. Fifteen, I think. Maybe sixteen. So she would only be twenty-five or six today?" Edward pondered that. "What does a twenty-five or six-year-old woman look like? Miss MacDougal says she is twenty, but she looks closer to fifteen to me."

Sir Arthur laughed, good-naturedly and slapped his massive knee. "Ah, Lord Edward! And I suppose you can tell me how old my eldest daughter, Anne, is. Go on. You danced with her last month, at Ashbury House. How old would you guess?''

Edward tried to hide his irritation. It was bad enough that he was constantly being called upon to entertain his father's estate executor, but to have to dance with his half dozen daughters as well. . . . He tried to remember which one was Anne. The horse-toothed wench, or the one with the freckles? Then he remembered. The passably pretty one.

"Seventeen," Edward shrugged, knowing he'd get it wrong.

He did. Sir Arthur slapped his knee again in delight. "One-and-twenty," he cried. "One-and-twenty. You shaved off four years, there, sir. Virginia would be thrilled to hear it."

Edward stared at his boot-toes, scuffed now from a day's worth of riding. He thought of the impossibly pretty upturned face that had regarded him with such disdain just moments ago. He would never, ever, be able to picture a face like that cradled in his brother's hands, hands that Edward had seen commit atrocities that even now, years later, made him shudder to remember.

Edward was about to resume his pacing when a low knock sounded on the door. He barked, "Come in," and his valet calmly entered the library, glancing just once at his lordship's scuffed boots. "My lord, Evers informs me that dinner will be served shortly. I've taken the liberty of drawing your bath and laying out your evening clothes."

"Yes, yes." Edward waved him away, distracted. "I'll change presently."

The valet appeared unruffled by this brusque dismissal. He bowed and withdrew. Alistair, with a long, loud sigh, heaved himself up out of his chair and said, "If Daniels is anxious for you to dress, Edward, then my Knowlton must be frantic. I'll see both of you gentlemen downstairs for dinner." He paused on the threshold, looking back at

Edward. "Am I to understand that the lovely Miss MacDougal won't be joining us, then?"

"I think it hardly likely," Edward replied with a composure that surprised even himself. "We'll see what Parks has to say about it. He's with her now."

"Too bad," Alistair sighed. "Liberal or no, she seems a jolly sort." He left, not being too careful about closing the door behind him.

"A jolly sort," Edward echoed, as if he couldn't quite believe what he had heard. He went to the liquor cabinet and poured himself a generous glass of spirits. He had a feeling he was going to need a lot to drink for the next few days.

Chapter Seven

Mr. Parks, Pegeen realized the following morning, hadn't been exaggerating when he'd informed her that her head might ache for a while. That ache, coupled with the fact she'd been shaken awake every two hours by an anxious Lucy, left her feeling as if she really *had* fallen off Lord Edward's horse and that the damned beast had trod upon her several times for good measure.

What the surgeon failed to predict was that the hours Pegeen spent in the wind and snow, along with the beating her body had taken in the carriage accident, not to mention her wild ride across the moor, would result in a head cold of such severity that when Lucy roused Pegeen for her morning bath, she found her mistress unable to utter a sound through her raw, swollen throat, let alone rise out of bed.

One look at Pegeen's pale, feverish face sent the red-haired lady's maid running for Mrs. Praehurst. The housekeeper arrived with alacrity and was instantly alarmed at the sight of Pegeen sitting up in her bed, her dark hair in wild disarray, her eyes glowing indignantly as she tried in a barely audible whisper to explain that she felt fine, really.

It was just a little cold. What was everyone so upset about? Hadn't they ever seen a woman with a cold before?

Try as she might, Pegeen was unable to convince Mrs. Praehurst that she wasn't seriously ill. The housekeeper put a hand to Pegeen's forehead, felt the fever there, and immediately dispatched one of the footmen for Mr. Parks. Pegeen raged that it was ridiculous to send for the surgeon when all that was wrong with her was a simple cold, but since she'd lost her voice, no one paid her any mind. Pegeen's wishes were unilaterally ignored as the entire staff of Rawlings Manor, or so it seemed, rushed to her room with warming pans and garlic poultices and other even more aromatic home remedies.

By the time Mr. Parks arrived, Pegeen had given up all hope of ever being allowed to get out of bed. The surgeon was as businesslike as he'd been the night before, giving Pegeen's head wound a perfunctory exam before looking down her throat. His prognosis was quick and to the point: severe inflammation to the throat, in particular, the tonsils, caused no doubt from overexposure to the Yorkshire elements.

"Quinsy," Mrs. Praehurst said emphatically. "I should have known." And she clapped her hands and sent several housemaids scurrying down to the kitchens for hot tea with honey.

"You'll live," Mr. Parks informed Pegeen, who made a sour face at the news. "Bed rest and all the tea she can drink for a week. Keep her warm, Mrs. Praehurst, and make sure she sleeps. The laudanum will help with that. I'll be back in a few days to check her progress."

Pegeen wanted to ask the surgeon how long it would be before she got her voice back but rasping out so many words seemed like too much of an effort. Disgruntled, Pegeen settled back against the piles of down-filled pillows and tried to count her blessings, though they seemed, at that moment, few and far between. To Pegeen, who'd spent the better part of the past nineteen years rising every day at dawn and working steadily until sunset, this sudden bout of enforced bed rest was most inopportune. Finally she was freed from the fetters of housework and the demands of her father's parish. She had all the time in the world to read and write letters and work for the betterment of the lot of the poor. . . .

And she was so weak she couldn't even cross the room without help.

At least, she told herself, Jeremy was being well taken care of. Though she couldn't help worrying about who was going to look after him during the course of her illness. She wasn't so much concerned about Jeremy as she was about the welfare of his caretakers.

For nearly a week, Pegeen endured a throbbing head and aching throat, spending considerable amounts of her time sleeping. It was as if, now that the burden of Jeremy's care had been lifted from her, Pegeen's body was trying to make up for all the sleep it had lost over the years. When she felt well enough, Pegeen dipped into the pile of books Lord Edward had supplied from his library and couldn't help laughing. She suspected that he'd purposefully chosen light romances over reading material of weightier substance to annoy her.

Pegeen couldn't, however, complain about her nurses. Lucy hardly ever left Pegeen's bedside. She was willing to dart down to the kitchen at any time, day or night, to fetch her mistress 'a nice cuppa,' and tried to tempt her into eating confections from the pastry chef. She also regaled her with stories about the goings-on belowstairs. Mrs. Praehurst, too, proved to be an unfailingly cheerful companion with a natural inclination towards chat, from whom Pegeen garnered certain interesting facts concerning the Rawlings family, or, more precisely, what was left of it.

It seemed, for example, that Lord Edward Rawlings was one of the most sought after bachelors in England, who'd narrowly escaped marriage several times by fleeing to Europe at the last minute, and once even winging a prospective fiancée's brother in a duel. He had mistresses all over the Continent, as well as in England, and was regularly seen in all the places where young men of titled wealth ought to be seen. Pegeen was immensely gratified that her assessment of Edward's dissipation had been correct, and she looked forward to teasing him about it just as soon as she could speak again.

When Pegeen felt well enough to sit up but was still not allowed out of bed, she requested newspapers with which she might pass the time, eschewing the reading material Lord Edward had thought suitable for her. Mrs. Praehurst, though she clacked her tongue in disapproval, managed to produce an armful stolen with some difficulty from Lord Edward's library. Pegeen pored over them, taking copious notes while selecting the charitable concerns that she intended Jeremy to sponsor. This led her to wonder just how much wealth Jeremy possessed, and Pegeen's next request was for the household and estate account books.

Despite Mrs. Praehurst's evident anxiety over the matter, Pegeen did not particularly care what Lord Edward was going to say when he discovered what she was up to. Since she'd managed her father's parish accounts, Pegeen felt perfectly capable of tackling those of Rawlings Manor. It was the extravagances she saw there that shocked and alarmed her. While it was perfectly understandable that a house the size of Rawlings Manor should go through a ton of coal a month during the winter, there was absolutely no reason why, when there were people starving on the streets, a *champagne fountain* needed to have been erected on a dining table while Lord Edward entertained a few friends from London.

A champagne fountain? Why, the cost of its operation for one night only was more than Pegeen's mother had left her per annum! And then there was a notation about something called charades. A good deal of money had spent on costumes and sets for this, but when Pegeen asked about it, Mrs. Praehurst told her charades was a game Lord Edward and his friends played. A *game* that cost more money than it took to run the entire Applesby orphanage for a year? Pegeen could hardly believe her eyes.

When she compared the costs incurred by Lord Edward's last party from London with the cost of operating the Ladies Seminary from which Lucy had been hired and of which the Rawlings estate was the primary benefactor, Pegeen found that it was cheaper to run a boarding school for forty girls for half a year than it was to entertain a group of the haute monde at Rawlings Manor for a fortnight.

Pegeen was so angry that she nearly broke her pen in two.

What on earth was Lord Edward thinking? Was the man a dandy without a thought in his head save his own enjoyment? She had felt that his behavior during the carriage accident had been nothing short of heroic, slogging through all that snow to find a horse with which to conduct her to safety. Hardly a dandyish act, that. Yet he'd spent over a hundred pounds this year on cravats alone! This, Pegeen felt, with no small amount of indignation, was ridiculous.

She tried, however, to be fair. Lord Edward had a right to spend his share of the Rawlings fortune however he saw fit. And it was not the vast amounts he spent on horseflesh that annoyed her. She did not even mind so much that he entertained so extravagantly. But when she saw a notation indicating that two dozen gold napkin holders, monogrammed with the letters E and A, had been ordered for the upcoming hunting party, she very nearly, in the words of Jeremy, spontaneously combusted. The cost of those napkin holders was equal to the cost of the stained glass windows in her father's church in Applesby. Over her dead body would Lord Edward entertain with napkin holders engraved with his own and his mistress' initials.

Pegeen was so enraged by this expense that Mrs. Praehurst grew rather fearful for the girl's health, seeing only
that Pegeen's face had gone quite pale yet her cheeks
burned as if with fever. The plump housekeeper had rushed
out into the hallway with the intention of sending one of
the footmen for Mr. Parks straight away, when she happened to bump directly into his lordship, who'd come reluctantly and only after a good deal of needling by Alistair
Cartwright, who was anxious for the pretty Miss Mac-
Dougal's recovery, to inquire after Pegeen's health.

"Oh, my lord," Mrs. Praehurst cried worriedly,
wringing her hands. "I'm afraid Miss Pegeen's taken a turn
for the worse. Quite a sight she looks, with fevered brow
and eyes hard as great green emeralds!"

Edward looked alarmed. "Have you sent for Mr.
Parks?"

"I was on my way to do so. Oh, dear, I'm afraid it's
all my fault. She's been looking peaked all morning, ever
since I brought her the household account books . . ."

Edward, who'd been about to rush down the stairs and
bellow for Evers—something he did invariably whatever
the nature of a crisis—froze at the top of the stairs, leveling
his housekeeper with a gaze that might have frozen fire.

"The household account books?" Edward's dark
brows rushed down into a frown that sent Mrs. Praehurst
back a step, one hand flying to her bosom. "Did you say
you brought her the *household account books*?"

Mrs. Praehurst nodded, her spectacles quivering on the
end of her nose. "Was that so wrong, my lord? She asked
to see them, after all . . ."

Edward's frown flattened out into a grimace, and he
started back up the stairs, striding purposefully down the
hall towards the Rose Room. Mrs. Praehurst tripped after
him with a little squeak, holding up the hem of her black
wool dress.

"Oh, my lord," she called querously. "You can't go in there, my lord! It wouldn't be at all seemly. The young lady is abed, my lord!"

But Edward had already stalked into his mother's former bedroom, noting with disapproval that the fire was too high and the room roastingly hot.

Pegeen sat in the center of the great canopied bed, her dark brown hair loose about her shoulders, her nose tucked into a ledger that was nearly as large as she was. About the bed were littered more ledgers and papers upon which the blasted wench had been taking notes. Notes! Though the rest of the chamber had the appearance of a sick room— there were fresh-cut flowers everywhere along with multitudes of bottles and tonics and poultices—the bed looked like the desk of a very promising young businessman.

Pegeen had not so much as lifted her head at Lord Edward's entrance and didn't do so until Mrs. Praehurst, who had hurried in behind him, cleared her throat.

"Oh, Miss Pegeen," the housekeeper coughed. "You have a visitor."

Pegeen looked up, her eyes, as Mrs. Praehurst had said, very large and very green. Without registering the slightest surprise that Edward was in her bedroom, Pegeen said, "I'm canceling your order for the monogrammed napkin holders."

Edward stared at her. "I beg your pardon?"

"What you do with your personal life is your concern, of course," she went on. "But Jeremy is a young boy and worships the ground you walk upon. I'll not have him grow up thinking it is quite all right to carry on love affairs with married women."

Edward heard Mrs. Praehurst inhale rather sharply behind him. He himself hadn't the slightest idea how to react. The girl looked perfectly harmless in her high-necked cotton nightdress with the lace trim and her hair hanging down her back like a schoolgirl. And yet she was speaking to him as coolly as if she were Queen Victoria herself.

Torn between rage and laughter, Edward settled for asking curiously, "What napkin holders?"

Pegeen frowned at him. Taking a bit of pencil from behind her ear, she pointed at an entry in the ledger she held.

"It says right here that you ordered two dozen solid gold napkin holders with the letters EA entwined upon them. Perhaps I was wrong, but I assumed the A stood for Arabella. Does it, perhaps, stand for Alistair?" Her gaze was steady. "I had heard of such things, of course, but I must say, I hadn't expected it of *you*, Lord Edward."

Edward flushed. "Now, see here——"

Mrs. Praehurst coughed again softly. Both Edward and Pegeen looked at her, and the housekeeper bobbed an embarrassed curtsy. "I beg your pardon, my lord, miss, but those napkin holders were ordered by the viscountess." Flashing an appealing look at Pegeen, the woman explained, "Lady Arabella Ashbury, I mean. She sometimes orders things for the Rawlings household, and Lord Edward told me that whatever her ladyship wanted, I was to please purchase."

Pegeen flipped back a page of the ledger. "The viscountess wouldn't happened to have ordered costumes for charades and a champagne fountain, would she?"

"Why, yes! Bless you, she ordered both those things!"

Pegeen slammed the ledger shut with a bang. "Lord Edward, I'd like a word with you in private. Mrs. Praehurst, could you excuse us for a moment?"

Mrs. Praehurst hesitated. "Oh, dear," she said, her eyes filled with dismay. "It wouldn't look at all right, my lord, for you to visit with Miss MacDougal alone in her bedchamber——"

"Under the circumstances," Edward replied with a grin he couldn't restrain though he was trying very hard to glare, "I think it would be permissible for you to leave us alone for a bit, Mrs. Praehurst. Though at your peril you stay away too long. Miss MacDougal looks as if she'd like nothing better than to run me through with a hot fire iron."

"Oh, my," Mrs. Praehurst said. But she bustled from the room with many a nervous glance back at them over her rounded shoulders. "I'll be right outside the door, then."

The door had no sooner clicked shut than Pegeen said in her hoarse voice, "I mean no offense to you, Lord Edward, but you simply cannot allow the viscountess free rein with the household expense account. She is quite exorbitant in her tastes, and the money she spends on frivolities would be better spent elsewhere, like improving conditions in the homes of your tenant farmers or building a new roof for the Ladies Seminary."

Edward looked down into the heart-shaped face and tried to remember that he ought to be angry, murderously angry at the little chit's impudence. But something about being called upon this hearth rug for a scolding, where he'd stood so many times in his childhood, filled him with amusement, and it was all he could do to keep from bursting out into loud guffaws.

Trying to smother his mirth, Edward frowned and eyed the girl, who, he noticed, looked absurdly fetching for an invalid. There was color in her high cheekbones and with her hair down she looked much the way she had the first time Edward had ever laid eyes on her that afternoon he'd mistaken her for a parlor maid. It was exceedingly difficult for him to glower at her when all he wanted to do was throw back the duvet covering her and crawl into bed beside her.

"That's your opinion on the matter, is it?" he snapped, dissembling annoyance. At her crisp nod he asked, "And might I inquire what possible right you felt you had to rifle through my ledgers?"

"They aren't *your* ledgers at all," Pegeen sniffed haughtily. "They are Sir Arthur's ledgers. And now that he has been installed as the new duke of Rawlings, they are *Jeremy's* ledgers. And as I am Jeremy's guardian, I have every right to look over what has been left to him. And that includes all household accounts." With a cough Pegeen continued, "Really, Lord Edward, but I was prodigiously surprised to see how wasteful you are. One hundred pounds a year on cravats? Are you so foppish that you cannot wear one more than once?"

Edward felt himself turning red with embarrassment at the reproof. Foppish? *Him*? Alistair Cartwright, maybe, but not—

"Of course you have the right to spend your inheritance however you see fit, my lord." Pegeen shrugged as she flipped back through the pages of the ledger. "But it seems merely ludicrous that you try to pass off Claire Lundgren as a new mare . . ."

Edward was so startled that he choked. "*What*?"

"Honestly, Lord Edward, do you think no one reads the papers? I know perfectly well that Claire Lundgren is no mare but an actress, and that this stable you've hired for her in Cardington Crescent is in actuality a house."

"Now, see here," Edward cried when he'd recovered himself. "That was . . . That was a necessary expense!"

"Oh?" The corners of Pegeen's mouth turned up. "I see. You tired of her and had to buy her off, did you? I'm quite ashamed of you, my lord. I'm sure she would have settled for something in a less expensive neighborhood."

Edward was so astonished by the girl's gall that he could only let out a bark of sarcastic laughter. "Well!" he cried, folding his arms across his chest. "We're certainly seeing your true Scottish colors today, aren't we? I didn't notice any of this parsimonious penny-scrimping when it came to purchasing a new wardrobe for you!"

"Considering," Pegeen interrupted hotly, "that before

now I never in my life owned more than two dresses at a time, I believe I'm deserving of the mere two dozen you so generously had made up for me in London. If you'll remember, that was one of the conditions stipulated before I even agreed to come to Rawlings, an act which I am beginning to regret, since I've had nothing but misery——''

''Oh, you certainly look miserable, tucked up in that great bed with roses all around you, doing nothing all day but poking your nose into other people's business!''

''And as for Scots being stingy,'' Pegeen cried, throwing back her bedclothes and rising to her knees as if the slight to her countrymen had only just sunk in, ''I'd rather be associated with a country that knows how to save money than one that squanders it on champagne fountains!''

Edward strode towards the bed, leaning down to rest two fists upon the abandoned ledger so that his face was just inches from Pegeen's. ''You ought to try a little champagne sometime,'' he suggested maliciously. ''If you ask me, you need it.''

''What is that supposed to mean?'' Pegeen demanded. She reached up and poked him in the chest with an index finger. ''I could drink you under the table any day of the week. Just name the time and the place.''

Edward looked down at the finger pressing upon the buttons of his starched white shirtfront. It was a small finger, the nail short but well sculpted. But it wasn't the finger that interested Edward so much as the hand attached to it. What would she do, he wondered, if he snatched up that hand and placed it where it would do him the most good?

He shook his head. What in God's name was the matter with him? He simply could not allow this ingratiating weakness to continue. He had spent a week assiduously avoiding this room, trying to deny the existence of a Miss Pegeen MacDougal. But there was no denying that since she'd set foot in Rawlings, bringing with her that incorrigible boy, Edward's life had been turned upside down. Mrs.

Praehurst, who'd normally seen to his household's daily affairs, was too absorbed with nursing the girl to pay attention to matters like Edward's lunch and dinner menus. He and Alistair had been forced more than twice to dine at the village pub. Evers was so busy chasing that brat away from the banister on the staircase in the Great Hall that he couldn't be bothered with seeing that Edward's liquor cabinet remained fully stocked.

Even Daniels, Edward's valet, had forgotten to pick up one of Edward's waistcoats at the village tailor because he'd been busy fetching some sort of medicine for Pegeen at the apothecary. And when Edward had berated him, Daniels hadn't even had the grace to look guilty. He'd stared straight at Edward and said in indignant tones, "Miss MacDougal needed her medicine, m'lord. Ye didn't expect me to fetch yer waistcoat when the wee lass was wastin' away on account the quinsy, did ye, sir?"

And the stableboys! What was Edward going to do about the stableboys? Each and every one had his eye blackened by the new duke, and all of them were too frightened at the prospect of punishment to hit back. What if they all up and quit the day before hunting season opened? Where was he going to find trained stablehands so late in the season?

But these concerns paled in the light of Edward's most serious problem. Which was what in God's name was he going to do about the fact that no matter how hard he tried, he could not quite rid his mind of the memory of this irritating virgin's kiss?

In a voice gruff with suppressed emotion, Edward growled, "I wasn't talking about whiskey, I was talking about champagne, and a drinking contest was not what I had in mind."

"What did you have in mind, then?" Pegeen's pointed chin thrust out in stubborn challenge.

"You _would_ need to ask," Edward sneered. "I never

saw such a missish little thing as you. If you can't think what a man and a woman might do together over a bottle of champagne . . ."

The thick fringe of lashes surrounding those green eyes lowered suddenly, and Pegeen regarded him suspiciously. "Is it my imagination, or are you suggesting that I might serve as a replacement for the discarded Claire Lundgren?"

Edward laughed wickedly. "All I'm suggesting is that perhaps if you thought less about saving the poor of the world and more about having fun, you wouldn't be here at all, living off your nephew's inheritance, but in your own home with a husband and a houseful of brats keeping your mind off me and my affairs."

He saw the green eyes widen in surprise and knew he'd gone too far. He didn't know whether to expect tears or a slap across the face, and in an effort to ward off both, he seized the hand Pegeen had placed against his chest and pulled her towards him. Placing a steadying arm around her narrow waist, Edward lowered his head, planting a hearty kiss on her upturned lips.

Chapter Eight

This was precisely what Pegeen had hoped to avoid. She knew from past experience that she was powerless to resist Edward's kisses, and this one was wreaking havoc with all her good intentions.

Drawing her towards him in an inexorable grip, Edward eased her lips apart with his tongue, as effortlessly as the heat from his hands burned her tender flesh through the thin material of her nightdress. She groaned in frustration as she realized that her thighs were again melting, just as they'd done that day not so long ago in Appleby. The sudden throbbing readiness between them, leaving her slick with desire, was all too familiar.

And yet she couldn't push him away. Indeed, she clung to him like a shameless hussy, kissing him as if her very life depended upon it . . .

It was then that Edward realized Pegeen had nothing on beneath the thin cotton nightgown. He could feel the hard buds of her nipples against his waistcoat. The kiss Edward had intended to be mocking had turned into something he could no longer control. He had forgotten how wanton she was, how little she cared for convention, despite her missish ways. He could feel her firm young body pressed against him, and with a groan, forgetting all else, his hands moved to cup her rounded buttocks through the transparent material, bringing her pelvis hard up against his throbbing erection.

Pegeen drew back with a cry like an injured animal. Edward kept a firm grasp on her, however, anticipating her retreat.

"No," he growled. "Not this time. You'll damn well finish what you started. . . ."

"What *I* started?" Pegeen cried indignantly. "*You* kissed *me*!"

His fingers, moving to grasp her shoulders, bit into her flesh. "You encouraged me. Admit it. You feel something for me. Don't deny it."

"Of all the conceited—"

"You want me, Pegeen, every bit as much as I want you."

"What nonsense!"

"Nonsense? What's nonsense is your prudery!" Edward shook his head in disbelief. "What sort of woman are you? You claim not to believe in the institution of marriage, and yet you kiss with the enthusiasm of a Covent Garden whore!"

Pegeen blinked as if he'd slapped her. "How dare you! Have . . . have you gone mad? You forget yourself, Lord Edward!"

Perhaps it was the genuine look of shock on her face. Maybe it was the catch in her voice. But most likely it was the reminder of his title that stopped him. He realized that she genuinely did not know what he was talking about, that she honestly had no idea the effect her touch had on him. And how could she? He was the son of a duke, pampered and cosseted from birth, with a vast amount of experience in the art of lovemaking. She was an impoverished vicar's daughter, a virgin ten years his junior, who, despite her

shrewish tongue, had until recently known nothing but
hardship.

Reality returned. It was mid-morning, and Mrs. Praehurst was right outside the door. With a smothered curse,
Edward released her.

Diving beneath the coverlets, her cheeks flaming, Pegeen glared at him, noting the bulge in the front of his
breeches with disapproval.

"What's the matter with you?" she hissed. "Supposing your housekeeper walked in?"

"She's seen worse," Edward said mildly. He wasn't
exactly displeased with himself. Missish she might have
been, but with each kiss, she seemed to have more and
more difficulty resisting him. It didn't seem possible, but
he felt he might wear down her resistance after all. That
thought, despite the uncomfortable chafing he felt in his
trousers, was momentarily cheering.

"I'm not one of your mistresses," Pegeen declared,
sniffling into a handkerchief. She wasn't crying, however,
he noted with relief, just blowing her slightly reddened
nose. "Kindly keep your hands to yourself in the future."

"For a woman who claims to hate men of my class,"
Edward observed, "you certainly don't seem to mind my
kisses."

"Get out," Pegeen snarled.

"Tell me something, Pegeen. Since you don't believe
in the institution of marriage, why are you so against people
conducting love affairs outside of it? I would think a
woman of your convictions would be quite a proponent
of—"

"Get out!" she yelled, though her raspy voice didn't
carry far.

"But you aren't done chastising me. Remember? The
ledgers?"

Exhaling gustily, Pegeen said coldly, "I intend to tell
Mrs. Praehurst that all household expenses are to be ap-

proved by me before purchase. Jeremy is the duke of Rawlings, and I am responsible for seeing that *some* of the Rawlings fortune remains for his use in adulthood.''

Edward smiled. ''Well done. You, my dear, are already a shrewish wife, and you haven't even been wed yet! I congratulate you. It takes some women years to achieve your level of—''

''Get out!'' Pegeen yelled again, and this time, chuckling, Edward obeyed.

Chapter Nine

Striding into the pale blue morning room of Ashbury House, Edward slapped his gloves against his thigh, his cloak billowing out behind him. Lady Ashbury was seated at the breakfast table, perusing the society pages and looking angelic in a green silk gown trimmed with pink rosettes. She glanced up when Edward entered, and smiled. The viscountess of Ashbury's smile had been known to send weaker men to their knees. Edward did not even sit down.

"Well?" he demanded, not exactly rudely, but not in a friendly manner, either. "What is it? It had better be important. Alistair and I were intending to ride out to Knox Ridge this morning, to see how the snowfall had affected the gamekeeper's strategies for Saturday's hunt."

"I've finished the list," Arabella said regally, waving a slip of paper in the air. At Edward's blank stare, she said in measured tones, "The list. For Mrs. Praehurst. Regarding the guest room arrangements. Really, Edward, what's the matter with you? You've gone quite stupid suddenly."

Edward stepped forward to take the page from her white fingers, folded it without a glance, and slipped it into an inner pocket. "You might have sent it," he said testily, "rather than that cryptic message that I was to come as soon as possible. When I got your message, I thought . . . Well, it doesn't matter what I thought."

The viscountess laughed, a tinkling sound that at one point had sent shivers of delight up Edward's spine. Now the affectation only irritated him.

"But if I'd sent it, I wouldn't have the pleasure of breakfasting with you this morning." The viscountess dimpled at him in a manner that someone once must have told her was charming. "And I know what you thought. You thought the worst, I'm sure. Tell me, which frightens you more: Ashbury finding out about us or me finding someone else?"

Edward eyed the breakfast buffet on the side table. There was ham and pheasant and eggs, along with crispy bread rolls and several pots of jam. He picked up a plate and helped himself. "It would take someone a bit fiercer than your husband to frighten me, Arabella," he said, shoveling eggs onto his plate. "And as to your finding another, I might find my life considerably less complicated were that to occur."

Arabella pouted attractively. "Poor Edward." She eyed him as he moved along the buffet table, dwarfing it with his powerful bulk. "It seems as if I haven't seen you in ages, darling," she said, trying to keep her tone light. "It's been over a fortnight, I do believe. Have your new relations put a crimp in your social life?"

"New relations?" Without removing his cloak, Edward sat down at the breakfast table and picked up a fork. "Oh. You mean the boy."

"Yes, the boy. And his spinster aunt."

Edward smirked and tasted the pheasant. Not bad. Arabella's cook was French and tended to go to extraordinary lengths to complicate a meal far more than necessary.

Breakfast she managed to do fairly well. No mysterious sauces or creams.

"Well, let me see," Edward said, chewing meditatively. "It's Thursday, is it? In a space of one week, the new duke of Rawlings has frightened off three nursemaids, gotten into over a dozen fistfights with the stablehands, smashed a china tea set that was a gift to my mother from King Edward, poured ink on the head of his French tutor, and sent Evers into apoplectic fits by cursing fluently at the dinner table."

Lady Ashbury laughed. "He sounds like a Rawlings, all right. And the Liberal spinster?"

"I beg your pardon?"

"The Liberal spinster. How is she? Priggish and prudish? You ought to introduce her to the vicar. They ought to get along famously."

"I don't think so." Edward grimaced. "She hasn't had much luck with vicars. I walked in on her being proposed to by one. The man was nursing a shin that had met rather forcefully with her boot's toe."

The viscountess of Ashbury blinked her pale eyes at him and asked with evident confusion, "She was being proposed to by a vicar?"

Edward scraped ham from the bone china plate. "Yes, that's right." He chewed, gazing out the morning room windows, at the unbroken blanket of white that covered Ashbury House's grounds. "Is there coffee?"

Quite uncharacteristically, Lady Ashbury made no move to pour. She seemed to be in a state of some distraction. She sat with a silver spoon raised motionless in the air. Edward eyed her, then helped himself with a shrug to a steaming cup from the silver pot on the table.

"But I don't understand," Lady Ashbury said slowly. "I thought this Miss MacDougal was an old maid."

Edward tasted the coffee, discovered it was still piping hot, and added cream to it. "Maid, yes. Old, no. She's all of twenty and looks fifteen, if you ask me.''

"Twenty!" Arabella frowned. "But Edward, she's just girl!''

"Hmph," Edward agreed with his mouth full.

"But you can't let her stay at Rawlings with you! A young, unmarried woman, unchaperoned—''

"She's chaperoned. There's Mrs. Praehurst.''

"Mrs. Praehurst! Oh, Edward. Our party this weekend! How are we to have our party this weekend with a young girl about?''

Edward shrugged again, a little irritated by her histrionics. "What else can I do, Arabella? Throw her out in the snow?''

"Can't you send her to some relations in London or something?''

"No, I can't send her to London. In the first place, she's not out, and I'll be damned if I'm going to sponsor a season for her, however troublesome her presence at Rawlings might prove. Have you got any idea what it costs to get a girl decently married these days? And even if I were willing, she'd never leave the boy. That's why I had to bring her here in the first place, remember?'' He shook his head disgustedly. "What's the matter with you? You've gotten quite dim-witted since I saw you last.''

"I'm quite sure *you've* taken leave of your senses.'' Lady Ashbury's voice took on a strident note. "What are you thinking, allowing a young girl like that to take up residency at Rawlings? She's going to ruin everything!''

Through the wide bay windows, Edward noticed a half dozen or so deer picking their way through the leafless trees down by Ashbury Stream. He gazed at the brown, slender creatures, his mind unaccountably summoning up a vision of Pegeen MacDougal. Like the deer, she was long-legged and reed thin, thinner, really, than he generally liked his women. But one hardly noticed this detriment when accosted by her flashing green eyes. And Edward knew better than anyone that despite her slender frame, she was soft where it counted. . . .

"Edward? Are you listening to me?" Lady Ashbury had raised the silver spoon to knock off the top of her soft-boiled egg, but she used it to bang the table instead. "Edward!"

He tore his gaze away from the deer. "I beg your pardon." Edward smiled self-consciously. "What were you saying, Arabella?"

Lady Ashbury's eyes narrowed into twin slits of milky white. "I was saying that I don't understand why you don't throw her out."

"Throw her out? I can't throw her out, Arabella." Edward chuckled and tasted his coffee again. Better. "The staff's all become devilishly fond of her. Besides, if I turned her out, the boy'd never give me any peace. The only time the house is ever quiet these days is when he's with *her*." He shook his head in genuine wonder. "I've never seen anything like it. Every footmen in the house is in love with her, the maids all worship the ground she walks on, and Cook announced to me the other day that from now on I'll have to go to the Goat and Anvil if I want tripe, since Miss MacDougal doesn't like it and Cook will no longer be preparing anything His Grace's aunt doesn't like. If I didn't know better, I'd say the wench had bewitched them all—"

"Wench?" Lady Ashbury's rouged lips pressed into a very thin line. Following Edward's gaze out the window, she stared unseeingly at the deer ruining her willow trees. "And this wench. She's a typical Scotswoman, I take it? Gangly and snaggle-toothed? Awkward? Mealymouthed?"

Edward shook his head, his eyes still riveted on the deer. "Not at all. She's a pretty little thing, actually. But with a temper. Speaks her mind. At least she did, until she came down with quinsy—"

"Quinsy!"

"Quinsy. From exposure to the Yorkshire elements, Parks said. There was an accident. The carriage overturned, and stranded us all out on the Post Road for hours. Didn't Alistair tell you? I borrowed a horse from your stable . . ."

Arabella reached for a napkin and delicately wiped her mouth on it. She said, "Edward, would you be so kind as to tell Mrs. Praehurst to expect me to dine tonight?"

Edward tore his gaze from the deer and stared across the table at the viscountess of Ashbury. "What?"

"Don't say 'what,' Edward. It's vulgar. There are some things I want to discuss with Mrs. Praehurst before our guests arrive tomorrow, so I think it's best if I come to stay at Rawlings tonight. You'll remember to tell her to expect me, won't you?"

Edward continued to stare. "Arabella," he said, cautiously, "what are you up to?"

"Up to? I don't know what you mean." Arabella daintily sipped her tea.

Chapter Ten

Mr. Parks' declaration that Pegeen was well enough after a week's bedrest to leave her room brought a smile of satisfaction to many faces, but no one was happier than Pegeen, who fairly sprang from the bed that had become her prison. Her head had healed along with her throat and though her voice was still hoarse, she felt better than she had in a long time—no doubt due to the fact that the move to Rawlings had dramatically improved her mental health. She had no more worries about paying the coal bill or where the money for Jeremy's next pair of shoes would come from.

The surgeon wouldn't leave without extracting from her a promise that she'd refrain from going outdoors for another week, which meant she couldn't join in the weekend's hunt. Pegeen rejoiced over this fact, since it gave her an excuse for not mounting the mare Lord Edward had purchased for her in a fit of misguided generosity.

She was, however, well enough to take over her self-appointed duties as hostess, and she was delighted when Mrs. Praehurst said shortly after the two of them had shared a luncheon of roast quail before the Rose Room's hearth,

"I know you might still be feeling tired, Miss Pegeen, but I thought that if you weren't, you might like a tour of the house. You know that during the summer months, Rawlings Manor is open for public touring. Of course we don't show all the rooms, just the Great Hall and the conservatory—the late duchess was very proud of her yearround roses—and the dining room and, oh, a few other rooms, if Lord Edward is away in London, as he usually is. If you'd rather rest, of course, I'd understand."

Pegeen readily agreed to the invitation. But Lucy, who seemed intent upon proving that although not French, she could fuss as much as any great lady's maid, wouldn't hear of Pegeen setting foot outside the Rose Room without first luxuriating in a hot, scented bath. Then, again at Lucy's insistence, Pegeen's long hair had to be brushed and arranged, and Pegeen had to be helped into one of the fashionable, tight-waisted dresses designed for her by Mr. Worth.

When Pegeen was finally dressed in a long-sleeved confection of raspberry colored silk, Lucy took a step backwards and gazed at her mistress dreamily.

"Oh, miss," the maid sighed. "I never saw anyone look so lovely, and that's only one of your day gowns." Then the auburn eyebrows slanted downwards in concentration. "You're needing ear bobs."

Pegeen's fingers flew to her ear lobes. "Oh," she said. "I don't have any."

"Don't have any ear bobs?" Lucy's voice cracked. "What're you sayin', miss? Didn't Lord Edward buy you any, I mean, back in London?"

"No, of course not. Why should he . . . ?" Pegeen broke off, aghast at the thought. The very idea of a man buying jewelry for her set her cheeks aflame. Of course Lord Edward had paid for her entire wardrobe, but that had been part of their agreement. No mention had been made of ear bobs.

Pegeen glanced at her reflection in the oval, gilt-framed mirror that graced one of her wainscoted walls. She hardly recognized herself. The woman staring back at her with the infinitely small waist, the enormous emerald eyes, and the swan-like neck, looked like a lady of fashion, not a penniless Scottish spinster. The effect was so startling that Pegeen let out a nervous laugh.

"You'd best speak to 'is lordship, miss" Lucy said confidently. " 'E's got all 'is mother's jewelry locked up somewheres, and it's a shame not to use it. Diamonds was made to be worn, not shut up in a safe in the accounting room."

Pegeen laughed again, her nervousness forgotten. Moving towards a window, she said, "Oh, I don't need diamonds, Lucy. I'm a vicar's daughter, remember, not a princess."

Outside, unbroken snow lay like a carpet over the lawn. Beyond a clump of trees just past the lawn's end, Pegeen could see a church spire scraping the low-lying, grey clouds. So there was the village. She'd been right about being able to see it from the upper windows.

Mrs. Praehurst's timid knock interrupted Lucy's insisting that Lord Edward be queried about Miss Mac-Dougal's lack of ear bobs, and the housekeeper's pleasure at seeing Pegeen looking so well was quite genuine. Mrs. Praehurst came bearing messages from various members of the household. Jeremy wanted Pegeen to come by the day nursery as soon as she was able. The other message was an invitation: Lord Edward would take great pleasure in Miss MacDougal's company at dinner this evening, where they would be joined by Mr. Alistair Cartwright. This pleased Pegeen very much, though she tried not to show it. Her first opportunity to illustrate to his lordship that she was very capable of having fun!

The first stop on the tour was, necessarily, the day nursery. Jeremy was ecstatic at seeing Pegeen, and he took her by the hand and showed her around the bright, colorful room as if he'd lived in it all his life. He proudly displayed his newly constructed fort and the metal soldiers that inhabited it, and he introduced her to Ellen, his fourth nursemaid, a girl just a little older than Lucy who looked as if helping to construct wooden forts was the least of her talents. He prattled on about the horse Lord Edward had, as promised, purchased for him, inquired hopefully as to whether or not Mr. Parks had bled her, and shrugged philosophically at the negative answer.

Loathe as she was to spoil his euphoric mood, Pegeen asked Mrs. Praehurst and Ellen to leave her alone with Jeremy for a few minutes, and as soon as they withdrew, she commenced to delivering the speech she'd been planning all week, when her swollen throat hadn't allowed her to speak.

Jeremy took the scolding manfully, with bowed head but straight shoulders. Pegeen's voice was still not quite up to its usual strength, but she more than managed to convey her displeasure with Jeremy's recent behavior. If she happened to hear that Jeremy had committed any more offenses, she would pack up both their belongings and drag him back to Applesby.

"You wouldn't," Jeremy declared but weakly.

"I would," she informed him severely. "Because if you're going to behave like a street urchin, then that's where you belong. On the other hand, if you intend to behave like a duke, we'll stay here, where dukes belong. Now, if you want to keep your lovely new horse and nice new clothes—" Jeremy made a face and pulled expressively on his lace collar "—and brand new toys and all of that, you have simply got to behave. Do you understand me, Jeremy?"

Jeremy nodded mutely. Then he asked her very politely if there wasn't the slightest chance that Mr. Parks had, at any point during her illness, ever employed leeches.

Secure in the knowledge that Jeremy was healthy, and, at least presently, happy, Pegeen left him in Ellen's capable hands and continued her tour with Mrs. Praehurst, but not before the new duke had extracted a promise that Pegeen would return after dinner to read him a bedtime story. Apparently, children at Rawlings were expected to dine in the nursery, a practice Pegeen was going to have to abolish. How would Jeremy ever learn adult manners if he wasn't allowed to observe them being practiced? She made a mental note to speak to Lord Edward about it.

Mrs. Praehurst was obviously fond of both her job and her employer and talked nonstop of Rawlings—the house, its furniture, its upkeep, its place in history. Pegeen trailed along, enjoying Mrs. Praehurst's enthusiastic monologue, particularly when she dropped references to Lord Edward, which she did at frequent intervals. Every room in the house seemed to inspire a Lord Edward story. Why, Lord Edward had been the most even-tempered child Mrs. Praehurst had ever encountered. Always unfailingly polite and kind to servants and animals. Had Pegeen ever heard about the time Lord Edward had rescued one of their hunting dogs from a sinkhole at the expense of his place in the hunt? She hadn't? Well, Lord Edward had carried the poor creature home himself and said he didn't care a whit that his older brother was the one who ended up bagging the fox.

Pegeen listened with amusement. Mrs. Praehurst was quite obviously enamored of his lordship. It seemed that Lord Edward rendered every female in his acquaintance smitten with him. In this, she supposed, he was not unlike his father. The duke had been rumored to have had quite a way with the ladies. Pegeen saw why as soon as they entered the long portrait gallery.

Standing before the late duke's portrait, Pegeen realized at once that the resemblance between father and son was uncanny. Like Edward, his father was dark, with broad shoulders and a piercing gaze. But the skillful artist who'd rendered the likeness had been unable to disguise the florid lines of dissipation in the late duke's face, the sarcastic glint in that brooding gaze. Pegeen felt sorry for the artist who'd painted the duke's portrait. How difficult it must have been to render such an unsympathetic person in a manner which would please him! And how very much like the late duke Jeremy's father had looked! It was unfortunate that there wasn't a portrait of the duke's eldest son. John, Mrs. Praehurst informed her, had never been able to sit still for more than a minute.

Mrs. Praehurst squinted up at the portrait of her former employer and said nothing, which astonished Pegeen. It was the first time she'd ever seen the woman at a loss for words. This in itself was telling, and Pegeen took a step sideways, to stand before a painting of the late duke's wife, Edward's mother. The late duchess had been a beauty, as fair as her husband was dark, and Pegeen recognized those grey blue eyes, so like Jeremy's, as well as his uncle's. But Edward's eyes, though they glowed sardonically as often as not, were more intelligent than his mother's, and softer, somehow.

Mrs. Praehurst moved onto the next portrait and let out a contented sigh. "This is my favorite," said the housekeeper, gazing up fondly at the painting. "You know, Lord Edward didn't want to sit for this at all. The duke forced him into it. I remember the day it was unveiled, and Lord Edward was so embarrassed. He said to me, 'Mrs. Praehurst, can't you stage a faint or something so we can all go about our ways?' But that's just like him. Lord Edward's got no patience for pretense, not him."

Pegeen swallowed involuntarily. Staring up at the portrait of Jeremy's uncle, she felt almost as if she were looking up at the man himself. Never had she been able to gaze so long at Edward's face, however, without risk of being caught staring. Now that there was no such danger, she gazed long and hard with narrowed eyes.

The painting was beautifully rendered and highly accurate. She could count each fleck of silver in those grey eyes. Comparison between the portrait of the son and those of his parents was inevitable—and startling. Though Edward had inherited his father's good looks and his mother's eyes, the resemblance went no further. There was warmth and good humor in Edward's face and thoughtfulness in his gaze. And yet the painter had also managed to capture the slightly sarcastic twist of Edward's lips, the potentially dangerous strength in his large, tanned hands, the shrewd intelligence in his eyes. Mrs. Praehurst had told Pegeen at the beginning of their walk through the house that she knew nothing of art, but by choosing Edward's portrait as her favorite, she'd proven that she did indeed have an eye for beauty—and the sense to see that there was more to her master than just a well-chiseled profile and a fondness for dogs.

But before Pegeen could say a word in admiration of the painting, she heard the ring of boot heels in the corridor and turned in time to see the object of the portrait himself striding towards them at no mean pace. Edward looked as if he'd just come in from riding—he still wore his long black cloak and carried his gloves and crop. His face was wind-chapped and his hair in disarray, curling in dark locks across his broad forehead. Pegeen, glancing from the painting to its subject, decided that the portrait fell short in one respect: Edward, in reality, was far more physically intimidating than the artist led one to believe.

"Mrs. Praehurst," Edward called.

The housekeeper beamed with pleasure. "Why, if it isn't his lordship himself! We were just admiring your portrait, my lord."

"Really?" Edward strode up to them, and Pegeen was conscious that he smelled of the outdoors—of leather and of cold, wintry air. He was smiling in that strange, lopsided way of his, as if he were thinking of a private joke.

Abashed at having been caught staring at his portrait, and even more embarrassed over the fact that the last time she'd seen him, Edward had had his hands upon her derriere, she kept her gaze on the toes of her shoes, willing her cheeks to stop burning.

"Good afternoon, Miss MacDougal," Edward said, and with his customary gallantry, he clicked his heels together and gave a little bow. A broad smile had broken out across his handsome face. "Mr. Parks told me you were feeling better. You look uncommonly well. I trust you've recovered completely from your unfortunate illness?"

She eyed him, trying to look as if the sight of him did not send her heart into beats so rapid she felt as if she'd been running.

"I'm quite well, thank you, my lord," she said coolly. Of course, the fact that her voice was still several octaves lower than usual did not strengthen her case that she was fine, but at least she'd managed to get out the words without coughing.

"Excellent. And your head? It's better?"

"It's tolerable."

Mrs. Praehurst, perhaps noting Pegeen's lack of enthusiasm at this chance meeting, rushed in with, "I've been escorting Miss MacDougal on a tour of the house, my lord."

"Ah," Edward said, his dark eyebrows arching. "And what does Miss MacDougal think of Rawlings Manor?"

Pegeen tugged nonchalantly on the lace cuff of her sleeve. "I find Rawlings Manor quite charming."

The eyebrows inched even closer to that jet black hairline. "I beg your pardon?"

"It's a charming home," Pegeen said again. She could tell the answer surprised him, coming as it did on the heels of her lecture concerning his spending habits. But she cer-

tainly couldn't tell him the truth, not in front of Mrs. Praehurst. The truth, of course, was that she was quite shocked
over the fact that while entire families were starving in
London, homes like Rawlings Manor even existed.

They stood in awkward silence for a moment, Pegeen
gazing at his muddy boot tops, excruciatingly aware that
he in turn was staring at her, until Mrs. Praehurst inquired
politely, "Was there something you wanted, sir?"

"Oh, yes, of course, Mrs. Praehurst." Edward tore his
gaze from Pegeen and said loudly, "I'd appreciate it if
you'd tell Cook there'll be one more to supper. The viscountess plans to join us."

"The viscountess!" cried Mrs. Praehurst, genuinely
startled. She glanced hastily at Pegeen, then recovered herself and stammered, "Of course, of course, the viscountess.
I'll tell Cook. Do—Shall we expect her to stay the night,
sir?"

"I believe so."

"Forgive me, my lord, but I wasn't expecting the viscountess until tomorrow, with the rest of the party from
London . . ."

"Nor was I," Edward said, and Pegeen couldn't tell
whether or not the change in plans pleased him—or if perhaps they'd been at his instigation. "But she's expressed a
desire to meet you, Miss MacDougal." Edward's grey-eyed
gaze fastened on Pegeen's face. "You've become the object of a great deal of curiosity in the neighborhood, I've
discovered, madam."

"I don't see how," Pegeen replied mildly. "Unless
someone has been riding about spreading wild tales about
me." She looked pointedly at his mud-spattered boots.

Edward followed her gaze, and she was infinitely gratified to see that he began to look slightly uncomfortable.
Edward Rawlings wasn't about to let a slip of a girl get the
better of him, however. He grinned at her.

"I think the neighboring gentry are understandably ill

at ease, knowing there's a Liberal in their midst. I believe they are going over their household ledgers, checking for any telltale champagne fountains.''

Caught off guard by his casual reminder of their argument from the day before, Pegeen replied with a lifted chin, ''Perhaps that's just as well. I'm certain there are any number of charitable causes in the county that might benefit from their guilt.''

''You're uncommonly skilled with figures,'' Edward observed. ''I wonder if you wouldn't have thought my father paid too much to the fellow who painted that.'' He nodded his head towards his own portrait. ''Do you think it like me?''

Turning towards the painting, she looked up at it. She was still discomforted by the directness of both the portrait and its sitter's gazes and a little irked by his reference to the champagne fountain. It was for that reason that she answered with a sniff, ''No, I'm afraid I don't.''

Edward as well as his housekeeper looked startled.

''Not like?'' Edward glanced from the portrait to Pegeen's face. ''Whatever do you mean? Everyone tells me it's astonishingly like.''

''Well, I'm certain they were just being polite,'' was Pegeen's acerbic reply. ''I think the painter has made you look much more . . .'' She glanced at him, wondering what she could say to irritate him most. He was a man whom she considered to have many faults, but to society in general, he was all that a member of the haute monde was supposed to be—handsome, titled, and, most importantly of all, rich.

''Much more . . . masculine than you are in reality,'' she finished with some satisfaction.

''Much *more* masculine?'' Edward took a step forward to stare at the portrait. ''I'm afraid I don't see—''

''Don't you? You really have quite a remarkably feminine air about you, my lord.'' Pegeen smiled sweetly up at his astonished face. "Your brother always said you were something of a fop."

"A fop!" Edward's bewilderment was complete. "John said that? Damn his eyes, I—"

"Well, I'll admit, you don't look it now." Pegeen took a bold step towards him and reached up to adjust Edward's cravat, which was askew from his ride. She stood close enough so that the tips of her breasts brushed against his chest. "In fact, you look rather . . . well, scruffy, just at the moment."

"Cartwright and I've just been riding," Edward said lamely. She saw his nostrils flare and knew that he was smelling her perfume. She smiled winningly up at him and gave his cravat a final pat.

"There," she said, stepping back. "That's a little better." But the way she said it indicated that it wasn't much better at all. "Well, Mrs. Praehurst, we'd better hurry along if we're to get through our tour before supper."

"Oh, uh, y-yes," the housekeeper stammered. "Yes, if you'll excuse me, my lord, I'll just let Cook know about Lady Ashbury . . ."

Edward recovered himself enough to bow, but the slant in his eyebrows indicated that he was more than a little disturbed about something. He stalked away, his boot heels ringing on the stone floor. Inwardly, Pegeen rejoiced. She certainly hadn't acted the blushing virgin there. With any luck, he'd brood over her little barb at his masculinity until dinner.

Mrs. Praehurst, however, had ruffled feathers that needed smoothing. Pegeen turned towards her, her eyes wide with injured innocence. "Oh, dear. Did I say something I oughtn't to?" she asked. "He seemed rather tiffish . . ."

The housekeeper shook her head, looking after her departing master. "Oh, Miss MacDougal, I'm afraid you might have nettled him. Lord Edward is the gentlest person alive, except when he's been nettled. His only fault is that he inherited his father's temper. Well, your sister must have told you that. Lord John inherited it as well.''

Pegeen nodded. She remembered John's temper tantrums well. One of them had led to his getting killed. ''Yes,'' she sighed.

''I'll be sworn, miss, when Lord Edward and his brother fought, you could hear it for miles around. And all they ever did was fight, you know. I can't say as I'm surprised Lord John told you that his brother was a fop.'' Mrs. Praehurst gave a little chuckle. ''He probably knew it would anger his younger brother no end! Lord Edward's as far from a fop as any man I've ever known. Quite a way with the ladies he has, not unlike Lord John.''

Pegeen pursed her lips. ''So I've been led to understand. How long has the viscountess been one of Lord Edward's . . . friends?''

Mrs. Praehurst looked down at Pegeen in surprise. She tried to laugh off the question, but Pegeen saw the uneasiness in the woman's face. ''Oh, bless you! I don't think . . . Well, I suppose Lady Arabella's been friends with Lord Edward ever since her husband, the viscount of Ashbury, purchased an estate a few miles down the Post Road.''

''But the viscountess is coming to stay here without her husband?'' Pegeen asked.

''Well,'' Mrs. Praehurst said. ''Yes.'' Suddenly, her voice took on a conspiratorial tone. ''Between you and me, miss, the viscountess is quite a beauty, and her husband is . . . well, the viscount is considerably older than his wife. They've been unable to have children, poor souls. And the viscountess, well, she has a love of society that her husband simply does not share . . .''

The housekeeper's voice trailed off, Mrs. Praehurst having no wish to be disloyal to her employer. But by reading between the lines, Pegeen quickly saw how it was: A beautiful, bored wife; an older, unobservant husband; and a man like Edward Rawlings, all within a stone's throw of one another's front doors? *Of course* they were having an affair! Pegeen felt a little stab of disappointment, but that was easily explained: She'd only had such a brief time to enjoy Edward's pique, and soon the viscountess would flatter him right back into complacency. Pox!

Mrs. Praehurst wasn't flustered enough over the viscountess' addition to dinner to postpone the rest of their tour. She dutifully—and quite happily, it seemed to Pegeen—led her through morning, dining, and sitting rooms, libraries and parlors, chattering away about silver patterns and embroidered fire screens, until they came to the hallway that led to the conservatory. Then Mrs. Praehurst's tone turned boastful, and there was no mistaking the pride in her eyes as she launched into yet another story about her employer.

"Her ladyship, the late duchess, loved flowers," the housekeeper said, leading Pegeen down the long, somberly lit corridor. "She loved them so much that it quite depressed her during our long Yorkshire winters when there wasn't any color on the moor. So the duke had this place built out of the wind, where the sun would hit it, and imported the most beautiful plants and flowers I'd ever seen, and paid a rather extravagant amount of money to see that the place was heated November through March. But when the duchess died, well, the late duke, perhaps understandably, allowed the room to fall into disrepair. It was locked up, never used again . . . until the duke himself passed. Then Lord Edward had the room redone by a man from London. Such flowers he brought, and plants, and even little trees and a fountain! Well, you can see for yourself. It stands now as a tribute to Lord Edward's affection for his mother . . ."

With the dramatic flair of a born thespian, Mrs. Praehurst threw open a pair of heavy wooden doors at the end of the dark hallway down which they'd passed. Pegeen, passing through them, could only gasp in delight, first at the warm, moist wave of air that hit her, then at the rich, scintillating odor of soil that assailed her senses, and then finally at the brilliant hues that filled her eyes.

The hothouse quite took Pegeen's breath away. She had never in her sheltered life seen anything like it. It seemed so odd to see flowers blooming in the dead of winter, to see so much green against a vista of white. The glass-encased room was far larger than Pegeen had expected, large enough to entertain a garden party. Indeed, there were wrought iron tables and benches scattered about the flagstone floor, some set up around bubbling fountains of plain water—not champagne. Roses, lilacs, lilies . . . Pegeen had never seen so many flowers, even in her own garden, which had been envied by many an amateur horticulturist in Applesby. It was astonishing, the amount of time and tender care that had been put into keeping so many plants alive in so bitter a season. Time, tender care . . . and a good deal of money.

But, Pegeen admitted grudgingly to herself as she strolled down the scented paths between the flower boxes, money well spent. That Edward had gone to such trouble and expense to correct a wrong of his father's seemed strangely like him. Hadn't he done much the same thing in having Jeremy brought to Rawlings at last? Much as she hated to admit it, Edward did not *always* spend frivolously. Some of his expenditures were quite justifiable. This one in particular, despite the enormous amount of money he must have invested in it, she could not help but approve. The conservatory quickly became her favorite room of the house. It took a good deal of coaxing on Mrs. Praehurst's part to get her to leave it to dress for dinner.

Chapter Eleven

When Mrs. Praehurst finally returned Pegeen to Lucy's charge, Pegeen saw that the maid had already laid out her dress for dinner, an off the shoulder evening gown of the palest pink satin. It was one of the gowns that Lady Herbert had selected, despite Pegeen's protests that it was far too elegant for her. As if wearing such a low-cut garment wasn't mortifying enough, Lucy insisted on weaving some of the white roses from the vase beside Pegeen's bed into her hair, an act which Pegeen felt might lead certain parties to accuse her of putting on airs.

"You haven't any jewels, miss," Lucy declared, with not a little indignation. "You've got to have *something* in your hair, and about your neck as well." The 'something' Lucy had come up with was a black velvet ribbon, upon which she had pinned a perfect, half-blown rose. Its whiteness paled against Pegeen's opalescent skin when she finally allowed Lucy to tie it around her slender neck.

When Pegeen's toilette was complete, she examined herself critically in the mirror. She wondered briefly whether or not she ought to tuck a bit of lace over the rather shocking bit of bosom the cut of her gown displayed. Mr. Worth had known quite well she was unmarried, and Pegeen had insisted strenuously, ignoring Lady Herbert's laughter, that she intended to remain so. Yet despite her protests, the designer had given all of Pegeen's evening gowns scandalously low décolletage.

"It is a sin," the great clothier had declared, "to hide what the good Lord saw fit to give you, Mademoiselle MacDougal."

Pegeen wasn't quite certain she agreed with the illustrious Mr. Worth, but she supposed that since Edward's attention would be engaged elsewhere, she was safe enough. Applying a few more drops of expensive French perfume to her wrists and throat—the cost of even the smallest bottle of the stuff had scandalized her, and yet it smelled so divinely, she hadn't been able to resist its purchase—Pegeen was about to go downstairs when Lucy stopped her, and gave her cheeks two hard pinches.

"There!" cried the girl. " 'o needs diamonds? You 'ave somethin' better, miss. . . . Roses in your cheeks!"

Pegeen, suddenly nervous, could only smile weakly in response.

Recalling Mrs. Praehurst's tour, Pegeen remembered that dinner guests always gathered in the Gold Drawing Room. She hurried downstairs, smiling at the various servants who greeted her cheerfully on her way, and paused outside the doors to the drawing room. The voices she heard inside were pleasantly harmonious; tinkling, feminine laughter was foremost among them.

Pegeen fingered the rose at her neck, gulping. Whatever was wrong with her? What did she care what a silly viscountess thought of her? So what if she hadn't any title? She had her pride, at least. The MacDougal clan was as ancient as any English duchy, and a thousand times more noble. What's more, she had every confidence the viscountess couldn't stomach as much whiskey as *she* could.

Still, she remembered only too well how she'd been treated by the other girls back in Applesby. As if it weren't bad enough that she'd been the vicar's daughter, eccentrically fonder of books than of chasing after the village boys, she'd been cursed with looks just good enough to cause the other girls to envy her. Pegeen sincerely hoped the viscountess considered her beneath notice, so that she would not have to speak to her overly much. Pegeen knew no more what to say to a viscountess than she'd known how to talk to Maureen Clendening, the innkeeper's daughter.

Evers appeared from out of nowhere, bowed, and politely opened the door to announce her arrival to the group assembled within the sitting room. Lucy had pinched her mistress' cheeks for nothing: Pegeen found herself blushing furiously when the cultured voice called out, "Miss Pegeen MacDougal."

Oh, Lord, she prayed. Please don't let me do anything stupid. And then she was angry with herself for even caring what anyone thought. Oh, why had she agreed to leave Applesby in the first place?

Opening her eyes, she smiled queasily at Evers, who bowed again, this time, Pegeen noticed, with a slight pinkening of his own gaunt cheeks. Oh, dear, she thought. Perhaps vicars' daughters oughtn't to smile at butlers. But he was so sweet! How could she help it? Lifting the hem of her skirt with her left hand, Pegeen hurried past him, hoping the regal tilt of her nose would distract everyone's gaze from her crimson cheeks.

If she'd hoped to make a subtle entrance, however, she couldn't have been more disappointed. Conversation in the Gold Drawing Room abruptly halted, and three sets of eyes swung in her direction. Pegeen, abashed, ducked her head, aware that both Lord Edward and his friend Mr. Cartwright climbed hurriedly to their feet only after a moment's hesitation. She didn't know that the hesitation had occurred because both men had been momentarily awestruck by the vision she created in the doorway with her pink cheeks, slender figure, and shyly lowered gaze.

Courage, Pegeen, she said to herself, and rallying her spirits, she threw back her shoulders and lifted her head. Then she smiled, crossed the room, and held her hand out to the first person she came across, who happened to be Alistair Cartwright.

"Mr. Cartwright," she said. "How lovely to see you again. It seems as if it's been an age since we met."

Alistair Cartwright took Pegeen's hand and bowed over it, apparently speechless, though Pegeen couldn't think why. Tearing her worried gaze from his friend, Pegeen turned towards Lord Edward. He'd changed from his riding clothes into a distinctly unfoppish ensemble that included another perfectly tied cravat and a rather somber waistcoat. Though his grey eyes raked her, his expression was inscrutable, and Pegeen could not tell whether or not he liked what he saw.

"Miss MacDougal," he said, his deep voice distantly polite, as if he were addressing a mere acquaintance, and not someone with whom he'd been more than a little intimate upon occasion. "May I present the viscountess of Ashbury, Lady Arabella?"

Pegeen found that she had to tilt her chin up rather far to get a good look at the viscountess, who, though she'd inclined her head politely in greeting, was quite a bit taller than Pegeen. Taller, and, Pegeen realized with a sinking heart, more beautiful than she could ever hope to be, despite all of Lucy's efforts.

Considerably older than Pegeen had expected—Lady Arabella was a very well preserved forty at least—the viscountess possessed a delicate beauty that was distinctly English. Everything about her was as pale as a faded tea rose. Her hair, in ringlets down to her shoulders, was almost white, it was so blonde. Her eyes were such a light blue that the irises seemed to fade into the white parts, but they were shrewd eyes, whose knowing gaze took in everything, including, Pegeen noticed with a blush, her own lack of jewelry. Dressed in the height of fashion in a gown of azure silk with a skirt so wide it was a wonder to Pegeen that she could fit through the door, the viscountess nevertheless looked as fragile as a piece of delicate china. Hers was the kind of beauty writers like Tennyson and Browning raved about in their poems. And women like Pegeen could never hope to rival.

"How do you do, Lady Ashbury?" Pegeen asked diffidently.

"I'm well, thank you," Lady Ashbury replied. Rising out of her curtsy, the viscountess gave Pegeen the same sweeping, head-to-toe glance that Edward had given her. What she saw, she apparently didn't like, because her lips—made pink through artifice, Pegeen saw at once—turned into a smile so false that Pegeen wondered whether Lord Ashbury was blind. The woman was so bad at hiding her true feelings that it was rather ill-advised for her to be traipsing about having affairs with the neighbors.

"I do hope you've recovered from your illness, Miss MacDougal, and from the unfortunate accident that Edward was telling me about."

Pegeen smiled. "Oh, I'm feeling so much better. But what else could one expect with such an attentive host?"

Pegeen turned her brilliant smile on Edward, who only raised his dark eyebrows in response. He obviously didn't know what to make of her sudden flattery, since just hours ago she'd accused him of effeminacy in a fit of pique.

Beside Edward, Alistair Cartwright could restrain himself no longer. He stepped forward, seized Pegeen's hand once more, and, gazing down at her, said, "I'm so glad to see you up and about, Miss MacDougal. I do hope you'll be joining in the activities Edward's got planned for this weekend. . . ."

Pegeen made a moue of disappointment. "Mr. Parks

absolutely forbade me from riding,'' she said, as if this was the worst news she'd ever received. Pegeen couldn't think of anything she'd least rather do than gallop about the winter countryside after a poor, starving little fox.

"But he didn't say a word about dancing, did he?" Alistair demanded eagerly.

Pegeen looked puzzled. "No, sir, he did not, but—"

"Then you'll save a waltz for me?"

"Mr. Cartwright!" Pegeen couldn't help but laugh. "Are you always so forward with your host's female relations?"

"I hardly know. Up until last month, he hadn't any," Alistair said. He tucked her hand into the crook of his arm and steered her towards the low couch upon which he'd been lounging. Pegeen sank down upon the velvet cushions a little nervously. She had an uneasy feeling she was being courted. Never in her life had she been courted, unless one counted Mr. Richlands . . . and Lord Edward, of course. Except that one could hardly call Lord Edward's advances *courting*. They were more insulting than anything else. But Alistair Cartwright was in every sense of the word a gentleman. Pegeen didn't know if she was to take his gallantry seriously, or if he was simply being polite to his host's poor Scottish relation. . . .

"I've decided," Alistair was explaining to her, "that since this is your first stay in Rawlings, you'll be needing a guide, and I've nominated myself for that duty—"

"I believe Miss MacDougal has already been given a tour," Edward growled. But when Pegeen glanced over at him, she saw that he wasn't even looking at them. He was gazing into the fire, as if determining whether or not it needed poking. "Mrs. Praehurst took her round this morning," Edward finished mildly.

"Ah!" Alistair bounded from the couch to pour Pegeen a generous glass of sherry. "And what did you think,

Miss MacDougal? Was it everything old Edward promised?''

"Everything and more," Pegeen assured him with a laugh, accepting the glass he held out to her. "Why, I hardly believed Lord Edward when he told me that Rawlings Manor was quite renowned for its winter roses, but now that I've seen them myself, I can only say that even Lord Edward's praises didn't do them justice."

Across the room, the viscountess appeared to have been admiring her own reflection in the night-darkened glass of the casement windows. Apparently satisfied with her toilette, she straightened and strolled in Pegeen's direction, an arch expression on her lovely face. "I wonder, Miss MacDougal, that your sister never mentioned the roses of Rawlings to you. Surely it must have been quite the coup in your village when Kathy MacDougal managed to snag the Rawlings heir."

Pegeen raised her eyebrows. She had no idea, not knowing the woman well, whether or not the viscountess was being purposefully insulting. "Oh, well," she said, trying to keep her tone light. "Perhaps the Rawlings family isn't quite as well-known as they'd like to think. I had certainly never heard of them before Kathy brought home Lord John. And *he* certainly never said a word about the conservatory."

"I can believe that!" Alistair laughed. "What man would be thinking about hothouse flowers with a genuine briar rose in his grasp?"

Pegeen smiled at him before directing her attention back towards the viscountess, who was frowning. "Besides," Pegeen shrugged, "My sister's late husband hadn't the slightest interest in anything beyond horseflesh. He was quite a man's man, if you know what I mean." She cast a quick, mischievous glance at Edward, who looked right back at her steadily, and, if she wasn't mistaken, angrily. Good! Let him be angry with her. Better that than making more of those advances she was too weak-willed to resist.

But the viscountess didn't seem particularly happy, either. She kept up her little pace about the room, her tall figure very much at an advantage in an upright attitude. Lady Ashbury's décolletage, Pegeen had noticed, was even more dramatic than her own.

"Well, I simply cannot tell you, Miss MacDougal," the viscountess said with obviously forced gaiety, "how lovely it will be to have a woman about Rawlings again! I'm afraid that while Edward is quite good at managing the stables, he doesn't have the slightest idea how to run a household. He really is quite hopeless at anything else."

"Oh, I can't believe that," Pegeen exclaimed, forgetting in her haste to rush to Lord Edward's defense that she was supposed to be trying to keep her host hostile. "He was so thoughtful during my illness, arranging to have books and flowers brought to me . . ."

Edward cleared his throat a little too noisily at the sharp glance Lady Arabella shot him. "Well, what man wouldn't have wanted to help speed Miss MacDougal's recovery?" Edward declared gallantly "So that she could sooner grace these drafty halls with her lovely countenance."

Pegeen didn't even notice Edward's compliment. She was still busy trying to prove the viscountess wrong. "And for someone supposedly so hopeless at managing a household," she chattered on, "Lord Edward *did* plan this weekend's hunting party—"

"Oh, but that's all Lady Ashbury's idea," Alistair chimed in. "Come, Arabella, 'fess up. You haven't got a great hall at Ashbury House, and you delight in using Rawlings' as if it were your own—"

"Nonsense," said Lady Ashbury, a distinct chill in her tone.

"It's true," Alistair assured Pegeen. "She's had all

her friends down from London at least twice this season alone.''

"Provoking puppet.'' Lady Ashbury frowned at him. ''I don't have the slightest idea why Edward allows these month long visits of yours. You are nothing but a nuisance.''

"Cartwright,'' Edward growled from the mantle. ''Behave.''

"Dear me,'' Pegeen said, turning to Alistair with a bemused air. ''Do they always abuse you so abominably to your face? I wonder why you stay!''

Alistair looked delighted. ''By faith, she's defending my honor. Your brother John stumbled upon a treasure trove up there in Scotland, Edward. Do you suppose there are more like her? I quite want one of my own!''

Pegeen had no chance to glance back at Edward to see how he took this assertion, since Evers suddenly entered the room and announced that dinner was served. But to Pegeen's very great surprise, the arm that was offered to escort her into the dining room wasn't Alistair's, but Edward's. He stared grimly down at her, as if it was the last thing he wanted to do. But he placed her fingers into the crook of his arm and pulled her, none too gently, to her feet.

"Why, Lord Edward,'' Pegeen said, glancing over her shoulder to see the viscountess glaring balefully into Edward's back, her pale eyes deadly as daggers. ''How gallant of you.''

"Not at all,'' was Edward's cool reply. ''You are my sister-in-law, after all. It's my duty to escort you into dinner.''

Pegeen blinked at his coldness, instinctively trying to draw away from him. ''Excuse me, my lord,'' she said, when he tightened his grip on her hand. ''But I am hardly in need of your charity—''

"That's rich,'' Edward observed. ''Considering that

without it, you'd be back in that miserable cottage in Applesby.'' When she gave her fingers a wrench, however, his expression softened and he said, "Don't cause a scene. I've been wanting to talk to you."

She narrowed her gaze suspiciously. "About what, pray?"

"About what you said this afternoon." Edward stared straight ahead of him, and when Pegeen looked up at him, she saw a tiny muscle twitching in his lean jaw. "About how I strike you as having—" he cleared his throat "—feminine qualities."

"Oh," Pegeen said, attempting not very successfully to hide her smile. "That."

"Yes, that. I've been giving it some thought."

"Dear me," Pegeen said, restraining herself from gasping they passed into the vast dining room. Though she had already seen the room that afternoon on her tour, the table had not yet been set with the Rawlings silver nor had the candelabras been lit. The resulting play of reflected light on the high, arched ceiling was breathtaking. Pegeen came quite close to losing the track of the conversation. "If I had known what an impression a thoughtless comment like that would make," she said distractedly, "I'd have kept my mouth shut."

"No," Edward said. He steered her towards a chair just right of his own at the long dining table but close enough, she noticed, to the vast fireplace and its blazing fire to keep Pegeen from catching another chill. "You wouldn't have. I believe you made it up and said it to purposefully vex me. And I think I know why."

Pegeen lifted her delicately arched eyebrows once more. "Do you?" she asked. When a footman hurried forward to hold her chair for her as she sat, Edward waved him away, and held the back of Pegeen's chair himself.

"I do," Edward said. He leaned down and spoke in a low voice directly into her ear as she smoothed the ruffles of her satin skirt over her lap. "I believe it was a barb intended to put me at my distance."

Pegeen almost snorted, then remembered herself just in time. "Whatever can you mean?"

"Don't play the innocent with me. You know what I'm referring to. Our, er, conversation yesterday in your bedroom . . ."

Pegeen glanced around quickly, her cheeks instantly going scarlet. "Lord Edward!"

"Yes, it was quite shocking, wasn't it?" Edward sounded infuriatingly smug at her reaction. "Unmarried ladies and gentlemen like myself aren't supposed to engage in such activities, are they? But I think you're more shocked over the fact that you quite like my advances, rather than that I make them—"

Pegeen nearly choked. "Don't be ridiculous!"

"You're the one who's being ridiculous." All the smugness disappeared from his deep voice, replaced by something that sounded to Pegeen like anger. "Can you deny that there's something between us, Pegeen? Can you?"

"I most certainly can," Pegeen lied without a moment's hesitation. "Do sit down, they'll be here in a moment—"

"Well, I can't," Edward said flatly. All at once, Pegeen stiffened, feeling his cool fingers on the back of her neck. He seemed to be stroking the soft tendrils of hair that had escaped from the coiffure Lucy had designed. His touch, mingled with his next words, sent gooseflesh up and down her spine. "I want you, Pegeen. And you seem to forget that I'm used to getting my way."

"Then I'm afraid you're going to be disappointed," Pegeen said promptly, though her mouth was so dry, she was surprised she could even speak.

Edward stared down the slender column of her ivory throat. "I don't know what you mean."

"Well, you see, I'm used to getting *my* way." Pegeen noted the direction of his stare and involuntarily glanced down at the front of her dress. Though she was certain Mr. Worth could not have done so on purpose, Pegeen realized belatedly that when someone stood above her, he could look directly down the bodice of the gown and get an unobstructed view of her tip-tilted breasts. Only thankfully her pink nipples were hidden from sight by the lace cups of her corset.

Pegeen swallowed hard. She went on with temerity, giving her head a little toss to bring Edward's attention back to her words and away from her breasts. "And if both of us are used to getting our own way, that means one of us is going to be disappointed, eventually."

"I certainly hope not," Edward said softly, still speaking into her shell-like ear. Suddenly, she felt his strong fingers move from her neck to her bare shoulders. "There's always the possibility we could work out an arrangement that would be amicable to the both of us."

Pegeen twisted in her chair to look up at him, her eyes narrowed suspiciously. "Lord Edward," she said. "Are you making love to me?"

His smile was decidedly devilish. "What if I am?"

She said primly, "Then I think I ought to remind you that I'm here under your protection, and that it would be a scandalous thing were you to attempt to seduce me."

Reaching for her napkin, Pegeen unfolded the linen square with a resounding snap, a sound Pegeen had meant to effectively end the conversation. But Edward continued to stare down at her, his expression not unlike Jeremy's when he'd been denied dessert. He couldn't, for the life of him, begin to fathom what this girl was up to. Was it her intention simply to drive him mad? Because if so, she was succeeding. He had never met such an exasperating woman in all his life. She clearly enjoyed his kisses and yet steadfastly refused to admit it! Well, he undoubtedly deserved such treatment, having allowed himself to become so enamored of her. After all, it was exactly the sort of behavior he ought to expect from a virgin.

Alistair Cartwright, entering the room with the viscountess on his arm, caught sight of Edward leaning over Pegeen's chair in an intimate manner and cried out, "Heigh-ho! What are you two whispering to one another? You know what my nurse used to say about whispering at the table: 'Whisperers at the table shall breakfast in the stable.'"

Edward's smoldering gaze swung from Pegeen to his loud-mouthed guest. Seeing the murderous glint in his host's stare, Alistair let out a startled laugh. "I say, Edward! Why the dirty look? Have I snuff on my face again?"

"We'll discuss it," Edward rumbled as he strode to his seat, "after dinner."

Alistair deposited the viscountess in the chair to Edward's left, then sauntered to his own seat. Edward didn't say another word, but went directly to work on his soup. Alistair, his blonde hair falling boyishly over one eye muttered quite audibly, "My nurse also used to say, 'Faint heart never won fair lady.'"

A look from Edward silenced him, and Alistair sought comfort in his wine glass.

Edward proceeded to attack course after course of succulent, savory meats, delectable vegetable dishes, truffle pates and fish and meringues with wordless singlemindedness. The viscountess, sensing her host's foul temper, took it upon herself to introduce a topic of conversation the whole table could share.

"Miss MacDougal," she began, delicately slicing through a piece of mutton on her plate. "I can't help wondering what a change Rawlings Manor must be for you after life in the convent."

Pegeen swallowed a mouthful of claret and met the older woman's gaze with a polite smile. "The vicarage, you mean? Oh, yes, it's quite different. At the vicarage, I never had a minute to myself. I was always busy with chores of one kind or another. If I wasn't baking bread or mending clothes for our poorer parishioners, I was tending to the sick or helping write out lesson plans for the Sunday school . . .''

Pegeen didn't mean to sound pious. She was merely stating a fact. She realized how pedantic she must have sounded to the others, however, when Alistair burst out, "Good God! You had to do all that? What kept a little thing like you from dropping dead of exhaustion at the end of every day?''

"Her devotion to the Lord, I'm certain,'' Lady Ashbury muttered, her gaze safely on her plate.

Pegeen let out a gentle laugh to show she took no offense at the older woman's sarcasm, though it had actually mortified her a little. "Well,'' she said. "I enjoy helping those less fortunate than myself, but whether or not I do it out of devotion to the Lord, I don't know. I feel that I do it because it's only fair that those of us who have so much share it with those who have so little. None of us can ever be sure that what we have won't be taken away one day, leaving us no better off than those we once pitied—''

"Quite right,'' Alistair said, his mouth full of foie gras. "Quite right. The Lord giveth, the Lord taketh away, and all that.''

"Did your beloved nurse teach you that, Allie?'' sniffed Lady Ashbury. "What nonsense.''

"I beg your pardon, but it isn't nonsense.'' Pegeen laid down her fork, no longer caring whether or not she sounded prim. "After my father died, Jeremy and I had nothing but what the church could provide us. We were receiving charity from the very people to whom *I'd* once been a benefactress—''

"How absolutely scandalous,'' Alistair said, vigorously shaking his head. Noticing that the viscountess glanced sharply in his direction, he cried, "Well, Arabella, it *is*. It's absolutely scandalous that a Rawlings should have been living on the charity of the church."

Pegeen, realizing for the first time what she'd said, gasped, "Oh, no! I didn't mean to accuse—"

Edward interrupted. His voice was stern. "The fault is mine. I ought to have kept better tabs on the welfare of my brother's family."

Pegeen, much to Edward's surprise, rushed to his defense. "But how were you to have known?" She looked guiltily at the others. "I didn't mean to imply that the Rawlings family was in any way negligent—"

"But we were." Edward regarded her bemusedly. He didn't know whether to be encouraged or chagrined by Pegeen's occasional displays of loyalty. It seemed like only a few days had passed since she'd so liberally abused his family name to his face. It appeared that now, however, maligning Edward Rawlings was a pastime reserved solely for herself and not something to be done in front of strangers.

"You oughtn't blame yourself, Edward," Arabella said. "It does seem slightly incredible that John would have left his wife and child penniless. You really couldn't have known."

"But I should have." Edward didn't know it, but a dangerous light began to shine in his grey eyes. "I, of all people, should have expected it. I knew what John was."

"Well," Pegeen said brightly, trying to put an end to the rather uncomfortable twist the conversation had taken. "In any case, it's all worked out for the best in the end, hasn't it? This venison is simply delicious, don't you—"

"But I still don't understand why you never contacted Edward about your circumstances, Miss MacDougal," Lady Ashbury interrupted, her pale eyes deceptively expressionless. "It seems odd that you'd accept charity from strangers, but not your own brother-in-law's family."

"Well," Pegeen began falteringly. "I—"

"After the way my father behaved when her sister married John," Edward said, returning the favor by coming to Pegeen's defense in his own turn, "it's no mystery that the MacDougals balked at asking anything of us. Now, if it's all the same to you, Arabella, can we talk about something else?"

Lady Ashbury looked more than a little taken aback. She blinked rapidly, staring at Edward as if he were a beloved pet that had suddenly, without provocation, bit her. Pegeen began to feel a little sorry for her. In order to change the subject, Pegeen asked her about the activities that had been planned for the hunting party.

Recovering herself, the viscountess began to chatter animatedly about the number of people they were expecting, where each of them would be sleeping, how long they'd be staying, what their food preparation preferences were, and exactly which card games they most enjoyed. Pegeen listened with only half an ear, finding it hard to pay attention to anyone but her saturnine dining partner.

Edward had eaten heartily but silently, and Pegeen noticed that he'd drunk an entire bottle of claret by himself. Whenever she dared, she risked a glance at his face, and almost always found him gazing steadfastly at her. But no sooner did their eyes meet than he looked away, as if he'd only accidentally glanced in her direction. Surely, she thought, with a growing sense of unease, he hadn't *meant* all of those things he'd said before dinner. He'd only been flirting, hadn't he? Wasn't that what society people did, flirt outrageously with one another? None of it *meant* anything. . . .

Or did it?

"And tomorrow night . . ." To Pegeen's surprise, she found that Lady Ashbury was still cataloguing the weekend's itinerary, though no one, as far as Pegeen could tell, was listening to her. ". . . after dinner, we'll have a game or two of charades. I've got a lovely tableau for you, Edward. It will require you to dress up like an Arab sheik. Don't you think Edward would make a dashing Arab sheik, Allie? His hair is such an inky black. I can almost envision him in a moonlit oasis.''

Alistair waved a glass of madeira. ''And I assume he's sharing that oasis with you, eh, Arabella?''

The viscountess fluttered her eyelids. ''But of course.''

''And you'll be a member of his seraglio?''

''Oh!'' Lady Ashbury pretended to be offended, but not even Pegeen, who was completely unused to society, was fooled. ''You rapscallion!''

Alistair held his glass of madeira aloft and examined its murky depths in the soft glow of the chandelier. ''I'll wager your husband would pay a pretty penny to see you dressed as a harem girl, Arabella.''

The viscountess let out a delighted little shriek at his forwardness. Pegeen, who was growing rather irritated at Lady Ashbury's proprietal attitude towards both Rawlings Manor and at least one of its inhabitants, could hold her tongue no longer. Without pausing to think about what she was doing, she dropped her fork with a clatter and stared across the table at the pale, lovely viscountess, an expression of open-mouthed astonishment on her face.

''You're *married*?'' Pegeen gasped.

The viscountess stared right back, her nearly invisible eyebrows raised to their limits. ''Yes, of course I'm married,'' Lady Ashbury said, more than a trace of sarcasm in her voice. ''To the viscount of Ashbury.''

''But I thought . . .'' Pegeen glanced from Edward to the viscountess and back again. ''But from the way you seem to manage Lord Edward's household, I thought . . .''

She didn't need to finish. Her eloquently raised eyebrows spoke volumes.

Alistair had already dissolved into silent laughter, his shaking shoulders the only outward sign that he found humor in the situation. But both Edward and the viscountess continued to stare at her, the former expressionlessly, and the latter with absolute hatred.

"Yes," Lady Ashbury said at last, after a certain amount of hesitation. "I do manage Ed—Lord Edward's household affairs from time to time, since Rawlings Manor lacks a chatelaine. But—"

"But it doesn't anymore, does it?" Pegeen's smile was all youthful vivacity. "I believe I'll be able to lift that burden from your shoulders, Lady Ashbury. Then perhaps you'll be able to spend more time with your husband. I'm certain he must miss you when you are away from home so much."

Alistair's laughter could no longer be contained. He burst out with a guffaw that made Pegeen start. Alistair's dining partner was not so amused. The viscountess stared at Pegeen through eyes that had been narrowed to slits of pale blue. "Thank you for your concern," Lady Ashbury said, her voice dripping with venom. "But I believe we should allow Edward to decide who he wants to manage his household."

"Actually," Pegeen said, before Edward could say whatever it was he'd leaned forward to add, "I don't believe it's up to Lord Edward. Wouldn't it be up to the duke of Rawlings?" The cold hatred that swept over Lady Ashbury's face was answer enough for Pegeen. She leaned back in her chair and said, "I imagine Jeremy will agree with me that it's asking entirely too much of you, sacrificing so much of your time for Rawlings Manor, Lady Ashbury. I know that if *I* were married, I'd want to spend all the time I could with my husband, not managing someone else's household."

The viscountess rose, her generous bosom heaving, and threw down her napkin as if it were a gauntlet. Edward, who'd leaned back in his chair, his arms folded across his chest, tore his inscrutable gaze from Pegeen and eyed Arabella Ashbury with irritation.

"Sit down, Arabella."

His voice was not loud, but it was deadly serious. Edward's bark may have been worse than his bite, but his bark was very, very frightening indeed.

Blanching so that she was even paler than usual, the viscountess sat down heavily, her gaze openly resentful. Edward unfolded his arms and leaned forward in his chair to reach for his glass of madeira, which he quickly drained and placed back upon the table.

"Miss MacDougal is perfectly correct," he said in an entirely different voice. His tone was controlled but still commanded total attention. When he spoke again, his gaze, as well as his words, were directed at Pegeen. "There's no reason for you to run my household as well as your own, Lady Arabella. It's too much to ask of one woman, even one as capable as you."

Arabella blinked disbelievingly. "But Edward," she began, "I don't mind—"

He cut her off. "We'll discuss it later, Arabella. More madeira, anyone?"

Pegeen, who'd watched the little drama unfold before her with something like incredulity, could not help smiling, suddenly and involuntarily, at her brother-in-law. *This* was the Edward she had come to know, the one who had promised her roses in winter back in Applesby, and who had braved a blizzard to rescue her. It seemed that, despite his tendency towards lechery, he was quite capable of thinking of others besides himself, even at the risk of alienating his own mistress. Feeling quite happy, Pegeen held out her glass to be refilled, and only then raised her gaze to meet Edward's, the smile still playing about her lips.

Unaccountably, when their eyes met, blood rushed up into *his* face. . . .

Chapter Twelve

But that was ridiculous! Pegeen looked quickly away, abashed. It had to be a trick of the candlelight, or maybe it was a result of how much Edward had had to drink with dinner. Still, there was no denying that Edward's face had a distinctly ruddy appearance to it. Pegeen wasn't the only one who noticed it, either. Alistair had finally stopped laughing and was squinting at his host with disbelief plainly written all over his face.

"Now that that's settled," Edward said, looking coolly away from Pegeen, "may I suggest, Alistair, that we retire to the billiard room for a glass of port? Ladies, coffee will be served in the Gold Drawing Room."

Pegeen was ready to run from the table. She had never in her life experienced such a horribly uncomfortable meal. Edward, his complexion returned to normal, coldly held her chair for her, staring down at her as if she were an escaped lunatic. Pegeen, feeling the beginnings of a blush at the back of her own neck, fairly catapulted out of the dining room.

In the Gold Drawing Room, she breathed a little easier—until the viscountess came in. A plague on the woman!

Pegeen wanted to be alone. Could she beg tiredness and retire to her bedroom for the rest of the evening? How vexing society was! Pegeen would much rather spend her time in the company of Myra MacFearley and her brood back in Applesby than with a coldly calculating creature like the viscountess.

After a considerable amount of silence, during which Pegeen played with a cup of coffee she did not want, the viscountess said, "So, Miss MacDougal," as if she were continuing a conversation that had been interrupted, "you must forgive me if I sound forward, but you seem extraordinarily, er, outspoken for a vicar's daughter. Particularly such a . . . young one."

Pegeen bit her lower lip, uncertain how to respond. Finally, she said carefully, "I, um, thank you, Lady Ashbury."

The viscountess blinked in surprise. She obviously hadn't intended for Pegeen to take her bald statement as a compliment. "Uh, of course," she said. "Edward tells me that the new duke is quite a . . . headstrong young man. I can see where he inherited *that* trait."

Pegeen smiled politely. "Oh, really? From whom?"

"Well, you must admit, Miss MacDougal," the viscountess purred. "You are rather . . . willful."

Stung, Pegeen burst out, "So is Jeremy's uncle!"

Lady Ashbury laughed. Her laughter had quite an unpleasant ring to it, Pegeen found. "Oh, come, Miss MacDougal. Lord Edward is authoritative, as a man of his rank in life should be!"

"Why is it," Pegeen demanded, more to herself than to the viscountess, "that when a man states his mind, he's authoritative, but when a woman does so, she's perceived of as willful?"

Lady Ashbury looked down at her curiously. "What a strange little thing you are, Miss MacDougal," she said, as if she had just discovered a new species. "I wonder, would you mind, my dear, reminding me how your brother-in-law died? I'm afraid I've forgotten.''

Pegeen was so astonished that for a moment she was struck dumb. When she did find her voice at last, she could only stammer, "I . . . I beg your pardon?''

"Lord Edward's brother John. I was wondering if you were aware of how, precisely, he'd died.''

Pegeen stuttered, "Uh, no. I mean . . . No, I don't know.''

The Viscountess raised her pale eyebrows and busied herself with her coffee. Pegeen, thinking the topic had been effectively dismissed, rose and hurried across the room to stand by the fire. Off-the-shoulder evening gowns, she was discovering, were flattering to the figure, but quite chilly on snowy November nights.

"I'm sorry if I've offended you, Miss MacDougal,'' the viscountess said, after another short silence. "It's just that Edward never discusses his brother. I get the impression that the two of them didn't get on so well together. And he never told me how Lord John died, though I did hear a rumor—''

Pegeen, suddenly exhausted, closed her eyes and leaned her forehead against the green marble of the mantelpiece. The heat from the flames, however, did nothing to warm the growing chill in her blood.

"—I did hear a rumor that John was killed in a duel.''

Pegeen swallowed. She had known all along that this was coming, and so she was not particularly surprised by it. "If you knew how he died, why did you ask me?'' she asked, softly, her eyes still closed.

"Well, I didn't know for certain. . . .'' The viscountess had the grace to pretend to be embarrassed. "I told you, I heard a rumor.''

Pegeen opened her eyes and replied in a half-whisper, "My brother-in-law was killed in a duel. Shot through the heart, leaving my sister a widow and her son without a father. I hope that satisfies your burning curiosity."

She heard the sound of silk rustling and the next thing she knew, Lady Ashbury was at her side, a warm hand on her bare shoulder. "Miss MacDougal," the viscountess said softly. "I can't tell you how sorry I am. I did not mean to upset you. You mustn't blame your sister for Lord John's death—"

Pegeen turned her face away from the fire and stared up at Lady Ashbury with wide, astonished eyes. "Blame my sister? Why on earth would I blame Katherine for her husband's death?"

Lady Ashbury's smile was not at all kind. "Well, I'm afraid the rumor that circulated at the time was that when he died, Lord John was fighting for your sister's honor."

Pegeen's wide green eyes went dark as the sky outdoors. "Whatever . . . whatever do you mean?"

"Well," Arabella laughed airily. "Your sister was very young and very beautiful, and everyone says she took up with another man in Venice, and that John Rawlings found them together one night and challenged the fellow to a duel."

Pegeen could only stare at the viscountess in mute horror.

"And of course, John was murdered and your sister ran off with the fellow, leaving behind her infant son." Lady Ashbury gave Pegeen a brilliant smile. "In fact, they say she isn't dead at all, but—"

All at once, Pegeen found her voice. "That is a lie!" Pegeen shouted, quite forgetting where she was. "That is nothing but a damned lie!"

The door opened just then and the men came in. Pegeen, whirling around, took one look at their astonished faces, realized what she'd done, and sank with a groan onto a couch, her face hidden in her hands.

"I say," Alistair exclaimed with some alarm. "Was it the fish?"

"Don't be an ass," Edward advised him, brushing past Lady Ashbury to kneel at Pegeen's side. "Miss MacDougal? Are you all right?"

"I don't know what's the matter with her," the viscountess said with a slightly nervous laugh. "We were simply talking about her sister and then all of a sudden, she went quite out of her head—"

"Miss MacDougal?" Edward laid a hand on the bare shoulder nearest to him and wasn't particularly surprised to find that it was trembling. "Is there anything I can get you? A . . . A glass of whiskey, perhaps?"

"I told you, Edward," the viscountess hissed, loudly enough for Pegeen to hear. "This is what you get for taking in obscure relations. You ought to have left well enough alone . . ."

"That's enough, Arabella," Edward snapped. His dark eyebrows had slanted downwards, his scowl intimidating. "Alistair, instead of standing there like a stick, ring for Evers and have him send someone for Miss MacDougal's laudanum—"

"No," Pegeen gasped. Recovering herself with an effort, she raised her head. Fortunately, she'd gotten her tear ducts under control. Now, if she could only recapture a little of her lost dignity. "No, it's all right. I'm sorry. I don't know what came over me. I don't suppose I'm as well as I thought . . ."

"Arabella, I'm quite ashamed of you," Alistair declared, turning on the viscountess indignantly. "Can't you pick on someone your own size? It's quite unsportsmanlike of you, what with the poor little thing just getting over quinsy."

"I don't know what you're talking about," Arabella said with a sniff. "Miss MacDougal and I were merely—"

"I said, that is *enough*." Edward's cold voice cut off Lady Ashbury's explanation. "Alistair, give that bellpull a yank and send someone for her maid."

"I don't need laudanum and I don't need my maid," Pegeen insisted, appealing to Lord Edward only because her voice wouldn't carry any further. His sudden fits of temper frightened her, because they seemed to be triggered by the smallest of irritants. She reached out and grasped the large cool hand that rested on the seat cushion beside her. Edward glanced down at her small fingers, then into her eyes. There was no way she could control the blush that crept across her cheeks this time. She could only ignore it and say, in the steadiest whisper she could muster, "Really, I'm fine."

"Her color's better," the viscountess observed. That made Pegeen laugh, in spite of herself. The fact that Lady Ashbury, the palest woman in Yorkshire, should point out that someone else's coloring was improving struck Pegeen as somewhat ironic.

"Well, if she's laughing, she must be better," Alistair declared. He let the bellpull dangle and approached the couch, doing a not bad imitation of Mr. Parks, the surgeon. "Hmmm," he said, assuming the very same stance Mr. Parks had assumed while examining Pegeen. "You'll live."

Pegeen laughed again. Edward looked up at Alistair, his lips quirked sarcastically. "If you're quite through . . ."

Alistair bowed. "I yield the stage to Lord Edward Rawlings."

"Thank you." Edward glanced from Pegeen to Lady Ashbury as if he wanted to say something, then changed his mind. Instead, he gave Pegeen's hand a brotherly squeeze, then dropped it as he climbed to his feet. "I think Miss MacDougal's had enough excitement for one evening," Edward announced to the room in general. "She's only just recovered use of her voice, and we don't want to cause her to lose it again."

To Pegeen, he said, a strange twist to his lips that Pegeen realized was genuine amusement untainted by cynicism, ''I believe if Parks were here, he'd prescribe tea with honey and order you straight to bed. I, however, know of your preference for strong drink. May I pour you a whiskey, Miss MacDougal? The stuff we keep here at Rawlings lacks the kick of your Applesby brew, but it's a rather pleasant blend, just the same . . .''

Pegeen grinned up at him and for one moment she saw it in his eyes, those silver-grey eyes that at first she'd thought cold, then later realized were only cautious, like a hawk's. She was given a glimpse of Edward Rawlings as he really was. Not the devil-may-care rogue or heartbreaking Lothario he pretended to be, but the Edward Rawlings that Mrs. Praehurst spoke of, the one who'd carried a wounded dog home from the hunt, the one who treated his servants so kindly. The Edward Rawlings who'd promised a young boy a horse, then faithfully delivered on that promise.

What kind of childhood had Edward had, growing up in the dark shadow of his cruel older brother, his mother dying when he was ten, his domineering father too self-involved to take an interest in his youngest son's life? It was no small wonder that Edward was quick-tempered and even churlish at times. What was remarkable was that he hadn't turned out more like John—and a more selfish, evil-minded person than John Rawlings had never walked the earth.

Then, in a split second, the contact was broken. Edward tore his gaze away first and went to the sideboard to fetch her a whiskey. And Pegeen, who'd felt as if his glance had set her very soul on fire, sat still, a little shaken by the intensity of the moment that had passed between them. Was she losing her mind? Could this man break down all of her defenses with a single glance and render her, in spite of her firm resolve, in love with him? No. It wasn't possible. It was Pegeen's overactive imagination playing tricks on her.

Edward Rawlings was good-looking and possessed a magnetic quality she couldn't quite explain, but he could not make women fall in love with him against their will. At least, not Pegeen.

Chapter Thirteen

She was still telling herself this as she made her way up the stairs to the second floor, the whiskey—and Edward's smile—having warmed her in a way the fire could not. Not having wanted to spend a minute more than necessary in the company of Lady Ashbury, Pegeen had jumped at Edward's suggestion that she retire early to save her throat. She'd even allowed Edward to give her a good night kiss—not that she'd had much choice in the matter. When Edward had bent to stiffly kiss her hand, Alistair Cartwright exclaimed that as Miss MacDougal was Edward's sister-in-law, it was only fitting that he kiss her on the cheek instead of the hand. So under Lady Ashbury's blazing eyes, he had done just that, bending to graze Pegeen's soft pink cheek with his lips. She was proud to say that his kiss hadn't ruffled her in the least. It was the whiskey, not Edward's kiss, that had made her feel all rosy inside. . . .

Of course, she couldn't possibly go to bed. She had an appointment with Jeremy and she meant to keep it, Lady Ashbury or no Lady Ashbury. The boy was still wide awake when she arrived in the night nursery, and the nurse looked relieved to see her, retiring immediately when Pegeen entered the room. Pegeen told Jeremy his bedtime story, an ongoing saga concerning a pirate named Jeremiah and his pet parrot Pickles. It was nearly an hour later when Jeremy finally nodded off. Pegeen, feeling drowsy herself, tucked him into his boat-shaped bed, gave his ferret—also named Pickles—a good night pat on the head, and slipped back out into the hallway.

She ran right into Lord Edward and the viscountess.

Well, almost. Lord Edward was carrying a candelabra to light their way, since the chandeliers hanging in the Great Hall had been snuffed out. Pegeen nearly stepped into the circle of light cast around the couple, but at the last minute, she was able to pull back into the shadows, praying that she hadn't been spotted.

"Oh, Edward," the viscountess was saying, in a throaty voice quite unlike the one she'd used in the dining room. "Why ever not? You can't care what Praehurst thinks. She's got to know, after all this time—"

"I just don't think it's appropriate tonight, Arabella." Edward sounded as if he were speaking through gritted teeth. "We've got a number of guests arriving in the morning, and—"

"Oh, pish-posh, Edward. They all know, too. What's come over you? I think having a child in the house has rendered you positively—"

"Miss MacDougal?" Edward had stopped midstride and peered into the shadows. "Is that you?"

Bother! Pegeen reached behind her and rattled the knob to the night nursery as if she were only just now leaving it. "Oh, good evening," she tried to say, affecting an air of nonchalance, but her scratchy voice ruined the effect.

Edward's brows knit. "But I sent you off to bed an hour ago . . ." he began, as if she were a child in need of chastising.

Irritated at his condescending tone, Pegeen pointed towards the door she'd just closed. "Jeremy," she said simply.

Edward, his gaze following the direction of her slender finger, said, "He has a nurse, Miss MacDougal. Let the nurse put him to bed."

Pegeen shrugged helplessly. What she really wanted to do was run as fast as she could to the safety of her bedroom. "The nurse doesn't know Jeremy's bedtime story. We've been working on this particular installment for over a year."

The viscountess, squinting at her in the dark, said in tones of great ennui, "How touching. It must be wonderful to have such a creative imagination, mustn't it, Edward? How I do envy you, Miss MacDougal."

Lady Ashbury managed to make what ought to have been a compliment sound like an insult. Not that it mattered. Pegeen was already mortified enough to have stumbled upon the pair, who were clearly on their way somewhere together . . . bed, most likely. Angry at herself for caring, Pegeen muttered good night and turned to head down the hallway, not even certain she was going in the right direction. She'd hardly gone three steps, however, before her bare arm was encircled by a set of strong fingers. She found herself pulled up short and whirled around, not very gently, to face a glowering Lord Edward.

But he wasn't, she realized with relief so great that it almost caused her knees to sag, angry at *her*. He was looking back over his broad shoulder at Arabella, at whom he'd thrust the candelabra.

"I believe Mrs. Praehurst has put you in the White Room, Arabella," he said in a voice that was even colder than the wind that seeped into the Great Hall from the moor. "You know the way. I'm going to see to it that Miss MacDougal finds her way safely to her room. Good night."

Arabella, the candelabra hanging dangerously loose in

her grasp, stared at them, her mouth slightly ajar. Pegeen could almost see the swift calculations going on inside that pale head, as Lady Ashbury weighed possible retorts and dismissed them.

Edward, however, did not seem of a mind to stay to wait for the right one. His fingers biting into Pegeen's flesh, he hauled her off down the dark hallway, his boot heels resounding heavily on the parquet while Pegeen's high-heeled slippers made only the faintest clacking sound.

They rounded the corner of the gallery where the double staircases curved downwards and Pegeen could stand it no more. She gave the arm Edward clung to so tightly a convulsive little twist and said irritably, "Let go of me. You're hurting me."

Edward abruptly loosened his grip on Pegeen's arm, then released her altogether. She couldn't help glancing down at her arm to see if his fingers had left a mark on her ivory skin. Striding beside her, Edward noticed the surreptitious look and said in the deepest voice Pegeen had ever heard him use, "I'm sorry. I didn't mean to hurt you."

Pegeen examined the creamy skin of her upper arm. She could hardly see in the dim light, but the angry red finger marks were obvious even in the semidarkness. She looked up at Edward through her dark eyelashes and saw from his guilty expression that he, too, had noticed the welts.

"I can find my own way back to my room, thank you very much," she said primly. Only because her voice was so hoarse, she wasn't sure whether or not the primness came through. "I hardly need an escort."

"I'll just accompany you through the gallery," Edward said stiffly. "It's late. Young ladies shouldn't be wandering the halls by themselves at this hour."

She flashed him a shrewd glance. "Oh? And what, precisely, ought I be afraid of in Rawlings Manor? Winter drafts? Lurking footmen? I think it likely that the only thing

I have to fear in Rawlings Manor is standing here before me.''

Edward smiled, but it was a tight-lipped, humorless gesture. ''Your low opinion of me is probably well earned, madam, judging from the way you've been treated tonight. However, I insist upon seeing you safely to your room.''

''You certainly don't seem to care whether or not the viscountess makes it safely to *her* room,'' Pegeen pointed out.

Edward's smile grew a little more genuine. ''Do I detect a note of jealousy in your voice, Miss MacDougal?''

Pegeen tossed her head, and one of the rose blossoms in her hair, limp now from lack of water, lost a petal. The small white leaf spiraled down past her bare shoulders, over the side of the balustrade and into the darkness of the Great Hall below. Pegeen, watching its gentle descent, swallowed.

''Jealous?'' She turned her attention back to Edward. ''Of the viscountess? Certainly not. She may be the wife of one of the richest men in England and the mistress of another, but what has she done with all of that wealth? Worked to help alleviate the suffering of women less fortunate than she? No. She spends her days gossiping and her nights playing at charades. No, Lord Edward, I am not *jealous* of the viscountess. If anything, I feel sorry for her. And for you, for being so enamored of her. Good night, my lord.''

Hoping he hadn't noticed the tremor in her voice, Pegeen turned away from him and continued down the gallery, dragging her gloved hand along the balustrade as she went. Edward followed her, his grey eyes, she could see even in the half-light, glinting strangely.

''Pardon me, Miss MacDougal,'' he called after her, ''but it seems to me that for someone who disparages gossip so strongly, you were quite affected by that piece Lady Ashbury told you.''

Pegeen halted, leaning her back against the balustrade, and spread both her arms out wide in an elaborate gesture meant to illustrate her contempt for the discussion.

"And why shouldn't I have been affected by it? It was about my sister, after all. And your brother, too. I don't know about you, Lord Edward, but I don't care to hear my sister's character slandered. Our siblings, in case you haven't notice, were not exactly saints . . ."

He was at her side in two strides, his mouth still twisted with amusement. Pegeen saw his gaze drop to where the bodice of her gown gaped a little in the front. "I think it safe to say, Miss MacDougal, that neither you nor I fall into that category either."

He was standing close enough to Pegeen that she could feel the heat from his body, but she wouldn't move away. She kept her hands on the balustrade, her chin turned up so that she could look into his frank, laughing eyes.

"I beg your pardon, Lord Edward," she said. "But speak for yourself. I may not be a saint, but at least I'm not a lecherous spendthrift."

"And at least I," Edward said, suddenly uncrossing his arms and laying one hand on the balustrade on either side of Pegeen's waist, effectively trapping her within his broad, muscular arms, "am not a penny-pinching hypocrite."

"And what is that supposed to mean?" Pegeen thrust out her chin indignantly, her emerald eyes blazing. She tried to ignore the fact that his face loomed just inches above hers, and that one of his knees had insinuated its way between her thighs despite the sturdy wires of her crinoline.

"I think you know very well what I mean," Edward said with another one of his devilish smiles. "For all your missish protestations, you want me, Pegeen, every bit as much as I want you."

Pegeen inhaled gustily, ready to berate him with a

stream of denials, but the sudden rise of her bosom caught Edward's attention, and he glanced down at the ivory swells of her breasts. Her cheeks pinkening at Edward's bold appraisal of her décolletage, Pegeen thought fast, knowing that if she let him touch her, she'd crumble. She drew back her arm to launch a well-aimed blow to his cheek with the flat of her palm. . . .

But Edward hadn't been as engrossed by her cleavage as she'd hoped. He saw her quick movement and caught her gloved wrist, stopping its upward momentum just inches from his face. Before she could utter a sound, Edward had twisted her slender arm behind her back, leaning forward so that her body was pressed up against the balustrade.

Finding herself suddenly molded against Edward's body, her senses assaulted by a hundred different sensations—the brandy and tobacco scent of him, the feel of his crisply starched shirt beneath the soft skin of her breasts, the long, hard line of his thigh between her legs, the iron grip of his cool fingers curling around her wrist and waist— Pegeen could not even cry out, she was so surprised. And then, when she'd gathered enough of her scattered senses to draw breath to protest against this rough treatment, her words were stifled by Edward's lips, which he lowered over hers in a kiss that robbed Pegeen of breath . . . and thought.

Edward's possession of her didn't stop at her lips, however. The fingers that had captured her wrist loosened, and Edward's hand slid up the length of her bare arm, caressing the soft curve of her shoulder, then circling the column of her throat, while the arm around her waist pulled her even closer to him. Pegeen was totally and inexorably gathered to him until she could feel the buttons of his shirt burning into the tender flesh of her chest. His need for her became alarmingly apparent as his rigid erection pressed against her abdomen.

It was when his lips began sliding down her throat that

Pegeen knew she was lost. She had never felt anything like the burning sensation his mouth made on her smooth skin. Her hands, which had been fanned against his chest as she'd tried to push him away, suddenly circled his neck, yearning to pull him closer. But when his head dipped lower so that his mouth was suddenly burning on her breast, she gasped, her back arching against the balustrade.

Had Pegeen not known better, she'd have accused Mr. Worth of designing her dress to Lord Edward's specifications, since under his questing fingers, the material over her breasts gave way easily. Her straining nipples were bared at once, each pink peak greeted by Edward's tongue and lips. Pegeen, throwing her head back with a groan she couldn't suppress, closed her eyes, caught in an eddy of desire from which she couldn't escape. She strained his head closer, her gloved fingers tangled in his dark hair. The thigh he'd inserted between her legs came up against the slick and swollen crevice there, and it was all Pegeen could do not to press herself against that firm limb to release some of the throbbing tension she felt there.

Then Edward's hand replaced his lips, his fingers kneading the soft flesh of her breasts as his mouth recaptured hers. She clung to his coat collar as he ravaged her lips, and then one of her hands, as if of its own volition, embarked upon a bold exploration of his hard, masculine body, so unlike anything she'd ever known before. She felt the firm muscles of his chest through his shirt and waistcoat, and then her hand dipped lower, across his lean, flat belly, and then lower still, until her fingers brushed against that muscular organ that pressed so demandingly against the front of his breeches.

At her touch, Edward lifted his head with a gasp. "Pegeen," he whispered raggedly.

Pegeen felt his need pulsating against her hand. She stared up at him with eyes half-lidded with desire, and all at once, his own hand pushed aside the layers of silk and lace and steel that separated her from him and came up against the jointure of her thighs, hot and moist against her cotton drawers.

Pegeen nearly bucked from the explosive sensations his fingers on her caused. Trembling with an emotion she couldn't understand, she clung to him, an incoherent exclamation tumbling from her lips.

"Damn," Edward swore against her neck. "We can't do this in a drafty hallway. Come, my room's just down the corridor—"

But his words had broken the spell. Suddenly Pegeen realized that she was indeed standing half-naked in the gallery over the Great Hall of Rawlings Manor.

What had she been thinking? Had she completely lost her mind? Turning her head sharply, she managed to evade his questing mouth, and by pressing both her hands against his broad, firm chest, she was able to push him, staggering, away from her. Clinging to the balustrade as she panted for breath, Pegeen opened her eyes and saw, in one corner of the Great Hall below them, a flicker of candlelight as someone disappeared through a side door. Pox! As if it wasn't bad enough that she'd been manhandled by her brother-in-law. Someone had been spying on them! Now it would be all over the house by morning that Lord Edward and Miss MacDougal had been seen . . .

"Come," Edward said, his hand on her arm gentle. "It's just this way—"

But Pegeen pulled away from him, shaking her head with so much energy that more rose petals went flying.

"No," she said firmly. "No, we can't."

"Pegeen." His voice was incredibly gentle, softer than she'd ever heard it. She felt his fingers slide up her bare shoulders to cradle the back of her neck beneath her heavy hair. There was something in his touch, something other than the chill in the air that caused goose bumps to rise on the skin of her arms. "Pegeen, listen to me—"

But Pegeen was too upset to listen. She was a hussy, a shameless hussy, and she'd led him on and now he could, with perfect justification, call her a hypocrite. Oh, but how she wanted him!

"Pegeen, listen, I swear to you, no one will find out, if that's what's worrying you. My friends are all very discreet—"

Whirling around to face him, Pegeen's hand found its target this time. Her aim was true, and her arm strong, and the resulting slap echoed throughout the Great Hall as noisily as if some wayward kitchen maid had dropped a pile of dishes. Edward stared down at her, his lips parted in disbelief, his left cheek red from the blow she'd delivered. Pegeen contemplated giving him another, then saw the growing anger in those grey eyes, like storm clouds brewing on the horizon on a summer morning, and decided to seek shelter while she could.

Fleetly as a deer, Pegeen gathered up her skirts and ran for the safety of her bedroom, not looking back even when she heard him bark out her name in a tone as menacing as it was desperate. She wasn't sure how she managed to find it in her distressed state, but all at once she was in front of the door to her room. She heaved it inward and then slammed it closed behind her with all her might. She made haste to bolt it from the inside, relieved that the late duchess had seen fit to have a lock installed. Had Edward's mother felt the need to lock out the duke from time to time? Pegeen supposed so. He'd been a Rawlings, after all.

"Miss?"

Pegeen whirled around, then put a hand to her chest in relief when she saw it was only Lucy, rising sleepily from a couch in the corner. "Sorry to startle you, miss. I waited up to 'elp you out of your things."

Pegeen crossed the room and sank down onto her bed, heedless of the limp flowers in her hair or the creases she was making in the skirt of her gown. "Oh, Lucy," she sighed.

"Miss Pegeen! Your voice! You get right into bed this instant, and let me make you a hot drink. You've gone and lost your voice again!"

Pegeen couldn't help but let out a rueful little laugh. "Oh, Lucy," she said again. "I certainly hope that's the only thing I've lost tonight."

Because she was very much afraid that what she'd actually lost, finally, was her heart.

Chapter Fourteen

Pegeen was wakened the next morning by a series of soft thudding sounds. At first, she thought someone was pounding on her bedroom door, but after sitting up, she realized that the dull thumping was coming from something being thrown up against one of the large casement windows that lined the southern wall of her room. After rubbing the sleep from her eyes, Pegeen threw back the heavy coverlets and padded barefoot to the windowseat, shivering a little in the chill that the dying fire had been unable to disperse from the room.

A glance at the wintry, grey sky told her that she'd slept well into the morning, and she wondered why Lucy had allowed her to doze so long. Probably the poor girl had thought a rest would do Pegeen good, never knowing that it was her mistress' heart that was suffering now, not her body.

As Pegeen knelt on the silk cushions of the windowseat, a large white projectile thudded against the windowpane, and Pegeen realized that she was being bombarded by snowballs. Jeremy, she thought, and heedless of the thinness of her cotton and lace nightdress, she pushed the window open and leaned out, just as another ball of snow smacked against the side of the house.

Below her, mounted on an enormous black horse and half-hidden behind a large evergreen, Jeremy called up a greeting and waved. "Good morning, Pegeen!"

"Good morning, Jeremy," she called down to him, trying to keep her long, loose hair from getting wet in the snow on the windowsill. "I supposed that's your new horse?"

"Yes." Jeremy gave the magnificent animal a mighty smack on the neck. The horse whinnied appreciatively. "This is King."

"King?" Pegeen clutched her arms, trying to retain some warmth in the chill wind that swept through the window. "That's a curious name. Why King?"

"Because I'm the duke. And Uncle Edward told me he'd buy me a horse fit for a king. So I named him King, of course."

Pegeen nodded as if this explanation made sense to her, which, of course, it didn't. "And where are you and King going this morning?"

"Well," Jeremy said slowly. "We're going to ride around a bit and see the lay of the land."

"Not by yourself, I hope."

"Oh, no. Uncle Edward is coming with us." Jeremy turned and looked at something that was hidden behind the branches of the evergreen. "Aren't you, Uncle Edward?"

To Pegeen's dismay, another horse and rider came into view beneath her bedroom window. It was Edward on his massive black stallion. And there she was, leaning out the window with her hair tumbling wildly about her shoulders and nothing on but a practically transparent white nightdress.

"Good morning, Miss MacDougal," Edward called cheerfully, acting for all the world as if what had occurred between them last night had been a figment of someone else's—hers, presumably—imagination. "Sorry to wake you, but His Grace insisted upon showing off his new steed."

"Oh." Pegeen tried to keep her tone light. "Well, King is a very lovely horse. Did you thank your Uncle Edward, Jeremy?"

Jeremy rolled his eyes dramatically. "*Pegeen*," he said with a great deal of disgust. "Of *course* I thanked him."

"Well," Pegeen said. When Edward continued to do nothing but sit on his horse and stare up at her, she said, "Well, have a pleasant ride, gentlemen," and started to pull the window closed.

"Wait," Edward called out, suddenly coming to life.

Pegeen gave him a perfunctory glance over her shoulder. "What is it? It's cold out, you know."

"I just thought you'd like to know that some of the guests for tomorrow's hunt have already arrived. The ladies will be gathering for luncheon in the drawing room in about an hour."

Pegeen stared down as if he'd taken leave of his senses—and perhaps he had. "I'm afraid I won't be able to join them. I planned upon calling on the headmaster of the Ladies Seminary this morning. Perhaps another time—"

"They're very anxious to meet you," Edward shouted up to her.

She released the window latch and stared down at him some more. "I'll do my best not to disappoint everyone," she said acidly. And with that she gave the window a vicious tug and slammed it shut.

When Lucy arrived to help her mistress bathe and dress, Pegeen's spirits weren't much improved. True, she'd survived an encounter with Edward without bursting into tears, blushing, or slapping him—a first, given their recent history. But did that prove that she hadn't fallen in love with him? This thought had irritated her excessively for the

better part of an hour after she'd gone to bed the night
before. It really would have been most inopportune for Pegeen to fall in love with Edward Rawlings, seeing as how
he had a reputation for being a bounder.

When Pegeen fell in love, it was going to be with a
nice, serious man, a man interested in science or letters—
a man like Mr. Parks, the surgeon, in fact. Mr. Parks, Pegeen felt, would make an excellent husband. He didn't intimidate one with his size. He wasn't outlandishly
good-looking. He didn't tease or rage at one. That was the
kind of husband Pegeen wanted. An ordinary-looking, safe,
quiet husband. Edward Rawlings would never make anyone
a very good husband. He was too wild, too flippant, too
quick-tempered. Too handsome. Too rich. And much, much
too quick with his hands.

When she'd finished buttoning Pegeen into a flattering
velvet gown of the darkest midnight blue, Lucy let out a
little giggle and skipped over to the late duchess' dressing
table.

"Oh, miss," Lucy called, rooting around in drawer.
"Will you be wearing your rubies or your diamonds today?"

Pegeen was gazing at herself in the gilt-framed mirror,
trying to decide whether to wear her hair up or down.
"What are you talking about, Lucy?" she asked distractedly.

"Your ruby or diamond ear bobs?" Lucy held out her
hands, unable to stifle a delighted laugh. She was holding
a large leather box, its lid open to reveal a jumble of beautiful, expensive jewels. The light that hit the precious stones
reflected upwards onto Lucy's freckled, laughing face.
"What do you think of his lordship now, miss?"

Pegeen reached out and lifted a long strand of pearls
from the box's confines. "Where . . . ?" she breathed. "Oh,
Lucy! Where did you find this?"

"I didn't," Lucy giggled. "Find it, I mean. I just 'appened to mention yesterday to Sukie, the cook's apprentice, about you not 'avin any ear bobs, and Sukie mentioned it to Cook, who mentioned it to Mrs. Prae'urst, 'o tol' Mr. Evers, 'o tol' Lord Edward's valet, who musta tol' his lordship, 'cause early this mornin', as I was comin' up the stairs to check on you, miss, I met Lord Edward in the gallery, an' he give me this.''

"This box?" Pegeen stared at the younger girl in confusion. "He just handed it to you?"

"Well, not quite. He said, ' 'Ere, Lucy. See that Miss MacDougal gets this. It's my mother's jewelry collection.' Then he laughed, kinda funny like, and said, 'Tell'er if she wants to donate it all to the local orphanage, she can be my guest.' '' Lucy reached up and scratched her nose. "At least, that's what I think 'e said.''

Pegeen took the heavy jewelry box from Lucy's arms and sat down with it at the dressing table. Her astonishment was complete. Lord Edward Rawlings was an enigma Pegeen would never unravel.

Lucy pinned Pegeen's hair on the top of her head with ringlets curling down her back, so that her long neck showed off her new sapphire ear bobs to an advantage. Satisfied that at least she didn't look as virtuous as she actually was, Pegeen took out a sheet of paper and penned a quick note to the headmaster of the Ladies Seminary, asking if she might be able to meet with him some other time. Today, she wrote, she was going to be unfortunately detained. . . .

Chapter Fifteen

Try as he might, Edward could not keep a song from warbling in his throat. As he was no singer, and as he and the rest of his male guests were trudging through the woods on his estate looking for game to shoot at, this was not particularly appropriate behavior. It seemed to irritate Alistair Cartwright more than anyone else, a fact that bothered Edward not at all, since Alistair himself was the most irritating of human beings at times.

"Damn," Cartwright swore at another missed shot. A flock of pheasant took flight at the report of his rifle, and by the number of echoing reports, it appeared that Edward's other guests, spread across the woods and meadows of the Rawlings estate, also were taking futile shots at the birds. Cartwright turned to glare at his host. "I would have hit one, if it wasn't for that blasted humming."

"I don't know what you mean." Edward continued to hum, his own rifle perched on his shoulder, where it had sat all afternoon. He hadn't fired a single shot. Couldn't bring himself to do it, somehow.

"You know what I mean, you insufferable git. That. That humming."

"This?" Edward hummed some more. "Is that what's bothering you?"

"You know damned well that's what's bothering me." Alistair shoved some of his long blond hair from his face and glared up at Edward, who was both taller and a better shot. "Let me tell you something, Rawlings. You and I have been through a lot together."

Edward began to trudge through the snow toward a low ravine that looked promising, and Cartwright followed him, still yapping.

"We survived that god-awful boarding school together, suffered through the same tutors, studied under the same lecturers at Oxford, even bedded the same wenches now and again. I've seen you morose, and I've seen you drunk, and I've seen you in blinding white rages, but I have never, in all my life, seen you like this."

Edward continued to hum. Yorkshire winters might be too cold for some, but not him. He had his wool-lined jacket and his heavy cloak, his thick boots, his best hunting dog, and a flask of brandy in his vest pocket. He felt warm and contented as a baby. Nothing Cartwright could say would dampen his mood. He was happy.

"Now," panted Cartwright, climbing after his host. "I've asked myself, what is it that's making Edward behave so peculiarly? What changes have taken place in his life to make him so insufferably smug? And I stumbled upon an answer. It's the girl, isn't it?"

"Girl?" Edward smiled to himself as he made his way down a particularly steep and icy slope. "What girl?"

"You know what girl I mean. There's only one girl in our acquaintance that I'm aware of. I'm not blind, you know. I saw the way you looked at her last night—"

"Last night? What are you talking about, my friend?"

"You know damned well what I'm talking about. I'm telling you right now, Rawlings, that you had just better steer clear of her."

"Oh, had I? And why is that?"

"Well, for one thing, because nothing can come of it. You're either going to have to marry her or forget her, because she's not going to fall into your bed like a dockside doxy."

"And what makes you think that?"

"She's a vicar's daughter, isn't she? Besides, you saw her last night. The way she stood up to Arabella like that." Edward was surprised at the tone of genuine admiration in Alistair's voice. "Thing like that takes character, Edward. I know how you feel about Arabella, but I also know I won't be the first to tell you the woman's a veritable bitch when she wants to be. And the way that girl looked her square in the eye and told her she need not trouble herself managing your household anymore—" Alistair hooted appreciatively. "Lord, that was rich. Wish I could go back and see it again."

Edward continued picking his way down the ravine, a smile of amusement on his face. "And that's it, Alistair?"

"Well, damn. No, it isn't just that, you know. I mean, look at her. I know you were looking at her last night, but I mean, really, look at her. The girl's got beauty, brains— hell, she even makes *me* laugh, and it's damned rare that I laugh *with* a woman, rather than *at* her. She's a rare one, Eddie. If her sister was anything like her, your brother had the right idea."

Edward, at the bottom of the ravine, turned to look up at his companion, who was still only two-thirds of the way down. He wasn't smiling anymore. "If I didn't know better, Cartwright, I'd say you talk like a man in love."

Alistair grasped onto a leafless sapling as he slid the last few feet into the hollow. He brushed himself off, his breath coming in great white puffs from his cold-reddened lips. "Damn your eyes, Rawlings," he panted. "We're talking about you, not me. Arabella caught me this morning at the crack of dawn and told me how you'd put off paying her your usual midnight visit. She even managed to squeeze out a tear or two. She tried to get me to believe that you and the girl are, shall we say, cozier than in-laws ought to be—''

''The deuce you say!'' Edward stormed past a rocky, icicle-strewn outcropping and glared balefully up into the woods in the direction of the manor house. ''Damn! I knew I never should have taken up with Arabella in the first place.''

Alistair leaned his backside against a boulder and looked more pained than entertained. ''Oh, yes. She told me she saw the two of you in the wee hours last night, kissing madly in the gallery—''

''Damn!'' Edward felt as if he might explode with fury. ''Of all the conniving—''

''Of course, I didn't believe her.'' Alistair had laid down his gun and folded his arms across his chest. ''Until now, that is.'' With real feeling he cried, ''Really, Rawlings, how could you? The girl's hardly been in the house a fortnight, and already you're out to ruin her? Haven't you any sense of decency whatsoever? She's your sister-in-law, for God's sake!''

''I couldn't help it,'' Edward ground out, his eyes on the icy rivulet that come spring would be a pleasantly burbling stream. ''You don't know how it is. I'm telling you, the girl keeps provoking me—''

''The hell she does! You expect me to believe that the great Edward Rawlings has met his match in that rosy-cheeked slip of a girl? Why, she's barely twenty years old, and prim as a schoolmistress!''

Edward snorted rudely. Alistair raised his eyebrows. ''Are you suggesting she's not?''

Edward paced up and down the gorge once, then whirled upon his companion and growled, ''No, damn you. Unfortunately, she's even primmer than a schoolmistress. She's a goddamned nun. At least, she tries to be. But I'm telling you, Alistair, underneath that missish facade—'' Edward clamped his mouth shut. What was he doing? This was not something he needed to reveal to Alistair Cartwright.

Alistair Cartwright's curiosity, however, was already aroused. "And how," he asked, with elaborate nonchalance, "might you know that?"

Edward groaned. He'd never been able to keep a secret. "Because Arabella, damn her spying eyes, was telling the truth when she said she saw me kissing the girl in the gallery last night!"

Alistair shook his head. "Cad."

"What Arabella didn't see, apparently, and was unable to report back to you, was that after I kissed her, the girl delivered such a mean right hook that I could hardly shave this morning."

Alistair started laughing so hard that he had to lean forward and grasp his knees. "No, no, say it isn't so! Edward Rawlings gets rebuffed! I never thought I'd live to see it."

"Now do you see what I mean, about her provoking me? I swear to you, one minute, the girl's looking out at me from beneath those long black eyelashes, and the next, she's slapping me. Or even worse, telling me she thinks I'm a fop! I ask you, Cartwright, do I strike you as remotely foppish? Do I?"

Alistair was laughing so hard he couldn't reply.

"I can't think what ails the girl." Edward paced back and forth again. "I've paid her every kindness I could think of, sent her flowers and books. I even bought that brat of a nephew of mine a stallion for over five hundred pounds, thinking it would please her, and what do I get for my efforts? A slap in the face!"

"Well, what did you expect, Edward?" Alistair wiped tears of laughter out of his eyes. "What we have here is a girl of uncommon spirit and beauty, a Scot *and* a vicar's daughter, to top it all off. She's not going to tumble into bed with you, my friend, not without a ring on her left middle finger."

Edward snorted. "Not her. Says she doesn't believe in the institution of marriage. Says it's enslaved women throughout the ages—"

"No!" Alistair let out a bark of laughter. "You must be joking."

"I've never been more serious in my life."

"Well, there you go, then." Alistair shook his head. "She's thrown down the gauntlet. You've no choice but to take up the challenge. Though, frankly, I don't believe you are quite up to it."

"And you are, I suppose?" Edward glared at him belligerently.

"I believe I'm capable of stealing a kiss without getting my face slapped."

Edward took one long stride and planted himself in front of his laughing companion. The hand that he placed upon Alistair Cartwright's shoulder was heavy, and he pressed upon it to better relay the seriousness of his intent to his old friend. "You are going to stay away from her, Cartwright," Edward said, in careful, measured tones. "If I catch you anywhere near her, I'll see to it that you suffer a painful, but unavoidable hunting accident, which will render you bedridden for the remainder of the season. Do you understand me, old bean?"

Alistair wasn't laughing anymore. But then, Edward wasn't humming anymore, either.

"I understand," Alistair said sullenly. "You needn't press down on me like that. I quite get the picture."

Abruptly, Edward released him. Spinning on his heel, he headed blindly towards the far side of the gorge, his jaw set angrily. What was the matter with him? Alistair was his closest friend, one of the few human beings he could tolerate for more than an hour at a time. And here he was, threatening him. . . .

"But I just want to say for the record, Rawlings, that I object to this whole thing." Alistair had risen to his feet and was adjusting his heavy cloak about his shoulders. "I don't want to see that girl hurt."

Edward, startled, glanced back at Cartwright over his shoulder. "And why do you assume I'm going to hurt her?"

"For God's sake, Rawlings. They don't call you The Heartbreaker for nothing, you know."

Edward grinned without humor. "Is that what they call me?"

"Yes," Alistair admitted, then added with considerable venom, "when they aren't calling you something even worse."

Edward's smile broadened. "Good," he said.

Chapter Sixteen

The area in which Pegeen was least afraid of failure turned out to be the one in which she was most assured of success. With very little effort on her part, she managed to win over nearly all of Edward's female guests. It was surprisingly easy, Pegeen discovered, to charm these jaded society ladies. Some of them, of course, she'd already met: Lady Herbert, Sir Arthur's wife, and her five daughters knew Pegeen from the night she and Jeremy had spent at their estate on their way to Rawlings. From five-year-old Maggie Herbert to her twenty-one-year-old sister Anne, they were all delighted to see her again.

It was the Herberts' warm reception of Pegeen alone which caused several of the titled matrons to give her the benefit of the doubt. "If Virginia Herbert likes her," Pegeen overheard the wife of the earl of Derby whisper to the marchioness of Lynne, "then she must be decentish."

To Pegeen, whose hostessing experience was limited to mission society teas in her father's rectory and the occasional church bazaar, the prospect of entertaining a dozen society ladies and their children was daunting. There was no use turning to the viscountess of Ashbury for help either.

By so blithely informing Lady Ashbury that she need no longer trouble herself with the management of the Rawlings household, Pegeen knew she'd made an enemy.

But she found that by behaving naturally—the way she would have around her father's parishioners—she was able to captivate even the starchiest matron. Pegeen's outgoing personality and striking beauty lent her an advantage in just about any situation, and her youthful enthusiasm was contagious. By the end of the day, she had nearly every guest in stitches at her stories of Applesby, had organized a rowdy game of loo, and had managed to convince nearly every lady present that the Rawlings Ladies Seminary was in dire need of donations, such that they all agreed to call upon the school in the morning.

Not everyone, however, was so easily charmed. Though Pegeen made a great effort to treat the viscountess civilly by including her in conversations and asking her opinion on banal subjects every once in a while, Arabella made no attempt whatsoever to hide her sneering contempt for Pegeen, from rolling her eyes at the younger woman's jokes to 'cutting' Pegeen whenever she entered a room— that is, by not acknowledging Pegeen's presence.

Pegeen had never been cut before, and though it did not seem particularly to shock the ladies present that the viscountess of Ashbury actively disliked the new duke's aunt, Pegeen herself was secretly horrified by the older woman's antipathy.

When the gentlemen finally returned from their shooting expedition, the ladies scattered to their various rooms in order to bathe and dress for dinner. Pegeen paid a brief visit to the nursery, where she was not particularly surprised to learn that Jeremy had met his match in pigtailed Maggie Herbert. The five-year-old termagant had turned Jeremy's fort into a castle, and she was ruling over it and the eight other children in the playroom with queenly grace. Jeremy had been relegated to the tiresome role of King and was complaining steadily about the sad lack of pirates in the little girl's game. Seeing that for once, Jeremy was staying out of trouble, Pegeen retired to the Rose Room, where Lucy had another luxurious bath waiting.

Dinner was a formal affair in which the ten courses that were to be served to the eighteen adults in attendance played only a small part in the overall scheme of things. Pegeen was only half-dressed when Mrs. Praehurst came bustling into her room, worrying about the seating arrangements.

"Lady Seldon just caught me in the gallery and told me that under no circumstances did she wanted to be paired with Sir Thomas Payton, as he's recently joined a society that promotes the health benefits of opium and of course Lady Seldon can't abide opium eaters . . ." The housekeeper was all but wailing, pushing her spectacles more firmly up the bridge of her nose. "I don't mean to interrupt your toilette, Miss MacDougal, but I'm at my wit's end. I can't put Lady Seldon with either of the earl of Derby's sons, as they have that bad habit of throwing small pieces of fruit into large ladies' décolletage—"

Pegeen smiled sunnily up at Mrs. Praehurst. "Well, it's quite simple, isn't it? Pair Lady Seldon with Mr. Cartwright, and give Mr. Cartwright's partner to Sir Thomas."

Mrs. Praehurst exhaled so mightily that her wrinkled cheeks expanded like a hornblowers. "But you see, Mr. Cartwright isn't titled, and Lady Seldon is very conscious of such things—"

"Could we try seating her with the son of the marquis of Lynne?"

Mrs. Praehurst sighed. "I suppose we'll have to. But he's so young—I can't think what they'll have to say to one another."

Pegeen shrugged. "Make sure an epergne is set on the table between them. Then Lady Seldon won't have to speak to him at all."

"Perfect! Thank you, Miss MacDougal."

Pegeen, still smiling, turned back to her reflection in the dressing room mirror. Lucy was engineering a complicated coif on the top of Pegeen's head, and she glanced at the loosely curled tendrils skeptically. "You know what you're doing Lucy, don't you?"

"Oh, yes, miss. We practiced this one ever so much at the Seminary. It's called a frizzed coronet."

Seeing that Mrs. Praehurst hesitated in the doorway, Pegeen glanced her way—a difficult thing to do, since Lucy was holding several fistfuls of her hair. She asked, "Mrs. Praehurst? Was that all?"

"Well, actually, miss, there's just one other thing."

Pegeen smiled. "What is it? You act as if it were a major catastrophe."

"Well, you see, Miss MacDougal . . . I don't mean to sound impertinent, but the viscountess has always been seated at Lord Edward's right . . ."

Pegeen raised her delicately arched eyebrows. "Yes?"

"But I—well, like I said, I don't mean to sound impertinent, but Lady Ashbury stopped me in the hallway and inquired as to the seating arrangements, and said I was to make certain that she's still seated on his lordship's right—"

Pegeen finished for her. "And you don't feel that's appropriate?"

Mrs. Praehurst, like a bursting dam, let loose a torrent of pent up animosity towards the viscountess. "I feel it's *highly* inappropriate, miss. The viscountess is a married woman. Her place is with her husband, not with Lord Edward. And as her husband won't be in attendance, and as you're the lady of the house now, I feel strongly that the seat to his lordship's right belongs to you until such a time as he's married, or His Grace, the duke, assumes the head of the table—whichever comes first."

Mrs. Praehurst looked slightly shocked at herself for having said so much and with such vehemence, but she didn't apologize for her outburst. Instead, she held out both her hands in helplessness. "Really, Miss MacDougal, I'm at my wit's end."

"I have an idea." Pegeen waggled her eyebrows at her own reflection. "You say Sir Thomas Payton is an opium eater?"

"Yes, but—"

"Let's seat the viscountess with Sir Thomas, and I'll take the seat to his lordship's right." The twinkle in her eyes was impossible to disguise, and Mrs. Praehurst couldn't help but smile in return.

"Quite right, miss," the housekeeper said as she withdrew, a distinctive bounce in her step that hadn't been there before.

Lucy, whose mouth was stuffed with hairpins, said only just intelligibly, "I understand the viscountess'll be wearin' pure black satin tonight, miss."

"Oh, she will, will she? And what will I be wearing, Lucy?"

"White silk. And the late duchess' diamonds, I think."

Pegeen laughed some more. She was still laughing to herself an hour later as she appeared at the top of the double staircase to the Great Hall. There was no one below but Evers and a few of the footmen, but the moment her foot, shod in a velvet, high-heeled slipper, touched the first step, they ceased speaking amongst themselves, looking up at her with astonishment plainly written on their faces.

Pegeen's gown, of the most dazzling white, was both off-the-shoulder and daringly low cut. With a dazzling diamond brooch fastened between her breasts, and matching diamond pendants swinging from her ears, she didn't look a bit like the dowdy vicar's daughter she'd been the first day Edward had met her. The footmen gaped up at her, completely forgetting their duty, which was to escort the ladies to the drawing room, where the guests were to gather before dinner was served. Pegeen smiled down at them—by now she'd managed to learn just about every Rawlings' staff member's name—and continued her descent, pausing only when she heard a door open. Lord Edward Rawlings, himself resplendent in evening wear—black pants, waistcoat, and jacket, white shirt, and cravat—came barreling out into the hall to complain to Evers about the lack of sherry in the sherry decanter. He halted at once when he noticed Pegeen on the stairs.

Pegeen didn't feel like laughing anymore. This was the first time she'd seen Edward Rawlings up close since their tiff the night before. She had no idea how he was going to greet her, sarcastically, politely, or even at all. True, he'd sent her the jewels, but that had been an act of self-preservation. He couldn't very well let the servants go on talking about how poor Miss MacDougal hadn't a single ear bob, when everyone knew in the manor safe rested a fortune in jewelry. Suddenly, Pegeen's victory over the matrons didn't seem like much. Whether she wanted to admit it or not, what she really wanted to win wasn't the hearts of a lot of titled society women, but the heart of just one duke's younger son.

Keeping her chin in the air, Pegeen finished her descent of the great staircase, grateful she hadn't stumbled or tripped over the hem of her voluminous skirt. She glided across the smooth parquet floor to Edward's side, giving him the briefest of curtsies before turning her attention to Evers.

"Is there a problem with the sherry?" she inquired.

Evers, for once nonplussed, stammered, "Er, yes, miss. I'm afraid the decanter needs to be refilled. I'll see to it straight away." He took off at an astonishingly fast clip for such an old man, the footmen hot on his heels.

Edward, meanwhile, was gazing at Pegeen with an inscrutable glint in his grey eyes. She glanced at him over one bare shoulder and inquired pertly, "Have I grown warts suddenly, my lord? You're staring."

"I beg your pardon." Edward's smile was all that was charming—whether it was gentlemanly was another story. There was more than a hint of lechery in his glance. "I'm merely admiring the fairest maiden that has ever graced this ancient hall."

Pegeen lowered her gaze modestly. "I'm sure you say that to all your sisters-in-law." A glimpse out from under her eyelashes showed her that he was smiling at the barb.

"Ah," Edward grinned. "I see that an afternoon spent in the company of some of the grandest ladies of the realm has done nothing to temper that sharp tongue of yours."

Pegeen was quick with a rebuttal. "If you think I'm such a shrew, why did you send me the jewels?"

"To keep my household staff happy. Although I don't agree, they apparently think your beauty needs such adornments."

"You coddle your staff in the same way you coddle your nephew." Pegeen shook her head so that the diamond pendants on her ear lobes danced, but her voice was only gently chiding. "Really, Lord Edward, you are far too extravagant in your gifts. The boy would have been happy with a pony, yet you give him a thoroughbred. What could you have been thinking?"

"I was thinking that when I was about his age, all I wanted was a hunter of my very own." Edward managed to do a very good imitation of a man looking wistful over his childhood. Pegeen wasn't fooled. She knew he was trying to soften her towards him, and the fact that he was so blatantly using Jeremy to do so amused her. "I never got one. It makes me happy to give a little boy some joy—"

Pegeen rolled her eyes expressively. "I can see why Lady Ashbury thinks you're so well-suited to charades. Your flair for the dramatic is rather pronounced."

"Do you think I'm lying?" He made a grand sweeping gesture with his powerful arm. "Ask anyone here—ask Evers—and they'll tell you I spent my childhood pining away for a horse like King."

Pegeen nodded tolerantly. "And a good thing, too. All that practice you received in pining away as a child will serve you in good stead now, as you pine away for various and sundry other things you'll never get."

"Madam," Edward said, with mock dignity. "You emasculate me."

"I hardly see how that's possible, considering that your lack of masculinity has already been well-established."

Quick as lightning, Edward snaked an arm around Pegeen's narrow waist and pulled her to him, as boldly as if he were some lovesick shepherd and she a passing milkmaid. "I think you had a handful of evidence to the contrary last night," he reminded her teasingly.

Struggling in his embrace, her heart thumping wildly at his sudden proximity, Pegeen twisted her head about, frantically looking to see if anyone was watching. "Edward!" she hissed, giving his oak-hard chest a bang with her fist. "Stop it! This isn't funny! Someone might see!"

"Let them see," Edward declared, gazing down at her with teasing lights in his silver-flecked eyes. "What does it matter? Any man who saw us would understand my actions completely. You, Pegeen, have a waist that fairly cries out to be encircled by a pair of callused hands, and lips begging to be kissed heartily and often—"

Craning her neck to keep her lips as far from his as possible, Pegeen gritted her teeth in anger. Did he really think she was some common housemaid whom he could snatch up and kiss whenever the desire seized him? Did he honestly think she'd let his pretty compliments go to her head, knowing, as she did, his reputation? Why, he was nothing more than a Lothario, in the game for the hunt alone. Well, she wasn't about to be any man's prey. . . .

"You great fool," Pegeen snapped. "Let go of me." She was uncomfortably aware that his rough treatment of her person had caused some disorganization to occur within the bodice of her gown. She was afraid her décolletage might have slipped a little *too* low. "It's one thing if you ravish me in private, but it's quite another if you ruin me in front of all your friends—"

"Ah, of course." Edward released her so abruptly that she fell away from him and stumbled a step or two. "We must think of decorum. It's always decorum with you, isn't it . . ."

Edward's voice trailed off as he turned and saw that Pegeen was in a most interesting sort of distress. His eyes widened when he realized that his manhandling of her had resulted in the disarranging her gown so that one of her full, rosy-tipped breasts had been dislodged from the lace cup of her corset, and even, he saw with delight, from the front of her gown itself. Blushing furiously, Pegeen was attempting to set things right, chewing on her lush lower lip as she did so.

"Miss MacDougal!" Edward couldn't help himself. The opportunity was too rich. "Are you in need of aid?"

"No!" Her cheeks burning hotly, Pegeen presented him with her tantalizingly bare back. "You've done quite enough, thank you very much. Don't come near me."

"I'm offering my services as a gentleman—"

"Ha!" Pegeen finally managed to get things under control. Tugging on her bodice to see that they stayed that way, she whirled back around to face him, her eyes flashing with fury. "A gentleman, you? Why, I've seen hogs with better manners than you!" She held out a warning finger as he stepped towards her, his arms outstretched beseechingly. "No, not another step closer. You stay away from me. You take one step closer and I'll scream so loud, they'll hear me all the way to London."

Edward folded the arms he'd held out to her across

his chest. "Well, this is certainly going to make things difficult, isn't it? After all, I'm your escort this evening."

"You just escort me from there," she said, pointing to a spot a good three feet away from her. "You cross that line, and by God, you'll regret it."

Edward looked speculatively at the place on the floor that she'd chosen. "That's rather an arbitrary spot, isn't it? I fancy I could still reach you from there, if I tried—"

Pegeen stamped her foot petulantly. What was the man trying to do, drive her to distraction? Was it his bed he wanted her in or Bedlam? Before she could stop herself, Pegeen blurted out, "If this is an example of how you've treated your previous lady loves, it's no wonder you ended up stuck with a cold fish like that viscountess of yours."

Edward's face took on the same expression he'd worn the night before, after she'd slapped him. Recognizing his cold white anger, Pegeen beat a hasty retreat, stumbling backwards towards the door to the drawing room. She wished she could take her hasty words and stuff them back into her mouth, but she'd always had a problem with thinking before she spoke. She was used to getting into trouble for her thoughtless remarks. But having her mouth washed out with soap was the worst punishment she'd ever suffered for her past sins. From the look on Edward's face, she'd be lucky to escape with her hide intact.

But she wasn't about to apologize. She continued backing away from him as he strode inexorably forward, his grey eyes hard as steel. They fastened on her with an intensity that suggested he'd like nothing better than to strip off the rest of her clothes and dunk her into something very cold, and preferably not let her up for air until she lay inert. . . .

The door to the drawing room popped open, and Sir Arthur Herbert cried out, "Ah, my dear Miss MacDougal! There you are! We've all been waiting for you!"

Pegeen gathered up her heavy skirt and practically ran

towards the corpulent solicitor. "Oh, Sir Arthur," she cried. "How are you? I'm so sorry I'm late. Evers should be here directly with the sherry. How good it is to see you. Are you quite recovered from our dreadful accident?"

Sir Arthur beamed down at her, all smiles and plump wine-reddened cheeks. "I'm quite well, quite well. I heard about your terrible illness. I hope—Oh, and Lord Edward." Sir Arthur turned his wide grin towards the glowering duke's son. "And how are you, sir? I see that you got a little wind-chapped out there today. Your cheeks are almost as red as mine, ha!"

Smiling up at her protector, Pegeen slid by him and into the safety of the Gold Drawing Room, which was crowded with men in evening wear and women in brightly colored skirts stretched over the most enormous crinolines Pegeen had ever seen. As she stepped onto the rich red Oriental rug, a distinct and audible sigh swept through the assembled party, though whether it was due to appreciation over the vision she created or surprise at her unannounced entrance, Pegeen wasn't certain. In any case, she was eagerly greeted by cries of "Oh, Miss MacDougal! Sit by me!" and "Miss MacDougal, you simply must sit over here." She didn't dare dawdle in the doorway—Lord Edward was directly behind her, and she intended to put as much distance between the two of them as she possibly could.

This proved to be almost impossible. When Evers announced that dinner was served, Edward appeared at her side as if he'd never left it, tucking her hand into the crook of his arm and half-dragging her to her feet. Pegeen managed to keep smiling, though inwardly, she was seething with emotions that had nothing to do with the polite expression she wore on her face. As if he'd glimpsed these inner fires through her blazing eyes, Edward commented as he led her through the Great Hall to the dining room, "Chin up, Pegeen. It'll all be over in a few minutes."

"Stop calling me that." Impertinent cuss.

"Why? It's your name, isn't it?" Edward kept his own chin in the air, his eyes level, but the corners of his mouth had a distinct upward slant to them. "I happen to like the name Pegeen. I can't abide calling you Miss MacDougal. MacDougal's such an ordinary name. It lacks character. Unlike you . . ."

"Would you—" Pegeen closed her eyes for a moment. Think before you speak, she said to herself. She lifted her lids, and found Edward gazing down at her curiously. She threw caution to the wind. "Would you please just leave me alone?"

"You ask the impossible." The corners of his lips had definitely twitched into a smile. "I've tasted those sweet lips of yours, remember. You can't expect me to be satisfied with a mere peck like the one we shared last night—"

"Peck!" Pegeen laughed bitterly. "That *peck* nearly turned my lips black and blue."

"You should have seen my cheek after you clobbered me."

"Ha! You think that hurt? If you continue to maul me about the way you did in the Great Hall just now, I'll give you a lot worse than just a slap on the face."

Edward raised his eyebrows. "Dire threats from a wee lass."

"I may be small, but I know how to fight. Jeremy and I were on our own for a year, you know—"

"Oh, yes, I heard all about it." Edward looked down at her with amusement twinkling in his grey eyes. "You accused me of possessing dramatic flair, but I believe that honor belongs entirely to you, Pegeen."

"I told you to stop calling me—"

"Yes, and you also want me to stop 'mauling' you, as you put it, but if I'm not mistaken, Pegeen, there was a moment or two last night when you were enjoying yourself—"

"Why, I never—"

"Yes, yes, but virginal protestations aside, you can't tell me that you felt nothing when we kissed. You forget, I was there. I felt your heart drumming like a bird's beneath your breast."

"Of all the—"

"And I felt the passion in your lips, Pegeen. You can affect maidenly airs all you want." He guided her to the chair to the right of his at the long dinner table. "But we both know that there's an undeniable fire between us."

Sitting down, Pegeen reached blindly for her napkin and shook it furiously with crisp snapping sounds. She was oblivious to the people that milled about them, chattering gaily and glancing curiously now and again at the attractive, bickering couple at the head of the table. "I'll tell you what's undeniable," Pegeen hissed, leaning towards him so that her bosom, of which he'd already had more than an eyeful, swelled.

"Oh?" He had seated himself as well, and placed an elbow on the table to better hear her *sotto voce* communication. "And what's that?"

"Your self-centered, conceited, coldhearted, selfish ego." Pegeen leaned back and fluttered her eyelashes at him. "That's what." Then she turned to the man seated at her right, who happened to be the earl of Derby and smiled brilliantly at him. "My lord, you're not eating! Don't let your soup go cold on my account. Please start."

The evening wore on, and Pegeen, who'd always thought of herself as an open-minded person, began to realize some curious things about the gathered company. After having spent the day with all of the women present, Pegeen had thought them genteel ladies of quality. But did genteel ladies of quality flirt quite so openly with men who weren't their husbands? Did genteel ladies of quality wear quite so many flashy jewels, and so much rouge? Did genteel ladies of quality comment on how much a certain champagne that was being served cost, and how extravagant Lord Edward was being in serving so much foie gras? And did genteel ladies of quality cut one another off in order to make some witty observation to a gentleman?

Pegeen couldn't say that every woman present proved as cruelly vindictive as the viscountess. Certainly Lady Herbert and her daughters were polite, prepossessing individuals. But the dowager lady Seldon and her lewd connotations! And the earl of Derby's wife, thrusting her bosom at the marquis of Lynne's face, under her husband's nose, no less! And how could she forget the viscountess, who had apparently taken her new seating assignment with good grace, but now was laughing loudly at some joke of Sir Thomas Payton's, and remarking about how much Edward had spent on the claret.

And the questionable behavior wasn't reserved solely for the women in the party either. The earl of Derby, on Pegeen's right, started off the evening by leering at her gown and remarking to Edward that he was a lucky man, a very lucky man indeed, to have such a fetching sister-in-law. He'd then progressed to reciting limericks of such poor taste that Pegeen's ears began to burn. Across from her, the marquis of Lynne's eldest son was eating his peas with a knife, and his dining partner, Anne Herbert, didn't know where to put her horrified gaze. At one point, Pegeen met her eye, and the two girls exchanged sympathetic grimaces.

Pegeen supposed that after dinner, things would get better, but she was wrong. After the men withdrew to smoke in the billiard room, the viscountess clapped her hands and commanded the footmen to help her set up a stage in the Great Hall for charades. While a number of the women squealed delightedly, Lady Herbert at once declared that she had a headache, and, gathering her two daughters who were 'out,' she retired. Pegeen realized later that she ought to have taken Lady Herbert's early departure as a sign that she was not going to approve of the proceedings, but never having played charades before, she wanted to see how it was done.

The return of the gentlemen signalled the commencement of the game, and the party settled into chairs the footmen had dragged into the Great Hall for the occasion. The 'stage' was the area between the curves of the double staircase, and the viscountess and a mildly protesting Edward were the first to act out a tableau. Pegeen already knew that the scene had to do with a seraglio, so she wasn't shocked when Edward appeared on stage with a bared chest and a scimitar at his side. But when the viscountess pranced out from the dining room in a dress that was so transparent it might well have been made of gauze, and then proceeded to perform some sort of bizarre dance that harkened back to Salome, Pegeen had had enough.

Because she'd asked to be seated in the back and since she wasn't playing, Pegeen's departure was easy enough. She couldn't very well go up the double staircase to the second floor, not while the performance was underway, but she knew now how to duck through the kitchens to the servants' stairs. Her sudden appearance in the kitchen caused a minor sensation—Evers, Cook, and Mrs. Praehurst were having their dinner with the lesser staff waiting on them, and everyone jumped to their feet when Pegeen stepped into the room. She begged them to go about their business, stating that she just wanted to go upstairs and see to Jeremy and explaining that she couldn't use the main stairs.

Mrs. Praehurst looked at her a little too intently, Pegeen thought, as if she could tell that she was lying, but Pegeen hurried on her way without pausing to discuss it. She really did want to look in on Jeremy before retiring, and when she did, she found him already asleep, tired out by a hard day of playing. He was going to have an even harder day tomorrow: his first fox hunt. Pegeen didn't exactly approve of allowing children as young as Jeremy on a hunt, but while she'd been ill, Edward had promised the boy, and she couldn't very well make Edward break his word. Still, she worried that Jeremy might become upset when the hounds actually caught the fox. After all, it wasn't as if they let the creature go after finally running it nearly to death.

Lucy was waiting up for Pegeen in the Rose Room and looked surprised to see her mistress return so early. She said nothing about it, however, except to ask Pegeen how she'd enjoyed her dinner. Pegeen lied and said she'd liked it very much. After seeing that her mistress was dressed for bed, her long dark hair brushed to a sheen, Lucy withdrew, leaving Pegeen to gaze thoughtfully into the fire, mulling over her not very successful day.

She fumed over the fact that Edward had again seen her bare bosomed, an indignity she wouldn't have wished on her worse enemy. His own chest, she'd noticed, in the brief moment she'd stayed for the charade, was as muscular as it was wide, and covered with a delightful mat of thick, black hair. It was the kind of chest a girl could lay her head upon. It was the kind of chest that would warm one on a wintry November night. It was the kind of chest . . .

Shocked at her train of thought, Pegeen rolled over and resolutely refused to think of Edward any longer. Instead, she thought about how awfully much she'd like to ask all of his odious friends to leave. She pictured herself at the massive double doors to Rawlings, pointing imperiously out into the snow, and giving the earl of Derby a good swift kick in the pants on his way out.

Chapter Seventeen

The viscountess laughed throatily as she plucked off her earrings and threw them casually into a silk-lined box on her dressing table. "And where do you suppose your little charity case disappeared to, Edward?" she inquired, admiring her own reflection. "I don't even think she stayed long enough to admire your manly physique."

Edward, standing before the fire in the White Room, scowled and said nothing. He was dressed in his evening clothes again, and held a snifter of brandy in one hand. The game was over, the participants scattered to their various rooms, and he was feeling restless, even a little moody. Perhaps it was only the enormous quantity of spirits he'd consumed throughout the evening. More likely it was the prospect of getting up at the crack of dawn tomorrow morning to ride with the hounds.

Arabella removed her gloves and examined her perfectly manicured fingernails. "Do you know, Edward, I believe we shocked the little thing tonight."

Edward looked up from the flames upon her hearth. "What?"

"I've asked you before not to say 'what,' Edward. It's

so coarse.'' Arabella began removing the complicated head-dress she'd worn throughout the night, pin by pin. ''I was saying that I think we shocked your little vicar's daughter. I don't think she knew quite what to think of us.''

''What do you mean?'' She had Edward's full attention now.

''Well, she's quite obviously unused to sophisticated society. She'd never played charades before. She organized a ridiculous game of loo this afternoon. I hadn't played loo in ages, darling. Lady Seldon nearly died laughing at the very idea. But we played it, just the same. I can't wait to see what thrilling games she has planned for tomorrow. Of course that Herbert woman will approve. I can't think why you continuously invite Sir Arthur to all of your functions. They are so starchy, he and his oh-so-proper wife.''

Edward downed the contents of his brandy glass and looked around the room. It was the White Room, so called because all of the furnishings, including the walls and car-peting, were ivory colored. It was a strangely appropriate room for Arabella, as it actually managed to give her the appearance of having color.

What the White Room lacked, unfortunately, was a liquor cabinet. It was a long walk to his library, but Edward saw nothing for it. He needed another drink, and fast.

Arabella was brushing out her long blonde hair. It was thin hair, silky smooth, and he remembered a time when it had fascinated him, when she'd let it hang loose and it brushed against his bare chest. He wondered if she had purposefully unplaited it to tempt him. Knowing Arabella as he did, he knew the answer well.

''And her face, darling! Did you see her face whenever Derby spoke to her? It was like to put me in stitches, I was laughing so hard. I wouldn't be at all surprised if the little chit were to get a surprise midnight visitor this evening.''

''She'll have locked the door,'' Edward said with a shrug and then realized, when Arabella looked up from the stocking she was rolling down, that it had been the wrong thing to say.

"How do you know she keeps her door locked at night?" The viscountess' smile was wide, but it wasn't reflected in her pale eyes. "Have you tried the knob?"

Edward turned away, still holding the empty glass. Damn Evers for not providing brandy decanters in all the guest rooms. Edward would have to speak to his butler about it. "Of course not. Don't be ridiculous. But what else would you expect from a girl like that? She isn't stupid."

"No," the viscountess said, slowly. "She isn't stupid. But she is appealingly innocent, isn't she, Edward?"

Edward glanced back over his shoulder at her. Arabella was dressed only in a diaphanous peignoir of the palest blue, and with her hair all about her shoulders, she looked far younger than her forty years. Only a decade older than Edward, but ages and ages older than the girl they were discussing.

"I don't know what you mean," Edward said finally.

Arabella laughed musically. "Oh, don't lie to me, Edward. You know you were never any good at it. I saw you last night, you know. You and that girl. And I can't say that I blame you. I'm sure there's something delicious about debauching a virgin. Tell me, have you ever had one before, or will she be your first?"

Before he knew what he was about, Edward had thrown the empty brandy snifter against the wall, where it shattered into a thousand tiny shards of glass with a loud crash. Arabella, startled, stared up at him with eyes that had become so enormous, he could see the whites all around them.

"Edward, dear," she said through lips that had gone pale beneath the rouge she wore on them. "Did I strike a nerve?"

Without another word, Edward left the room, slamming the door quite forcefully behind him.

Chapter Eighteen

Pegeen woke feeling relieved, and at first could not remember why she felt so. Then she recalled that today was the Rawlings Manor fox hunt, and that Edward and his friends—including the viscountess—would be gone all day. This would give Pegeen an opportunity to do exactly as she liked, which was to spend the day with Lady Herbert and her daughters, none of whom were sportswomen with the possible exception of the youngest, though at five years old, Maggie was considered too young to ride with the hounds. Pegeen sought out Lady Herbert at once, and a pleasant scheme—a shopping trip to the village, a charitable visit to the Ladies Seminary, and then luncheon—was decided upon with alacrity.

After luncheon, a tour of the Rawlings Manor gardens was proposed, though the gardens, of course, were snow covered: nothing lived in the flower beds, and the trees were all leafless. Nevertheless, snug in their mittens and capes, the younger Herbert girls dashed about the hedge maze, laughing until they were as red-cheeked as their father had been the night before. Lady Herbert and her older daughters behaved with a little more decorum. As they walked briskly along a path that had been recommended by the gardener—"Lovely icicles this time o' year"—Anne Herbert asked how Pegeen was getting along in her new home. Pegeen answered her honestly, "I think I'd like it better if I didn't have to share it with Edward Rawlings."

Lady Herbert could not restrain a laugh at this bald statement. "Whatever do you mean, Miss MacDougal? I've never found Lord Edward to be anything but charming . . ."

"Oh, he's charming," Pegeen agreed, kicking at a chunk of ice that had fallen from a drainpipe. "Charming as a snake."

This piece of news pricked up the ears of all three Herbert women. "Has he made advances towards you?" Anne asked excitedly.

"Anne!" Her mother was shocked, but she looked expectantly at Pegeen for a reply, just the same.

"Well," Pegeen said, keeping her hands snug inside her fur muff. "Let's just say he has a rather curious attitude towards women."

"Not all women, Miss MacDougal," Lady Herbert said. "Only pretty women, like yourself."

"Oh, quite," Anne said. "He's never behaved the least inappropriately towards me."

Her sister, Elizabeth, chimed in, "Oh, Anne, you're not so plain."

"I am, though. Otherwise, why wouldn't Lord Edward have made advances towards me? I believe he's made advances towards every single attractive woman in the county—"

"Girls," Lady Herbert said severely. "Stop gossiping. You're going to give Miss MacDougal a bad impression of her brother-in-law." Looking down at Pegeen, Lady Herbert spoke with gentle care. "I have heard that Lord Edward is a bit of a man about town. But one can hardly blame him. He's good-looking and quite rich, and he has, as we've already mentioned, a charming way about him. I wouldn't go so far as to say that he's made advances towards *every* attractive woman in the county, but I will say this, Miss MacDougal: He's found a good many willing partners in his day, and though Sir Arthur and I have long hoped he'd settle down, I have never yet seen him serious about any woman.''

"He's been quite serious about the viscountess for a bit," Anne said.

"Anne!"

"Well, Miss MacDougal has eyes in her head, Mamma. I'm sure she's noticed.''

Pegeen grinned ruefully. "I've noticed.''

"But I must say," Anne went on, "I saw him looking at you, Miss MacDougal, all through dinner last night—''

"Anne!"

"Oh, Mamma, please. We're all adult women here. Why can't we talk about it? And I did wonder to myself what it could mean. If I were to hazard a guess—''

"Please don't, Anne," Lady Herbert warned.

"—I'd say he's fallen in love with *you*, Miss MacDougal.''

Pegeen shook her head and was thankful that the blush suffusing her cheeks would be mistaken for color brought out by the intense cold. "No, Miss Herbert. If Lord Edward seems interested in me, it's only because, unlike those women you were speaking about, Lady Herbert, I resist him. I doubt he's had many of those. Rejections, I mean.''

Lady Herbert nodded. "Yes, I'm certain rejection would be something quite novel to Lord Edward. How astute of you to see that. Many women would have been so flattered by his attentions, they'd—'' She broke off, noticing seventeen-year-old Elizabeth's fascinated gaze on her. "I mean, er . . .''

"Don't stop!" Elizabeth protested. "Oh, do tell me, Mamma. I'm old enough—''

"You're not," Anne said, then wisely changed the

subject. "How many guests are expected at the ball tonight, Miss MacDougal?"

"Oh, the ball." Pegeen had all but forgotten. "I don't know. I believe Mrs. Praehurst said something about fifty—"

"Fifty!" Elizabeth's wide blue eyes lit up. "How lovely!"

Pegeen smiled at the younger girl's enthusiasm. How wonderful it would be to be Elizabeth Herbert, Pegeen thought enviously. To have such a kind, sensible mother, and so many happy, good-tempered sisters. Of course there was the drawback of having Sir Arthur Herbert for a father, but that was easily tempered by the domestic tranquility that reigned over the Herbert estate. What Pegeen wouldn't give for a little of that kind of familial stability! She'd never experienced it in her life, having lost her mother when she was born. Her father had placated his sorrow at losing his beloved wife by throwing all of himself into his work, and there'd been little left for his daughters.

"We ought to be heading back," Lady Herbert said with a glance at the darkening sky. "They'll all be changing soon."

Pegeen didn't have to ask who 'they' were. Reluctantly, she headed back indoors, where Mrs. Praehurst met her with a few minor household problems that had arisen. Lady Herbert and her daughters retired to change for the ball, and Pegeen had ironed out nearly all of Mrs. Praehurst's difficulties when Evers announced with some indignation, "His Grace, the duke of Rawlings."

Jeremy, his face and clothes smeared with mud and what looked like blood, came hurtling into the Great Hall, screaming Pegeen's name.

"Good God," Pegeen cried as the little boy flung his arms around her legs and fell sobbing to his knees. "Jeremy, what's wrong? What has happened?"

Sinking down onto the first step of the curving double staircase, Pegeen gathered the hysterical boy into her arms, heedless of the blood and dirt that stained the dark wool of her day dress.

"Jerry, what is it? Are you hurt?" She tried unsuccessfully to lift his chin so that she could look into his face, but Jeremy clung even more tightly to her, his entire body racked with sobs.

Pegeen held onto him, gently rocking him in her arms and murmuring incoherently into his damp, dirty hair. She had never in all the time she'd known him seen Jeremy so upset, and the strength of his despair frightened her to the core. Hearing the familiar sound of Edward's boot heels ringing on the flagstones, Pegeen looked up, her face white with apprehension.

It wasn't just Edward who entered the Great Hall through the massive front doors. The entire hunting party was returning, all of them mud-spattered but none of them looking particularly out of spirits. In fact, the vast majority of them, including the viscountess, were laughing rather drunkenly. Pegeen, stroking Jeremy's hair, began to feel the spark of a deep, dangerous anger awaken within her. When Edward approached with an expression on his face that could only be called abashed, Pegeen looked up at him and demanded in an deadly quiet voice, "What happened to Jerry?"

Edward's gaze was on the dark-haired head on Pegeen's shoulder. For the first time since she'd met him, Pegeen saw that Edward was at a loss for words. Alistair Cartwright had shuffled up behind him, and a glance at his face told Pegeen he was as embarrassed at his host.

Pegeen glared up at them. "One of you tell me what happened to Jerry. Don't just stand there, gaping down at me like the great oafs that you are."

It was Alistair who spoke up first. "Well, Miss MacDougal, you see, I don't think Lord Edward was aware that His Grace had never been on a fox hunt before . . ."

Pegeen shot a sharp glance at Edward. "Oh, really?

And precisely when did you think Jeremy attended his first hunt? The day he was crowned King of Siam? For God's sake, he's a ten-year-old boy who grew up in a vicarage! Of course he's never been on a hunt before today.''

"I didn't know," Edward snapped. His face had lost the abashed expression and now he looked defensive. "I swear to you, I thought he knew—''

"Knew what?" Pegeen demanded. When neither man spoke, Pegeen snapped, "Would somebody please tell me what happened to Jeremy?"

Alistair started to speak, but Edward cut him off. "No," he said to his friend. "It's my fault. I accept full responsibility." He turned back to Pegeen and set his jaw. "Jeremy apparently didn't know that when the hounds catch the fox, they well . . . eat it."

Pegeen stared up at him, biting her lip to keep from bursting into giggles. Really, it was not a laughing matter. On the one hand, it was perfectly ridiculous of Jeremy to suppose that during a hunt the quarry is simply let go. On the other hand, the boy loved animals and probably had been genuinely horrified to see the fox he'd pursued devoured by hounds. Then she tightened her hold on him guiltily. She remembered sitting at Jeremy's bedside the night before, wondering if he'd known that very thing. And she hadn't said anything, because she'd assumed Jeremy had known. But how could Jeremy have known? Jeremy, who up until a few weeks ago had divided his time between bullying all the neighbor children and playing pirates with Pegeen, could have had no idea. All desire to giggle vanished, and Pegeen lowered her head until her forehead rested against Jeremy's. "Oh, Jerry," she sighed. "I'm so sorry."

Jeremy's sobbing formed into words. "They k-killed him," he stammered. "The dogs k-killed the fox, and Un-Uncle Edward just stood there and let them!"

Pegeen didn't look up. She whispered to Jeremy,

"But, darling, that's what dogs do. You know that."

"But Un-Uncle Edward let them! And it was a sweet brown fox with a sp-spotted tail. It l-looked like Pickles!"

Pegeen saw out of the corner of her eye that Edward had settled himself onto the stair beside them, sitting so close to Pegeen that she could feel the heat of his hip against hers. She was conscious of the odors of damp wool, horse, and very subtly, whiskey.

"Jerry, old chap," he began. "I'm sorry about all that mess back there. I didn't know you felt that way about foxes—"

Jeremy lifted his head from Pegeen's bosom and glared at his uncle with more malice in his eyes than Pegeen had ever seen. "You put its blood on me," he accused shrilly. "I told you not to, and you did it anyway!" Sobbing again, Jeremy once more buried his face between Pegeen's breasts.

Now she did look up, and she cast Edward a glance that was so scathing his jaw fell open. "You blooded him?" she demanded unbelievingly.

"It was his first hunt," Edward insisted. "We always blood boys on their first hunt."

"Excuse me. I thought I heard you say just a minute ago that you didn't think it was his first hunt."

There was no sensible reply Edward could make to that, and, knowing it, he lowered his gaze to the weeping boy in Pegeen's arms. She felt such all-consuming rage that she could hardly breathe, but her anger was directed at herself, not Edward. If she hadn't been spending all of her time thinking about the uncle, instead of looking after the nephew the way she ought to, none of this would ever have happened. Disgusted with Edward, his guests, but mostly with herself, Pegeen looked up, caught the eye of a nearby footman, and called to him.

"Could you help me, please?" she asked, nodding her

head to the boy in her lap. "I think I need to put him to bed, but I can't lift him."

Edward immediately reached out and tried to take the boy from her arms, but Pegeen cast him a withering glance and said in her most imperious voice, "No. Not you. You've done enough."

"I'm his uncle," Edward said, just as imperiously.

"Are you? Too bad you didn't remember that earlier." Pegeen felt Jeremy being lifted from her lap. She looked up and smiled politely at the footman who deftly slung the weeping boy over his shoulder.

Climbing to her feet, eschewing the hand Edward stretched out to help her, Pegeen looked for the housekeeper, who stood quite close by, wringing her hands worriedly. "Mrs. Praehurst, could you see that we get some hot water and a dinner plate in the night nursery?"

"Of course, miss," Mrs. Praehurst said, curtsying, her face pinched with concern. "I'm so sorry, miss."

"So am I." Without another word, Pegeen started up the stairs, not glancing back at anyone except the footman, who followed with alacrity.

Chapter Nineteen

Two hours later, Pegeen had bathed and fed Jeremy, and watched him fall tearfully to sleep. She'd left his bedside only when she was assured that he wouldn't awaken again, and then she went her room, feeling bone tired, even though it was only seven o'clock in the evening. All she wanted to do was have her bath and her dinner and go to bed.

But when she entered her room, she found Lucy busy spreading a pure white ball gown across her bed. The maid looked up upon hearing Pegeen's footsteps, and her face crumpled with relief. "Oh, miss! I thought you'd never be coming. I heard what 'appened with 'Is Grace. It's a right shame, that is."

"Yes," Pegeen said. Lucy gasped when she saw the blood and dirt on Pegeen's dress. She immediately dragged the offending garment from Pegeen's body, wrapping her in a ridiculous, feather-trimmed dressing gown, and sat her down in the pink armchair that sat in front of the fireplace. Pegeen gazed unseeingly into the flames as Lucy undid her hair and gave it another thorough brushing.

"Lord Edward's been by twice, miss," the girl informed her mistress, with excruciating nonchalance. "He wants to talk to ye. He told me to tell 'is valet as soon as you come in. You want me to tell'im you'll see'im?"

"No," Pegeen said shortly.

"Well, miss, I know you're probably feelin' peevish with 'is lordship right now, and I can't say as I blames you." Lucy brushed Pegeen's hair with unaccustomed savagery. "Seems as if every time he has folks up from London, there's trouble. I 'ardly got a wink of sleep last night meself, what with all the slamming doors and whatnot."

Pegeen craned her neck to look around the back of the chair. "What are you talking about, Lucy? What slamming doors?"

"Well, you know, miss." Lucy blushed prettily. "It seems as if nobody was spendin' the night where they were supposed to. Soon as the candles in the chandelier went out, everyone was runnin' to someone else's room. Mrs. Praehurst doesn't like it any, but 'o is she to tell'is lordship how 'is guests oughter behave? Sukie says 'er ma worked here, back when the duke was alive, an' it was even worse then. Men and women runnin' about at all hours of the night, dressed in nothin' but their skivvies, like as if the staff were blind—"

Pegeen shook her head. She had never considered herself a prude, but such casual adultery shocked her to the core. She'd had no idea such practices existed, except in the penny dreadfuls she'd sometimes perused when her father wasn't paying attention to what she happened to be reading. She didn't want to pass judgment on Edward's friends—God knew, she wasn't one to be casting stones—but the very idea of, say, Lady Seldon in bed with the earl of Derby made her feel a little sick.

"Beggin' your pardon, miss," Lucy interrupted her musings. "But there isn't much time for sittin' and gossipin'. The guests for the dinner dance arrive at eight. You'll 'ave to 'ave a lightnin' quick bath—" Lucy peered down at her mistress curiously. "Miss? You do want a bath, don't you?"

"Yes, I do. But I shan't be going down tonight." Pegeen lifted her slippered feet and rested them on the tapestry-covered stool in front of the armchair. "I'd like my dinner in here, and then I'm going to bed."

"Oh, Miss Pegeen!" Lucy's face was a caricature of shock. "But you *'ave* to go downstairs tonight . . . there's more'n fifty people coming for the ball!"

"I can't help that, Lucy," Pegeen said, evenly. "I didn't invite them. They aren't my guests."

"Oh, but, miss!" Lucy twisted her head to look at the gown on the bed. "I laid out your prettiest dress of all, the one with all the diamanté on the skirt. It'll be a burnin' shame if you don't wear it. I was goin' to put that diamond tiara in your hair, too—"

Pegeen couldn't help laughing at the younger girl's chagrin. "Lucy, I'm not going. I'm sorry. There'll be another time to wear the tiara, I'm sure. Now, please won't you see about getting me some dinner? Just some soup and bread, and maybe a little cheese. I don't think I could face anything in aspic jelly right now—"

A loud thumping on the door to the Rose Room interrupted her. Pegeen stared at the portal with suspiciously narrowed eyes. Lucy lowered the hairbrush and went to the door, opening it just enough so that she could look out, but the person on the other side could not see in.

"Yes?" she asked, and Pegeen saw the girl's shoulders straighten perceptibly as she realized to whom she was speaking. "Yes, m'lord?"

Edward's voice was softly persuasive. "May I speak to your mistress? I know she's in there—"

Lucy's head started shaking no before he'd got out the first word. "No, sir. Miss Pegeen is indisposed . . ."

"Then I'm just going to wait out here until she'll see me."

"Please, m'lord. Miss Pegeen's not feelin' well—"

"I don't imagine she is. I still want to speak to her—"

Sighing, Pegeen got up from her armchair, pulled her robe about her body and tied the satin sash securely around her narrow waist. Flicking her long, loose hair behind her back, she went to the door, seized the knob, and pulled it all the way open. Standing beside the taller Lucy, Pegeen looked up at Edward, who had changed into his evening clothes but didn't appear to be any less agitated than he had in the Great Hall a few hours earlier.

"Pegeen," he said, hurriedly. "I'd like a word with you."

Lucy drew breath to repeat her litany that her mistress was indisposed, but Pegeen stopped her by laying a gentle hand on the younger girl's shoulder, saying, "Lucy, why don't you run downstairs and see about a dinner tray?"

Lucy looked reluctant to leave her mistress alone with the clearly discomposed Lord Edward, but Pegeen's appealing glance sent her on her way. Edward stood awkwardly in the entranceway, his eyes looking everywhere but at Pegeen. She said, coolly, "Well, come in and say what you've come to say."

Edward stepped into the room, and Pegeen closed the door behind him. She went back to her comfortable chair before the fire. She felt oddly calm for the first time ever in Lord Edward's presence. She wondered what that meant. Was it possible that she didn't care for him as much as she had feared? She sincerely hoped so. Falling in love with Edward Rawlings would be the worst mistake she could ever make.

The chair in which she sat had a mate directly across from it, and Pegeen gestured to it, but Edward shook his head, his somewhat disheveled, ink black locks falling over one eye. He pushed the wayward strands from his face and set to pacing the room from the door to the casement windows and back again, several long strides each way.

"I don't mean to take up much of your time, Pegeen," he began, his eyes on the carpeting as he tread through the thick pink pile.

"Miss MacDougal," Pegeen corrected him. "If you don't mind."

Without glancing in her direction, he waved a dismissal of the name. He paced towards the windows and paused beside them, lifting a mauve curtain and peering out into the black wintry night. "I want to apologize for what happened today with Jeremy," Edward said, to the windowpane. "I take full responsibility."

"It's not all your fault." Pegeen couldn't disguise the weariness in her voice. "I should have been paying more attention to him."

Again, Edward waved at her dismissively. "Nonsense. It's entirely my fault. I had no idea he was so sensitive. I don't know much about ten year old boys—"

"Or anyone else, for that matter," Pegeen muttered, darkly.

"I beg your pardon?" He was looking at her finally, his eyes glowing in the firelight. "What did you say?"

Pegeen held out her hands to the warmth of the fire, and boldly returned his gaze. "I said, you don't know much about anyone else, either."

"What is that supposed to mean?" His tone was sharp.

"It means," Pegeen said, with a haughty toss of her waist-length hair, "that I think you're a sorry judge of character."

"Oh, do you?" Edward looked amused rather than annoyed. "And are you referring to the viscountess again?"

"Not just the viscountess," Pegeen said. She pushed herself up from the chair and faced him with her chin held high. "Do you have any idea how completely without scruples your so-called friends are? They are the most ill-bred people I have ever had the misfortune to meet. I am shocked, completely shocked, at the things that have been going here at Rawlings this weekend, and I don't consider myself a person who shocks easily.''

"Is that so?" Edward's mouth twitched sarcastically. "You've certainly spent most of our acquaintance in a state of indignation . . ."

"Because I certainly never expected to come to Rawlings Manor and be pawed about like a common serving wench!" Pegeen shouted the words, she was that angry. Suddenly, she lost all control of herself, and, with fists balled at her sides, she let Edward Rawlings have it, at the top of her lungs.

"Since my arrival here, the only people who've treated me with anything remotely resembling courtesy have been the servants!" Pegeen declared. "*You* seem to think I'm nothing but some kind of entertaining diversion, placed here solely for your carnal amusement."

Edward blinked slowly. He had quit pacing, and was standing stock still, looking down at her with incredulity written all over his face. Pegeen continued loudly, "Well, for your information, Edward Rawlings, I do not appreciate it! I think you're forgetting that I was raised in a rectory, and I do not take things like adultery very lightly. I cannot believe that you would allow that kind of thing to go on under your roof, particularly now that there's an impressionable child living here, who up until today worshipped the ground you walked upon."

Pegeen drew a deep breath and continued berating him before he could interrupt. "I thought when I came to Rawlings that I would be associating with people who knew better than to 'cut' someone they hardly know, or throw pieces of fruit down the front of a lady's gown, or tell bawdy stories in the presence of young women, or—"

Edward raised a hand, his expression far from furious. "Enough," he said, in a quiet voice. "You've made your point."

But Pegeen wasn't about to let him off that easily.

"You don't seem to understand that your guests' behavior reflects back upon you, and not very flatteringly, I might add. Lucy, my Lucy, was just telling me that she was up all night because of all the door slamming and bedroom hopping that was going on beneath your very nose—"

"Pegeen."

"Can't you see that with the exception of the Herberts, these people are using you? They comment on how much every dish you serve costs, they talk of nothing but the quality of the Rawlings china and the Rawlings sheets and the Rawlings horses. They don't even like *you*, Edward. They like the fact that you let them abuse your hospitality. Mrs. Praehurst told me that someone even broke into the champagne last night and stole three bottles, and that one of the earl of Derby's sons was caught trying to compromise the laundress—"

"Enough!" Edward had to shout to be heard above her tirade. Pegeen immediately shut her mouth, and stood with her fists still clenched at her sides, panting hard. She glared defiantly up at him, her green eyes bright anger.

"Well?" she demanded hotly, when he only stood and looked down at her, a strange expression on his face. "Haven't you anything to say for yourself?"

Edward, instead of shouting back at her as she'd expected, was grinning down at her with an expression on his handsome face that could only be called wistful. This was hardly the reaction Pegeen had expected, and she rubbed one bare foot with another nervously. She would have preferred a temper tantrum to this mysterious behavior.

"Do you know," Edward said in a quiet voice, "that I haven't been chastised quite so roundly in twenty years? And that the last time it happened, it happened right here in this very room?" He chuckled. "Though I must say, my mother never owned quite as fetching a dressing gown as the one you're wearing."

Pegeen looked down at herself. Good Lord! She'd completely forgotten she was wearing nothing but a peignoir, the one with the ridiculous feathered robe that Lucy had picked out for her! What on earth was she doing, entertaining a gentleman in her boudoir in her nightclothes? If Mrs. Praehurst found out, she'd be shocked to her very core!

"I apologize," Edward said, breaking in on Pegeen's self-remonstrances, "for any mistreatment you might have suffered here at Rawlings, Pegeen." Though his eyes in the shadows cast by the firelight were unreadable, Pegeen suspected from the deepness of his voice that he was sincere. "I know you've been insulted, both by myself and at least some of my guests, and I want you to know that it won't happen again."

Pegeen lifted an eyebrow skeptically but said nothing. She was surprised by Edward's complete capitulation, and a little suspicious of it as well. He hadn't denied any of her accusations—including the one she'd leveled at him about her being nothing but an entertaining diversion for him. Was that really all he thought her?

"Well?" Edward moved from the shadows, and Pegeen saw that his chiseled features had been twisted into the picture of contriteness. "Am I forgiven?" He looked so much like Jeremy when he was begging Pegeen's pardon for some malefaction that she had to laugh.

"Honestly," she said, shaking her head. "You Rawlings men. I don't know what to do with any of you."

"Does that mean you'll join me downstairs?" Edward took another quick step towards her. She wouldn't have exactly called his expression eager, but there was something there that hadn't been there before. Then again, perhaps he was just impatient for his dinner. . . .

Pegeen grudgingly agreed to attend both the dinner and the dance. "But," she said, raising an admonishing finger at him. "You keep those friends of yours away from me."

Edward laid a hand upon his heart and spoke with mocking earnestness. "I swear to you that I won't let anyone offend your honor this evening, my lady."

"Including you," Pegeen said, escorting him to the door.

"But of course." Pausing at the threshold, Edward seized one of her hands and planted a hearty kiss upon it. Before releasing her fingers, he looked down at Pegeen with unfathomable eyes and said, quietly, "Thank you."

Pegeen felt the warmth of his hand course up her arm. Her eyes dropped beneath the intensity of his gaze, and suddenly she realized she wasn't in control of the situation anymore. She uttered some inanity, hardly knowing what she said, and then he released her, and was gone.

Chapter Twenty

"What have you done to Edward?" Alistair Cartwright demanded later that night, when he was finally able to claim Pegeen for the waltz she'd promised him.

Smiling up at her outspoken dance partner, Pegeen gave an elegant shrug. "I haven't done anything to him," she insisted. "Why? Do you think he's acting strangely?"

"By God, *yes*." Alistair swung Pegeen expertly across the highly polished floor of the Great Hall, where dozens of couples were waltzing to the music from the eight piece orchestra in one corner. "Everyone's been asking me what's come over him. He's already sent Sir Thomas Payton packing for eating opium at the billiard table, and now I understand he's given the earl of Derby notice that if he doesn't keep his hands off the household staff, he'll have him barred from Claridges'. . . ."

Pegeen raised her eyebrows, impressed in spite of herself. "Can he really do that?"

"By faith, he can. With hunters like his, and the Prince of Wales so crazy about horseflesh? Edward can do just about anything he damned well pleases—" Alistair looked down at her guiltily. "I beg your pardon. I didn't mean to swear."

Pegeen laughed, feeling wonderfully light-headed from both the champagne she'd consumed with her supper and the momentum of the dance. "Swear all you want. I don't care."

"Don't you?" Alistair looked delighted. "By God, you *are* a jolly sort. Now, seriously, won't you tell me what you did to Edward?"

"I didn't do anything to him," Pegeen insisted. "Honestly, I don't know what you're talking about!"

"Liar," Alistair said. "Anyone with eyes as bright as yours is up to no good. Even a fool like me knows *that*."

Pegeen just shook her head with a chuckle. She knew her eyes were shining as brightly as the diamonds in the tiara she wore on top of her elaborate coiffure, but there wasn't anything she could do to control that. In her beautiful white ball gown, sparkling all over with diamanté, Pegeen knew that thanks to Mr. Worth she looked like a princess out of one of Jeremy's storybooks. She'd seen the raised eyebrows of the viscountess and her friends when Evers had announced her entrance, and she'd descended the double staircase with all the regality of a queen.

But if anyone had expected her to *act* like a queen, they were in for a surprise. Because she was determined to pay back every slight she'd received from the viscountess and her friends . . . only with kindness instead of bitterness. So when Edward met her at the bottom of the stairs, his grey eyes frankly admiring, she'd done just that. She smiled graciously at all of Edward's guests, taking special care to compliment Lady Arabella on her attire, even inquiring prettily where she had purchased her fan. The viscountess responded monosyllabically, white with anger, while Edward looked on, candidly entertained by the proceedings.

No one could have said that Pegeen acted anything but the most gracious of hostesses.

Being the highest-ranking gentleman in attendance, it was necessary that Lord Edward open the ball by dancing with the hostess. As Pegeen had pointed out often enough, his guests were his own, not hers, so she hardly ranked herself as hostess of the gathering and expected him to ask the viscountess for the first quadrille. Pegeen was swallowing a mouthful of meringue when suddenly he approached. Bowing low to her, he casually asked if she would care to dance. Pegeen was so shocked she very nearly choked.

Pegeen soon learned that she wasn't the only one surprised by this turn of events, though, with the exception of the Herberts and possibly Alistair Cartwright, she was the only one to whom the shock was pleasant. She noticed the viscountess darting from cluster to cluster of guests, whispering menacingly behind her fan and casting dark looks at Pegeen and her various dancing partners. Pegeen was far from concerned, however. She was enjoying herself too much to let Arabella Ashbury spoil her evening.

Turning her attention back to Mr. Cartwright, Pegeen realized he was again accusing her of having 'done something' to his friend.

"I beg your pardon," she said. "But I don't know what you can be talking about. Lord Edward and I are hardly even friends. We fight more often than not. Perhaps he's still smarting from some insult I inadvertently dropped."

"Oh, you think that's it, do you? Why one minute he's humming, and the next he's hopping mad?" Scrutinizing Pegeen's face, Alistair grew serious. "You honestly have no idea, do you?"

Since Pegeen didn't believe Edward's transformation was due to anything she might have said, she shook her head. Surely he was merely keeping his part of their recent bargain and that was all. Still, it was enough. Pegeen felt happier than she had since her arrival at Rawlings.

As Alistair whirled her around the dance floor, they passed Anne Herbert, who smiled at Pegeen as she was swept by. A devious but well-meaning plot formed in Pegeen's brain, and she said to Alistair, "You ought to ask Anne Herbert to dance next, you know."

Alistair looked confused. "Who?"

"Anne Herbert. Sir Arthur's eldest daughter. Such a sweet girl."

Alistair glanced in Anne's direction. "That girl, you mean? The plain one?"

"She isn't plain," Pegeen said, offended. "She's got a beauty that's too subtle to be spotted with a casual glance like that. You ought to ask her to dance next, you know."

Like a typical male, Alistair balked at being told what to do. "Why should I?"

"Well, because she was telling me earlier today how handsome she thinks you are," Pegeen lied easily. "And she thinks you're amusing."

Alistair all but preened. "Does she, now? Handsome, too?"

"Oh, very."

When their waltz ended, Alistair bowed to Pegeen, then made a beeline for Anne Herbert, who looked more than a little surprised to be asked to dance by such a distinguished gentleman. Such a thing had never occurred to her before in her life.

Without a partner for the first time all evening, Pegeen scanned the dance floor, her eyes seeking out one black coat in a sea of many. She found Edward instantly, dancing with a large woman she didn't recognize and looking rather miserable about it. Pegeen stifled a giggle. She knew that the ball was an extravagant waste of money, but, oh! She was having so much fun!

Feeling that the combs in her tiara were slipping, Pegeen stole the few minutes she had free from the demands of a partner and hurried upstairs to her bedroom so that Lucy could repair what all the waltzing had damaged. After she'd freshened up and exchanged pleasantries with her maid, Pegeen left the Rose Room, eager to return to the dance. But in the hallway, she heard unfamiliar voices. One of the bedrooms near Pegeen's had been turned into a ladies cloakroom for the evening, and a number of women had just left it, speaking in low voices amongst themselves. Seized by a sudden bout of shyness, Pegeen ducked into a doorway to avoid having to converse with these great ladies, something she wasn't feeling particularly up to after all the champagne she'd consumed.

"It can't be true," one of the ladies cried. "I simply refuse to believe it."

"Arabella insists," another woman said firmly.

"But where could she have heard such a thing?"

"She claims that Ashbury was there when it happened. In Venice."

"But if it's true, why doesn't Edward know it?"

"Perhaps he does."

"Then why ever does he allow the hussy's sister to come and live here?"

Pegeen felt her heart begin to hammer. They were talking about *her*!

"What can he do? Whether it's true or not, the boy is still the new duke of Rawlings. And they say the boy wouldn't come without his aunt."

"And you know the last thing Edward wants is to be saddled with a title—"

"But that Lord John was murdered by his wife's lover—really, it's simply too much to be believed! It's like something out of a novel."

"It's got to be true. Why would Ashbury make it up?"

The first woman snorted. "Arabella's jealous. Any fool can see the sister's caught Lord Edward's eye."

"She's not making it up," an older woman's voice declared. "I recall hearing something similar at the time of Lord John's death—"

"My *dears*! You know what this means, don't you? Why, that boy might not be a Rawlings at all!"

The women's voices faded as they moved out of Pegeen's hearing. In the shadowy doorway, Pegeen stood trembling, her shoulders sagging.

It couldn't be true. It couldn't be true. How could the viscountess have been so cruel? To tell everyone . . . *everyone*! Someone was sure to say something to Edward, and then what would happen? Oh, God!

Walking blindly down the gallery, her head ducked, Pegeen passed the double staircase and headed down the hall towards the servants' stairway. She needed to be alone for a while, somewhere where she could avoid rumors and speculative gazes. Instinctively, she headed for the conservatory, taking a roundabout route that passed through the kitchens, where everyone was too caught up in food preparation to notice her glide by.

In the relative darkness of the conservatory—the only light was that which spilled through the glass roof from the moon—Pegeen began to feel a little better. She paced the walkways between flower beds, inhaling the pungent odor of roses mingled with peat. It seemed strange, seeing such beautiful blossoms when outside snow lay all about. She could only just hear the orchestra in the Great Hall. Occasionally there was a tinkle of glass or a peal of laughter from a nearby hallway.

How far, how very far she'd come from her quiet life in Applesby! She'd gone from owning two dresses to more than twenty, from worrying where her next meal was coming from to fearing that she'd eaten too much. This was her first ball, her first evening 'out.' And what a fine job of it she was doing, hiding here with the lilies and ferns! But she couldn't go back in there, not with the viscountess spreading those rumors. Supposing someone mentioned it to Lord Edward? What was he going to say? What would he do?

A sound from nearby caused Pegeen to pause in her meandering and look up. There was a great shadowy form by the rhododendrons. Pegeen heard heavy, labored breathing. Good Lord, she thought, feeling gooseflesh rise on the backs of her arms. It's one of the ogres from those storybooks of Jeremy's. . . .

"Miss MacDougal!" It was an ogre who evidently knew her name, but Pegeen didn't recognize the voice. "How appropriate that I should stumble across you here with all of the other exotic flowers."

Pegeen squinted into the darkness. Her initial instinct was to run, but she was unwilling to show cowardice if she could help it. "Who is that?" she demanded. "Show yourself."

Obligingly, the ogre stepped into a patch of moonlight, and Pegeen found herself staring with some surprise at the earl of Derby.

"Oh," she said. "It's you."

The earl took another step forward and said, "Yes, it is I. Sorry to disturb you. Were you expecting someone else?"

Pegeen blinked. "No."

"I only ask because it seems odd, you being here, while all the dancing is going on in the next room." Something in the earl's manner struck Pegeen as strange. She could not for the life of her figure out what it was. "You're sure you weren't meeting anyone? A lover, perhaps?"

Pegeen felt her cheeks flame. "Of course not!" she cried.

"How fortuitous, then," the earl said, "that we should meet like this."

Pegeen stared up at the earl. He was a large man, not yet middle-aged, but his features had become florid from habitual dissipation. At one time, he'd been muscular. Now the muscle had gone to fat, leaving him with an extremely thick neck and a bit of a paunch. Looking at him, Pegeen thought of his eldest son, a twenty-year-old cuss who had already managed to insult most of Rawlings Manor's female staff. Like father, like son, Pegeen told herself, and took a wary step backwards.

"Quiet little thing, aren't you?" Lord Derby pressed closer. "I like that in a woman. Don't care much for yelping and giggling."

"Lord Derby," Pegeen said, still backing up. She was frightened now and not certain why. "I . . . I was just heading back to the dance. Perhaps you'd like to escort me?"

"What's the hurry? I like it in here. Nice and quiet." He slurred the words so that they came out sounding as if he'd said 'nishanquite.' Pegeen knew he had to be fairly well intoxicated to wander so far from the food and drink. She said to him, "Perhaps you'd like to stay here, then, while I go and get you another drink. Would you like that?"

The earl of Derby shook a thick finger at her. "You won't come back. I know women like you. Teasing! You're all of you always teasing!"

"But of course I'll come back," Pegeen lied sweetly. "I like it here in the quiet as well. Would you like champagne or wine, Lord Derby?"

"What I would like, my girl, is for you to stand still a minute." The Earl passed a thick-fingered hand over his eyes. "You're makin' me light-headed, flittin' about like that—"

Pegeen attempted to flit right past him, thinking that he might just be intoxicated enough to lack the reflexes to stop her. She thought wrongly. Quick as a cat, Lord Derby's arm shot out and captured her narrow waist in an iron grip. With surprising strength, he dragged her towards him until her face was nearly smothered by the soft folds of flesh beneath his black waistcoat.

"Lord Derby!" Pegeen cried out, more surprised at the suddenness of his attack than angry. "What—"

"I've had my eye on you, my girl," the earl declared loudly. "You remind me of someone, someone I met in London last year. You're a peg prettier, but you've got the same rosy cheeks—"

"Lord Derby!" Pegeen's cheeks were burning not with indignation but with shame. It was quite possible that he *had* met someone in London who reminded him of her—someone to whom the type of behavior he was currently displaying would be quite appropriate. If he suddenly happened to recall . . .

She pounded a furious fist against the earl's broad chest. "How dare you! Release me at once or I shall tell Lord Edward!"

Lord Derby laughed. "You think old Edward would blame me? Damned if he doesn't have the same thing on his mind!"

A cool voice sounded from the darkness. "That's quite enough, Derby. Release the girl."

The earl of Derby let go of her so quickly that Pegeen stumbled backwards and would have fallen if her arm hadn't been caught up in Lord Edward's firm grasp. He looked down at her, his eyes unreadable in the shadows, but his lips quirked into a smile that had little humor in it. The fingers that encircled the bare flesh of her arm were like ice.

In a controlled, even voice, Edward said to Lord Derby, "Well, old boy, you seem to have forgotten what I told you would happen if you laid a finger upon Miss MacDougal."

"But he didn't," Pegeen said quickly. The last thing she wanted was to cause further trouble between Edward and his friends. "Lay a finger upon me, I mean."

"Didn't he?"

Pegeen shook her head quickly. She had never seen an expression on anyone's face like the one Edward wore. It quite frightened her.

"He's fortunate, then," Edward said. His cold gaze never once left the slightly swaying figure of Lord Derby. "Because if he had, I'd have no choice but to call him out. Right, old boy?"

"I s'pose," the Earl hiccupped, not looking very concerned. "Leastways, if you say so, Rawlings."

After delivering a final warning glance in the earl's direction, Edward slipped his fingers from Pegeen's arm to her waist, steering her from the conservatory into the dim hallway that led back to the Great Hall.

"What," he demanded almost at once, "were you doing in there alone? Haven't you the sense God gave a goat? Why didn't you tell me where you were going? I've been looking high and low for you."

All of Pegeen's fear disappeared in a burst of indignation. "I didn't know I had to ask your permission to leave a room!"

"You don't have to ask my permission," Edward said with infuriating reasonableness. "But you might have let me know you were leaving the ball. Pegeen, this isn't exactly the Applesby Harvest Festival. These men are . . . used to getting their way. It isn't wise for a young woman to wander about without an escort while these gentlemen are in their cups."

Pegeen glared at him. "Gentlemen! That's using the term loosely!" Then, seeing that he was walking her towards the Great Hall, she suddenly balked. "Oh, no!"

Edward looked down at her, bemused. "What? You're not ready to go back?"

"I . . ." Pegeen looked up at him desperately. She liked the feel of his arm around her waist, the warmth of his partial embrace. In fact, she was afraid she liked it a little too much. It wouldn't do for her to start getting used to Edward's attentions. The minute he heard the rumors that were circulating, they'd stop. And what about what Lord Derby had said, about her reminding him of someone? Supposing when he sobered up he remembered who it was she resembled? Pegeen made a small nervous gesture to be free, and Edward instantly released her, as if she were an iron that had grown too hot to handle.

"I really ought not to go back," Pegeen stammered. "I think I'm ready to retire for the evening—"

"Ah," Edward said knowingly. "Had a little too much champagne?"

"Y-yes," Pegeen whispered. "That's it. If you'll excuse me—"

"No." Edward took hold of her elbow. "I'll escort you to your room." When Pegeen started to protest, he held up a hand. "Now, now. Remember Lord Derby. We wouldn't want you to run into another one of my drunken companions in the corridor. I insist."

Pegeen had no choice but to allow him to guide her to her own room. They took the back stairs and encountered no one. It wasn't until they were just outside the door to the Rose Room that Edward asked curiously, "May I inquire what prompted that visit to the conservatory?"

She looked up at him. His profile was all she could see of him in the dim light and that looked a little forbidding. She sighed and unaccountably her eyes filled with tears.

"Here, here," Edward said suddenly. He slipped his fingers beneath her chin and brought her face towards his. "Are those tears I see?"

Pegeen blinked, ashamed of her own weakness. "No," she said, in a voice choked with sobs. "I just . . . have something in my eye."

"I don't believe it." Edward extracted a white linen handkerchief from his waistcoat pocket and dabbed one end of it at the corners of her glistening eyes. "Pegeen, what is it? Can't you tell me?"

Moved by the warmth in his voice, Pegeen looked down. "I daren't," she whispered.

"Tell me. I chased away the dreadful vicar, didn't I? And the loathsome Lord Derby. Perhaps I can chase away this as well."

"You can't," Pegeen said, and all at once the tears came, a veritable flood of them.

Edward was as startled as if it had suddenly started to rain indoors. He swore softly, then, glancing up and down the hallway, reached for her bedroom door. "In here," he said commandingly. "We're having this out, you and I. Right now."

Pegeen was far too upset to protest. For the life of her, she could not stop crying. Without thought, she headed straight for her bed, flinging herself upon it to sob into the softness of her pillows. She didn't give a thought to what Edward might be doing while she cried. Lucy had apparently gone downstairs for her supper, leaving the room dark except for the glow of the dying fire on the hearth. Pegeen heard Edward lock the door behind him to ensure they would not be disturbed.

If Edward thought her behavior unusual, he didn't say anything. When she finally regained control of herself and lifted her head from her now thoroughly damp pillow, she saw him standing a foot or two away from the bed. He was staring down at her with an inscrutable expression on his face, his arms crossed over his chest.

"Now," he said. "Would you mind telling me what this is all about?"

Pegeen gulped. There was no sense avoiding it anymore. He'd hear it from someone eventually. Taking a deep, shuddering breath, Pegeen said, "I . . . I overheard some ladies gossiping."

"Did you?" Edward's tone was only distantly interested. "Ladies have a tendency to do that. What, precisely, were they saying?"

She couldn't help letting out a last little sob. "That . . . that your brother John died in a duel over my sister Katherine."

She glanced up at him swiftly to see how he bore the news. His jaw tightened a bit. "I see," he said carefully. His tone was impassive. "And where would these ladies have heard a tale like that, I wonder?"

"I-I don't know," she lied. She didn't dare tell him that the viscountess had been the one spreading that rumor. He'd only accuse her of jealousy again. . . .

Edward uncrossed his arms and approached the bed. Pegeen, starting to tremble a little under the directness of his gaze, refused to be intimidated. She held her chin high, staring defiantly right back up at him, though she knew he had the advantage, since he was standing and she was sprawled on her back on her bed, her skirts ballooned around her.

"Is it true?" was all he asked.

Pegeen glanced down once, then rallied her courage and looked him in the eye. "Yes," she said.

He stared down at her, the muscles in his jaw twitching as he wrestled with some inner emotion. When he had finally mastered control of himself, he demanded, his voice rough, "How do you know?"

"She told me so."

"But your sister died just months after John, in Italy. . . ." Seeing that she was shaking her head, Edward's voice trailed off. "What . . . what are you saying? That she . . . your sister isn't dead?"

"Yes," Pegeen replied, struggling to keep her own voice from shaking.

"Why? Why the pretense?" The words were swift, enunciated as if each one had been wrung out from his gut.

"It's better." Pegeen sat up, holding out both of her

gloved hands in a gesture of helplessness. "It's better that people think she's dead. Believe me."

"Why?" Edward could no longer restrain himself. He reached out and seized her bare shoulders with hard hands. "Why should you go about pretending your sister is dead when she isn't?"

"Because she *is* dead" Pegeen insisted. "Katherine MacDougal *is* dead, don't you see?"

Edward's grip tightened on her shoulders, and he stooped to look more closely into her face until his mouth was just inches from hers. "Where is she?" Edward gave her shoulders a shake with each syllable. "Where . . . is . . . Katherine . . . Rawlings?"

Pegeen shook her head so violently that the tiara slipped and fell to rest rakishly over one eye. "I can't tell you! Please, don't make me tell you. It's better this way. Please, Edward. Don't make me tell you."

Edward, seeing the tears that were spilling from beneath her long eyelashes and the way her mouth was trembling, abruptly let go of her shoulders. With a groan that seemed to be of frustration mingled with rage, he all but threw himself against a far wall, where he leaned silently, his forehead resting against a clenched fist.

Pegeen, her thoughts jumbled and confused, rolled over onto her stomach and buried her face in her arms. Why, oh, why had she told him? She had meant to keep it all a secret, the deepest, darkest secret she'd ever held. And with one question, he had managed to get her to reveal more than she'd ever told anyone, ever.

Well, she could comfort herself that he didn't know the worst of it, and, God willing, he never would.

But what would happen now? She'd been a fool from the very beginning, thinking she could come to this place and live in peace with this man. From the very first moment she'd laid eyes on him, she'd known he was trouble. Not just for her, but for the world she'd built up so carefully from lies, lies of every conceivable kind.

Lifting her head, Pegeen saw that Edward was standing quite still, his face turned toward the wall, his broad shoulders stiff with tension. Pegeen glanced uncertainly towards the door he'd locked. Downstairs the orchestra had broken into yet another waltz. Down that hallway was another world, a world of gently bred, albeit unscrupulous, ladies and gentlemen, a world to which Pegeen didn't belong. She'd never wanted to belong to it. Especially not now.

She realized now that she'd been a fool to ever think the charade would work. Perhaps it was better to admit defeat and return to the world she knew, the world of scrimping for coal and preparing food baskets for people who were no poorer than herself. . . .

Shoulders sagging, Pegeen sat up. She would ask Lord Edward to go, and then she'd ring for Lucy to help her pack her trunk. She could order the carriage for first thing in the morning, before anyone else was awake, and slip out unnoticed. She wouldn't say good-bye to Jeremy. She couldn't bear that. But she'd leave him a note. Yes, a note. She wouldn't blame Edward. It wasn't his fault, after all. She'd simply say she'd been so homesick for Applesby, she'd had to go back. Yes, that was it. Jeremy would be hurt, but he'd get over it. He had his uncle Edward now, after all.

And even if they tried, they wouldn't be able to find her. Because she wouldn't go back to Applesby. She'd go to London and find work as a nurse, or a governess, or even a midwife. It would be difficult, but Pegeen had faced difficulties before. She'd be all right.

"Where are you going?" Edward's words lashed out at her from the shadows in which he'd been leaning. She'd barely risen from the bed before his menacing growl stopped her in her tracks.

Not looking back at him, Pegeen said to her slippers, "To ring for Lucy."

"Why?" His voice was harsh, accusatory.

"I'm going."

"Going? Going to bed?"

Pegeen turned towards him. She couldn't see him very well in the dimly lit bedroom, but her heart began hammering just as furiously as it did when he stood just inches from her.

"I'm going, all right?" She managed to sound imperious, in spite of her shaking voice. "I'll be gone in the morning. You'll have to lend me the use of your carriage for a day."

Edward was out of the shadows in a single step. He stared down at her, frowning. "What are you talking about?"

"I'm going. Before you throw me out. It was a stupid plan, a childish plan, me thinking that I could hide the fact that Katherine isn't dead from you. It's one thing to hide it from Jeremy. But to do it to you. . . . Well, I'm sorry." Pegeen stared down at Edward's shoes, though her vision was still blinded with tears. "I don't know what else to say except . . . good-bye."

She glanced up through her eyelashes briefly and found her eyes locked on his by the sheer intensity of his gaze. He was frowning even harder now, two deep grooves on either side of his wide, sensuous mouth.

"It's good-bye, is it? And where will you be going in my carriage, may I ask?" His voice held a mocking note in it that caused Pegeen to tilt her chin up at him defiantly.

"Back to Scotland."

"The devil you will!"

Pegeen was taken aback by the intensity of Edward's objection. He reached out and took her by both shoulders again.

"You aren't going anywhere in my carriage tomorrow

morning, do you understand? And if you try to, I'll find out where you've gone and I'll fetch you back myself, even if I have to sling you over my shoulder and carry you home to Rawlings every step of the way. Do I make myself clear, Pegeen?''

Alarmed, Pegeen nodded mutely. But Edward wasn't finished. His fingers digging into the bare flesh of her shoulders, he cried savagely, ''How dare you? How dare you threaten to leave, you heartless little scamp? My God, do you think I *care* what your sister did to my brother, or what my brother did to your sister? You're all I've been able to think about for days and days. From the moment I saw you on that doorstep in Applesby, I've wanted you. And I'll be damned if I'm going to play your ridiculous games anymore. . . .''

Lowering his head until his mouth collided with hers, Edward pulled her roughly against him. Pegeen put out both her hands to ward off the onslaught of his lips and tongue and encountered only starched shirtfront and the hard muscle beneath it. Edward slid both his arms around her slim waist and bent her body backwards against the bed pillows with his sheer weight. Never once did his mouth leave hers. The heat from his thighs singed her legs, the razor stubble on his chin grazed the softness of her face, and all she could think of were his words: He wants me to stay, she thought, dizzy with happiness. He wants me!

Then his hands were sliding over her body, dexterously moving over the fastenings to her ball gown, the ties to her crinoline. His fingers brushed the taut peaks of her round breasts as he plucked at her corset strings. Everywhere he touched her burned with the sensation, every inch of her seemed to spring to life at his fingertips. And though she knew that what they were doing was wrong, and that later she would regret it, she could not bring herself to utter the words that would stop him. Her lips had parted beneath his, and his tongue was probing the inside of her mouth with feverish intensity, while his rough hands pulled at the muslin of her chemise, as if even this thin boundary between them was too much.

A rending sound nearly startled her from her ardor, and Pegeen realized Edward had torn her undergarments asunder. His hot mouth moved from her lips down the smoothness of her throat to the rosy nipple of one breast, the other straining beneath his questing fingers. She gasped as his tongue teased the pink bud it found there, her fingers tangling in his ink black curls. She couldn't think, she couldn't breathe, she couldn't do anything but writhe with pleasure. When Pegeen felt Edward's fingers slide down her flat stomach to find the moistness between her legs, she could only gasp, arching her body against him. Never had anything felt so right.

Cupping her bare buttocks, Edward pulled her to her knees upon the mattress, holding her so tightly against him that his chest hair grazed her sensitive nipples. He, too, had risen to his knees, and now he struggled to remove his shirt without taking his hands from her. He seemed to be endlessly whispering her name, "Pegeen, Pegeen," into the curve of her neck, his hot breath sending chills up and down her spine. Pegeen spread her fingers against the hard muscles of his thickly haired chest, inhaling the earthy fragrance of him, feeling the stiff urgency of his need against her hip. In the firelight, his skin was dark as a pirate's against her almost translucently pale body.

"Pegeen," he said again, and she felt him guide her hand to the buttons of his trousers.

With no more modesty than Myra MacFearley might have exercised, Pegeen pried at his breeches, and when his erect manhood sprang free from the constraining material, she encircled it with her fingers, causing Edward to groan against her lips. Marveling at the size of the organ in her hand, Pegeen gasped as Edward's fingers again moved between her legs. This time, he laid the heel of his hand flat against her pubic bone as he inserted first one, and then another finger inside of her. Pegeen arched against the pressure of his hand, the sensations the friction created within her causing her to mewl with pleasure.

Edward could take no more. Pushing her back against the mattress, he lowered himself between her silken thighs. When the tip of his penis prodded her, Pegeen instinctively arched her back, bringing herself more fully against him, and he entered her with a groan.

Once inside her, Edward found himself enclosed in the tightest sheath he had ever encountered. Pegeen's maidenhead was merely a barrier to his complete fulfillment, and without conscious thought, he quickly eliminated that barrier. Pegeen's cry of pain reminded him of what he'd done, and Edward, instantly ashamed, cupped her thrashing head in his hands, whispering meaningless words of comfort.

But as quickly as the pain had come, it left her, and in its place was a mounting urgency that Pegeen reacted to by pressing herself more fully against him. Edward, realizing her pain was gone, started to move away, but Pegeen snatched at his shoulders, her green eyes wide.

"Don't go," she said, softly, pleadingly.

Edward smiled. Never in his life had he bedded a more charming partner. "I'm not going anywhere, love," he said, and when he thrust deeply inside her, Pegeen, instinctively raising her hips to meet him, understood.

And then Edward could control himself no longer. His arms trembled with the effort he'd made to go slowly with her, and now he drove himself deeper and deeper into her tight warmth, pounding her body back into the mattress. Pegeen clung to his broad shoulders, her long dark hair fanned out on the pillows beneath them. Suddenly, her back arched off the bed as she climaxed, shuddering with ecstasy from her scalp to the arches of her feet. Edward followed a second later, heaving himself so deeply into her that she thought he'd break her in half. Instead, he collapsed on top of her, and the two of them lay in the semi-darkness, breathing heavily, their bodies slick with perspiration.

It seemed like hours later, but perhaps only minutes passed, before a timid knock sounded on the bedroom door, and Pegeen heard Lucy call, ''Miss Pegeen? Are you in there? Why is the door locked?''

Chapter Twenty-One

"I don't believe it." The viscountess of Ashbury put down her tea cup with a little crash. It was sheer luck that she didn't spill any on her lavender morning dress. "You've *never* spent the holidays in London. There is still at least six weeks of good hunting left!"

Edward, his own cup of coffee quite steady in his hand, shrugged elaborately. "A man has the right to change his habits, Arabella," he said mildly, but he was aware of the startled looks that were passed across the dining table at his words.

"I say, old chap." The earl of Derby was looking the worse for wear after his midnight prowl through the conservatory. He had dark circles under his eyes in spite of the fact he'd slept 'til noon. "This—this sudden decision of yours wouldn't have anything to do with our, ahem, conversation last night, would it?"

Edward blinked at the older man, affecting light-hearted disconcern. Secretly, of course, he wanted to bash Lord Derby in the head with an epergne.

"I should say not, Derby. No, I think outdoor sports have simply lost their flavor for me early this year. I'll be off to London this evening, and those of you game to come with me are welcome. The rest of you'd better clear out. Things'll be deadly dull around here, I can tell you.''

The viscountess gave a disparaging snort. ''I never heard anything so ridiculous,'' she said into her ruffled fichu. ''No one goes up to London so early. The season doesn't start 'til February.''

''Oh, I don't know, Arabella,'' Alistair Cartwright chimed in, casually leaning back in his chair. ''Just think: London, without the crowds. We'll have the theaters and restaurants to ourselves for a change. I rather like the idea.''

Arabella glared at him. What was the point, her look plainly stated, of having the theaters and restaurants to oneself? There wasn't anyone to admire one's new gowns, new hairstyles, new lovers. . . .

Edward, however, shot his old friend a glance full of gratitude. It hadn't been easy coming up with an excuse to rid himself of his unwanted houseguests, and the scheme to go up to London had occurred to him in the wee hours of the morning, after hours of berating himself over his own weakness. He'd promised the girl that he'd spare her from further insults from his friends, and since his friends didn't know any better, he had to send them packing. But they wouldn't leave without dire provocation, and short of setting the house on fire, Edward couldn't think of any other way to get them to go than to go himself.

The viscountess wasn't the only one who looked upon Edward's sudden announcement with suspicion. Though outwardly he supported his host's plan, Alistair knew something was afoot. After lunch, when everyone else had gone upstairs to bid their maids and valets to start packing, he caught up with the duke's son in the servants' gallery, where Edward had gone to inform Mrs. Praehurst of his plans.

''It isn't like you, old bean,'' Alistair exclaimed, keeping stride with his taller host. ''You hate London this time of year. In fact, I always suspected that you rather hate London all times of year.''

Edward kept his face turned resolutely forward, fearing if he looked at his friend, he'd give away something he was trying to keep to himself. "I don't know what you're blathering about, Cartwright. I'm a man of independent means and can go up to London whenever I so desire—"

"No one's disputing your right, man. What they want to know is your reason—"

"Why do I have to supply reason for my actions?" Edward's long strides had taken them up the back stairway and towards his private chambers. Despite his protest over having to make excuses for his actions, Edward reluctantly provided one. "I want to rid my home of these parasitic complainers, and this is the only way I could think of to do it, all right?"

"Rid your home . . . ?" Alistair followed Edward into his private study and sank onto a leather couch. "Does this have something to do with what happened yesterday, with the boy?"

"Boy? What boy?"

"Your nephew."

Edward had gone to the door of his bedchamber and called to his valet to start packing. Then he went to the mantel and found a cigar that he immediately began to smoke energetically. "It doesn't have anything to do with the boy," Edward growled, the cigar clamped between his teeth.

Alistair, who was well-enough acquainted with Edward to know that he only smoked under duress, clasped his hands behind his head and leaned back against the sofa cushions meditatively. "The girl, then."

Edward coughed, plucked the cigar from his teeth, and said, "Don't be an ass."

Alistair grinned at the ceiling. "I knew it. You're in love with her."

"Go to hell," Edward advised. A knock sounded on the door through which he'd barked to his valet. Edward threw it open and glared furiously at his manservant. "Well? What is it?"

"Excuse me, sir." Daniels appeared unimpressed by his master's ferocity. "But am I to understand that you wish me to pack for *London*?"

"That's what I said, wasn't it?" Edward jammed the cigar back into his mouth and began to pace the room in long, loose-limbed strides. "Which part didn't you understand?"

Daniels blinked impassively. "But, sir . . . London? In *November*? The hunting season's barely begun—"

"Not you too, Daniels," Edward roared. He turned his back on the valet and appealed to the ceiling. "My God, can't a man go to London whenever he takes a fancy to do so?"

"Certainly, sir," Daniels said, unruffled by all the yelling. "Might I ask how long we'll be staying there?"

"I don't know." Edward glared into the fire. "Better bring a month's worth of shirts at least."

"Very good, sir." Daniels left the room cloaked in an air of disapproval. Edward noticed it and swore.

"Can't a man give an order without being questioned by his own servants?" he demanded, and though he did not seem to require an answer, Alistair provided one.

"Of course he can. If he seems to be in his right mind. But you, Rawlings, seem to have become bedeviled overnight. Might we return to the possible source of this fever? I was wondering if you'd finally admitted to yourself that you've got feelings for that girl."

Edward let out another curse, this one much more profane than any of the others, and hurled his cigar into the flames in the fireplace. "Would you leave the girl out of it, Cartwright? It doesn't have anything to do with her.''

"Doesn't it?'' Unaffected by his host's violent display of temper, Alistair rose and went to the liquor cabinet for a drop of whiskey. "You heard what everyone was whispering about last night, didn't you? About how John died for her sister, et cetera.''

"I heard.'' Edward dropped into his leather armchair and propped his feet up on the hearth. "And *she* heard as well.''

"Ah.'' Alistair passed a glass to Edward, who downed its contents in a swift gulp and passed it back. Alistair refilled it, handed it back to Edward, then poured himself a shot and returned to his couch. "Would that, then, be the explanation for today's sudden departure for London?''

Edward glared into the fire. His face was dark with anger, his jaw muscles twitching beneath his lean cheeks. "No,'' he said succinctly.

Alistair shook his head. "I quite like her, Edward. You aren't going to cast her out, are you, old boy?''

"Don't be an ass.''

"Well, what *are* you going to do with her?''

"What do you mean, what am I going to do with her?'' Edward took his feet from the hearth and stood up. He took two long strides towards the window and pulled the curtain aside to peer down to the drive below. "I'm not going to do anything with her.''

Not after the verbal lashing she'd delivered shortly after their lovemaking had ended. Edward, slowly coming to his senses, had lifted his face from her breasts and suggested—merely *suggested*, mind you—that they might be wise to marry, as it appeared they couldn't keep their hands off one another.

Not that he wanted a wife. But since she nagged him like one already, and they bickered like a couple long married, it seemed to him it ought not to make any difference.

But he had forgotten Pegeen's resolution never to marry.

Not to worry. She'd reminded him, roundly.

"You give me entirely too much credit." Edward's laugh had no humor in it. "It's nothing to do with Pegeen. London's dismal this time of year, but I can't think of any other way to rid myself of these pathetic hangers-on—"

Alistair laughed. "Good Lord, Eddie! And I always thought you were genuinely fond of them!"

"They're Arabella's friends, you know that. I can't have them here, sniffing around, gossiping—" Edward went back to window and peered out again. "Ah, good," he said. "The marquis' carriage is coming round. I ought to go down and bid him good riddance."

"Before you go, Eddie—" Noticing the grimace on his friend's face as he turned from the window, Alistair raised his glass and said, "My apologies. I mean, Edward. Listen, about Pegeen, as you call her—" Alistair looked down at his empty glass. Edward was amazed to see his outspoken friend hesitate, and even more amazed at his words when he finally did speak. "About Pegeen, Edward. You wouldn't mind, would you, if I were to, uh, call upon her occasionally?"

"*What*?" The word slipped out before Edward could clamp his lips shut, and he was humiliated even further by the fact that his voice cracked, as it hadn't done since adolescence. "Are you serious?"

Alistair turned from hesitant to indignant in seconds. "Why? You don't think she'd have me?"

"Think she'd . . . think . . ." Edward couldn't believe what he was hearing. Had the entire world as he'd known it gone mad? What was Cartwright thinking? Had he taken leave of his senses?

"Oh, I know, I know," Alistair said, setting down his empty glass and holding up both hands as if to ward off blows Edward hadn't the slightest intention of delivering.

"I know, I'm too old for her. But what's ten years?"

"Try fifteen," Edward growled.

"All right, fifteen, maybe. But I do think she likes me, Rawlings. I make her laugh. So if you haven't any objection—"

"I have very strong objections," Edward ground out. "You make her laugh." He repeated the words mockingly. "What kind of basis is that for a relationship?"

Alistair looked taken aback. "A damned good one, if you ask me. You'll notice she hasn't slapped *me* yet."

"Oh, thank you very much, Mr. Cartwright. I invite you to my home, supply you with my best liquor, my best horses, and you turn around and ask whether you can court my—"

"Your what?" Alistair's lips twitched. He couldn't disguise his grin. "What *is* she to you, Edward?"

"She is my sister-in-law," Edward said, fully aware that he was grasping at straws but unable to help himself. "As long as she's under my roof, she's under my protection, and under no circumstances will I allow her to be courted by a ne'er-do-well like you, Cartwright."

Alistair, generally the easiest of companions, looked annoyed. "For pity's sake, Rawlings. I only asked your permission out of politeness. You can't stop me from seeing her, if she'll have me. What's wrong with you, anyway?"

"What's wrong with *you*?" Edward shot back. "You have the entire female population of London to choose from. Why do you have to court my sister-in-law?"

"Because I'm taken with her. You know I am. I told you from the start—"

"A passing fancy, like all the others." Edward waved a dismissive hand. "You'll get over it once we're in London. Now stop with this foolishness, Cartwright. I've got to bid adieu to my guests."

Edward was usually able to cajole his malleable friend out of any mood, but this time, Alistair wouldn't give up.

As Edward attempted to leave the room, Alistair barred with the door with a muscular arm. Edward looked down at him in amazement—and irritation.

"Cartwright, have you a death wish? Because I'll happily break off that arm if you don't remove it from my path."

"You want her for yourself, don't you?" The gentle hazel eyes were narrowed with suspicion. "That's it, isn't it? You want her, and you're trying to get rid of me with all this business about London!"

Edward sighed. It was going to be long day. "All right, Cartwright. Yes, I want her. I'm going to keep her here as my concubine, chained by the ankle to my bedpost." Seeing that the younger man saw no humor in this, Edward sighed again. "All right, Alistair. If you feel that strongly about it, you have my permission to court her. *If* she'll have you, which I know she won't, since the girl has some idiotic idea that marriage is an institution responsible for the subjugation of women throughout history. Now, will you start packing? I want to be off before dark."

Alistair, looking smug, removed his arm from the doorway. "Thank you, Edward," he said, smiling. "That's very generous of you."

Edward growled in response. He left the room and went downstairs to see that his guests departed without acrimony. It wasn't until Alistair reminded him, as he was pressing the marchioness of Lynne's gloved hand to his lips, that perhaps he ought to inform Pegeen that he was leaving, that Edward realized he'd have to see her one last time. Surely it wouldn't do for Mrs. Praehurst to mention something to Pegeen before he'd had a chance to explain.

The last person Edward wanted to see was Pegeen. But there was no avoiding it with Alistair standing there looking at him expectantly. Bowing reluctantly to the dowager lady Seldon and murmuring something about having an urgent business matter to attend to, Edward hurried back upstairs.

He found Pegeen, just as her maid had assured him that he would, with Jeremy in the day nursery. When no one responded to his knock, he opened the door and saw the two of them on the windowseat, watching the activity on the drive below with great intensity. Jeremy was saying in an assured voice, "That curricle the earl's son is driving just isn't the thing for the rough roads here in Yorkshire."

Pegeen, sounding amused, inquired, "And who told you that?"

"Bates, the coachman. He's in favor of the barouche. It's old-fashioned but holds up well in this part of the country."

Pegeen laughed at the boy's pompous tone. Edward was struck by the throaty richness of Pegeen's laughter in contrast with Arabella's high-pitched, tinkling titter. He cleared his throat.

Both figures at the window turned. Jeremy let out a little cry of delight at seeing his uncle, and, yesterday's hunting debacle apparently forgotten, jumped from the window seat and ran excitedly towards Edward, Pegeen following at a more sedate pace.

"Uncle Edward," Jeremy cried, colliding with Edward's legs and hanging onto his coattail. "Uncle Edward, shall we take out the horses today? King's going to need a good stretch after being cooped up inside all night."

"I don't think King's the only one who needs a stretch, little man." Edward ruffled the boy's hair, and Jeremy jerked his head away, annoyed by what he disparagingly called "being treated like a baby." "Why don't you run down to the kitchen? I understand Cook's just pulled a dozen of her world-renowned spice cakes from the oven. If you ask her politely, she might give you one."

Jeremy's grey eyes narrowed, and his freckled nose wrinkled. "If you want to talk to Pegeen alone," he said with wounded dignity, "you need only to ask. It isn't necessary to patronize me."

"Jeremy!"

A pink flush crept over Pegeen's smooth, ivory cheeks. Edward stared, fascinated by the play of color across the girl's face. As usual, she wore a highly fashionable gown that fit her slim figure perfectly. Except for the slight blush, she looked no different than usual, her long hair flatteringly arranged, her eyes bright without the aid of artifice. There was nothing in her demeanor to indicate that she'd spent the better part of last evening panting breathlessly in his arms, her lips clinging to his.

Laying gentle hands upon Jeremy's shoulders, Pegeen steered him bodily from the room. "And don't come back," she admonished the boy, "until you've learned some manners."

Disgusted, Jeremy slammed the door behind him. Pegeen turned towards Edward, and he was disappointed to see that the blush had vanished. She regarded him with eyes that were as green and cool and unfathomable as twin forest ponds. "Yes, my lord?" she asked, in her low, slightly hoarse voice.

Suddenly extremely aware of the fact that they were alone together, Edward stared down at his boot tops, abashed. What was the matter with him? He'd never before felt self-conscious in the presence of one of his conquests. Could Alistair be right? Could he have fallen in love with this impertinent minx? Impossible. She was hardly more than a child herself, and not at all his type. He liked cool blondes, not hot-tempered brunettes. And this girl, who *was* she? She wasn't even titled.

"Lord Edward?" The green eyes were appraising him curiously now, wondering at his silence. "Is something the matter?"

Edward shook himself. "No, of course not. Why should there be something the matter?"

"I don't know." Pegeen studied him expressionlessly. "But you certainly look bothered."

"I'm not bothered," Edward declared too quickly. This wouldn't do. He had to master control of the situation. As it was, the girl was manipulating the entire conversation. He realized his fingers were balled into fists. What was the matter with him? Perhaps he was only experiencing the normal anxiety one might feel after deflowering one's virgin sister-in-law.

"If I am bothered," Edward said, more evenly this time, "it's only because I've got such a lot to do. I'm leaving this afternoon, you see."

Though he watched Pegeen's face more carefully than was strictly necessary, considering that he had only the most remote feelings for her, he saw no change whatsoever in her expression.

"Oh?" she asked politely. "You're going away?"

"Yes," Edward said. "To London. I'm afraid I'll be gone for quite a while."

"I'm so sorry to hear that," Pegeen said, not sounding the least bit sorry. "I hope your business there isn't unpleasant."

What in God's name ailed the girl? Edward could not for the life of him figure it out. Last night had been one of the most incredible evenings of his life. Surely the girl must feel the same way. He flattered himself he was not an unskilled lover. And yet when he'd suggested marriage, the girl had recoiled, horrified. How perfectly ironic that the one time he proposed, he was turned down. Well, he wouldn't make the same mistake twice. He was going away so that he wouldn't risk the temptation of falling into her bed again.

And he could play the unconcerned lover every bit as well as she.

"Oh, I'm not going to London for business," he said. He tried to keep his voice light, a conscious imitation of her own tone. "I believe you know perfectly well why I'm going. Since you will not listen to reason and do the sensible thing by marrying me, I think it better to remove myself from Rawlings, lest what happened last night repeats itself."

He had the satisfaction of seeing Pegeen's mouth fall open a little in astonishment. She closed it almost immediately and said with admirable acidity, "I thought I explained to you, Lord Edward, that I do not believe in the institution of marriage, and that even if I did, I certainly wouldn't marry some man who felt compelled to wed me out of *duty*—"

"*Duty*?" Edward echoed.

"Yes, duty. That's what you call it, I'm sure. You only asked me to marry you because you feel responsible for besmirching my honor. Well, I assure you, my honor is far from besmirched. I quite enjoyed myself last night, and I suspect you did as well. I don't understand why this has to result in either our marriage or your leaving Rawlings."

"You don't understand—" Edward threw back his head and laughed mirthlessly. "Oh, what? You think I can stay after what happened between us?"

"Why not?" Pegeen shrugged. "The viscountess has been your mistress for years, and you don't feel compelled to marry her, or flee to London after making love to her."

Abruptly, Edward stopped laughing. He strode forward and grasped her arm. "You ignorant girl," he said, glowering down at her. "I'm trying to do the honorable thing. Why won't you see reason? Have you considered that you might be with child?"

Pegeen shrugged. "I won't name you as the father, if that's what's worrying you."

"Christ!" Edward swore, moving away from her. The girl was unnatural! She should be swooning with joy over her conquest, but instead, she stood there calmly as a cat, relieving him of all responsibility. Under any other circumstances, with any other woman, he'd have been overjoyed. The girl was all but granting him free license to make love to her whenever he wished, no conditions, no price. But that wasn't what he wanted. Couldn't she see that?

"The fact is, Lord Edward," Pegeen said blandly, "you're frightened."

Edward lifted his head to stare at her. "I beg your pardon?"

"You're frightened," she repeated. "That's why you're running away."

"You're damned right I'm frightened," he said. "I've never in my life met a woman like you. I don't know what you're going to do next."

"It's not me you're frightened of. It's yourself."

"Oh, I see." Edward nodded sarcastically. "Yes, I'm running away from myself."

"Precisely. You're frightened that you might actually come to care for me, and for The Heartbreaker, that's quite a burden to carry."

"And that's why I asked you to marry me?" Edward was furious now. "Because I'm afraid I might to come to care for you?"

"No. You asked me to marry you because you thought you had to. You're *running away* because you're afraid you might come to care for me."

With a haughty toss of her head, Pegeen whirled on her heel and began stalking towards the door, but Edward was too quick for her. He caught her arm just above the elbow and spun her around to face him, marvelling as always that such a slight body could contain so much force of character.

Pegeen stared angrily up at him, her lips parted to deliver another verbal lashing, but Edward pressed a long, hard finger to her mouth and said, "I want you to understand something. I'm coming back, and if, when I do, I find that you're with child, I'm marrying you, and there isn't anything you can say to stop me.''

"There most certainly is," Pegeen said, her lips soft but insistent against his finger. "I can tell the vicar I *don't*."

He pressed harder, feeling the smooth curve of her chin, aware that the anger hadn't yet left her eyes. "I mean what I say, Pegeen."

"I still don't see why you have to go away."

"I'll tell you why. You are an unattached young woman, wholly unrelated to me except by marriage. I am an unattached man without any female relations to act as chaperon. It is completely inappropriate for the two of us to remain together under one roof, especially considering what happened last night."

"But—" Pegeen reached up, and with surprising strength wrenched his hand away from her mouth. "Nobody knows about last night except you and me. Nobody will think anything of it!"

"*I* know," Edward said firmly. "And there's always the chance that someone may find out. Your maid nearly did. And while my reputation is such that there isn't much more damage I could possibly do to it, yours is, as yet, unsullied—"

"I don't care about my reputation," Pegeen said scornfully.

"You should care. I know all you've been thinking about lately is Jeremy's welfare, but eventually, you're going to have to give some thought to your own. You might want to marry someday, Pegeen—"

She snorted indelicately.

"Despite your absurd ideas on the subject," he went on carefully, "you're young and attractive, and there isn't any reason why—"

"I'll tell you why," Pegeen interrupted, hotly. "I saw what marriage did to my sister. It changed her. She came back from Europe hard and spiteful and mean—''

"It wasn't marriage that did that to your sister, Pegeen," Edward said tiredly. "It was my brother."

Pegeen shook her head truculently. "She was trapped, like millions of women in the world are trapped, in loveless matches from which they can't escape, because women aren't full citizens and cannot divorce, even if they are abused or abandoned—''

"Not again." Edward rolled his eyes. "Pegeen. I promise you it wouldn't be like that between you and me—''

"How could it not be? You only asked me to marry you because you feel guilty. What kind of basis is that for a relationship?"

"It wasn't purely guilt," Edward said hesitantly. "Obviously, I'm attracted to you."

"Attracted to me?" Now it was Pegeen's turn to roll her eyes. "You think because I'm young and pretty and female, I don't have a brain in my head. I know what I'm saying." The green eyes, glowing indignantly, met his gaze steadily. "*If* I were to marry, and that's a very big *if*, it will be for one reason, and one reason only: Love. I'll settle for nothing less."

Since it was quite clear from the heat in her gaze that love was the last thing she felt for him, Edward said stiffly, "Well, in that case, we have nothing more to say to one another."

"What are you going to do?" Pegeen demanded, stamping a small foot. "Stay in London for the rest of my life?"

"No," Edward said. He thought it might be prudent to end the interview before it got even more personal and turned towards the door. "Only until you're married."

He heard Pegeen stamp her foot again. "And just who am I supposed to marry? Who?"

Who, indeed, thought Edward, but he didn't say anything out loud except, ''Good-bye, Pegeen.'' He didn't look back at her either, because he wasn't at all certain that if he did, he'd maintain his resolve to leave.

Chapter Twenty-Two

By five o'clock in the evening the day after the hunt ball, there wasn't a single occupied guest room at Rawlings Manor. The viscountess and her friends departed shortly after lunch, though not without a few suspicious glances and dark mutterings in Pegeen's direction. Pegeen didn't care at all, she was so glad to be rid of them.

But despite the lack of concern that she'd dissembled for Lord Edward's benefit in the schoolroom, Pegeen was deeply unhappy about his removal from Rawlings. Though she understood the reasons behind his decision intellectually and emotionally, she was devastated. She had never, never intended to sleep with him, and still could not understand how it had happened.

Pegeen had always prided herself on the fact that she was ruled by her head, not her heart, but the night of the ball, it had been as if her body had taken over, leaving her head and heart in the cold. It would be wrong to say she regretted what had happened between her and Lord Edward, because it had been the most glorious thing Pegeen had ever experienced. But she regretted the inevitable aftermath of such an action. Because of course, Edward had felt compelled to propose.

And of course she had turned him down.

She knew she was probably the stupidest girl in England for having done so. Why, there were matrons all over London who'd have given their best diamond brooches to secure a wedding proposal from Lord Edward for their daughters. And Pegeen had shrugged it off as if it had been an invitation to tea.

But how could she possibly marry a man who'd only asked her out of some absurd sense of duty? What sort of marriage would *that* be? Marriage was bad enough without both partners being aware the union had sprung from a moment of ill judgment. No, Pegeen would have sooner died than accepted Lord Edward's marriage proposal.

But that didn't mean she wasn't dying now.

Because of course Pegeen was in love with him. She had fallen in love with him the moment she'd careened into him that day back in Applesby. What had happened that night at the hunt ball hadn't happened in an unguarded moment of lust. It had happened because Pegeen was unrequitedly, irrevocably in love with Edward, and his kisses had blotted out all reason.

She knew very well that he didn't love her. No mention of the word love had left his lips those dreadful moments in her bed when the horrifying reality of what they'd done had finally sunk in. He'd said a great many words of self-abuse and sworn quite a bit but never once had he looked at Pegeen and told her he loved her.

And that was why she couldn't marry him.

If she'd been a different sort of girl, perhaps she'd have married him anyway and hoped that over the years, he'd grow to care for her a little. But Pegeen's pride wouldn't allow such a thing. If he didn't love her, he wouldn't have her again, no matter how much she herself yearned for him. She had the memory of that single, wonderful night they'd spent together and that would be enough. Enough to sustain her for a lifetime, she hoped.

As the days stretched into weeks and the bitter winds of December buffeted the stones of the house, Pegeen hardly felt the chill. She was determined that though her heart was breaking, no one would know it. No, Pegeen decided that her love would be suffered in silence, a secret that she would never, ever share with anyone, least of all its object. She was perfectly aware that she was far from the first girl to have fallen in love with the handsome Heartbreaker, and she undoubtedly wouldn't be the last.

Pegeen had never been in love before. Edward's face was forever embedded in her subconscious, and at the oddest moments it would flash before her eyes. She could be paying a call upon one of Rawlings Manor's tenants and suddenly a memory of Edward's arms around her that night, his lips hard on hers, would stop her dead in her tracks, leaving her breathless. The longing to feel those arms around her again was almost overwhelming, but Pegeen had realized that Edward had been right to go away. It could never happen again. A moment's embrace could mean a lifetime of regret—especially since there was absolutely no reason for her to believe that Edward felt anything for her at all, except for the admiration her beauty aroused in nearly every man she met.

Pegeen kept her feelings to herself, not revealing them to anyone. Not to Lady Herbert and her daughters, who were frequent visitors in Rawlings during the month of December, nor to Mrs. Praehurst, in whom Pegeen had found a gentle, if rather dull, companion, and certainly not to Lucy or Jeremy. She held her secret close, allowing herself to think of it only in quiet moments by the fireside or at night before she fell asleep, though thoughts of Edward, his clear grey eyes, his smirking lips, often made sleep impossible.

She felt she hid her secret rather well, considering. Unlike heroines in novels she'd read, she didn't lose weight or grow pale. In fact, she remained quite hearty, so much so that Lady Herbert exclaimed each time they met that Pegeen looked more beautiful than the last time they'd parted company. Pegeen knew that the older woman wasn't trying to flatter her. She was speaking the absolute truth. Pegeen's new life at Rawlings Manor quite agreed with her. It was lovely to be able to spend the day entertaining orphans or writing letters to members of the House of Commons, rather than slaving over a hot stove or mending holes in trousers. If not for her secret passion for its master, Pegeen might have passed some of the happiest days of her life in Rawlings Manor. As it was, she willed herself to be satisfied with charity work and seeing Jeremy brought up properly.

Christmas came and went without the return of the master of the house. But then, Edward was no longer master of Rawlings Manor. When a shipment of gifts from his uncle arrived on Christmas Eve, Jeremy took no joy in them, loudly complaining that all he'd wanted was Edward, not another battalion of lead soldiers. Pegeen took not the slightest joy in the gift Edward sent to her, an emerald, diamond, and ruby brooch shaped like a rose. She gave it a single glance in its velvet box, and then she slipped it into a drawer and tried not to think about it again.

And then, just when she'd convinced herself that she could live perfectly well without him, that if she'd made the mistake of falling in love with him, she could certainly rectify matters by falling out of love with him again, Edward returned to Rawlings Manor. Alone. Without explanation. He simply appeared at the dinner table one evening as if he'd never been away.

By that time, a number of changes had taken place within the household, all at Pegeen's instigation. Jeremy no longer took his meals in isolation in the nursery. He ate at the dinner table like a normal human being. Mrs. Praehurst, despite some initial resistance, often joined them at mealtimes at Pegeen's urging to share some gentle gossip over

turtle soup. And at any given time, any number of Herbert
girls might be in attendance, as Pegeen enjoyed their company and Anne Herbert, in particular, had become a steady
companion.

So when Edward appeared in the dining room, Pegeen's shock at his return was somewhat less evident than
his surprise at seeing a dozen rather scruffy-looking orphans sitting round the table blinking at him and his own
place usurped by Jeremy. After all, Pegeen had Mrs. Praehurst and the Herbert girls to dissemble before. She
couldn't allow her true feelings to be known to anyone.
She simply greeted him coolly and ordered the orphans to
ignore the grumpy man and go right ahead finishing their
soup. Edward, slumped bewilderedly at Jeremy's left, was
left to draw his own conclusions about the lack of enthusiasm with which his return was greeted.

When Pegeen did speak to him, it was with gruff familiarity, her replies to his polite inquiries about her health
just bordering on the impertinent. Pegeen was convinced
that she wasn't the type of girl to sigh and stammer in the
face of her love, not when it was so clear that he hadn't
any feelings at all for her. Instead, she went to extravagant
pains to keep him from thinking she loved him, and that
entailed being as rude to him as possible without actually
insulting him.

Edward's return fell shortly after New Year's—a hol-
iday Pegeen and Jeremy had celebrated with the Herbert
family, Edward having been ''detained in London by inclement weather that made travel back to Yorkshire impossible''—and it was the morning after his sudden
reappearance into her life that Pegeen, arranging a bowl of
hothouse flowers in the Great Hall, happened to see Edward, Jeremy in tow, striding down the double staircase.

Jeremy, whose adjustment to life in Rawlings Manor
had been so rapid that even Pegeen had marveled a little at
it, had been a great deal more verbal than Pegeen in his

wonder over his uncle's continued absence. His lament—
"But why? Why does Uncle Edward have to be in London
so long?"—was heard all over the house, and more than
once Pegeen had told him to write and ask Edward himself
if he was so curious. Edward's replies on the subject—and
he wrote the boy regularly—were clearly unsatisfactory, for
Jeremy continued to harp on the subject.

But today it looked as if Jeremy was finally getting
his wish. Uncle Edward was deigning to spend a few of
his precious hours in the company of his adoring nephew.
Dressed to go outdoors—a brave attempt, as Pegeen could
hear the wind howling beyond the double portals. Though
it was past ten o'clock in the morning, the sun had yet to
appear in the thickly clouded sky. Nevertheless the two
Rawlings men swept past Pegeen without so much as a nod
in her direction.

Suddenly, finally, she lost her temper.

"And where might you two be going?" she demanded, her voice veiled in sweetness, but her green eyes
snapping fire.

Jeremy whirled about, startled. When he saw Pegeen,
his freckled face broke out into a proud, toothy grin. "Uh,
hullo, Pegeen," he said airily. "Uncle Edward and I are
going to look over some of my properties. I need to start
learning about my duties as duke, you know."

Pegeen thrust a prickly-stemmed yellow rose into the
vase before her with more force than was perhaps necessary. "I see," she said, casting a dark glance at Edward.
"How nice. And what about your German lesson?"

Jeremy made the appropriate—disgusted—face.
"German can wait," he said. "I've got all day for
German."

Edward, his hat in his hand, had been standing silently
at his nephew's side, and now he stepped forward, as if
coming to the boy's rescue. "It will only take an hour or
two, Miss MacDougal," he said with grave politeness.

"There's a tenant to whom I haven't yet introduced the new duke. He has a son Jeremy's age, and I thought—''

Pegeen raised her eyebrows. "And since when do you take an interest in the affairs of the Rawlings tenants, Lord Edward?" she asked coolly. "Correct me if I am wrong, but I thought the reason you went to such extremes to find Jeremy was so that you wouldn't have to perform duties just like this one."

Edward met her gaze impassively. "I thought perhaps that it was time I gave it a try."

"Good Lord," Pegeen said mildly. "London must have been dull indeed if it inspired in you a burning desire to get to know your tenants better." She could have bit her tongue off for saying it, but once it was out, there was no help for it. She did sound a petulant wife. A blush crept steadily over her cheeks, but she kept her eyes focused on the flowers.

"I'm sorry if *estate business*—" Edward's voice fairly dripped with sarcasm when he pronounced the two words "—has kept me away from Rawlings longer than you'd like, Miss MacDougal," Edward said. "However, it couldn't be helped."

"I could not possibly care less, Lord Edward, about your comings and goings," Pegeen said with what she hoped sounded like scathing contempt. "Except where it concerns Jeremy. I hope you haven't forgotten the last little outing you two embarked upon."

It was Edward's turn to flush. Pegeen, surprised, watched as his strong jaw turned a deep crimson as he recalled the unfortunate denouement of the fox hunt. "No, I haven't forgotten," Edward said, and he, too, sounded petulant. "But paying a duty call to a tenant farmer isn't like fox hunting, Miss MacDougal. No one is going to get hurt."

"Tell that to the farmer's son," Pegeen said pointedly. The duke of Rawlings, for all his newfound title, felt ob-

ligated to rub in the snow the face of any boy with whom
he came into contact. Pegeen was not certain whether Edward was aware of this new habit of Jeremy's.

"I believe I am perfectly capable of restraining His
Grace," Edward informed her, "should the need arise."

Pegeen didn't doubt it, but unlike Edward, she was
aware of Jeremy's propensity towards biting. "If you must
go," she sighed gustily, "I had better go with you."

"As you wish," Edward said. It wasn't so much Edward's resigned tone as the way he avoided meeting her
gaze that decided Pegeen. She stuck out her chin, an unconscious gesture that had during her childhood been a village joke, and glared at him.

"I will, then," Pegeen said, and she sent a maid off
for her cloak and hat, her heart thumping inwardly. Good
Lord! She was in a tizzy, and they were only going down
the road to visit a tenant farmer! Pull yourself together,
Pegeen.

But by the time the maid returned with her things,
Pegeen could hardly tie her own bonnet ribbons, her fingers
were shaking so badly. Fortunately, she had her muff to
hide them in. She fell in step with Jeremy and his uncle,
and even when Edward handed her into the carriage, she
was quite certain he didn't sense her nervousness at being
so close to him once more. She settled onto the leather seat
with an air of nonchalance, keeping her face averted from
his. She felt the springs beneath the seat sag beneath his
substantial weight as he lowered himself beside her. Jeremy, as usual, insisted upon sitting with the driver, so when
the carriage eased out of the snow-covered drive, Pegeen
found herself alone with Edward for the first time in over
a month.

In such a moment, much could have been said. Pegeen
kept her head stubbornly turned towards the window, her
face hidden within the wide, fur-trimmed brim of her bonnet. She vowed not to utter a word, not unless he spoke to

her first. He was sitting so close to her that she could feel the heat from his thigh against her hip, and occasionally, when the carriage wheels fell into a rut in the road, his shoulder brushed hers. At last, after nearly a minute of silence, Edward cleared his throat and ventured awkwardly, "Jeremy seems to have settled nicely since I've been gone."

Pegeen, still not averting her gaze from the window said, "Yes. He has."

When it became clear that no further information was forthcoming, Edward cleared his throat again and asked, "Excuse me, madam, but have I offended you in some fashion?"

This was enough to warrant Pegeen's full attention. She swivelled her head and looked up into his somber grey eyes. He seemed sincerely confused by her standoffish attitude. Good. "Offended me?" Pegeen managed to sound ingenuous. "I don't know what you mean."

"I realize that I was gone longer than I'd have liked—"

"Oh, la," Pegeen said airily. She turned her attention back to the passing winter landscape. "I'm sure you found much to amuse you in London. There are certainly more stimulating diversions there than in the wilds of Yorkshire." A sly glance back at him to see how he reacted to her words.

Edward looked uncomfortable. One of his gloved hands rested on his knee, the other on the seat between them. The fingers of both were clenched convulsively. Pegeen looked away again, satisfied that he was as nervous as she was.

"I spent a good deal of my time in London conducting business," he said stiffly.

"Oh, yes, so you said. That must have been quite a disappointment to Lady Ashbury." Pegeen smiled up at him sweetly but behind the smile she was calculating his reaction.

The little muscle in Edward's jaw, the one that started twitching whenever he was annoyed, the one that Pegeen had missed with feverish intensity while he'd been gone, began to throb. Pegeen observed it with raised eyebrows.

"I wouldn't know," Edward said, and now he was the one with the averted gaze. "I didn't see much of her in town."

"Didn't see much of the viscountess?" Pegeen felt ridiculously happy, and to hide her joy, she rapped on the roof of the carriage with her knuckles and shouted, "Jeremy? Aren't you cold up there?"

Jeremy's voice, disgusted, floated towards them. "No!"

"Well, if you get cold, ask Bates to stop and bring you inside."

Jeremy didn't respond. He hated it when Pegeen babied him. Inside the carriage, Pegeen settled back onto her seat, her hands buried in her soft fur muff, her nose and cheeks pink with cold, her heart thumping happily.

"Uh, Pegeen," Edward said. When she looked at him, she saw that his head was turned towards the window on his own side of the coach.

Anything might have been said at such a moment, and Pegeen, intensely conscious of his proximity, literally sat on the edge of her seat, her heart drumming with anticipation. Had a miracle occurred? Had Edward forsaken the viscountess because he'd realized his love for Pegeen? Had he finally realized that despite all the sophisticated and exotic women in his acquaintance, the one closest to his heart was the one closest to home? That despite their differences in age and experience, they were meant for one another?

Edward coughed again. "I've been meaning to ask you if . . . or, rather, whether or not you knew yet . . . if—"

Pegeen, observing his discomfort, realized with a feeling of horror that he was wondering whether or not she was pregnant. Her cheeks hot, she demanded, before she could stop herself, ''Don't you think I'd have told you straight off if I was?''

Edward looked visibly relieved, but not by much. ''Well, I wasn't certain. You were so adamant about . . . everything.''

Feeling as if her face was on fire with embarrassment, Pegeen turned the lever to slide open the window closest to her. The cold winter wind stung her eyes, but at least it was cooling her crimson cheeks.

''My offer from that night still stands,'' Edward said in his deep voice. ''In case you were wondering.''

Pegeen closed her eyes, feeling ice and snow against her forehead. She wished more than anything she hadn't been foolish enough to insist on joining him on this ridiculous outing. It was only going to result in making her more miserable than ever.

''And my answer remains the same,'' Pegeen said in a hard voice. ''In case you were wondering.''

Edward was quiet for several minutes after that, and the only sound was of the creaking of the leather seats, the jingling of the horse harnesses, and the crunch of the carriage's wheels in the snow. Pegeen prayed that he'd say nothing more. She had a feeling that despite her firm resolution not to, she might just turn around and accept his proposal, to hell with the consequences. So what if he didn't love her? She loved him enough for both of them.

Suddenly, Edward said, ''Well, I suppose you'll laugh when you hear this, but Alistair—you remember Alistair Cartwright, of course, don't you, Pegeen?'' At her cool nod, he continued, speaking rapidly. ''Well, it's damned awkward, you know, but Alistair has been hounding me these past few weeks. One of the reasons I came home was to escape his relentless whining, in fact. But I'm afraid Alistair's got it into his head that he's in love with you, and he won't be happy unless he's allowed to pay court to you.''

If Pegeen hadn't spent the past few weeks hiding her true feelings, she wouldn't have been able to dissemble as quickly as she did. Without skipping a beat, she smiled and said, ''Oh? Alistair Cartwright? How funny.''

''Funny?'' Edward's fists had relaxed. He leaned back against the leather seat and smiled. ''I don't know that Alistair'd be flattered by your reaction.''

Pegeen smiled automatically again. It had only taken her a few seconds to get used to the idea that Alistair Cartwright desired her. Alistair was a good-looking, kind-hearted, rather entertaining man. He wouldn't make a bad husband. Not at all. If she were marriage-minded, which, of course, she wasn't.

But why had Alistair asked Edward about it? Oh, because as her brother-in-law, Edward was responsible for her welfare. But Edward was more than just her brother-in-law. Did Alistair know that? Alarmed, Pegeen turned wide eyes up to the man seated beside her.

''Does he—'' She couldn't keep the anxiety out of her voice. ''Does he know? About us, I mean?''

Edward started. ''Good God, no! What do you take me for, Pegeen? I may be a fool, but I'm not a cad.''

Relieved, Pegeen leaned back in her seat. ''Well, what did you say to him?''

''What did I say to whom?''

''To Mr. Cartwright,'' Pegeen said through gritted teeth. Honestly, the man could be dense as a tree sometimes.

''To Alistair? About courting you? Well, I forbade it, naturally. But the man's a menace. He wouldn't let me alone—''

''You *forbade* it?''

Edward didn't take heed of the anger in Pegeen's

voice. "Of course I forbid it. It's perfectly absurd. Why, he's almost twice your age—"

"Don't you think *I* should have been consulted in the matter?" she demanded.

"You?" Edward's face swivelled towards her, his black eyebrows raised incredulously. Noting the grim set of her lips, he shook his head. "I'm surprised, Pegeen. You almost sound as if you're entertaining the idea of allowing him to—"

"And why not?" So long as she didn't look at him, it was easy to keep her tone light. "You said yourself, directly before you went away, that I should marry someday."

"And you insisted that marriage was something you'd never consider—"

"To someone with whom I wasn't in love," Pegeen corrected him quickly. "Or who didn't love me." Edward looked at her sharply, but before he could say another word, she added, "Besides, I've had a lot of time to think since you've been gone, and I've decided that perhaps it wouldn't be such a bad thing, were I to wed. It would be best for everyone, like you said. Silence the gossipers and lift the burden of my support from you."

"Burden! I'd hardly call you a burden!"

"It's perfectly ridiculous for you to go on supporting a woman who isn't even a blood relation to you. And if I married Mr. Cartwright, it would solve the problem of you and I living under the same roof without a chaperon, just as you said last month—"

"Marry him!" Edward squirmed on his seat. "I only told you he was interested in paying court to you because he kept insisting . . ." For once Edward appeared to be at a loss for words. Pegeen figured that he must be realizing she'd caught him in his own trap. "I never thought you'd take the offer seriously!"

"Why not?" Pegeen had pulled herself together

enough to glare at him challengingly. "Is the idea of a man paying court to me so ludicrous in your eyes? Am I some sort of witch or shrew that you couldn't possibly imagine any man falling in love with me?"

"No, of course not. You're—well, you're very attractive. But you're far too young to even think of marrying."

Now Pegeen was genuinely nettled. "Too young! I'm twenty!"

"Twenty," Edward echoed. He rolled his eyes. "You're a *child*. What do you know about marriage?"

"What do *you* know about it?" Pegeen challenged. "Except how to ruin someone else's."

The second the words were out of her mouth she regretted them, but there wasn't anything she could do about it. Edward stared down at her with disbelief plainly sketched across his handsome face. Hard fingers suddenly encircled her slim wrist in a crushing grip. "I beg your pardon?"

"Well," Pegeen explained, her throat suddenly dry. "The viscountess is married, and you—"

"That is enough," Edward barked. Pegeen was so startled at his sharp tone that she sank back into the corner of the carriage, her eyes wide. It was only Edward's grip on her arm that kept her from leaping from the carriage in fear for her life. "You know nothing about me and Lady Ashbury. Thank God. And I think it highly inappropriate for a girl your age to even mention such a—"

In spite of his fury, Pegeen couldn't help a grin. "Oh, you didn't seem to care about my tender age the night of the ball."

Edward stared at her with as much incredulity as if she'd spat at him. The knuckles on the hand that held her were white with rage. His mouth opened, but no sound came out of it, and Pegeen laughed humorlessly.

"Ha! Tell me, Lord Edward, why am I too young for your friend Mr. Cartwright but not for you?"

Edward said, with a patience that belied the leaping muscle in his jaw, "I believe I have made it clear to you that I could not regret what happened between us more. I have tried to do the honorable thing by asking you to marry me, but you've informed me on no uncertain terms that you'd scorn such a marriage. In light of that, I have removed myself from my own home in order to prevent what occurred between us from happening again. And yet now you say you'd welcome the prospect of marrying my best friend!"

Pegeen jumped as Edward gave the seat across from theirs a very vicious kick. The resulting impact caused Bates to halt the carriage and call down worriedly, "My lord? You all right down there?"

"Yes, Bates," Edward hissed, clutching his booted foot and cursing steadily beneath his breath. "Move on!"

"Aye, my lord," the carriage driver said, and the conveyance lurched forward once more.

Pegeen, who'd shrunk as far back into the corner of the coach as possible, studied Edward wordlessly through very wide eyes. She could not, for the life of her, determine why the thought of her wedding his friend should cause him so much distress. He had made it very clear that he wasn't in love with her, so why should he care? Unless he had come back to Rawlings entertaining ideas that they might pick up again where they'd left off . . . but that wasn't possible. He had to know she'd never again allow herself to lose her head. . . .

"I don't want to hear any more talk about you being courted by anyone," Edward said finally, releasing his injured foot. "I'm going to forbid Alistair Cartwright from—"

Pegeen let out an indignant cry. "You can't do that!"

Edward's expression was like one carved of granite. "I beg your pardon, Pegeen, but I can. As long as you are living under my roof, you are under my protection, and I will not have you subjected to the unsavory attentions of—''

''I thought he was your best friend!''

''He is.'' All at once, Edward seemed to realize that he was looming over her like some great bird of prey. He sat back, but his predatory gaze remained fastened upon her. ''He is my best friend. I know him better than anyone. And that's why I forbid it. You're to forget I ever mentioned it.''

Pegeen longed to point out to Edward that if he had such strong objections to his friend paying court to her, he oughtn't to have brought it up in the first place. Why had he?

Pegeen was left to mull over the problem for the rest of the day. The trip to the tenant farmer's cottage was uneventful, except for the fact that Jeremy's nose was nearly broken by the farmer's strapping twelve-year-old son, forever cementing a bond of friendship between the two boys, since Jeremy could only befriend someone physically his superior. Further discussion concerning Alistair Cartwright was curtailed by the fact that Jeremy rode home with them inside the carriage, Pegeen's handkerchief pressed against his swollen nose.

It was, perhaps, not surprising that when Evers admitted them to the Great Hall, the news he imparted as he took his master's cape and hat was not received with much enthusiasm by Lord Edward. ''Mr. Cartwright arrived not long ago, sir,'' Evers said. ''Mrs. Praehurst has put him in the Blue Room. He's currently playing at billiards, I believe.''

Edward swore. Pegeen stared at him with raised eyebrows, but Edward seemed oblivious of her presence. He stormed away, his boot heels ringing on the flagstones, and even Jeremy, his voice muffled beneath Pegeen's handkerchief, was perceptive enough to notice his pique. ''What's the matter with Uncle Edward?'' he asked plaintively.

''I don't know,'' Pegeen sighed. ''If you figure it out, be sure to tell me.''

Chapter Twenty-Three

Arabella Ashbury would never have been foolish enough to say out loud that she found London dull without the company of Edward Rawlings, but she keenly felt his absence, and had grown irritable because of it, irritable enough that friends had noticed and begun to wonder at it. It was bad enough, of course, that when he had been in town, Edward had declared himself too busy with "estate business" to so much as dine with the viscountess. Now he'd fled the city altogether, and there wasn't even a chance she'd run into him at the theater.

Not that there was any theater to be seen so early in the season. As if things weren't bad enough, Arabella and her friends had come down to London early at Edward's urging, only to be deserted by him. "Estate business." Never in her life had she been slighted quite so obviously— and so publicly.

Of course, now that Edward had evidently returned to Rawlings, it was all beginning to make sense. He hadn't any "estate business" in town. He'd merely wanted to get rid of them, Arabella and the earl and Alistair. The lot of them. Because of the girl, of course. Arabella could not think of Miss Pegeen MacDougal as anything else but ''the girl.''

That blasted girl, with her blasted green eyes and sooty black lashes, her peaches and cream complexion, her shining dark hair and seventeen-inch waist. What man wouldn't want to keep such a girl to himself? But then why had Edward spent such a long sojourn in town? Why not simply get rid of his guests and return, posthaste, to Rawlings? Arabella couldn't figure it out. But then, Edward Rawlings was a complicated man. She'd never been able to tell exactly what he was thinking.

But she was getting closer, she knew. Now that he'd returned to Rawlings, it was clear he considered himself through with the Lady Ashbury. Why, he hadn't even sent a note to say good-bye. Even the trashiest bit o' muslin usually got a note—a diamond bracelet at the very least— when her lover moved on to someone else. Edward hadn't even had the decency to tell her it was over. Well, there'd been that scene in the White Room at Rawlings. That might have been a sign that all was not well with their relationship. Arabella couldn't understand it. It just wasn't like Edward, usually so arrogant and devil-may-care.

And asking Alistair hadn't helped. Arabella had never really liked Alistair Cartwright. It seemed to her that he was forever smirking at her, not in a sexual way, which she might have understood, but as if he thought her stupid. When she'd asked him that night at St. James Palace whatever had come over Edward lately, he'd smirked rather more than usual and said he didn't know. Arabella knew he was lying, and in a rare display of ill judgment, she seized his sleeve and demanded, ''It's the girl, isn't it? He's in love with that girl.''

Alistair had blinked at her in that ridiculously laconic fashion of his and inquired innocently, ''Why, Arabella, whatever do you mean?''

''You know perfectly well what I mean. Well, he can't

possibly marry her. Do you know what people are saying about her sister?''

Alistair's smirk deepened. ''No, Arabella, pray tell me. What are *people* saying about her sister?''

She didn't like the emphasis he put on the word 'people,' but she continued, hoping he didn't know that almost all of the rumors had originated in her own parlor.

''That she killed John Rawlings, just as if she'd pulled the trigger herself. That the duel he was fighting was for her honor, and her lover won it. And that she's spent the last ten years in the Mediterranean with that lover—''

''*People* are talking quite a lot about things they couldn't possibly know, aren't they, Arabella?''

Alistair's smirk was unbearable, and it was then that Arabella realized that Cartwright, the fool, was under the girl's spell as well. It didn't seem possible that such a tiresome chit could have captured the hearts of *two* of Europe's most eligible bachelors, but then, her sister had done it as well, hadn't she? What was the name of that lover of Katherine Rawlings? If only Arabella could find out.

Arabella wasn't the only one wondering at Edward Rawlings odd behavior. The earl of Derby lamented the loss of his gaming partner, and spent entire meals sighing into his wine glass to the annoyance of his wife. He remembered only a very little of what had occurred in the conservatory the night of the ball, but what little he did recall bothered him. There was something about that girl, the vicar's daughter. Something familiar. If only Lord Derby could put his finger on it. He was quite certain the information, whatever it was, would cheer up poor Arabella.

And then one evening, he figured it out.

Despite a certain lascivious side to his nature, the earl of Derby was not an intentionally cruel man. It would never have occurred to him to share the discovery that he had come across with anyone, had he not been slightly in his cups later on that night, and fallen, in his usual hapless fashion, into hands far more intelligent—and manipulative—than his own.

Arabella Ashbury had little use for the earl of Derby and his wife. If it hadn't been for the fact that they owned the townhouse neighboring her own, and that at one time, before his physical dissipation had become complete, she and Lord Derby had shared a certain penchant for one another, she would have ignored them completely. True, they were gentry, but so dull . . . and all those children. It wasn't seemly to have so many children. But when Lord Derby ended up on her doorstep one evening shortly after New Year's, he was far too drunk to turn safely away. So she invited him in and asked him where he'd been.

"Kathy's," Lord Derby rasped, propping his feet up on Arabella's marble hearth.

Arabella rolled her eyes. Kathy Porter's was a notorious London brothel. If Derby thought she was at all interested in what he'd been doing there, he was in for a surprise.

"Well," she said crisply. Actually, she had her own company upstairs, someone she was fostering to replace the wayward Edward Rawlings in her heart, and she hadn't time to waste on fat, drunken earls. "You're welcome to stay the night if you feel you have to. I'll send a footman to your place to fetch whatever you'll need. We'll tell Bertha you're staying at your club for the night."

"You're so kind," Derby said, and Arabella was irritated to see that tears had welled up beneath his fleshy eyelids. Derby had always been a lachrymose drunk. "You're so lovely, Arabella. Almost as lovely as that little vicar's daughter."

Arabella was only half-listening to him. She was gazing at her reflection in the mirror above the mantel, adjusting her sapphire choker. "What little vicar's daughter?" she asked absently.

"The one at Rawlings. The one who looks so much like Kathy."

Arabella shot him a look that, had he seen it, would have frightened him. In three quick strides, she was leaning over his chair, her face just inches from his. "What do you mean, the girl who looks like Kathy? You mean Pegeen MacDougal looks like Kathy Porter?"

A fat tear squeezed out of the corner of one of Lord Derby's eyes. He nodded sadly. "The very image of her, only smaller, like in miniature, you know what I mean? They could be sisters. Kathy's older by a good ten years or so, and heavier by quite a few stones, but they might be twins otherwise." Lord Derby sighed. "It bothered me for so long. I knew that girl reminded me of someone, but I just couldn't think who. 'Til tonight, of course."

Arabella's fingers tightened on the brocade armrests she clutched. Her eyes had begun to glitter dangerously. "Katherine Rawlings is Kathy Porter. How utterly delicious."

The earl of Derby suddenly sobered up. He occasionally did this, and it never failed to surprise Arabella how quickly he could become lucid when he chose to.

"Arabella," he said, reaching out a hand that despite its girth was strong as a vise. "What are you thinking? I said they *looked* as if they could be sisters, I didn't say I knew for certain they were."

"Oh, shut up, Freddy," Arabella snapped. Her blue eyes had turned cloudy with thought. While Lord Derby had sobered up quite a bit, he had not sobered up enough to realize the significance of his discovery, and when Arabella did not mention the name Kathy Porter again, he relaxed, conscious only that the viscountess was being nicer to him than usual.

Chapter Twenty-Four

Edward Rawlings had known Alistair Cartwright for most of his life, and during that time, the two of them had rarely quarreled. The only significant fight they'd ever had been over a certain young lady who'd had the audacity to join a convent and marry the Lord instead of either of them, therefore settling the matter.

In Edward's opinion, one of Alistair's most appealing features was his malleability. He could easily be dissuaded from any course once embarked upon, and this lack of backbone made him an invaluable companion to someone like Edward, who needed to be in charge of every situation.

It was for this reason that Edward was so very surprised—and outraged—by Alistair's refusal to back down on the issue of courting Pegeen. Why, of all the issues in the world, Alistair had to pick *this* one to remain adamant about, Edward couldn't fathom. It just wasn't like Alistair to hold so firmly to a conviction. It was possible, Edward supposed, that his easygoing friend was really in love with the girl. If that was so, Edward was afraid he had no other alternative than to ask Alistair to remove himself from Rawlings forever.

It galled Edward that he was going to have to resort to this. He valued Alistair's friendship. Alistair was one of the few people Edward could abide for longer than five minutes. But he simply could not allow his best friend to court Pegeen. The very thought made him feel ill. Even now, watching the two of them together as they quarrelled over some book, Edward was quite certain he was going to lose his dinner. Right there, in the Gold Room.

It seemed that his days as master of his own household were finished. Pegeen had pointed out to him, quite sweetly that he had no right whatsoever to forbid Alistair from courting her, and that since she herself had no objection to it, he had better just mind his own business. And Edward, agreeing with her heartily, tried. He really did try. But the sight of the two heads, one so fair, the other so dark, bent over some ridiculous book of poetry quite inexplicably enraged him.

Edward thought he'd been a good enough sport so far. The three of them had spent nearly a week together in relative equanimity, Pegeen refraining from making the barbed sort of comments she seemed to feel compelled to make in his presence, Alistair pretending not to notice his host's hostile stares. As the weather was foul, there was no question of going outdoors, though had it been just a few degrees warmer, Edward would have insisted on dragging Alistair out for some shooting—anything to get him away from Pegeen.

Perhaps the most irritating thing of all was that Edward could not place his finger on the exact reason for his unaccountable anger. He certainly felt that Alistair was too old by far for Pegeen. And the fact that Edward had been privy to detailed accounts of many of Alistair's conquests made him nervous for Pegeen, who, easily arousable as she was, might be seduced by any of Alistair's more physical ploys.

The thought of Pegeen and his laconic friend in bed

together was thoroughly enraging, the more so because Edward knew that beneath the girl's prickly exterior was a profoundly sensual woman. Edward had never slept with a more demonstrative partner. The fact was that this twenty-year-old vicar's daughter could have given lessons in love-making to any one of London's most sought after courtesans.

But was being able to hold that delectable body of hers in his arms every night worth the cost of having to listen to that smart mouth? No.

So why not let Cartwright have her? Edward would find the girl of his dreams eventually. A nice, quiet girl, who'd sit by the fire and knit socks for him and not complain about the cost of his cravats and his drinking and his keeping company with married women. Surely she was out there, somewhere. And in the meantime, why not let Cartwright have what he wanted? Why couldn't one of them be happy anyway?

But as wrong as Pegeen was for Edward, she wasn't right for Alistair, either. Edward couldn't expect Alistair to realize it, since his foolish friend was obviously besotted by the dark-haired minx. But Pegeen ought to have realized by now that it would never work. What possible happiness would she find with a lazy ne'er-do-well like Cartwright? Not only did Cartwright let her walk all over him—he did, Edward had seen it—but he seemed incapable of saying no to the wench. She had only to flutter those inky eyelashes, and Alistair was putty in her hands. Well, it was ridiculous. It would never work. They'd both of them be miserable within a year. Edward was going to have to put a stop to it.

There was no use trying to talk sense to Alistair. Edward had already tried that. No, if he was going to make any headway at all, he'd have to speak to Pegeen, who, though she was damned stubborn, was at least intelligent enough to see reason. Of course, Edward was going to have to get her alone in order to have this discussion, and that wasn't going to be easy, since it seemed as if Cartwright was forever sniffing after her.

Finally, Edward decided he was going to have to wait until Pegeen had retired for the evening, and then approach her in her room, after Alistair had gone to bed. He knew she wasn't going to like it—she seemed as skittish as he was about the two of them being alone in a room together—but it couldn't be helped. To spare her from making the biggest mistake of her life, he was going to have to break some rules.

It was after midnight when Pegeen finally retired, and it was the work of but a moment to shake off Alistair. When Edward left him, he was snoring fitfully on a couch in the library, his arms wrapped around a decanter of brandy and his lips curled up into a ridiculously happy smile. Edward felt almost sorry that what he was about to do was going to wipe that smile away forever, but he didn't see that he had any choice. It was either that, or watch that smile fade into a grimace as the years wore on.

As he stood before the door to the Rose Room, Edward realized that he was nervous. He'd stood in front of that same door dozens of times in his very early childhood, experiencing a different kind of nervousness. His mother had always been a gentle but stern disciplinarian, and her punishments, though less physical than her husband's, were the ones that stuck in Edward's memory. Was it residual nervousness he was feeling now, or was he really not easy in his mind about what he was about to do? He wasn't sure. He knocked on the heavy door before he could change his mind.

Pegeen herself answered the knock. She looked more than a little surprised to see him. Her long, dark hair was loose, tumbling about her shoulders like a cape, and she wore the same diaphanous robe she'd worn before, the night of the hunt ball, the one with the feather trim. She looked ridiculously young but undeniably feminine. Edward felt something inside of him tighten and for a moment lost his nerve. Until he saw Pegeen's expression.

"Well, well, well," she said, one eyebrow quirked. "And to what do I owe this pleasure, Lord Edward?"

He realized that what he was doing was probably going to save Alistair's life. Maybe he wouldn't appreciate it today, and maybe not tomorrow, but one day, he'd thank Edward for saving him from this sarcastic wench.

"I need to speak to you," Edward said in a deep voice.

"Well, you can speak to me in the morning over breakfast," Pegeen said. "Good night."

She attempted to slam the door shut, but Edward was too fast for her. He placed his foot between the door and the jamb and Pegeen, though she pushed with all her might, could not close it.

After a while, she stopped trying. She looked up at him, clearly unimpressed, her hands on her hips. "Edward, you know I can't let you in. Think what happened last time."

"I'm perfectly aware of what happened last time. I was there, too, you know. But you needn't worry. I only want to talk."

"That's all you wanted to do last time," Pegeen pointed out.

"It's vital, Pegeen, that you let me in."

"What will the servants think? Mrs. Praehurst will—"

"Damn Mrs. Praehurst!"

Without warning, Edward kicked the door open, slammed it closed behind him, and stormed into the warm, cheerfully fire-lit room. Since he'd last seen it, Pegeen had made some changes. There was a portrait of his mother, painted before her marriage, over the fireplace, and there were even more bowls of fresh flowers scattered around. And on a side table lay that damned book of love poems

Cartwright had given her the day before, certain passages clearly marked with ribbon. Edward stalked over to it and held it up.

"This," he said, dramatically shaking the small, leather-bound book, "is what I want to talk to you about."

Pegeen, standing stock-still, her arms now crossed over her breasts, looked arch. "Oh? You wish to discuss Shakespeare's love sonnets?"

"I do not." Edward strode towards her, brandishing the book. "I want to talk about Cartwright."

One side of Pegeen's mouth twitched upwards. "Well, Edward, I can understand your jealousy. I admit, you saw him first."

Edward's fist crashed down on a small end table that wasn't strong enough to withstand the onslaught. It crumpled into a pile of inlaid wood and brass. Pegeen looked calmly down at the wreckage. Any other woman would have run for her life.

"Do you feel better now?" she asked drily. "Is there anything else in here that you'd like to smash? How about that vase over there? I understand it's an heirloom. Or perhaps you'd like to hit me instead."

"I've never struck a woman in my life," Edward replied automatically. He was still nonplussed by the collapse of the little table. He hadn't meant to hit it that hard. But he wasn't going to allow her to distract him. That was one of her ploys. He wouldn't be put off his mission. "Listen to me, Pegeen . . ."

"I don't seem to have much of a choice, do I?" Pegeen uncrossed her arms and went to her bed, which she'd clearly left to answer the door. Removing her high-heeled slippers, she slipped her bare feet beneath the heavy comforters. "I hope you don't mind," she said mildly, sitting up in bed and encircling her knees with her arms. "But it's quite chilly, you know."

She looked so small and innocent in that vast four-poster bed that for a moment, Edward forgot what it was he'd come to say. He pictured himself climbing into that bed with her, quite casually, as if they were a long-married couple who slept together every night. He pictured himself sliding the peignoir from her smooth white shoulders and kissing the silken skin beneath those sleeves. . . .

He saw the book in his hand. He started to speak, but his voice was so rough that his words were unintelligible. He cleared his throat. "Pegeen, I can't allow it."

She regarded him warily, her pointed chin cupped in her hands. "Can't allow what?"

"I can't allow you to marry Alistair."

"You can't." She was sitting half in shadow. The light from the fire didn't reach all the way to the head of the bed.

"No, I can't. You aren't right for one another. You'll only end up making each other unhappy, and I don't want to see that happen, not to either of you. So I've come to tell you—you've got to tell Alistair that you can't marry him."

Pegeen's voice carried strongly from the shadows. "In the first place, Edward, Alistair hasn't asked me to marry him. In the second place, if he does, what I decide to do isn't any of your business."

Edward took a few steps forward so that he could read her expression. Standing only a foot from her bedside, he could see that Pegeen was very angry indeed. Her green eyes sparkled like gemstones.

"But it *is* my business, Pegeen," Edward said, more quietly than he'd spoken thus far. "Alistair is my friend. I don't want to see him unhappy."

Pegeen lifted her chin from her hands and glared up at him angrily. "And what makes you so sure I'll make him unhappy?"

"You're too headstrong for him, for one thing. You don't know Alistair like I do, Pegeen."

It seemed natural for Edward to sit down on the side of the bed beside Pegeen. She didn't object, but that might have been because she was too busy being furious with him to notice. Once he was seated on the bed, Edward remembered that in spite of its deceptively soft look, the mattress was quite firm.

"You see, Pegeen," Edward said, tossing the little book of love poems onto the floor in a defeated sort of way, "I've known Alistair my entire life. And I know the kind of woman he needs. He needs a quiet woman, someone who'll look after him, who'll make sure he's wearing matching socks."

"I don't care what kind of socks a man wears," Pegeen said in a low voice.

Edward was a little disturbed to notice that beneath the diaphanous robe she wore only a thin gown that seemed to be made entirely of lace. He could see the curves of her pert breasts quite clearly.

"But you see, Pegeen," he said, dragging his gaze from her chest and fastening it on her dark, unreadable eyes. "That's the problem. What Alistair needs is a woman who *does* care about his socks."

"I think Alistair is a grown man," Pegeen murmured. Edward noticed that her eyelids had grown mysteriously heavy, and that she was looking at him through her eyelashes. "I think Alistair can make up his own mind about what kind of woman he wants."

"That's where you're wrong, you see."

It occurred to Edward that they were sitting entirely too close to one another. He could feel the heat from her practically bare body, and he could smell the flowery fragrance of her loosened hair. Her face was just inches from his own. He had only to lean forward and he could kiss her, taste the sweetness of those pink lips, bury his face in the softness of her neck. The image startled him. He stared down at Pegeen, realizing that she was speaking.

"—and I don't think it's fair," Pegeen was saying in her poignant, throaty voice. "You tell me you want me to marry and then when someone comes along who wants to marry me you tell me you want me to say no. Frankly, Edward, I'm beginning to suspect that you don't have the slightest idea what you want. It's like I said before you left for London. You're frightened."

"The only thing I'm frightened of," Edward snapped, "is the two of you ruining your lives. I didn't think I'd have to resort to this, but since I can see you're going to be nothing but stubborn, I'm going to have to. Pegeen, I'm going to tell him."

The green eyes flew open wide. "*What*?"

"I don't want to. It'll break his heart. But I don't see as how I've got a choice."

Quick as a cat, she'd flung back the coverlets and was kneeling beside him, both hands pressed to her cheeks. "Oh, Edward, you can't! Why would you do something like that? It would only hurt him!"

"Yes, it would hurt him very much. But it would also make him think twice about marrying you."

To his amazement, Pegeen's eyes filled with tears, and the next thing he knew, a small, white-knuckled fist pummeled him quite hard in the chest.

"How *could* you?" she cried wildly. "How could you do something so hateful?"

Edward, clutching at his solar plexus, gasped for breath. He'd forgotten what a strong right hook she had.

"You can't have me, so you're going to see that no one else does either, is that it?" Pegeen demanded angrily. "Oh, you arrogant man! And you wonder why I don't want to marry you!"

Then, before he had regained his breath, she attacked. Edward had never been assaulted by a woman before, and he didn't know quite how to react. One minute she was weeping beside him, and the next, she'd straddled him, shoving his body back against the mattress with surprisingly strong fists with which she continued to beat at him. Edward, conscious of the soft weight of her on his thighs, lay still for a stunned moment or two, eyeing the furious termagant above him, her green eyes flashing, her long dark hair spilling wildly about them.

It was the work of a second for him to seize both of those flailing wrists in fists of iron. Snarling like a tigress, Pegeen fought his restraining arms, until at last Edward pinned her to the mattress with the weight of his own body, keeping her arms raised over her head in his vise-like hold.

"Little cat," he growled. "Be still!"

Her chest heaving beneath him as she tried to catch her breath, Pegeen glared up at him, hatred glowing in her eyes.

"Let me go," she spat. "Let me go or I'll scream, I swear it."

But Edward's body was already betraying him, remembering another time when this same lithesome figure had lain beneath it, unresisting and pliant. Feeling the firmness of her nipples through the gossamer material of her gown, Edward groaned, even as he felt himself hardening against her flat belly.

Pegeen felt it, too, and the eyes she raised to his were no longer angry, but pleading.

"No," she moaned. "Let me go. Please, Edward. Let me go before things go too far—"

But it was already too late.

Chapter Twenty-Five

No. It couldn't be happening again.

But it was.

Prone beneath Edward's hard, heavy body, Pegeen fought against the rising tide of passion within her to no avail. She wanted him every bit as much as he wanted her. And though their heads told them not to, their bodies were proceeding recklessly, as if the first time they'd made love had only been a rehearsal for this.

Edward's mouth was savage on hers. It was as if his lips and tongue yearned to take possession of her. Not just her mouth, either, but her throat and her breasts as well. The peignoir lay in halves beneath her, Edward having rent the flimsy garment in two in his eagerness to bare her flesh to his questing mouth. Burning a trail of kisses from her mouth to her navel, Edward ravaged her breasts, mercilessly sucking on her tender nipples, his hands kneading the soft flesh until, arching beneath him, she mindlessly pressed her pelvis against his, whimpering in her longing to be filled.

Edward immediately dipped his head to the dark nest of hair between her thighs. The moment his tongue laved those swollen lips, Pegeen bucked against him, crying out in surprise, her fingers fisting in his dark hair. But he kept a firm hold of her undulating hips, his mouth clamped to her womanhood, his razor stubble burning the softness of her inner thighs. Reflexively, Pegeen closed her legs around him, cradling him within her thighs as she writhed against his face.

And then Edward could take no more. Raising himself from her silken stranglehold, he tore at his breeches until his massive erection sprang free. He buried himself in her tight, wet womb, raggedly murmuring her name, pounding her deeper and deeper into the bed, all control lost. Pegeen had flung up two hands as if to stop him, her eyes wide at the sight of his engorged member, but now those fingers curled around his hard biceps as her hips rose to meet each of his demanding thrusts. Her head flung back, her breath coming in short gasps, Pegeen moaned as he plunged himself into her, and with every stroke, she came closer to slipping over the edge of sanity. She tried to hang onto him each time he withdrew, to keep him from leaving her, teasing him with her lips, taunting him. . . .

And then he seemed to explode within her, spraying liquid fire into her, and battering her body with his own. Pegeen cried out hoarsely, arching against him and losing herself in her own shower of golden light. Her fingernails sank into his shoulders, but Edward didn't feel it, he was so caught up in his own climax. When Pegeen sank back against the pillows, spent, she was breathing hard, as if she'd run a great distance, and Edward, his head dropping to her breast, was no less breathless.

Bathed in sweat, they lay in the firelight, and it occurred to Pegeen that she ought to say something, but she was still luxuriating in the delicious sensations he'd aroused in her, and she didn't want to spoil the moment. Closing her eyes, she gently stroked his black curls, an unconscious gesture she performed even as she fell deeply asleep.

Chapter Twenty-Six

S leep did not so easily find Edward. Pacing the length of his bedroom, clutching a decanter of whiskey by its neck, he ran a hand through his long hair and cursed out loud.

The entire reason he'd gone to London, despite his assertions that the trip was merely to rid Rawlings of his unwanted guests, had been to forget about that little minx down the hall. His attraction to her had grown beyond all proportion, culminating in his seduction of her the night of the hunt ball. Afterwards, he'd attempted to do the right thing, first by proposing, and then by removing himself from the temptation.

And he'd thought he'd cured himself.

It had only been a passing fancy, he'd told himself. It was because she was something new, something fresh. She'd surprised him with her impertinence, impressed him with her intelligence, charmed him with her beauty. And staggered him by her passion in bed. He'd just needed a few weeks away from her to restore his equilibrium, and a few weeks to get his priorities back in order. He was lucky as hell that she'd turned down his proposal, luckier still that she hadn't gotten pregnant.

He'd thought he was cured.

He'd hardly been back a week. It wasn't any use playing games now. He wanted her. He would stop at nothing to have her. A thousand trips to London weren't going to cure that.

Edward paced his room, swigging generously from the whiskey bottle. A sheen of sweat glowed on his forehead. He'd opened all the windows in the room, but even the cruel winds from the moor couldn't cool his ardor. He didn't know what he was going to do. He certainly couldn't allow things to go on like this.

Exhausted, Edward sank into one of the black leather armchairs beside his hearth and stared unseeingly into the flames. Was this love? He couldn't think of any other name for it. He'd never felt anything like it. She was all he could think about. He had never felt this way about a woman before in his life. What was he going to do about it?

He didn't see any other way around it. He was going to have to figure out a way to get her to marry him.

Marry the sister of his brother's murderer? There was something distinctly distasteful about the idea. But then, she couldn't be held responsible for her sister's actions. Who cared what her sister had done? What was important was that he had to marry her, one way or another.

What was he going to say to Alistair?

Closing his eyes, Edward leaned his head back, and the memory of how he'd left Pegeen just an hour before, came flooding back to him. Her lips softly parted in sleep, her breathing gentle, Pegeen's fingers were still in his hair when he raised his head from the smooth skin stretched taut over her hip bone. She had stroked his hair for hours after they'd made love, probably not even aware she'd been doing so. But Edward had felt the gesture, and wondered at it. Was it possible that in spite of her avowed intention never to marry him, she loved him?

Edward was aware that she thought his proposal

stemmed from a sense of duty. At the time, it had. What else could he have done? She was a guest in his house, a decade younger than he was, and he'd taken advantage of her. Never mind that she'd been a more than willing partner in her own defloration. Gentlemen simply didn't sleep with their virgin sisters-in-law. Not that Edward had ever professed to be a gentleman, anymore than Pegeen had ever claimed to be a lady.

But he had tried to make things right, and she had thwarted all of his best intentions. And then, in the blink of an eye, it had happened all over again. And it had been even better, leaving him with a craving for more.

It was small wonder that he left the sleeping girl in search of whiskey.

It wasn't until dawn was streaking the sky that Edward finally fell into a troubled sleep, and his valet didn't wake him until lunch time.

When Daniels did wake him, it wasn't with pleasant news.

"Sorry to disturb you, my lord," the valet said, glancing critically at the boots Edward hadn't bothered to remove before he'd fallen asleep. "But I thought you might like to be informed that the Lady Ashbury is downstairs."

Edward, who'd been stretched fully clothed on his sofa, bolted to a sitting position upon hearing this news.

"Arabella?" Sleep had roughened his voice so that it was deeper even than his usual growl. "My God. Arabella's here?"

"Yes, sir." Daniels lifted his lordship's cravat from the floor and studied it with distaste. "She's asking to see you. May I suggest that you shave, sir, before going down?"

Edward leaned his elbows on his knees and unconsciously stroked his beard-roughed face. Arabella, here? Why wasn't she in London? Damn, if this wasn't the most inconvenient thing imaginable, her dropping by today, of all days. What was Pegeen going to think?

Damn! What was he going to do about Pegeen?

Glancing up at his manservant, Edward asked with elaborate nonchalance, "Is there anyone, er, with the viscountess at the moment, or is she alone?"

Daniels puttered around the room, gathering up various articles of clothing Edward had strewn about the night before. "I believe Mr. Cartwright is currently entertaining Lady Ashbury in the morning room."

"Is he? Are they alone? I mean . . . Do you happen to know, Daniels . . . Is Miss MacDougal with them?"

To Edward's immense relief, Daniels shook his head, though he might have been indicating contempt at the overturned brandy decanter he'd just discovered at the foot of the bed. "No, sir," he said distractedly. "Miss Anne Herbert came calling not long ago, and she and Miss Pegeen are in the conservatory, I believe."

Edward heaved a sigh of relief. At least Pegeen had been spared the indignity of receiving his former mistress the day after—well, the day after. Perhaps Alistair had somehow intercepted the message that Arabella had arrived and was keeping her out of Pegeen's way.

What in God's name was to be done about Alistair?

Ten minutes later, Edward, bathed, shaved, and dressed in fresh clothes, threw open the door to the morning room and tried to remove the grimace on his face. Better, he'd decided, not to antagonize Arabella overly much. She could be merciless when nettled.

"Arabella," he said. He made no attempt to hide the lack of enthusiasm in his voice. "What a delight."

Arabella turned from the window through which she'd been peering and smiled at him. She was dressed, as always, in the height of fashion, a high-necked, azure-colored gown ruffled all over with bits of white lace. Beside her,

Alistair wore an expression of almost comical misery. He brightened upon seeing Edward.

"Ah, Eddie," he cried. "You look wretched. Bit too much of the old Rawlings port last night, old bean?"

Edward gave him half a smile. The other side of his mouth was twisted into a frown of dismay. It had hit him all at once, at the sight of that trusting, crooked-nosed face. How in hell was he going to tell Alistair? *What* in hell was he going to tell Alistair? *Listen, Cartwright. Sorry, old bean, but I've fallen in love with the girl you're courting, and you're just going to have to lump it.* Edward wasn't at all convinced that Alistair was going to meekly back off. The last time they'd clashed over a girl, the two of them had come to blows. This time, Edward suspected it was going to be even worse. Pistols at dawn, most likely.

"Isn't it sweet of old Arabella, Edward?" Alistair was beaming unconvincingly in the viscountess' direction. "She's come to pay a call on Pegeen. Only that Herbert girl got here first, and I don't know where the two of 'em have taken themselves to. Mrs. Praehurst is tryin' to track 'em down."

Edward smiled tightly. "How nice."

Arabella wore the self-satisfied expression of a cat that's been up to mischief. There was an ulterior motive to this little visit of hers, and surprisingly, without preamble, Arabella revealed it, waving a lacy, gloved hand at them.

"The reason I've popped in so unexpectedly, Edward," Arabella purred, "is that I feel just terrible about poor Miss MacDougal."

Edward raised a quizzical eyebrow. "Oh? How so?"

"Well, here I live within a stone's throw of Rawlings Manor, and I haven't yet had my new neighbor to Ashbury House for so much as a cup of tea. I feel quite embarrassed."

Not embarrassed enough, unfortunately, to keep her away from Rawlings Manor altogether. Edward wondered how long she intended to keep him trapped here in the morning room. He wouldn't stand it for more than five minutes. He had to talk to Alistair alone and then find Pegeen. He was going to be damned if he had to hide his true feelings much longer. It was more than a man could bear.

Ignoring Edward's unencouraging silence, Arabella began to stroll about the room, her skirt swaying beckoningly. Edward recognized the ploy and stifled a yawn. Really, a bit of breakfast might be nice. And where was Evers with his coffee?

"So I said to myself, 'Arabella, darling'—" Arabella always referred to herself with endearments "—'You had better issue an invitation to Miss MacDougal to dine at Ashbury House posthaste.' " Arabella's stroll had taken her to Edward's side. She tugged on his coat sleeve and looked beguilingly up into his clear grey eyes. "And I'm here to do it in person, so it will be harder for you to refuse. And you won't refuse me, will you, Edward?"

Arabella's eyelids fluttered in a perfect imitation at abashment. Edward rolled his eyes.

"All right, Arabella, whatever you say. Now go home, will you? I want my breakfast."

Arabella released his sleeve at once. "Oh, Edward, you always were such a boor. I'll expect to see you all at eight o'clock precisely. And see that you two arrive sober, will you?" She turned to go.

"*What?*" Edward's thundering voice stopped her in her tracks. Arabella turned from the doorway, looking annoyed.

"Really, Edward," she said through pursed lips. "I've asked you not to say 'what.' It's so common—"

"We can't dine with you tonight," Edward said emphatically.

"Why ever not?" Arabella's tone was light. "Have you made other plans?"

"Yes," Edward said. "Haven't we, Cartwright?"

Alistair had slumped into an overstuffed armchair and was staring absently into the fire, fantasizing, Edward had no doubt, about Pegeen's slim white thighs—ridiculous, of course, because he had never seen them. Or if he had, Edward would have no choice but to kill him.

Crossing the room in three quick strides, Edward gave the armchair a kick, startling Alistair out of his lovelorn revery. "Haven't we, Cartwright?" Edward demanded menacingly.

"I don't know what you're talking about, old chap," Alistair said, blinking like someone who'd just woken from a nap. "Plans for this evening? We haven't any plans, no."

Arabella clapped her hands delightedly. "Lovely! Then I'll expect you promptly at eight. And don't forget to bring the young duke. I've so wanted to get to know that adorable child better. 'Til then, gentlemen."

She was out the door before Edward could draw breath to argue. Not that there'd be much point in attempting to argue with Arabella, of course. If she didn't like what you had to say, she simply ignored it anyway.

Damn, what an awkward situation. Now he was going to have sit through one of her insufferably dull dinners. He'd have to endure watching Cartwright making cow's eyes at Pegeen all night. Well, he wasn't going to stand for it. He'd have it out with Cartwright right now and to hell with the dinner. Turning decisively, Edward began in a rough voice, "See here, Cartwright—"

The door to the morning room was thrown open, and Evers appeared, bearing a silver tray laden with coffee items and hot plates. "Your breakfast, Lord Edward," Evers said.

"Yes, yes," Edward said, waving a hand. "Put it down somewhere."

Evers ignored his pacing master and calmly set the breakfast table. Edward observed his butler's painfully slow progress with a grimace on his face. Alistair, still slouching in the armchair, said distractedly, "I hope Arabella doesn't serve those damned jellied quail eggs again. Can't abide 'em."

Edward's shoulders gave an uncontrollable shudder. Damn Evers. He'd heard worse. "Listen, Alistair. About Pegeen."

Alistair looked up from the thumbnail he'd been examining. "Yes? What about her?" Observing Edward's pained expression for the first time, Alistair made a face. "Oh, Rawlings, please. You're not going to start in again about how I'm not to court her, are you? Because I can't stand your self-righteous mewling about how she's only a child and under your protection and—"

"My lord." Evers stood with his back ramrod straight. "Will that be all?"

Edward nodded his thanks and the old man withdrew but not without the subtlest of chuckles. So, now all the servants would know. Well, hang it, they all thought they knew everything anyway. Edward decided to try again.

"Listen, old boy," he began, and the door was again flung open, this time by the topic of conversation herself. Pegeen looked as taken aback at seeing Edward as he was seeing her. Her cheeks were instantly flooded with color, and he felt heat rising in his own face. He was unable to meet her gaze and kept his eyes fastened somewhere on the green velvet skirt of the dress she was wearing.

"Oh, I'm terribly sorry," she said, in that throaty voice that seemed so ill-matched to her delicate frame. "I thought . . . Evers told me that Lady Ashbury was here and wanted to see me."

"She was." Alistair had sprung nimbly from his armchair and raced to Pegeen's side. "And she did. But Rawlings got rid of her by promising to dine with her tonight."

Edward hastily raised his eyes to meet hers, anxious that she not get the wrong idea. "She invited *all* of us," he said quickly. "To Ashbury House. I couldn't think of a way to get out of it, and Cartwright here—''

"What did *I* do?" Alistair sounded offended. He had taken Pegeen by the hand and was pulling her towards a low divan, ostensibly so that the two of them could sit close together and whisper. Edward was relieved to see that Pegeen was exhibiting a certain amount of resistance to this plan.

"Really, Mr. Cartwright," she was saying, tugging at her fingers in an attempt to escape Alistair's inexorable grip. "I've got to get back to the conservatory. Anne is waiting for me—''

"Let the tiresome girl wait." Alistair was acting the part of lovelorn swain to the hilt. Edward glared menacingly at him and succeeded only in making Pegeen, who seemed acutely aware of his every gesture, even more nervous.

"No, I can't let her wait," Pegeen said, twisting her hand a little desperately now. "And I can't dine at Ashbury House tonight, either, because I've invited Anne to dinner here."

Edward could stand it no longer. In one long stride, he was at Pegeen's side. He reached forward and grasped Alistair's arm at the wrist and twisted it behind the smaller man, hard. Looking more surprised than pained, Alistair instantly released Pegeen's hand. She snatched her fingers away and examined them closely, as if he might have crushed them.

Bent nearly double by the pressure Edward was exerting on his arm, Alistair barked, "Rawlings! Have a heart! What do you want to do, break my arm?"

Keeping an iron grip on his friend, Edward grunted into his ear, "Wouldn't be a bad idea. Teach you to keep your hands to yourself, old boy."

"What are you talking about?" Alistair's voice broke. He was obviously in some pain. "I only—"

"Edward." Pegeen had stopped nursing her bruised

fingers and had her hands on her narrow waist. She'd overcome her initial shyness at running into Edward so unexpectedly and now her expression was impatient. "Don't be an idiot. Let him go."

"Listen to her, Eddie," Alistair said. At the word 'Eddie,' Edward gave Cartwright's arm another vicious twist, and Alistair cried out in pain.

Pegeen was upon them at once, like a mother cat berating her mischievous kittens.

"Edward," she snapped, giving him a surprisingly hard smack on the head with her open palm. "Let go of him at once! Honestly, you two—"

Edward was so astonished by her attack that he released Alistair, who stumbled away from him, clutching his sore arm. What was the matter with the girl? Ungrateful wench. It wasn't as if he *enjoyed* inflicting pain upon his best friend. Well, not very much, anyway.

At least she hadn't rushed to Alistair's side offering solace for his wounds. She stood still in the middle of the room, her hands back on her hips and her high cheekbones flushed pink. She was glaring at both of them, her lovely eyebrows knit with disapproval. Edward could have kissed her then and there, she looked so adorable.

Her tone, however, was acidic. "If you gentlemen, and I use the term loosely, don't mind, I am going back to the conservatory to entertain my friend. I will *not* be joining you for dinner with the viscountess, so I hope you have a very enjoyable evening. Good afternoon."

With a saucy little turn that sent her crinoline swooping up, rewarding them both with a glimpse of her slim ankles, Pegeen stalked out of the room. Edward glanced over at Alistair, saw that he was still sulking over his sore limb, and hurried after her. He caught up with her in the Great Hall, and, seizing a slender arm, pulled her into the shadows behind a large wooden support pillar.

Pegeen, her green eyes so large that she looked a bit

like a cornered animal, backed away from him until she was stopped by the pillar, but she kept up a brave front, keeping her chin high in the air and affecting an attitude of nonchalance.

"What do you want?" she demanded pertly, folding her arms across her small, but, as Edward was all too aware, perfectly shaped breasts.

Edward leaned a hand on either side of her narrow waist, trapping her against the pillar within the confines of his arms. He looked down at her, aware that his heart had begun to hammer dully within his chest. No woman had ever affected him like this diminutive, green-eyed witch. He wasn't certain how she'd accomplished it, but she'd stolen his heart, and Edward didn't care if he ever got it back.

"Listen to me," he said, his voice a deep rumble. He could smell the scent she wore, something light and clean and fresh, like wildflowers. It distracted him. He noticed that even though her lips were set into a thin line of disapproval, they were enticingly red.

"What?" she demanded impatiently. "What do you want? Anne Herbert is waiting for me in the—"

"I know, I know, in the conservatory." What in God's name was the girl made of, stone? How could she have forgotten the passion they'd shared only the night before? "Listen to me, Pegeen. You've got to say something to Alistair."

"*I've* got to say something to Alistair?" Pegeen's voice rose an octave. "Well, I like that!"

"Shhh!" Edward laid a finger over her indignantly set lips. "Not so loud, he'll hear—"

"He's *your* guest," Pegeen said through his fingers. "Why don't *you* say something to him?"

"I already did." He took his hand away from her mouth and quickly anchored it by her waist as she made a hasty motion to escape his embrace. What was the matter with the girl? He would have thought that after last night, she wouldn't have a shred of modesty left. Why was she acting so standoffish now? "Alistair won't listen to me, Pegeen. I don't want to hurt him—"

"Neither do I."

"But you're going to have to. Unless you want to see me pummel him into oblivion."

"I don't know why you're behaving so childishly." Pegeen had dropped her voice to a whisper, but she still sounded as if she were scolding a child. "What happened between us last night doesn't change anything, you know."

Edward stared down at her in disbelief. "Doesn't change anything? What are you talking about? It changes everything!"

"It doesn't." Her chin thrust out even more stubbornly than before. "We merely lost our heads again. It's best that we forget about it and go about our business as usual."

"Go about our business? Pegeen, are you mad? Don't you understand? I love—"

He didn't even see it coming. Like a flash out of the shadows, her hand appeared, palm side up, and then she slapped him, hard, a blow that wounded his dignity more than his jaw. Staring incredulously down at the fractious girl, Edward was stunned into silence. He'd tried to tell her that he loved her, and she'd slapped him! Was the girl mentally unbalanced? Her eyes were filled with tears, though, not hatred, and she let out a sob. Whatever was the matter with her? What had he done wrong?

Pegeen couldn't speak, she was so overwrought. Edward reached out to seize her shoulders, to keep her from running away, but she was too quick for him. She was gone in a flurry of velvet and lace, her high-heeled slippers clattering down the hallway. Completely baffled, Edward stared after her fleeing form, one hand on the cheek she'd slapped.

The girl was beside herself. He'd give her a little time to herself and then try again.

What else could he do?

Chapter Twenty-Seven

Pegeen flung herself onto her bed, having made certain that her bedroom door was locked and that Lucy was nowhere about. Oh, God! What was she going to do? She could hardly draw breath through her tears. Why was she behaving so ridiculously?

Wasn't this what she'd been waiting for, dreaming about, for weeks and weeks? Edward Rawlings was in love with her, and what had she done?

Slapped him!

Sobbing into her pillows, Pegeen tried to think rationally. There was no explanation for her behavior, save fear. She was afraid. But of what? Certainly not of Edward. After all, she'd been dreaming of this moment all her life, or so it seemed. Certainly since she'd first laid eyes on him that day so long ago in Applesby. And here he'd finally said it, what she'd been waiting so long to hear him say, and she'd run away like a fool. Oh, God!

After several minutes of fitful crying, Pegeen drew herself up and wiped her eyes with the back of a velvet sleeve. She knew now why she was afraid, and the knowledge of it clutched at her heart like icy cold tentacles.

She was going to have to tell him her secret, the dreadful secret no one, not even Jeremy, knew. The secret that would, when he learned of it, make Edward hate her, not love her. Hate her justifiably, too.

If only she'd never come to Rawlings. If only she'd never heard of Rawlings! If only she and Jeremy had stayed put in Applesby, none of this ever would have happened. She rued the day she ever clapped eyes on Sir Arthur Herbert. What was she going to do now?

A soft knock sounded on the door. Startled, and fearing it was Edward, Pegeen croaked, her voice ragged from crying, "Go away!"

"Pegeen?" Anne Herbert's kind, concerned voice came from beyond the heavy portal. "Are you all right? Lord Edward sent me to see if you needed anything. He said you weren't feeling well."

Giving a last, hiccupy little sob, Pegeen rose from the bed and unlocked the door. Anne looked as if she was trying not to seem startled by the sight of Pegeen's tear-stained, unhappy face.

"I'm sorry, Anne," Pegeen said, unable to meet the older girl's eyes. "I'm not having a very good day, I'm afraid." And she started to cry afresh.

Anne Herbert, sensible, plain, spinsterish Anne, proved to be an invaluable companion. Without asking for the reason behind Pegeen's pain, she tended to her, assuring her that everything was going to be all right, and encouraging her to take a small amount of laudanum from the bottle the surgeon, Mr. Parks, had left when Pegeen had been in the carriage accident.

The laudanum had a calming effect, and presently, Pegeen stopped crying. She apologized to her thoughtful guest, who smiled ruefully and said, "I have four younger sisters, Pegeen. I know quite a lot about drying up tears."

"I'm sorry," Pegeen said, again. She really was feeling much better. It was the laudanum, of course, but she almost felt as if everything would be all right. "I don't know what came over me. I feel such a fool. Do I look a fright?"

"You look beautiful, as always." Anne smiled down at her. "Now, why don't we ask Mrs. Praehurst to bring us some tea, and we'll sit by the fire and discuss what you're going to wear to Ashbury House tonight."

Pegeen let out a wail. "What? You must be joking. I'm not going to Ashbury House tonight!"

"Yes, of course you are." Anne's mouth had set into a determined line. "Lord Edward told me the viscountess invited all of you, and that there wasn't any way to get out of it."

"I just bet he did. Of all the cheek!"

Pegeen's fear turned to indignation. She might be hopelessly in love with him, but she still recognized the fact that Edward could be a complete and total manipulative wretch. Imagine, telling her guest that her hostess had other plans for dinner! And then sending the poor girl to Pegeen's room to stop her crying! Why, she didn't regret the slap one little bit.

"Well, I'm not going to Ashbury House without you," Pegeen said staunchly. Anne looked alarmed.

"Oh, no, Pegeen. I couldn't possibly. I wasn't invited—"

"I'm inviting you."

"But I haven't anything to wear—"

"You can borrow one of my gowns."

"It wouldn't fit. Your waist is so much smaller than mine."

"I'll get Lucy to let out the waist. You can wear my blue taffeta. It will go very nicely with your eyes."

Pegeen was resolute. She was not going to be alone with Edward and Alistair, not even for the short carriage ride to the neighboring estate. She was going to keep Anne Herbert by her side for the entire evening if necessary, and for the rest of the month, too, if she had to. She was absolutely not up to dealing with the two men's jealous tantrums. And as for dealing with either of them one on one, well, that was out of the question as well. She was simply at the end of her rope.

Pegeen dismissed all of Anne's arguments and sent for one of the footmen, asking him to let Ashbury House know to expect four for dinner from Rawlings Manor. Then she and Lucy set about transforming Anne from a prim spinster into a markedly attractive lady of fashion.

By the time Edward sent word upstairs that he and Alistair had been waiting half an hour and that if Pegeen didn't hurry they'd be late to dinner, Anne Herbert looked positively radiant, and Pegeen was almost calm once more. The two girls, Anne in turquoise blue taffeta, and Pegeen in peacock green, arrived simultaneously at the top of the curved double staircase and descended as one, Pegeen lagging a little behind her guest, afraid of meeting Edward's eye.

She needn't have worried. Edward seemed as reluctant as she was to repeat any of the afternoon's unfortunate proceedings. He merely eyed her critically, his sweeping gaze taking in the unnaturally bright spots on her cheeks and the feverish glitter in her eyes. She kept her gaze downcast, and only looked up when Edward wordlessly jostled Alistair out of the way to grasp her gloved hand in his.

She was about to rebuke him for this needlessly rude behavior when her gaze lit upon Jeremy in his best velvet breeches leaning casually against the ornate newel post.

"Jerry!" she cried, her voice still hoarse from weeping. "What are you doing in those clothes? Isn't it time for you to be in bed?"

"Certainly not." Jeremy looked scandalized at her ignorance. "I'm to dine with you all at Ashbury House."

The preposterousness of this notion and the pompousness with which Jeremy announced it struck Pegeen like a blow. She began to laugh helplessly. "You most certainly are not," she said between guffaws. "You get upstairs this instant and get into bed!"

While Jeremy glowered at her, his little hands balled into fists at his side, Edward said in a low voice, "I'm afraid he is coming with us, Pegeen. Arabella requested his presence especially."

Pegeen stopped laughing. "Well, I don't care what Arabella says. Jeremy is a little boy and should be in bed by now."

"Aw, Pegeen!" Jeremy lost his arrogant manner and stamped a petulant foot. "How come I can eat with the adults here in Rawlings, but I'm not good enough to eat with you at Ashbury House?"

"It isn't that, darling, it's just that—"

"Oh, let him come, Pegeen." Alistair, out of politeness, had offered his arm to Anne Herbert. He was clearly enjoying the fact that Pegeen didn't look at all comfortable about being escorted by Edward. "He's going to have to get used to it, eventually."

Edward, too, spoke up in support of his nephew. "It isn't much past his bedtime, Pegeen," he said in his deep voice, the one that rumbled so low in his chest. "And it will amuse Arabella, and keep her mind off . . . other topics."

Pegeen had to concede that Jeremy's presence guaranteed that the table conversation, at least, wouldn't slip into the obscene, as it seemed to have a tendency to do whenever the viscountess was present. She pursed her lips and finally shrugged her bare shoulders. "All right," she said. "Jeremy, you may go, but you are to be on your best behavior, is that understood?"

The boy nodded energetically, and after submitting to a search of his trouser pockets that resulted in the confiscation of a slingshot and his pet ferret, Jeremy raced the adults to the waiting carriage.

Pegeen soon found that though Edward didn't seem to intend to renew any of the afternoon's protestations of love, neither did he seem willing to relinquish her hand to anyone but himself. He kept her fingers pressed tightly into the crook of his right arm, handing her personally into the coach and seating himself possessively at her side. Had she any doubts as to the depth of his feelings, they'd have been dismissed by his proprietary behavior.

Alistair was obviously put out by this exhibition and spent the entire carriage ride glaring balefully at his host, but there wasn't anything he could do to rectify the situation. Pegeen was thankful for the presence of Anne, who good-naturedly pretended not to notice anything amiss. Jeremy, as always, rode up top with the driver, despite the near arctic cold.

When they pulled into the circular drive of Ashbury House, a dismal-looking brick mansion, Pegeen was relieved to see that theirs wasn't the only carriage present. Another vehicle, a rather gaudy contraption that Jeremy informed them through chattering teeth as Bates handed him down was a four-horsed brougham from London, was parked nearby. Pegeen wondered idly whose company the viscountess was going to inflict upon them. Certainly no one respectable, judging from the bright red trim of the brougham.

The footmen who greeted the party from Rawlings wore blue and silver livery and old-fashioned powdered white wigs, which Jeremy felt compelled to laugh at until Pegeen gave him a gentle cuff on the ear. The ladies were admitted into an upstairs bedroom to dispose of their wraps and repair whatever damage might have been done to their gowns during the short journey across the moor. While Pegeen was pinching her cheeks to make them redder, she noticed an ermine-lined cloak spread across the bed that must have belonged to the owner of the gawdy brougham. The cloak was deep purple, a costly and rather vulgarly ostentatious garment. Though she didn't mention it to the gentle Anne, Pegeen began to suspect that the viscountess' other guests were perhaps not gentry.

Anne, however, while she might not have noticed the vulgar cloak, had noticed Edward's odd behavior, and to Pegeen's dismay, she commented upon it, though in the most oblique manner imaginable.

"Miss MacDougal," Anne said, pretending to be absorbed in her own reflection in a full-length mirror in one corner of the guest bedroom. "I do hope that should you ever feel that you needed, well, to get away from—from Rawlings Manor for a little while, you'd consider coming to stay with us at Herbert Park." Anne blushed prettily. She'd meant 'get away from Edward Rawlings' but she'd found a more delicate way to say it.

Pegeen was touched by the older girl's perceptiveness. She smiled fondly at her and said, "You know, that might be just the thing. Maybe tomorrow, when your father sends his coach to fetch you, I'll pack a little bag and go along. Just for a few days."

"Oh, yes," Anne said, turning away from the mirror, her smile genuine. "We could have such fun, just as we did when you first came, you and Jeremy, on your way to Rawlings."

Pegeen squeezed the older girl's hand gratefully. How nice it was to have such a sweet friend. Yes, that's exactly what Pegeen would do, get away from Rawlings Manor for a little while. Maybe a few days away would give her a chance to really think. She was going to have to find some way to convince Edward that marrying her would be the worst mistake he ever made. Short of telling him the truth, Pegeen couldn't think of any way to do it, and she would never be able to tell him the truth—she'd go back to Applesby first.

When the two girls had finished primping, they left the guest bedroom and went back downstairs. Edward, Alistair, and Jeremy were waiting for them at the bottom of the stairs with the Ashburys' butler. Once again Pegeen found her hand seized by Edward Rawlings, and she couldn't help a small smile at his jealous behavior. He stared down at her, stony-faced, and her smile faded away at once. Poor man! What must he think of her? He tries to propose, and his intended flees from him as if he were a convict! If only she could tell him why!

"His Grace, the duke of Rawlings," the Ashburys' butler announced, and Jeremy, his chest puffed out with boyish pride, strutted into the sitting room in which the viscountess and her guests were gathered. Pegeen had to stifle a giggle.

The butler paused, then said, "Lord Edward Rawlings and Miss Pegeen MacDougal."

Pegeen felt Edward's arm tense beneath her gloved fingers, and then he was guiding her through the wide doorway, into a peach and white sitting room that was a little too hot. Pegeen had already plastered a gracious smile onto her face and was just turning to offer her hand to Arabella Ashbury, who was smiling, for some reason, very broadly, when her gaze fell upon the only other woman in the room, a woman who had risen abruptly to her feet at Pegeen's entrance.

The woman was obviously the owner of the purple cloak in the guest bedroom. Her gown was stylish but a little too showy, a fuchsia concoction with daringly low décolletage. There were matching fuchsia feathers in the woman's jet black hair, and the emeralds around her plump white neck shown as brightly as the woman's piercing green eyes. Those eyes widened when they met Pegeen's, and suddenly it seemed to Pegeen that the room grew dark, as if someone had extinguished all the lights and she stood alone, a roaring sound in her ears.

Because the woman who was staring at her was her sister, Katherine.

Chapter Twenty-Eight

Edward felt Pegeen's fingers clench his arm convulsively, and the next thing he knew, she was falling forward in a dead faint.

He caught her expertly before she hit the carpet, and with athletic precision, he scooped her slight form into his arms and moved to one of the settees, lowering her gently onto the white cushions and kneeling beside the low couch. He had no idea what had caused her to faint, but he did know that Pegeen wasn't one to faint easily. She hadn't lost consciousness that day he'd introduced himself, or when she'd been badly injured in a carriage accident, and despite her delicate appearance, she was strong as a pony. He could testify to that. His jaw was still sore from the smack she'd delivered to it hours ago.

Jeremy, of course, was at her side in an instant, his grey eyes wide with fear. "What's wrong with Pegeen?" he demanded tremulously, laying hold of Edward's coat lapels. "What's wrong with her? Is she dead?"

"No, Jerry." Edward felt Pegeen's smooth white forehead. It was icy cold. "She's just fainted. Arabella, your smelling salts—"

"Stupid me," Arabella said, biting her lip. She was peering down at Pegeen's supine form with something not unlike relish. "I should have anticipated that."

A tallish man Edward had never seen before was asking if they should send for the surgeon. Alistair had fetched a glass of brandy and kept insisting upon pouring it down Pegeen's throat. The dark-haired woman in the garish dress had backed off into a corner and stood there, looking angry. Only Anne Herbert seemed capable of behaving rationally. She struck a match at the fireplace and lit a piece of kindling, and she waved the smoldering stick beneath Pegeen's nose.

After a moment or two of this, Pegeen's eyelids fluttered, and then with a little sigh, she regained consciousness and blinked up at Edward, her pretty face perplexed.

"You fainted, darling," Edward murmured, brushing her forehead with his lips. He no longer gave a damn what anyone thought. "Give me that brandy, Cartwright."

But Alistair had seen the kiss and heard the endearment. He stared down at Edward, his handsome features twisted with astonishment.

"Bless me!" he cried. "I ought to have known! No wonder you were so resistant to the idea of my courting her! You wanted her for yourself all along!"

Edward glared up at him. "Not *now*, Cartwright. Hand me that brandy and stop acting like a child."

Rolling his eyes, Alistair passed the brandy snifter. Edward pressed the rim of the glass to Pegeen's lips, and she twisted her head away, making a face as the fumes from the spirits in the vessel assailed her senses.

"Drink it," Edward commanded. He was reminded of another time, months and months ago, it seemed, that he'd given Pegeen a similar order. Like that first time, she truculently refused to comply, keeping her face averted, her nose turned up.

"Drink it," Edward growled again. "It's brandy. You liked it, remember?"

"What's this?" The voice rang out from a far corner of the room, a strangely familiar voice, yet one Edward was certain he'd never heard before. He turned his head and saw that the garishly dressed woman was clutching the back of satin covered chair and laughing, a little hysterically, Edward thought.

"Faint, are you?" demanded the plump, heavily jeweled stranger. Her accent, like Pegeen's, had a hint of Scottish in it. She seemed to be finding something quite amusing. "Aren't you just the refined lady!"

Edward saw that, after hearing that voice, Pegeen downed the contents of the snifter with a neat flick of her wrist. She set aside the glass and stared with something akin to horror at the older woman. Jeremy had shrunk back against the settee and clutched Pegeen's hand so tightly his knuckles went white. He murmured something, and Pegeen nodded. Jeremy's face went as white as the snow outdoors. What he'd whispered, Edward knew, were the words, "Is that her?"

Realizing that it was this woman's presence that had caused Pegeen to faint, Edward rose angrily to his feet and demanded of Arabella, who was also staring at the jolly woman with a sort of simpering smile on her face, "Would you kindly introduce me to your charming guest over there, Arabella?"

"With great pleasure, Lord Edward." Arabella's smile turned devilish. He'd seen that smile before, right before the viscountess sprang one of her elaborate and mean-spirited pranks on some poor, unsuspecting soul.

Arabella gave a little flourish with her gloved hand, and, with infuriating calm, said, "Lord Edward Rawlings, may I present to you—"

"No!"

Edward turned and looked down. Miraculously, Pegeen was on her feet, pale as death but with a determined look on her lovely face. Her pointed chin was thrust out, her slender fingers clenched into small fists at her sides. She was breathing in quick, shallow gasps, her green eyes blazing. Edward had never seen her so angry—if, indeed, she was angry and not demented. Even Jeremy had shrunk away from her and was clutching Anne Herbert's skirts, his grey eyes wide.

"You," Pegeen said to the woman in fuchsia. Her voice was as flinty as rock. "A word. In private."

The woman had stopped laughing and was staring at the furious girl with raised eyebrows—eyebrows, Edward realized, that had been entirely plucked out and redrawn with a black pencil. "All right," she said in a strangely quiet voice after all the raucous laughter. Edward realized that the creature was a little cowed by Pegeen's fierce expression.

He, too, was alarmed by it. As Pegeen turned towards the door, he caught her arm and bent down to whisper in her shell-like ear, "Pegeen . . . What is it? Who is she? Let me come with you . . ."

But Pegeen, with an elegant, well-timed shrug, shook off his grip and disappeared through the open doorway. The larger woman sauntered after her, her head held high, but her gaze darting slyly at the strange man who'd kept insisting they send for a surgeon. The tall man's eyebrows were raised as well but with skepticism, not alarm. When the two women had disappeared through the doorway, Edward turned and lunged angrily at Arabella, grasping her arm in fingers that bit into her soft flesh.

"What is this about, Arabella?" He hardly recognized his own voice. "Tell me now, or by God, I'll wring that skinny neck of yours."

Arabella shrank from him, her face suddenly filled with fear. "Edward, you're hurting me!"

"I'll rip your damned arm off if I find you've done

anything to hurt Pegeen.'' He shook her in his grip to show
the validity of his claim. ''Now, tell me who—''

''Edward!'' Suddenly Alistair was pulling at him.
''Edward, let go of her. You're beside yourself.''

''She's Kathy Porter,'' Arabella panted, raising a face
that was every bit as furious as Edward's. Her pale blue
eyes blazed like sapphires. ''You remember Kathy Porter,
don't you, Edward?'' Arabella's smile was bitter. ''You've
visited her London establishment several times, if I'm not
mistaken.''

Edward grimaced. It was typical of Arabella to announce something like that in front of someone like Anne
Herbert, whose eyes had grown as large as Jeremy's,
though thankfully, she seemed to have no idea that Kathy
Porter ran one of the most expensive—and popular—bor-
dellos in London. Edward had never met the proprietress,
Mrs. Porter, though she was rumored to be highly skilled
at entertaining gentlemen. Why Arabella had felt compelled
to invite her to dinner, Edward couldn't imagine. And how
on earth would Pegeen know someone—

Edward felt a hard pull at his evening jacket, and,
glancing down, caught sight of Jeremy's pale face at his
elbow.

''Please, Uncle Edward.'' There were tears streaming
down the little boy's face. He was weeping pathetically.
''Please, Uncle Edward. You won't let her take me away,
will you? Please don't let her take me away.''

Abruptly, Edward released the viscountess, who fell
back into the arms of the tall stranger, disheveling her coiffure and looking as if she was beginning to regret her
scheme. Leaning down, Edward grasped both of Jeremy's
shoulders and gave him a shake.

''What's this, Your Grace?'' He spoke with a teasing
bravado he didn't feel. ''Why the tears?''

Jeremy could barely speak, he was sobbing so hard.
''She's come to take me away. I always knew she would.''

"Who's come to take you away, Jeremy? What are you talking about?"

"My m-mother." Jeremy hiccupped. "Oh, Uncle Edward, don't you see? That l-lady is my m-mother!"

Edward's fingers convulsed on the boy's shoulders, and Jeremy winced with pain but said nothing. It was Alistair who seized Edward's wrists and pulled his hands away from the boy.

"Take it easy, old chap." Cartwright's voice wasn't quite steady, though. "I'm sure there's a reasonable explanation . . ."

"There certainly is." Arabella had collected herself, smoothed out her gown and rearranged her hair, and now she spoke with brisk authority, and a certain amount of self-satisfaction. "Katherine Rawlings married your dead brother's murderer, one Thomas Porter, and became none other than Katherine Porter, notorious lady of the evening—"

Edward felt as if someone had poured a bucket of ice water down his back. "This is fiction," he ground out. "This is pure invention, Arabella, designed to hurt Pegeen!"

Arabella laughed, a cold, tinkling sound, like the tolling of a bell made entirely of glass. "You flatter yourself, Edward. Do you honestly think I care that you're bedding the bitch? It isn't any of my business if you choose to consort with the sister of a whore."

"That's enough, Arabella," Edward roared. He glared at the tall stranger who'd insisted upon calling for the surgeon.

"You," he said to the stranger. "You're Porter?"

"Your brother's murderer?" The tall man laughed, as if he found the suggestion genuinely amusing. "Would you really expect me to answer that question affirmatively, Lord Edward? You'd tear me limb from limb, I wouldn't doubt."

Arabella was still grinning like a cat who'd knocked over the creamer. "Thomas Porter died years ago, Edward, in a barroom brawl. This is Mr. Clyde Stephens. He's Kathy Porter's . . . accountant.''

Stephens clicked his heels together and gave a mocking bow. ''At your service, sir.''

''Well.'' Arabella sighed contentedly. ''Dinner will be served in a few minutes. Would anyone care for a drink?''

Edward stared at her, wondering how he'd ever sunk so low as to consider her a lover. Alistair, too, was looking at the blonde viper as if she were an oddity in a sideshow attraction. Without saying another word, Edward rose to his feet and left the room in search of Pegeen.

Chapter Twenty-Nine

Pegeen never once looked over her shoulder to see whether or not Kathy was following. She had never been to Ashbury House before, and of course she had no idea where she was going. She just kept walking, her heart hammering in her chest, her vision unsteady. A part of her wanted to turn around and head for the front door, and keep walking across the moor, back to the Post Road, all the way back to Applesby. The only thing that stopped her was the knowledge that, ill as she felt, she'd probably collapse after only a few yards.

It was in a dark gallery at the back of the house that Pegeen finally ran out of energy to go any further. The hallway was lined on one side with Ashbury family portraits, and on the other, with windows looking out over the snow-covered lawn of Ashbury Park. Moonlight filtered through the leaded panes, affording just enough grey light for Pegeen to see that her sister's face wore a smile. Pegeen restrained an impulse to wipe the smirk from Kathy's face with her fist.

"Well." Katherine strolled past Pegeen. She went right up to one of the windows and peered out at the wind-swept snow.

Katherine MacDougal Rawlings Porter was ten years older and nearly six inches taller than her sister. She had a figure that was voluptuous to the point of obesity, but she was still considered a great beauty in certain circles. Ten years ago, when she'd managed to trick Lord John Rawlings into marrying her, she'd been even prettier. Time, Pegeen saw, even in the dark, had treated her kindly in spite of the lifestyle she'd chosen to lead. Considering her profession, it was a miracle she was still alive, let alone in possession of her looks.

Katherine stared out the window for a moment, then turned her green-eyed gaze upon Pegeen.

"Hello, Peggy." Those eyes weren't warm. Not at all. Pegeen hadn't expected them to be. "You've certainly grown up since I last saw you."

"The last time you saw me I was ten years old." Pegeen's voice was low with emotion, and it rasped painfully.

"Really? Was it that long ago?" Katherine didn't sound as if she really cared, though. "I hadn't thought—"

"It was the night you brought Jeremy. You and that man." Pegeen spoke with a bitterness that surprised her. She hadn't thought she still harbored so much hatred for her only sibling.

"Oh, it couldn't be—"

"You didn't wait to see me that morning. I was at school, and you and that man came swooping back into town and dropped Jeremy off as if he was a parcel and took off again, like some kind of bat out of—"

"Please, Peggy. Let's not stoop to name-calling."

"Oh, no?" Pegeen heard her voice rising. *Don't get hysterical, Pegeen. Stay calm, or there's no hope at all.* "All right, then. I *won't* call you a coldhearted, vicious bitch."

Katherine's hand flew up from the shadows, but Pegeen reached out and caught the plump wrist before her sister's talon-like fingernails could rake her face. Katherine looked surprised at her little sister's reflexes.

"You see," Pegeen said, giving the soft wrist a twist that caused her sister to yelp. "I've learned a lot since you ran away. I had to learn to take of myself, as well as your son."

Katherine yanked her hand out of Pegeen's reach and looked at it unbelievingly. She'd taken a step backwards, and Pegeen knew she'd think twice before striking again.

"You're being ridiculous," Kathy said, but her voice shook a little. "You're acting as if Father wasn't around to look after you both—"

"Father?" Pegeen laughed abruptly. "Oh, yes, Father was there, physically, anyway. You broke his heart, you know, Kathy. You broke everybody's heart." She shook her head. "How *could* you, Kathy? I can understand your wanting to get out of Applesby, but how could you abandon Jeremy like that?"

Katherine looked uncomfortable. "I sent money—"

"I know you did, at first. Father sent it all back to you, remember? Father wouldn't accept money from a prostitute, you ought to have known that. If you'd bothered to write to me, to let me know where I could contact you, I'd have told you—"

Katherine shook her head so that her ink black curls—false curls, Pegeen was certain, for her own hair had never curled like that—swung. "It isn't my fault, Peggy. I did try, you know."

"Did you?" Pegeen shook her head again disbelievingly.

"What choice did I have?" Katherine cried with dramatic aplomb. "I never wanted a child. And God knows John never did. No one could be as bad a parent as I'd have been, not even Father, whose head was always buried in a book. And I knew *you'd* be there, Peggy. I knew you'd take care of Jerry. You were always finding sick and stray things, animals and such, and nursing them back to health.

It was in your nature to take care of things, I could tell that, even though you were only a little girl. So it wasn't as if I didn't think Jerry would be well taken care of—''

''That's right.'' Pegeen folded her arms across her chest. ''Good old Peggy, she'd raise your son for you. And when Father died, I suppose you thought I'd just get by without help from anyone?''

''Peggy, I never knew he died. He wasn't even fifty! How was I to know he'd died?''

''You could have written.''

''I could have.'' Katherine shrugged her round, sloping shoulders. ''But you know I'm not good with letters, Peggy.''

Pegeen threw her hands into the air. She didn't know what she'd expected. Her sister had never shown much sense before. Why would she start exhibiting it now? Placing her hands on her hips, Pegeen faced the older woman, her head cocked to one side. ''So what are you doing here, Kathy? Did you come just to humiliate me? Did you come to ruin your son's life?''

''Of course not.'' Katherine was examining her wrist where Pegeen had grasped it. There were red welts shaped like fingers circling the fair skin like a bracelet. ''I happen to be a friend of the earl of Derby—''

''Oh, no.'' Pegeen rolled her eyes.

''Yes. And he and Lady Ashbury informed me that there was a new duke of Rawlings. I never dreamed the old man would have changed his will, passing the title onto Jeremy. But when Arabella assured me it was so, well, I just had to come.'' Kathy smiled patronizingly. ''I just had to see my boy one last time.''

''Oh, yes! Now that he's a duke, you mean!''

It was Pegeen's turn to pace. She turned and walked quickly up the gallery, then back again, her hands clenched in tight fists at her sides.

"What is that supposed to mean?" Kathy demanded. "I don't like the implication in your tone."

"I'm not implying anything, Kathy. I just find it interesting that when Jeremy and I were living off the charity of the church, threatened daily with being sent to a workhouse, we didn't hear a peep from you. But now that he's master of one of the largest fortunes in England, you pop up at dinner parties!"

Kathy sniffed. "Of all the—"

Pegeen stopped pacing and whirled to face her sister. "Jeremy's all I have, Kathy. I didn't want him to find out about you. I mean, after all, Kath, you married the man who murdered his father!"

"Shh!" Katherine raised a fleshy finger to her lips. "Not so loud, if you please."

"Well, you did. It just seemed better if I pretended you were dead."

Katherine stared at her. "I suspect you're right," she said after moment. The response startled Pegeen. "Well, you certainly turned out better than I ever thought you would. You're actually pretty."

Pegeen made a wry face. "Thank you," she said, out of politeness only. She did not much value compliments from her sister.

"More than pretty, as a matter of fact." Katherine's eyes were calculating as they flicked over Pegeen, from her high-heeled satin slippers to the simple but elegant style of her hair. "You'd fetch quite a pretty penny in my place, you know."

Pegeen's cheeks began to burn. "Kathy! Really!"

"The idea shocks you, does it?" Katherine circled her younger sister, never taking her eyes off Pegeen's narrow waist and ripe bosom. "Still, I know men who'd pay a small ransom for the chance. You haven't let that Edward Rawlings into your pantaloons, have you?"

"Kathy!" Pegeen's cheeks were flushed scarlet. She

was losing the upper hand. This wouldn't do at all. . . .

"No, I can see by your virginal blush that you haven't.
Well, you always had more self-restraint than I had. I must
say Edward's turned out remarkably well, considering what
his father was. And his brother too, for that matter. A crueller pair of bastards you couldn't find. If Thomas hadn't
killed John, I probably would have."

This statement, made in the same bland tone which
Katherine employed for almost all of her conversation, was
chilling in its bald honesty. Pegeen stared at her sister, and
it occurred to her that she didn't know her sibling at all.
She'd thought Katherine capable of much, but actual murder? Never. Now she realized she'd have to reconsider.

Oblivious to Pegeen's shock, Katherine said casually,
"Edward's very good-looking, you know. Better looking
than John, that's for certain. And more civilized, you can
tell at a glance. Is he in love with you?" Without waiting
for Pegeen's reply, Katherine nodded. "I thought so. And
you? Do you love him?"

Pegeen stamped her foot. This was too much. "Kathy,
stop it!"

"Stop what? You think I'm a coldhearted, vicious
bitch, and maybe I am, but at least I know my place. You
don't honestly think that after all of this, Edward Rawlings
is going to marry you, do you?"

Pegeen swallowed. It felt as if her heart had been
pierced by a shard of glass. "I do not."

"Good. I'm glad to see you have some sense at least.
That woman. The viscountess. She loves him, and she
knows he loves you. That's why she arranged for this little
charade, don't you think? It's unfortunate, but it's the nature of the beast, isn't it? We must all know our place.
Now that you've been put back into yours, you ought to
come back to London with me."

Pegeen's eyebrows knit in bewilderment. "You can't
be serious."

"Of course I am. I'm a businesswoman, Peggy. I know a good investment when I see one. You would rake in a fortune. And you certainly can't stay here. Jeremy will be all right. It's you I'm worried about."

Pegeen let out an incredulous laugh. "And so you're going to take care of me by turning me into a *whore*?"

Katherine frowned. Frowning, she looked her age. "I don't like the word 'whore,' Peggy. It's so coarse. I prefer 'courtesan.' And I wouldn't laugh, if I were you. What other options do you have? You're not educated enough to become a governess, and you're far too headstrong to go into service. You're talented with numbers, I hear, but that's not women's work." Katherine sighed, and glanced down at one of the many large, jeweled rings on her fingers. "You could marry, I suppose, but isn't marriage a form of servitude in itself? Anyway, who'd have you? You've no dowry, no income of any sort. And your sister is a whore. No, Peggy." She looked up, and smiled very convincingly, almost—but not quite—warmly. "Come with me, back to London. We could leave tonight. I promise you, you'll make more money than you could ever imagine."

"I don't want money," Pegeen said.

"What do you want? Love?" Katherine laughed coldly. "Peggy, darling, you'll have more men worshipping at your feet than you'll know what to do with. Pin money, jewels, your own curricle, a matched pair of geldings, a townhouse—"

"That all sounds very tempting." The deep, masculine voice came from out of nowhere, it seemed. Pegeen whirled, recognizing the voice. In a shaft of light from a hall table candelabra, she saw the large figure of Edward Rawlings leaning against the stone archway that led into the gallery. It was evident from his relaxed posture—he was slumped against the wall, his arms folded across his powerful chest—that he'd been leaning there for some time.

Pegeen was still struggling to find her voice when Katherine said haughtily, "Sir, you ought to have made your presence known!"

"And miss your eloquent address on the benefits of prostitution?" He chuckled. "Perhaps my brother might have interrupted such a speech, but not I. No, I must confess that I find you to be quite an inspirational speaker, Mrs. Porter. Or should I call you Katherine? You are, after all, my sister-in-law."

Katherine eyed him warily. "You may call me whatever you wish. You'll excuse me if I sound rude, Lord Edward, but I was addressing my sister just now, not you. I'd appreciate it if you kept your opinions to yourself."

"My opinions? Oh, you mean my opinions on your profession." Edward nodded, stroking his jaw with his long, square-tipped fingers. "Well, yes, I could see how you'd want me to keep my mouth shut. I mean, after all, you've neglected to tell Pegeen what happens to—how did you put it? Oh, yes—*courtesans* who become too old to work anymore."

"I hardly think—"

"You know, don't you, Pegeen, that most *courtesans* don't live past thirty? You mentioned nothing of disease in your little discourse, Mrs. Porter. Or pregnancy. Or the fact that prostitution is, in fact, illegal. How many of your girls have been arrested in the past month, Mrs. Porter? And how many have fallen ill from sexually transmitted diseases? And how many have died from self-induced abortions, trying to rid themselves of an unwanted baby—"

Pegeen couldn't bear it any longer. She pressed her hands to her face and said in a tightly controlled voice, "Edward, for God's sake! Please stop!"

Edward left the wall upon which he'd been leaning and went to Pegeen's side. He put a heavy arm around her bare, quivering shoulders. "Come, Pegeen," he said, his lips brushing her hair. "Let's go home."

Pegeen's heart suddenly leapt to life, hammering hard within her breast. She lifted her tear-stained face to stare up at him, thinking she'd misheard him and praying that she hadn't. But it was Katherine who spoke.

"You can't be serious." Katherine was laughing in disbelief. "Don't you know who she is?"

"She is the aunt of the duke of Rawlings." Edward's face was so expressionless, it could have been carved from stone. "She raised him from a babe in arms because he was abandoned by his mother, if I understand correctly."

"She's the sister of a whore!" Katherine cackled. "And your so-called bloody duke of Rawlings is the *son* of one! What have you to say to that, eh? What have you to say about the fact that the duke of Rawlings has a *whore* for a mamma?"

"Only this," Edward said in a voice that was deadly calm. He paused inside the stone archway with his arm still around Pegeen. "If you ever come near Pegeen or my nephew again, I'll have you arrested, Mrs. Porter. I'll see to it that you are incarcerated for the rest of your natural life. Do we understand one another?"

Pegeen saw her sister's rouged mouth fall open. "*What*?" she gasped.

"Good night, Mrs. Porter," Edward said quietly. And then he was steering Pegeen away.

"What?" Katherine cried again. "Pegeen? You're going with him? Are you daft? Have you lost what sense God gave you, girl? He's no good, Peggy! He'll debauch you, just like his brother debauched me!" Katherine's voice had reached shouting pitch, since Edward had conducted Pegeen from the gallery. Still, she could not escape that shrill voice.

"Debauched me and then left me for his liquor and his gambling and his whores. Just you wait, Peggy! His brother will do the same to you, and then where will you be? Alone, like I was, except maybe he'll leave you with a little present, a little weeping, leaking present like John left me. We'll see how well little Pegeen takes care of herself then, won't we?''

Pegeen noticed that their shadows, cast from the light of the candelabra on a table in the hallway, were long upon the flagstone floor, and because she and Edward walked so close together, their two shadows mingled into one.

Katherine's furious screams followed them from the gallery. ''We'll see what becomes of pretty, pathetic Pegeen then, won't we?''

Chapter Thirty

The embers in the fireplace in the Rose Room were
dying. Pegeen, clad only in one of her muslin, lace-
trimmed nightgowns, tried to revive the fire, em-
ploying both poker and blower, but her heart wasn't in the
activity. When licking flames finally caressed the new logs
she'd laid, she wasn't even aware of it. She was sitting on
the hearth, both arms curled around her knees, hugging
them to her chest, staring unseeingly at a point in the center
of the carpet. There was no hope for it, she'd realized. She
was going to have to leave.

She'd gone directly to her room upon their return to
Rawlings. She had endured the carriage ride from Ashbury
House in silence, her arms wrapped protectively around a
weeping Jeremy. She had refused to make eye contact with
either Alistair or Anne, keeping her gaze upon the top of
Jeremy's dark head, not risking a glance even at Edward,
a brooding figure who took up much of the seat beside her,
silent and formidable in the darkness of the coach.

No one had said a word to her when she and Edward
had returned from the portrait gallery. Edward's command
that their wraps be collected had met with comment only

from the viscountess, who'd sucked in her breath and demanded to know why it was they couldn't stay for dinner after all. Edward had only glared at her. Their cloaks appearing with miraculous alacrity in the arms of the wigged footmen, the party from Rawlings left Ashbury House in silence, a silence that extended through the trip home.

Only Jeremy spoke, poor, inconsolable Jeremy, who clung to Pegeen as if she were a lifeline and kept asking her whether or not she was going to let his mother take him away. Pegeen could only kiss his forehead and assure him that his mother wanted him to stay at Rawlings.

"She only wanted to see you, Jerry," Pegeen told him. "She only wanted to see what a great big boy you've grown into." She could not convince him that there wasn't any danger of his mother taking him away.

Once in the Great Hall at Rawlings, Alistair seemed to recover some of his irrepressible good humor and suggested that they all raid the kitchens for something to eat— they had, after all, not yet had their dinner. But Pegeen declined, heading straight to the nursery with Jeremy. There, she was relieved to see his spirits revived by a cup of chocolate and one of Cook's puddings. If only, she thought wryly, watching her nephew's face as he fell asleep, her own problems could be solved by eating dessert.

She was perfectly aware that she was avoiding all sorts of confrontations by remaining in the sanctuary of the nursery. There was Anne Herbert, whose father Pegeen had purposefully lied to by telling him that Katherine Rawlings was dead. There was Alistair, whom she'd not only lied to but misled by making him think there was a chance she returned his feelings of admiration for her when in fact she knew perfectly well that she was in love with Edward Rawlings. And then, of course, there was Edward.

Well, she hadn't lied to Edward, though Lord knew she'd tried. No, her sin lay in omission. She had neglected to tell him that while Katherine Rawlings wasn't dead, she was a whorehouse madam, as well as responsible for his brother's murder. How could a man possibly love a woman whose own flesh and blood was capable of such evil? Even in the best of all worlds, a world where people were judged by their own merits and not by who their families were, Pegeen couldn't imagine that any man would be able to forgive something like that. Not even a man like Edward.

Of the three people she believed she'd injured most—and she wasn't even counting people like Mrs. Praehurst and Lucy, people who would be shocked and hurt when the truth came out (and the viscountess would see to it that the truth did get out as soon as possible)—she supposed that the person with the least reason to be offended was Anne Herbert. To make sure of this fact, Pegeen had stopped by the older girl's room on her way to her own after Jeremy had fallen asleep.

Anne had answered Pegeen's soft knock at once and had immediately made it clear to Pegeen that it wouldn't have mattered if she'd been Satan's own sister—Pegeen was Anne's friend, and would always remain so. Pegeen felt she owed the girl an explanation, but when she tried to make it, Anne wouldn't listen. She clung to Pegeen's hands and said only, "It doesn't matter, Pegeen. None of it matters. What you did, you did because you love Jeremy and wanted what's best for him. Everyone will understand that."

Relief and gratitude flooded over Pegeen like fresh rainwater. But she still had a favor to ask Anne, a great favor, considering everything that had happened. . . .

She asked it, and when Anne laughed and said, of course, don't be silly, Pegeen knew that in plain, gentle Anne Herbert she'd found a friend worth far more than her weight in gold.

But now there was Edward to contend with. And that, Pegeen knew, wouldn't be so easy.

He had come by her room several times since they'd returned from Ashbury House, knocking first, and then the third time she'd told him to go away, trying the knob, then kicking the door at finding it locked. Still, Pegeen wouldn't open it, telling him tartly that if he wanted to kick a perfectly good door to smithereens that was his business, but that she advised against it. Edward had tried reasoning with her, speaking in a voice so gentle and persuasive that Pegeen had felt herself weakening almost at once, then, remembering what had happened each other time she'd allowed him to enter her room, she turned deaf ears to his entreaties.

But now, nearly two hours later, she felt better prepared to face him. The servants, she knew, would have all gone to bed, so there was no chance that she'd run into Mrs. Praehurst or Lucy or Evers and have to endure their sympathy or snub, as the case might be. Alistair, she was certain, would have long since drunk himself into a stupor, and while there was a chance the same might have been said for the master of the house, Pegeen felt she'd most likely find Edward in his library, and that there they might be able to have a civilized conversation that wouldn't end up with a slap or a mad dash to the bed.

Donning a mannish, slightly tattered silk dressing gown that Pegeen hadn't found occasion to wear since her Applesby days but thinking it provided her with more protection against his rutting gaze than her sadly misused feathered negligee, she unlocked her bedroom door and peered out into the dark, chilly gallery.

There, sitting directly across from her door, was Edward, his long legs stretched out before him, a decanter of brandy on the floor beside the chair he'd carried from his library.

"Good evening, Miss MacDougal," he said casually, as if he often seated himself outside the bedroom doors of young women. But Pegeen realized immediately that there was an undercurrent of nervousness running beneath his teasing tone.

"If you're looking for your maidservant, I sent her to bed an hour ago. If you're in need of something, I'd be more than happy to fetch it for you. What, exactly, do you require at the moment? A glass of warm milk, perhaps? A book from the library to soothe your frazzled nerves? Or perhaps a manly shoulder upon which to weep?" He made a sweeping gesture with one hand. In the other, Pegeen noticed an empty brandy snifter. "Whatever you desire, it will be my pleasure to deliver to you."

Pegeen leaned in her doorway and studied him. He hadn't removed his evening coat, although the cravat was gone, and his shirt front was open to the waist. His dark, rich chest hair stood out in direct contrast with the crisp whiteness of his shirt, and Pegeen restrained an impulse to go to him then and there, and lay her head upon his invitingly broad shoulders. She said in a voice rough with emotion, "I was going to look for you."

He quirked a dark eyebrow ironically. "How propitious. It seems you found me."

"How long have you been sitting out here?"

"Long enough to have begun to suspect you were never coming out." He stretched his long, lean legs, and joints popped protestingly. "I don't suppose you'd let me come in, would you? It's rather cold out here, and this chair grows more uncomfortable by the second."

Pegeen glanced nervously over her shoulder. Her room, as usual, was cheerful and warm, and certainly more conducive to comfortable conversation than the hallway, or even, she considered, Edward's library, which was a bit threateningly masculine in all of its leathery decor. Still, the last thing she wanted was a repeat performance of last night's—had it really only been last night?—amorous adventure.

As if he'd read her thoughts in her troubled expression, Edward set down the empty glass and stood a little unsteadily. "Please allow me to assure you, madam, that these hands——" He held them out for Pegeen's perusal, shoving the massive, callused fingers under her nose "—— will remain at my sides at all times. Unless, that is, you require their services for something or other."

Pegeen did not care to venture what "something or other" he might have in mind, but after a few more seconds of hesitation, she sighed, and drew the portal open all the way to admit him. Edward looked neither pleased nor displeased to have won this small round. He seemed to Pegeen oddly nervous. Probably, she supposed, because he was going to ask her to leave Rawlings. Oh, yes, he'd put up a grand little show of solidarity for appearance's sake back at Ashbury House, but when it came down to it, actually living with a relative of his brother's murderer was asking a bit much. Well, she would set his mind at ease.

"Won't you sit down?" she asked stiffly, pointing at one of the soft, overstuffed armchairs before her merrily blazing fire.

"No, thank you." Edward bounced once or twice on the balls of his toes. She was always impressed by his size, but never more so than when he was in her room. He dwarfed all of the furniture, including the great canopy bed, the way she dwarfed all of Jeremy's toys. "I prefer to stand, if you don't mind. Been sitting down for quite a while now."

"It's your own fault if you're sore," Pegeen said with a flash of annoyance. "No one asked you to keep watch over my room as if it were a robber's den. What were you doing out there anyway? Afraid the criminal might escape into the night, were you?"

Even as she said it, she knew it was unfair, but indignation had brought hot color to her cheeks and triggered her temper. He stared down mildly at her, his expression amused.

"Actually," he said, putting both hands behind his back and assuming a relaxed stance, "I was taking your advice."

"*My* advice?"

"You told me it wouldn't be prudent to break down the door, and I agreed with you. How much more intelligent to simply wait until you came out. You'd have had to eventually. Your maid told me you hadn't any food in here." He grinned complacently. "And out you came. Eventually."

"You might have been there all night," she said, shaking her head with wonder.

"Spent many a night in chairs, my girl. Makes no difference to me." He was looking down at her, and she saw his brows knit critically.

"What are you wearing that horrid old rag for?" She saw that he meant the dressing gown. "What happened to that feathered thing? Why don't you put on that instead?"

Pegeen, her long hair swinging loose about her shoulders, shook her head wryly. "Oh, no. You'll recall what happened last time I wore that particular garment."

"I do recall it." He grinned down at her leeringly. "With relish."

Pegeen blushed at once, ducking her head so that her hair hid her flaming cheeks. This certainly didn't sound like a prologue to dismissal. Still, he'd been drinking. Better to get it over with herself, then.

Pegeen was in no mood to sit, either, and so she paced the length of the room, keeping her hands buried deep in the pockets of her robe, so that Edward wouldn't see that they were shaking. After several deep breaths and false starts, she said to the wind-battered window panes, "Edward, I can't stay here."

"Where do you want to go? There's a good fire in the library."

She shook her head, not taking her gaze off the swirling snow outside her night-darkened window. "No, no. I mean I can't stay here at Rawlings."

"Ah." Edward was pacing now. She could hear the floor boards creaking under his considerable weight. "And precisely why is it that you can't stay here at Rawlings?"

She turned at that, whirling around in disbelief. "Are you serious?" she gasped. "The reasons are—well, they're myriad." Her green eyes narrowed suspiciously. "Edward, please, don't patronize me. And don't pity me, either. I'll be all right. I've already spoken to Anne Herbert, and I'm welcome to stay with Sir Arthur and his family until I find a situation—"

"A situation?" Edward's hands weren't behind his back anymore. He'd taken several strides away from her, but now he turned and grasped the bedpost with a white fist. "Well, you've certainly been giving this matter thought, haven't you?" His voice dripped with sarcasm. "Already found a place to stay until you find a situation! And what, exactly, is a *situation*?"

She glared at him. "You know perfectly well what I mean. A position. As a governess, or something."

"Or something." Edward flung himself from the bedpost like an uncoiling spring, and Pegeen shrank back against the curtains. Fortunately, he strode towards the fireplace, not her. "Please enlighten me, if you would, because I'm still not certain why you can't just stay here."

Pegeen held both of her hands out, palms up, as if in supplication. "Edward, of course I can't stay here. Not after this. Lady Ashbury is going to tell everyone—"

"Of course she is. So what? What's a little more gossip about the Rawlings family? God knows there's been enough over the years."

"This isn't just a *little* gossip, Edward. I'm the sister of the woman who got your brother killed, a woman who owns a brothel—"

"Mrs. Porter has more than one establishment, actually," Edward said drily.

Pegeen glared at him. Why was he making so light of all of this? Didn't he realize that his place in society was being threatened if she stayed? Didn't he realize his reputation would be ruined?

"I lied to you," Pegeen said desperately. "I lied to everyone. Sir Arthur, Mrs. Praehurst—everyone. I can't possibly stay here after this. People will talk."

Edward wasn't looking at her. Instead, he picked up an iron poker and rearranged the logs in the fireplace. When he spoke, his voice was so quiet, she barely heard him. "And what about Jeremy?"

She inhaled and was surprised when her voice caught in a sob. She gulped, trying to control herself. "Jeremy will be all right with you. He'll just have to understand."

"He's already been abandoned once by his mother. Now you're leaving him too?"

Pegeen took a step forward, and now she held both her hands to her breasts, wringing her fingers in her dismay. "Oh, Edward! Please don't make this harder than it already is. Jeremy is going to be duke someday. I can't stay here and ruin any chance that he might have of gaining all the advantages of his rank in society."

Edward still wasn't looking at her. He'd propped one of his large feet on the hearth, and he had his arms folded across his broad, bare chest. "Is this my fire-breathing Liberal speaking? I never knew you were so concerned about what 'society' thought. It was my impression that you rather despised 'society.'"

"I hate your friends," Pegeen said shortly. "But they aren't who I mean when I say society. I mean, oh, I don't know. Real people. Good people. People like Sir Arthur and his wife."

Now Edward did look at her, and there was a strange glint in his grey eyes. "Didn't you just tell me that the

Herberts are going to be sheltering you until you find your mythical 'situation'?''

"Well. Yes."

"And if the Herberts are 'society,' and they still value your companionship enough to house you until you find somewhere else to stay, why are you so worried about my reputation?"

Pegeen opened her mouth to reply, then snapped it shut again when she realized that of course he was right. She didn't care one whit what people like the viscountess might say about her. It was people like the Herberts and Mrs. Praehurst, she cared about. And it was those very people who were the least likely to hold her in contempt for what she'd done. Why, Lady Herbert might have done the exact same thing under the same circumstances.

Defeated, Pegeen realized that none of the reasons she'd given Edward for leaving Rawlings were going to satisfy him. And she couldn't tell him the real reason, the reason she couldn't possibly stay was because she loved him irrevocably, unrequitedly, and she couldn't possibly remain under the same roof with him and not, eventually, share a bed with him again. Because he wouldn't renew that marriage proposal. Not now. Not knowing what he did about her.

Her sister's warning had echoed through her head all night: *We'll see what becomes of pretty, pathetic Pegeen then, won't we?* Why, even now Pegeen was sorely tempted by the sight of Edward's bare, thickly-haired chest, his flat, hard stomach, the ripple of muscles beneath the arms of his exquisitely tailored evening coat. Pegeen knew she had no self-restraint, feeling about him the way she did, and that the only way she could escape a fate similar to her sister's was to leave Rawlings Manor forever.

But she couldn't tell Edward any of this. What kind of woman would he think her? He had to know already that she possessed no more self-control than an animal, than a *man.* Women weren't supposed to harbor lustful feelings for men—well, women like Kathy were expected to, but women like herself? Never. Edward must think she was no better than her sister. And he was right.

Biting her lip and gazing embarrassedly at his boots, Pegeen tried to think of something to say, something, anything, besides the truth. She could think of nothing. Edward grew impatient by her continued silence, and suddenly removed his foot from the hearth. Placing both hands on one of the armchairs, he swung it around so that its wide seat faced her.

"Come here," he said in a deep, strangely menacing voice. "Sit down. I want to tell you something."

Pegeen was reluctant to approach him when his eyes were glittering so dangerously. But she dared not disobey him either, not when that muscle was twitching so violently in his lean, stubble-covered jaw. She pulled the lapels of the dressing gown more tightly around her slim body and took a few hesitant steps forward, then quickly sat down, her body tense in the soft cushions.

Edward circled the chair and approached the one that matched Pegeen's, but instead of sitting down in it, he chose to lower himself onto the hearth, his back to the fire. He sat so close that she could smell the leather and tobacco scent of him, and though he'd been drinking, he clearly wasn't drunk. She couldn't smell liquor on his breath at all.

Edward sat with his elbows on his knees, his fingers clasped loosely in front of him. His gaze was on his boot toes.

"Let me tell you something about my so-called reputation," he began in his deep, almost habitually sardonic voice. "Your sister wasn't exaggerating when she said one would be hard pressed to find a crueller pair of bastards than my father and brother. Her words, not mine, but I share the sentiment nonetheless. I know I've had a great many more advantages in my life than most men, and I'm certainly not complaining. Being the second son of a duke is hardly the worst existence in the world. But, and I thank God for this, you never knew my father and brother. If you had, you might understand why I don't entirely blame your sister for making the choices she did.''

Pegeen started to say something—what it was, exactly, she hardly knew—but Edward held up a hand, and she quieted.

Edward went on. ''I suppose that my childhood was happy, idyllic, even, up until my mother died. With her died whatever vestige of civility my father possessed. There was no warmth in this house, no compassion for anyone, servant or dog, and certainly no morality, after my mother passed. My father let my brother and I behave like wild things, encouraged us, even, to do exactly as we liked, whether it be seducing the scullery maids or torturing the farm cats— I'm sorry to upset you, but I'm afraid it's true.

''John was always more intelligent than I, and more creative, too, which I think is what also made him more dangerous, and crueller than anyone could possibly imagine. I won't disgust you with details of the inhuman behavior which he routinely exhibited. Suffice it to say that no one and nothing was safe from his whims.

''By the time I was old enough to realize that the way my father had taught my brother and I to live our lives was wrong, I was, in many ways, too far gone to change. I tried, though. I convinced the duke to send me away to the university, and after graduation, I stayed in London as much as possible. But my family's reputation had long since preceded me. There wasn't a matron in the city who'd allow me within fifty feet of her daughter, and most fathers weren't particularly glad when I took up with their sons. The only true friend I ever had was Alistair, who had no family to forbid him to be seen with me.

''Meanwhile, of course, the duke and John were spreading their reign of terror throughout Yorkshire until there wasn't a family in the county who'd send their children to work here, or a breeder in the country who'd sell us a horse or a hound. . . . My father and John'd killed that many of them between them. The horses they rode to death, the hounds they beat to death—Pegeen, don't look at me like that.''

Pegeen had been staring at him with tear-rimmed eyes, one hand over her mouth in horror. She'd known, of course, that the old duke had a formidable reputation—Mrs. Praehurst could barely stand to speak of him, and no one in Rawlings Manor ever mentioned John's name. But that Edward's father and brother had been guilty of such monstrous crimes . . . she'd had no idea.

She couldn't help but pity him, though she knew it was the last thing he wanted from her. To have lived so long bereft of love seemed a terrible thing to her. She'd never had to endure something like that. For as long as she could remember, she'd had her father and Jeremy. And that had been enough. That had been what saved her.

"I'm sorry," she said, removing her fingers from her lips. She wiped her tears away with the edge of a ragged sleeve. "I had no idea that living here had been like that for you."

"I'm not telling you this because I want your sympathy, damn it!" Edward was on his feet, striding away from her. When he turned to face her, she saw that his grey eyes were stormy with an emotion she couldn't identify. "I'm telling you this because I want you to know that what people say about me, about my family, can't be worse than the truth. And the truth is, as bad as they were, I wasn't much better."

He heaved a sigh, and Pegeen realized that whatever he was about to say, it was going to cost him something, something deeply and intensely personal. "I've been to your sister's houses, Pegeen. I've been to a lot of places I regret, I've been with a lot of people I regret. I could say it's because of my family, that no one in polite society would admit me to their home, but the fact is, Pegeen, I associated with people like Arabella and Lord Derby because, frankly, they were the only people over whom I could, in good conscience, feel superior. And because I knew myself to be so inferior to decent society, it was important to me that I be better than someone.''

Edward turned his back to her, his shoulders tensed. Then, in three quick strides, he was standing in front of her. Leaning down so that both of his hands rested on the arms of Pegeen's chair, he gazed down at her, his expression inscrutable. When he spoke again, his voice was carefully controlled. ''And so I lived for thirty years, and so I would have lived for thirty more, if I hadn't been standing in a cottage doorway in a little village called Applesby and had my stomach rammed into by you.''

Pegeen had shrunk back against the soft cushions of the armchair, conscious of the heat from his body, which was so much more intense than the heat from the fire beside her. He was so close that she could see the dark stubble on his cheeks, the strange ticking of the muscles in his jaw, the pulse beating strongly on the side of the neck, where his long, darkly curling hair met his shirt collar.

Pegeen felt frightened in a way she'd never been frightened before. It was a savage but oddly pleasant fear, a sort of aching anticipation for something she couldn't explain. She stared up at him, her green eyes wide, her breathing suddenly shallow. Her throat had gone dry. She couldn't have spoken a word even if she had been able to think of anything to say.

''Do you remember when we met?'' he wanted to know, his teeth flashing white and even in the firelight. ''Do you remember all the lectures you gave me on the evils of my class? You informed me, in a voice as clear and as frank as a child's, that I was responsible for subjugating the masses and keeping women from achieving equal status with men in our society.'' He quirked an eyebrow at her. ''To my utter amazement, this small, porcelain-skinned angel opened her mouth and proceeded to deliver to me a tongue lashing so full of venom that I thought to myself, 'This girl. This girl is different.' ''

Pegeen swallowed, and said with all of the light-heartedness she could muster, ''You ought to have sent me packing then and there.''

''Oh, no. Because the minute you started speaking, I knew you were someone I couldn't let slip from my fingers. How such a lovely creature could harbor such a warped mind, I couldn't fathom. But I believe I had hardly exchanged more than three sentences with you when I realized that I was in very grave danger of falling madly, deeply in love with you.''

Pegeen's jaw dropped. She stared at him, her lips parted moistly, her heart thudding heavily behind the thin muslin of her nightgown. She knew she ought to have said nothing, but Pegeen had never been able to hold her tongue at will.

''But that's impossible,'' she said, sitting up straighter in the chair so that her face was just inches from his. ''You can't be in love with me.''

''Oh, can't I?'' Edward's grin was lopsided, in sharp contrast to his passion-hooded eyes. ''And why not?''

Pegeen began to tick off the reasons on her fingers. ''You spent an entire month in London—''

''You wouldn't marry me. I couldn't live with you, have you sitting within arm's reach from me at dinner every night and know I couldn't touch you again. I knew I had to have you, but you were so adamant—''

Pegeen exploded indignantly, clutching the armrests of her chair. ''You only asked me to marry you out of an absurd sense of duty!''

''Of course I did. But don't think I wasn't relieved about what had happened between us. I spent every day in

London praying that you were pregnant so that you'd have no choice but marry me. You had that ridiculous idea about never marrying—''

"But I couldn't marry you!" Pegeen cried angrily. "My sister killed your brother and became a prostitute! Besides, you never mentioned a word about love!"

"Nor did you."

"But of course I loved you! I slept with you, didn't I?"

"Really, Pegeen, you unman me. Here I am, trying to propose, and you keep interrupting."

"Propose?" Pegeen gripped the armrests of the chair with white-knuckled fingers, her voice breaking on the second syllable. "Propose *marriage*?"

Edward pried one of her hands from the cushioned armrests in which she'd sunk her fingers and gripped it in a grasp that hurt, it was so tight. Lifting her eyes to examine his face, Pegeen saw that he was staring down at her, his jaw set determinedly, his grey eyes steely with resolution and lit with a strange inner light that glittered with febrile intensity.

"Yes, propose marriage," he said with a laugh, lifting her hand to his lips, and grazing the soft skin with the stubble from his day's growth of beard. "I daren't propose anything else, knowing your quick fists. Pegeen, you are truly the most exasperating, stubborn, sharp-tongued, beautiful, delightful woman I have ever met, and if you don't agree to marry me, I shall be miserable for the rest of my days. So say you will, won't you?"

Before she could say anything, he'd wrapped his inexorably strong fingers around her arms and pulled her against him. She flattened her palms against his bare chest, feeling through the thickly matted hair the heavy thud of his heart. Her head fell back against his arm, her hair streaming red-brown in the firelight, and then his lips were on hers, bruising her mouth with the violence of his emotion. His insistent kisses wiped Pegeen's mind clean of all thought save one: He loved her. He loved her. He loved her.

It seemed incredible, but he loved her, loved her enough to want to marry her. And then she was letting him kiss her throat, letting his quick fingers work the pearl buttons of her muslin gown, letting him whisper her name over and over, his breath hot on her skin.

"Say yes," Edward murmured, his lips tasting the soft skin behind one of her ears. The caress sent fevered chills running up and down Pegeen's spine, causing the peaks of her breasts to press resistantly against the fabric of her nightgown. "Say yes," he whispered again.

"Yes," she said, in a voice so laden with passion that she hardly recognized it as her own. And then she was kissing him as intrusively as he'd kissed her and almost as violently. She felt as if something deep inside of her had been released, something dark but lovely, something that suddenly made it all right for him to be dragging the old-fashioned dressing gown from her shoulders. He had pulled her up so that she knelt upon the seat of the armchair, her fingers splayed against the hard wall of muscle across his stomach, her chin level with his waist. When he had finally freed her from the constraints of the robe, Edward threw the offending garment to the floor, and Pegeen laughed at his vehemence.

But she stopped laughing when her gaze met his. Edward's grey eyes, half-lidded with ardor, glinted strangely. There was a flush on his dark features, and his breathing was as rapid and shallow as her own. His hands were in her dark hair, and though Pegeen wasn't aware of it, the firelight had cast her slim figure into silhouette through the thin fabric of her nightdress.

It wasn't just playfulness that caused her to raise her fingers to the buttons of his breeches. She had a woman's curiosity at her power over him, and though Edward hissed through his teeth as her knuckles grazed the wiry hair that surrounded his stiffening manhood, she ignored the warning. Taking the throbbing organ in her small hands, Pegeen marvelled at this instrument of pleasure, observing the veins and the ripe tip of his phallus closely in the firelight before slowly, delicately, tasting the engorged flesh with her tongue.

The contact caused Edward, held captive by her touch, to groan, his fingers curling into fists in her long hair. Encouraged by this reaction, Pegeen's lips followed her tongue, and she took as much of him into her mouth as she could, her lips forming a slick casing around his throbbing shaft. Edward's fingers dug into her scalp, and Pegeen moved her tongue along the stiff muscle, causing another groan to escape his lips.

With a suddenness that stole her breath from her throat, Edward drew away from her, dipping a hand behind her knees and lifting her bodily from the chair. Instinctively she circled his neck with her arms, her fingers tangling in his hair. His eyes never leaving hers, Edward carried her to the shadows of the wide canopy bed.

Placing her upon the yielding mattress as gently as if she were made of bone china, Edward took a step backward, and, his gaze on the womanly curve of her hips, threw off his evening coat and then his shirt until he stood bare-chested in the firelight. His tall black boots came off next, carelessly tossed aside. Pegeen watched as he reached for the waistband of his trousers, impatiently lowering the garment over his hips.

And then he was naked beside her, his sinewed arms drawing her to him, his lips capturing hers. Pegeen's breath grew short as she felt his fingers successfully navigate the multiple buttons on her nightdress, and then the slight protection the garment had afforded her was gone as he lifted the dress over her head and flung it aside. The beauty of her ivory skin in the firelight, contrasted so sharply against the darkness of her hair, was almost too much for Edward. He hid his dazzled eyes against the smooth skin of her swan-like neck, his hands moving to cup the perfection of her round, tip-tilted breasts, savoring the delicate tautness of their nipples.

Every place that Edward touched her, Pegeen felt as if she'd been branded by the searing heat of his fingers. She sank back against the down-filled pillows, dizzy with desire, pulling Edward down with her. Seeing that she was trembling, he moved to cover her slight body with his much larger frame, the darkness of his weathered complexion and the paleness of hers startling in the light from the fire.

The delicate skin on Pegeen's face was glowing from where the razor stubble on Edward's jaw had grazed it, and when she felt his mouth burn a trail of kisses down her throat, she knew that the porcelain skin of her breasts would suffer a similar fate. Her fingers strained his head closer as his lips teased a nipple, and currents of desire coursed through her body, sending her arching against him. His free hand strayed between her slim thighs, his fingers delving into her silken crevice. Pegeen gasped at the boldness of his exploration, but she could only cling more tightly to him, her own hand closing over the hard shaft of his manhood. Edward shuddered, and pressed his mouth harshly over hers, parting her satin thighs with a rough knee.

She knew that he meant to be gentle, but passion overcame intention, and suddenly, he was inside of her, filling her with his solid maleness. Pegeen couldn't help crying out as he entered her, as panicked as the first time they'd made love that she could not possibly accommodate him. Her fingernails dug into the firm muscles of his shoulders as she twisted beneath him. His lips silenced her inarticulate protest.

Her body arched against him as he thrust deeply into her. The need she felt for him could only be satisfied by pressing herself closer, ever closer, to his rigid body. She felt as if she were riding the crest of a steadily growing wave of desire, a wave that threatened to toss her to some barren shore, leaving her stranded and helpless. Clinging to what shreds of sanity still remained with her, Pegeen was conscious that Edward's thrusting had quickened, become more demanding, and she met him each time, thrust for thrust, instinctively tightening that part of her into which he pressed.

Suddenly, the crest Pegeen rode, rather than casting her aside, pinnacled, then crashed over her, soaking her in wave after wave of liquid relief. Crying out at the intensity of this bombardment of her senses, Pegeen clung to Edward, the only stable thing in her spinning, out of control universe. Dimly, she was aware that Edward, too, had cried out, and then, after a final, driving stab, his body sank heavily onto hers. She could feel Edward's heart beating as rapidly against her as if he'd had been running, and the strong but unsteady rhythm of it caused her to smile.

They lay panting in the firelight, their bodies deliciously relaxed against one another. It was several minutes before Pegeen felt able to speak, and then only because she thought the weight of Edward's body might crush her. He laughed at her whispered request and kissed her heartily, like a man who'd won an extremely valuable prize. Rolling from her, Edward pushed her languid body to her side, then spooned himself around her, his chest warming her back, one arm cradling her head, the other anchored firmly around her waist.

"This is how I want to spend every night for the rest of my life," he whispered in her ear. "Right here, with you in my arms. Tomorrow, I'll go to London to get a special license so we can be married at once. I don't want to wait."

"That's perfectly evident," Pegeen laughed drowsily.

Edward bent forward and kissed her temple. "I beg your pardon, young lady, but *you* were the one who attacked *me* a little while ago. I was quite shocked by your extremely forward behavior.''

''*Me*? Attack *you*? That's rich.'' Pegeen was so happy that she wouldn't even rise to the bait he set out for her. ''You can't stay here tonight, you know.''

''What do you mean?'' Edward pulled her even more firmly against him. ''I'm not going anywhere this time.''

''Oh, Edward! What will the servants think in the morning?''

''They'll think I'm a very lucky man, and that you're a very incorrigible young lady.''

''Oh, Edward,'' Pegeen sighed. But it was impossible to be angry with him, not when he drew her so close. He fell asleep thinking that their children, if they took after her, were going to be very good-looking indeed. Better have lots of boys, was his last conscious thought before slumber overtook him. Lots of boys to fight off the hordes of suitors their sisters would attract.

Pegeen, relishing the languid torpor that their love-making had cast over her, closed her eyes against the rosy firelight. Her last conscious thought, before she fell asleep, was *Kathy was wrong*.

Epilogue

The summer had been short but warm, and September brought, along with cooling breezes from the moor, a small, squalling bundle with Pegeen's stubborn chin, Edward's grey eyes, and a mass of blonde curls. They named her Elizabeth, after Edward's mother, from whom she'd inherited the golden hair. They spent hours simply staring at her, and then at one another, in blissful disbelief that something so infinitely precious could have been borne from their love for one another.

Jeremy was not so enchanted with his cousin but tolerated her presence as a necessary evil of seeing his Pegeen happy at last. The burden of his aunt's support having been lifted by Edward from Jeremy's shoulders, the duke was free to roam about the Yorkshire countryside finding boys to knock down and carriages to inspect. The only bane to his existence was young Maggie Herbert, a frequent visitor to Rawlings Manor, who, though years younger than the duke, stood a head taller and made much of this fact.

Edward was sitting in the conservatory, his month-old daughter sleeping soundly upon his shoulder while Pegeen thumbed through the local newspaper looking for stories about petty crimes that might well have been committed by her· nephew, when Alistair Cartwright came striding through one of the open sets of French doors that·led out into the fragrant gardens.

"Heigh-ho," he greeted the Rawlings family breezily.

Pegeen jumped up, throwing down the newspaper and rushing to Alistair's side to kiss his cheek.

"Hello!" she cried happily. "What are you doing back so soon? I thought you were spending two weeks in Florence. . . ."

"We were, we were," Alistair sighed, sinking down onto one of the cushioned, wrought iron benches Edward had ordered for the conservatory so that he and Pegeen could while away the long hours of summer more comfortably. "But I happened to glance at a copy of the *Times*, and saw that a certain piece of property was for sale—"

Edward, conscious of the sweet weight of his daughter's drooping head, grunted. "If you're talking about Ashbury House, you're damned right it's for sale. Arabella's married some Italian prince, if I understand correctly, and the two of 'em have hied off to Tuscany, or some such place."

"And the viscount hardly cold in his grave," Alistair said. "Tisk-tisk."

Pegeen had gone to the French doors and was peering curiously out them into the warm, lavender-scented evening. "Alistair," she said suspiciously. "Whatever have you done with your wife?"

"Wife?" Alistair folded his fingers behind his head and leaned back, gazing through the glass ceiling at the pink sky above. "What wife?"

Pegeen gave him a playful rap on the head. "The one you married last month. Don't deny it, I was there. Whatever have you done with Anne?"

"Oh, that wife," Alistair said. "Well, I believe she's at home, measuring things."

Pegeen sat down on the bench she'd abandoned, her pale green skirt billowing around her. "At home? You mean, you left her in London?"

"Oh, no." Alistair blinked lazily at the setting sun. "She's next door. Didn't I tell you? Ashbury House isn't for sale anymore. I bought it."

Pegeen's happy exclamation and Edward's hearty congratulations woke the baby, but she only sighed disdainfully at her parents' antics and went back to sleep.

"But this is marvelous!" Pegeen exclaimed, her green eyes sparkling. "We're neighbors! Oh, Sir Arthur will be so pleased."

Alistair raised a skeptical eyebrow. "Well, my father-in-law's happiness was not primary in my regard when I made the decision to buy the place, but I suppose if you put it that way—"

"Such an easy distance for Anne's family, Cartwright." Edward's tone was dry. "Thoughtful of you, old chap."

Alistair began to look more and more dismayed. "Faith, I hadn't thought of all that. I had better go and have a talk with Anne. We can't have her parents stopping by whenever they feel like it. I'll go right out of my head."

"Never mind, old man." Edward looked smug. "You can always sneak out the back door and seek solace here at Rawlings."

"Damn!" Alistair said. He jumped to his feet, murmured something about having to have a word with "the wife," and disappeared out into the purple twilight.

Still smiling, Pegeen rose and sauntered to where her husband and firstborn sat so contentedly. She leaned over the back of Edward's chair, encircling his neck with her bare arms, and laid her cheek upon his.

"Hello, there," Edward said, fondly stroking the silken skin of her arms. "Happy now, are you, you little witch? Not only did you get him to marry her, you get to see her everyday. Are you sure it's Scotland you're from and not Ireland? Because I could swear you're fey...."

"I'm no witch," Pegeen chuckled, kissing his lean cheek. "I haven't turned any princes into frogs lately."

"Are you sure? Because you've enchanted me." Then Edward glowered. "I'm not certain I'll like having that gadabout living next door to me. After all, he was in love with you for a while."

Pegeen laughed softly and ran a hand through her sleeping daughter's curls. "You have nothing to worry about, my lord. I'm as caught up in the spell of our love as you are...."

And they kissed in the shifting light of the setting sun, the heady fragrance of roses rich in the air.

Bestselling, award-winning author

Shirl Henke

takes readers on magnificent journeys with her
spectacular stories that weave history with timeless
emotion, breathtaking passion, and unforgettable
characters . . .

BRIDE OF FORTUNE

When mercenary Nicholas Fortune, amidst the flames of
war, assumes another man's identity, he also takes that
man's wife . . .

_____ 95857-9 $5.99 U.S./$6.99 Can.

DEEP AS THE RIVERS

Colonel Samuel Shelby is eager to embark on his mission to
make peace with the Osage Indians. The dangerous wilder-
ness is a welcome refuge from his troubled past — until he
meets beautiful, headstrong Olivia St. Etienne . . .

_____ 96011-5 $6.50 U.S./$8.50 Can.

KAT MARTIN

Award-winning author of *Creole Fires*

GYPSY LORD
_____ 92878-5 $6.50 U.S./$8.50 Can.

SWEET VENGEANCE
_____ 95095-0 $6.50 U.S./$8.50 Can.

BOLD ANGEL
_____ 95303-8 $6.50 U.S./$8.50 Can.

DEVIL'S PRIZE
_____ 95478-6 $5.99 U.S./$6.99 Can.

MIDNIGHT RIDER
_____ 95774-2 $5.99 U.S./$6.99 Can.

If you crave romance and can't resist chocolate, you'll adore this tantalizing assortment of unexpected encounters, witty flirtation, forbidden love, and tender rediscovered passion...

MARGARET BROWNLEY's straight-laced gray-suited insurance detective is a bull in a whimsical Los Angeles chocolate shop and its beautiful, nutty owner wants him out—until she discovers his surprisingly soft center.

RAINE CANTRELL carries you back to the Old West, where men were men and candy was scarce...and a cowboy with the devil's own good looks succumbs to a sassy and sensual lady's special confectionary.

In **NADINE CRENSHAW**'s London of 1660, a reckless Puritan maid's life is changed forever by a decadent brew of frothy hot chocolate and the dashing owner of a sweetshop.

SANDRA KITT follows a Chicago child's search for a box of Sweet Dreams that brings together a tall, handsome engineer and a tough single mother with eyes like chocolate drops.

For The Love of Chocolate

YOU CAN'T RESIST IT!